All Roads To Trinity

By

Paul James O'Donnell

Contents

Prologue 5

New Mexican Desert 18th July 1945, shortly before sunrise. 5

Chapter I 9

Charles University, Prague, March, 15th, 1939 9

Prague outskirts, March 15th, 1939 11

England September 1939 12

Cabinet War Room, Whitehall, Central London 15

Cabinet War Rooms, Whitehall, London, the same day 18

Palace of Whitehall, London April 1941 20

Spring, Dublin, 1941 22

London May 1941 25

Chapter II 28

Havana Central Jail, Cuba, early summer, 1941 28

American Embassy, Habana, 10:30 pm 43

Havana Central Jail 45

US Embassy conference room, 3 am 47

New York City, summer, 1941 49

Chapter III 75

Chichely Hall, Buckinghamshire, England, July 1941 76

6 pm, Main Reception room, Chichely Hall 85

11 am, following morning, Chichely Hall 89

London, 1 week later 90

Charleston, South Carolina, July 1941 95

Chapter IV 99

Baltic Sea, autumn, 1941 99

Hamburg Rathaus 105

Chapter V 123

Soltau POW Camp, October 19th, 1941 123

Quedlinburg POW Camp, October 21st, 1941 124

Spangenberg POW Camp, October 24th, 1941 126

Eichstatt POW Camp, October 27th, 1941 130

Wetzlar POW Camp, October 28th, 1941 132

6 am Hotel Arnou dining rooms, October 30th, 1941 133

Holzminden POW Camp, October 30th, 1941.. 137

Chapter IV.. 144

Berg Els, 30th October 1941.. 144

Chapter VI.. 168

Munich, November 5th 1941 168

Munich, 12th November 1941 181

Imperial Japanese Fleet, North Pacific, 500 miles from Hawaii............................ 203

6th of December. Munich 204

The Carolinas, USA 6th December 1941... 206

Chapter VII... 208

Theresienstadt, 6th of December, 1941... 208

North West Pacific, 7th December 1941... 214

Munich, 7th December, 1941... 215

Prague, 7th / 8th December 1941 217

Chapter VIII.. 255

Prague, 8th December.. 255

Deeper in the forest 266

Chapter IX.. 280

Theresienstadt.. 280

Chapter X... 287

Transcript W4453 Telephone conversation... 287

Farmyard Barn, 50km to Prague, 4km to the nearest village 289

Prague, 15th of December 297

Chapter XI.. 301

Czech countryside, 16th December.. 301

Back at the Farmyard 306

Deep in the Czech countryside.. 311

Gestapo HQ, Prague, Radio Incident room 319

Same time 60 miles away near Jedovice.. 322

Chapter XII... 333

Flight Control Tower... 333

Flight 90 minutes in... 355

Chapter XIII.. 357

January 4th, 1942, Maltese coastguard lookout point. 357

Epilogue 1: Berlin SS headquarters, Late January 1942 361

Epilogue 2: Sidi Haneish airfield, south of Alexandria, Egypt, Sept. 14th 1942 366

Epilogue 3: Wolfs lair, Eastern Ukraine, Nov. 12 1942 367

Epilogue 4: Los Alamos, New Mexico 18th July 1945, 8:13pm 371

Epilogue 5: October 1926 Prague University 373

Epilogue 6: Checkpoint Delta, Berlin, August 1947 375

Epilogue 7: Trinity College Dublin, summer, 1932 376

Prologue

Mission control's main observation point miles from the blast point was located near an old farmstead which had become a small village in the weeks leading up to the test. It was teeming with people who all wanted to be present to see the culmination of four years of work and billions of dollars in taxpayer's money. Everyone had been issued with dark goggles to filter the intense bomb blast expected and most were nervously fiddling with the straps like schoolboys before an excursion. Some shivered in the open air as the cool desert night had yet to dispel and they were dressed in shorts and sleeveless shirts de-rigueur apparel for the scorching daytime temperatures. The witnesses were out in the open as that would give the best view; small ridges had been ploughed to act as blast barriers, as seats and to separate the participants in orderly lines. They had been advised to sit and turn their backs at the last moment; only the most fortunate and the most involved had been allowed this close. Far in the distance, visible only by binoculars and only a pinprick at that, was the "gadget", the first of the bomb prototypes built and the one designed to be used as the tester. Fifty meters off the ground, held in a metal skeleton of a platform, it too was surrounded by trucks, a house, a caisson and all manner of cameras, microphones, instruments and detectors placed close by and all the way to the control centre. There was only one test and everything had to be ready the first time.

The hard work had been done all through the night and now as the sun came up the test was ready. No one knew if it would work or fizzle out or do nothing or create a black hole and devour the earth as one physicist had predicted could occur. But the paymasters were expecting results and politicians and top brass badly needed the weapon. Germany was beaten and the three months wait, stipulated at Yalta, that the Russians had before acting against Japan would be up on the 8th of August. The Americans were desperate to blast Japan out of the war before the Russians could take too many easy spoils now that the USA had done all the hard work. A bit similar to the recent race to Berlin that the Russians felt they deserved to win and that the Americans had nearly stole in on them, only to stop at the Elbe at the last minute. Comrade Stalin and his massive armies needed to be impressed if only because communist internationalist doctrine said they should keep going all the way to the river Tagus on Lisbon's shore regardless of who is in the way. After all, they had tried that once already in 1920.

- Sir!

The senior technician spoke to one man among a group of five or six, that figure, tall and gaunt in his pre-war suit now two sizes too big was unmistakably Robert Oppenheimer.

- Yes, keep the countdown going – Oppenheimer confirmed, if no one indicated it should stop for some reason then onwards it must go - With your permission General of course – he said to General Gates beside him, the military head of the Manhattan project, the biggest one-off expense in the history of the United States government.

- Robert, I've been waiting three years for this. Let's do it, please.

Everything was in place; calls to all personal to position themselves for detonation went out. The final countdown started after those areas had been alerted. The reporters, high powered guests, staff and scientists held their breaths as the countdown went on.

- The mattresses still there? – Groves asked.

The gadget had been hoisted up the 50-meter metal tower and in the event that it fell they had put a truckload of mattresses below. The irony wasn't lost on anyone, the highest technology yet developed by mankind surrounded by something as mundane as the spring mattress.

- Never mind them I hope you told the Air Force to take the day off – Oppenheimer joked as a way of dealing with the tension.

The Trinity test site was on an Air Force live testing range and was so secret that no one had told the Air Force. The village on the site had been bombed twice.

- They're the least of my problems; if this fizzles I'll have to explain to Congress the loss of one billion dollars worth of plutonium. I'd never even heard of the word billion before this war - The countdown was reaching its conclusion.
- We need this test General Groves or otherwise you might be explaining to Congress how you gifted Japan that billion dollars worth of plutonium when Fat Boy piles into Japanese soil instead of exploding.

- Harry Truman needs to see a result, he arrives at Potsdam the day after tomorrow - Beside Groves, his young driver looked extremely agitated and nervous.
- Corporal, we physicists like to think of all the possibilities however remote and you're thinking of the one about the atmosphere catching fire burning all the planets oxygen aren't you?

The young Corporal nodded shyly, they were surrounded by young NCOs and rank and file. Part of the community of 450 men and women the test site had grown to since it had been chosen the previous year.

- What you're going to see is history not the end of the world.
- 8,000 ton TNT delivery is my bet for the yield – Teller said.
- Okay, everyone on the ground lying down and facing away, two minutes – the excitement made full-fledged scientists behave like giddy schoolboys.
- I'm watching it - said Teller who stood up - this I have to see.
- Where's Feynman?
- In a truck over there, he said he's going to watch it without glasses from there.
- Damn fool, be the last thing he'll see – Groves thought if they're like schoolboys then he'd been the schoolmaster making them pay attention to their lessons and getting results not just interminable scribbling on blackboards which is what most had been doing in Harvard, Yale, Oxford, etc..
- He said the tinted windshield will stop the gamma rays.
- I hope he's right, scaled plutonium enrichment was the secret, Martin here said it a million times – Oppenheimer said this to Groves but was overhead by the self-same Martin Kessler, a renowned Czech scientist and expert in radioactive elements – I knew it from the start and which was why we were damn glad when you walked in the door. I didn't know you had got out of Prague after 1939 but we were sure glad you did.
- Things were bad there back then but now that the Russians have taken over things should improve – Kessler said.
- I doubt it – Groves was openly scornful.
- I know it is funny when Russians are an improvement but believe me it was really bad from 1939 on. I got out just in time – Kessler said wistfully.
- You must tell me all about it – Oppenheimer said.
- It's a long story – 'ONE MINUTE' came an urgent announcement.

They had worked closely together for three years and Oppenheimer had never asked till now. Kessler had never told him how he'd got out nor would he, he owed his escape to one man and that man had asked him never to reveal a word of their escapades, 'keep your fat gob shut right' had been the exact words.

- Better lie down – Oppenheimer said - You know the most expensive part of the most expensive project known to man was getting the plutonium and we got over the biggest hurdles thanks largely to you solving the problems you did, if it hadn't happened it might have been the Germans doing a test, not us.
- '10 SECONDS'.

The cold nighttime desert was shrouded in shadows, the sun was beginning to show but was suddenly upstaged for the first time by a man-made effect. A dazzling light lit up the whole area, brighter than any of the sunniest of days, then came a crashing noise followed by shock waves sweeping over them knocking Teller to his knees, an apt position given the look of awe on his face.

The whoops and hollers started as the sky was filled with a huge dome-like cloud ballooning upwards. People started dancing and singing, it was euphoria all around.

- The atomic age gentlemen, you made it happen and its America's – Groves shouted.
- Wait till Congress sees this home movie – Tennessee's Senator Bush shouted.

Kessler looked over at Oppenheimer who had truly made this moment happen more than anybody no matter what he had said about Kessler's contribution. Oppenheimer had a contemplative look, one out of kilter among the congratulations and revelry around. A distracted air as if thinking beyond the moment, on what mankind had just done, harnessing the power of the atom and not for good ends but destructive, indeed murderous ones. Kessler took his hand and shook it.

- *Bhagavad Gita* – said the project leader still not fully himself.
- Pardon?
- An Indian proverb sorry. What have we done what have we become but did they give us any choice – he said absentmindedly over Kessler's shoulder as he held his hand. Then as if returning he looked straight at Kessler and said firmly – You were a God send.

8

Chapter I

Charles University, Prague, March, 15th, 1939

Maria Kessler was in the physics faculty of the university when the news has been announced over the radio. Half a dozen researchers and technical staff crowded around the Philco 90 cathedral-style radio found in her father's office, grown men had tears in their eyes as she observed reactions ranging from shock to resignation, Karel instinctively slipped his hand into hers and squeezed it. They had grown close over the past six months this doctorate student of her father, some years younger than her but in the more liberal environs of a university that fact decreased in importance. No one was talking happy ever afters. It was more the primal need to have someone to hold at night especially important given the tumult of events over the last year. They had become secret lovers while at the time trying to maintain a professional distance during the working day. The moment overcame her, she took his arm and moved to his side, Karel understood the double anxiety felt by Maria, not just about the invasion, she and her father were also Jews, everyone knew what the Germans thought of Jews. Their newsreels, films, magazines and newspapers left people in no doubt what they thought.

The official statement was read out, the announcer speaking with a pronounced accent, it spoke of welcoming our Aryan brothers; great German lands joining together; glowing futures together....

- How can they possibly do this, turn the country over to a bunch of thugs? – Maria's voice quivered.
- I never thought it would happen.
- Why didn't the British or French stop them, didn't we sacrifice enough with the Sudeten land.
- Maybe the British will make them withdraw – Karel said hopefully.
- You're clasping at straws, the Nazis aren't the types to give up anything – Maria instinctively knew what she was dealing with.
- What next? Will you flee with your father to the Hungarian border?
- You know my father, he will never leave and if he doesn't I can't

- Please take this seriously Maria, you still have time, it will take the Germans weeks to get everybody under control, I can help you and your father over into Hungry, I have friends who 'exchange' goods in, shall we say a manner that's outside the auspices of the state customs authorities.
- I don't want to do anything illegal - said Maria.
- Illegal! This is no time for cowering law abidance. – Karel was nonplussed
- I don't know, I'll have to talk to my father - Maria conceded.
- Your father's a brilliant scientist, they will want to use him, don't worry about him – Karel knew this reading of realpolitik was at odds with stated Nazi doctrine but he wanted to reassure Maria.
- But how can I just up and leave without him, he's the only family I have, I'm the only family he's got.
- Maria – Karel spoke with pleading in his voice.
- I'll speak to him I promise.

The radio announcer continued his discourse cloaked in language that was meant to calm the population. '*Centres of transport and power will continue to function as normal, education and public offices are to close today*'. At the same time, the announcer did his best to make the whole drama something of a new public holiday, celebrating the triumphal arrival of National Socialism in Bohemia, brother lands of the Greater German Reich and so on.

- Bohemia! I woke up in Czechoslovakia – Maria said – they don't waste their time, do they? Take over a country in the morning, wipe it from the maps by the afternoon and erase the name by night time.
- Maybe they think it will wipe out their crime, people won't associate the name with a country brutally expunged from the list of free nations – Karel pointed out the bitter truth.
- Maybe the Russians will intervene, they can't be happy about what's happening on their doorstep – Maria said forgetting who their allies were.
- Old Joe Stalin to the rescue, now that's a contradiction in terms if I ever heard one. He's too busy liquidating the party apparatchik's to take any notice and he's afraid of Hitler anyway. Some of the group are going down to the street, let's go with them – Karel suggested.
- Why not. Let's go see history being made, the day the Germans came and stole my country – Maria said bitterly.

Prague outskirts, March 15th, 1939

Ernst Kaufman was enjoying another great day in the vanguard of the German tidal wave that was sweeping across Europe. Ernst had never travelled before but recently he had been to Austria and now he found himself driving across the famous Charles Bridge. Wait until he told his mother, his German army motorbike had carried him and Rolf Werner his pillion passenger all the way from the border that morning. The exhilaration of the moment was all the greater as they hadn't known until right before the invasion whether the Czechs would offer resistance or not. They hadn't, the fools and so what could have been a hard battle had turned out to be a glorious bloodless procession. Just like the entrance to Vienna, the onlookers displayed the whole gamut of emotions at what they were seeing; surprise, loathing, shock and fear. Mostly fear though unlike Vienna but even here a good portion of the population seemed resigned and more and more Heil's and Nazi salutes appeared, often to the disgust of the person beside.

Ernst eyed the new reluctant citizens of the grand Reich, tonight was going to be fun if Vienna was anything to go by, there the beer had been plentiful and free-flowing, the girls had been receptive to a soldier's advances, to the victor the spoils. Careful though, Rolf got more than he'd bargained for in the Imperial city the regimental doctor had nearly put him on a charge but in the end, the Captain had smoothed things over. *'A lesson learnt'* and all that the Captain had said. A lesson indeed, Rolf had sworn that the next time he would stick it where there was no risk of infection! Rolf had taken the dose very badly and so had the poor Jews who'd crossed his path while the itch had gone untreated. Ernst didn't understand fully why he should hate Jews so much. In his class he had been friendly with a couple of them, Weinberg and Goldstein he remembered and they had seemed perfectly 'German' not the horrible caricatures they portrayed Jews as in the press and newsreels. Even Rolf, who loved to go Jew-baiting when he was bored, admitted one time after several pilsners that his widowed mother had worked for a Jewish doctor as a receptionist until they were forbidden to practice. Maybe that was the root of his hatred for Jews, the shame of having been helped by them. Ernst reasoned their superiors knew what they were doing and if that was hard on the Jews well they must deserve it somehow after all hadn't another victory been achieved at no cost what so ever. *'Yet again demonstrating the super invincible qualities of the Aryan'* Ernst thought as the column turned up the hill to the Cathedral and Presidential palace.

England September 1939

The war was only days old but people were still in a state of semi shock. Many of those who remembered the previous conflict were at a total loss. How could you explain how the same nation's bled dry only twenty years before could once again embark on such follies? As if the slaughter and horrendous carnage of the trenches had been but a dreamy poem imagined into existence by Siegfried Sassoon. Inexplicable as it all was it hadn't been completely unforeseen by the British government. Events over the previous years had brought home the threat and certain organizations have been planning and now in just the second week of the second month of autumn as German panzers closed in on Warsaw those hastily made plans began to swing into action.

The Germans were playing for keeps but the situation was deceptive or so the black humour of the moment went. England has the *Boche* surrounded no less. Malta, Gibraltar and Cyprus were on one side and England covering the other, all we are waiting for was a place to strike the dazed public told themselves with tongues firmly in cheeks. The pessimists were advocating German lessons such was the tidal wave that was *Blitzkrieg*. The government just got on with it, there was now much unfinished business in Europe but the profound lack of intelligence made picturing the situation on the ground a very inexact science. Our guide relevant to our narrative is one Jamey Millrose, Jamey was taking his time walking the five minutes from Charing Cross underground station tastefully attired in a lovely sandbag finish, the station not Jamey, to his 'office' in a small street near Piccadilly. Jamsy was as an Oxford double first, somebody who had taken the trouble to master not only the notoriously difficult Czech language but also Slovak at the same time. Like the country the languages had given their names too, it was a difficult and uneasy partnership. This rare and special combination had been noted in places not usually spoken about, by people not usually seen. So one day in early September part of those plans, a small part, saw the bursar of St Paul the Evangelist's College Oxford crossing over the central quad to climb the stairs leading to a small half-hidden set of steps up to the garret. He had two letters to deliver to the startled honours student. This postgraduate in Middle Slavic languages was rightly startled by the imperious puffed up as only a college bursar can be acting as mere messenger boy! This could only mean something serious thought our dishevelled noon riser. As he looked at the two letters reverently held in the hand of the bursar he wondered if he was being rusticated for moral laxness and deservedly so. If the bursar had happened to time his arrival shortly before he would have had the pleasure of meeting an illicit overnight guest, a certain young woman from the drapers' shop on the high street. Midnight visitors were risky but not unusual episodes for our aspiring gallant. St. Paul would never have approved, Saul definitely. But the twist was the second letter, he couldn't think of a reason why it takes two letters to get sent down?

The bursar may have missed making a new acquaintance but he did note a faint air of what he thought was perfume which surprised him. Perhaps this sorry academic specimen in front of him was one of that band of certain young men who wouldn't be interested in meeting his daughters, though he couldn't fathom it, if rumours were anything to go by he should try and avoid any introductions taking place between his romantically inclined Brontian reared daughters and the Byronic styled Don Juan he saw opposite him.

This train of thought almost led the bursar to neglect his important official business. His apparent blank look of superiority was down to his constant daydreaming. His daughters reminded him of a good Cotswold stew, strong, hearty, richly flavoured but heavy on the system. They were also a source of constant worry to him, he mused on how exactly he could bring the independent spirited too close to thirty for his liking gals to a matrimonial state. The word 'state' brought him back from his revere to the immediate business at hand which had all started a short time before with a mysterious dark-suited man knocking on the door of his lodgings. Ironically given the gulf in position, an abode not much superior to the one he found himself in now. The English higher educational institution seemed to glory in the public, the visible, the grand halls, wide commons, geometrically perfect quads, immense vaulting libraries and then slum it in the private domain. The quiet serious man had come on government business of the highest sort, business that couldn't wait till his breakfast had finished. The slice of toast had slid from his hand at the surprise intrusion and had neatly landed jam side down on the threadbare carpet. 'Damn it' he thought 'but what were porters for except to stop this sort of unwelcome intrusion. This time as the bursar handed over the letters they'd already changed hands four times in twenty hours.

Jamey tried to organise a chair for his guest, check to see if he had any dry sherry left over after his bit of fluff had downed half the bottle the night before, discard any of the remaining garments she hadn't had time to scramble back into and generally rearrange himself in a comfortable manner meanwhile the Bursar just settled on a table. He didn't seem to mind sharing it with a Mongoloid selection of documents, articles torn from newspapers, learned journals, crosswords and assorted odds and ends but he did wonder briefly at the vase filled a whimsically protruding skeletal arm and hand, the arm didn't occupy his thoughts so much, 'borrowed' from a medical student no doubt, as the stocking draped from the curled up bony forefinger. Looked like real silk too he thought, might slip it in my pocket while this whipper snapper isn't looking, the wife would be pleased as she had any number of mismatched stockings bereft by a laddered partner that would welcome a new mate.

Eventually both parties overcame the circumstances and got to business. The chain of events as follows, the Bursar hands over the letter to the postgraduate fellow of the College, postgraduate looks surprised, porters delivered the post, not bursars but opens the letter and reads, a startled look begins to form on his face, now Bursar briskly hands over a second letter. This time the recipient is somewhat slower to respond still winded by the contents of the first, not that the second letter is such a surprise as the first made reference to it, the second letter is opened and the contents revealed. This caused so much consternation that the legerdemain the Bursar employed to pocket the mislaid ladies stocking went completely unobserved.

The Bursar knowing some of the details just revealed to the astonished ex-postgraduate coughed.

- It is beholden of me as the college representative to do two things; one on behalf of the college authorities in this most irregular graduation ceremony is to offer our most heartfelt congratulations on your recently awarded Doctorate and following on we wish you luck in your future career.

Jamey, Oxbridge's most recent former postgraduate, mumbled his gratitude mainly because he thought he should and it gave him time to absorb the facts he had just been presented with, to figure out what on earth was happening and frame a suitable response.

A feeble - Thanks again - as the facts began to have some real-life meaning, the first letter he read was about his grad com Laude doctorate awarded by the college without recourse to exams, written or oral or thesis, written or oral, solely given by invoking obscure statutes written in the original royal warrant giving the sovereign the right to award degrees where 'God's work be exalted', i.e. the king needed knights in a hurry as there was a war on. This was document given to him twenty minutes before by the shadowy functionary to which the

Bursar had shakingly countersigned the signature of the current head of the house of Windsor.

Having finished his postgraduate career rather abruptly Jamey of course was free to pursue other interests. That freedom had lasted from the end of the first letter until the opening of the second; this invited Jamey to become part of the civil service. The invitation contained an address that Jamey didn't know but would lead him to a small backdoor in a small side street close to Whitehall palace Monday morning. Lest Jamey feel any doubts as to his intentions to accept this kind offer of work for the civil good the letter was signed by his father, contained his new social security number and told him he started work at 08:30 (sharp).

Having slumped against a dusty stack of back copies of the Prague *Prognosis* newspaper dating back to the turn of the century Jamey pulled himself upright with the aid of a bust of Ernest Benes. Well-meaning but formulaic words floated between the two men.

- I say young man are you alright? – Bursar noncommittally.
- Fine I just lost my footing - Doctor J.M Esq. nonchalantly.
- Yes, I dare say, all this 'material' underfoot could undermine the surest of goats. – Bursar nail head bangingly.
- Off to London. Well looks like I'd better get packing then – Dr J.M. Esq. excitedly.
- Hadn't you aught. – Bursar grudgingly.

A smile crept into the corner of his mouth at the realization that the damp dreary fens and quiet cloistered life of Oxford was about to fade into the background while an exciting and mysterious adventure was coming to the fore. One and a half hours on the mainline train. Capital of an empire, a citadel at war. Boyfriends, husbands and brothers were faraway doing the hard work of winning or at least fighting the war. Their womenfolk at home, pining, alone, afraid and best of all bored, in short perfect working material for the amorously inclined, The Slavic language expert and would be Don Juan would never have such a clear field again.

Cabinet War Room, Whitehall, Central London

He wasn't much to look at but greatness comes in all sizes, big and small or in this case short and pasty - though he couldn't be blamed for being pallid given he spent most of his time thirty feet underground. At least he could empathize with the miners he mused to himself. He was bald as a coot, hair being something he'd said goodbye to in his twenties, snub-nosed, bottle glasses, portly and a messy eater. The remains of the two partridges roasted in a rich grenadine sauce were simultaneously on the plate in front, between the plate and the edge of the table, on the napkin around his neck and the jowly chin.

Removing the napkin to dap his lower jaw he pushed the plate away. In its place an orderly set down a decanter of prize vintage cognac and a humidor of his favourite deep rich Cuban cigars. While most Britons made do with what they could, powdered eggs and Woolton pie, Winston Leonard Spencer Churchill had aristocratic tastes, hardly his fault being the scion of one of the most ancient families in the land and along with the sense of 'noblesse oblige' he could fall back on the logical argument of it being his duty to take the utmost care of himself as to better serve the interests of his beleaguered people.

A short knock on the door resulted in the appearance of his senior communications clerk, a small figure who walked with a slight limp, courtesy of a German shell fragment, red hot at 2000°C intersecting his right knee at 400mph. That had been in 1917 at the battle of Campier having miraculously survived by that stage years of trench life, rats, fleas, bad food, major pushes, minor offensives, numerous sorties and three heart-stopping over the tops, our clerk had been genuinely grateful to the German gunner for blowing his right knee cap off.

- ·That was the first time we used tanks you know - Winston said addressing the clerk with some pride in his voice, as First Lord of the Admiralty he had come up with the idea. One more of history's endless ironies, the man in charge of the world's biggest navy being responsible for the biggest development in land warfare since the invention of gunpowder. Strange but the thinking was of ships on land hence the first tanks had a prefix very much like their aquatic sisters. HMLS, His Majesty's Land Ships.

The clerk knew all this and by now a consummate civil servant was adept at handling his 'charges' and humouring their pet likes and dislikes.

- Yes, Prime Minister and it was another right royal cock-up by the general staff if you don't mind me saying so sir - both being veterans of the trenches he felt he could take a certain amount of liberties with his gentlemen.

Winston, who fancied himself as a bit of a military innovator, rated the Western high command in much the same light.

- Yes, it was a bit - he replied.

One of his better ideas he thought tanks, as they were now called, just look how far they had come along, it hadn't been his fault that back then others hadn't used this evolution in warfare properly but instead had managed to completely throw away the advantage. Like inventing the rifle and using it as a club. The Germans had taken the message on board though, all too well, had Blitzkreig'd their way through Western Europe right to the Spanish border. Sods law though Winston.

- What do you have there? - asked the first lord of the treasury, 21st occupant of 10 Downing Street and at the age most people were retiring Supreme Warlord during some of the darkest days Britain had seen since the Black Plague.
- Diplomatic communiqué from Washington Prime Minister - replied the discreet valet before adding - it came through the Q channel.

This resulted in a minor growl from the seated figure who quickly reached over to the proffered silver tray upon which the precious telegram rested. The Q channel was the holiest and most sacrosanct level of communication between the two Atlantic countries. It existed almost as one to one connection that bypassed the entire diplomatic establishments on both sides of the three thousand mile wide U-boat infested pond that separated them.

Putting on his glasses hastily Winston began to read the page. He was dealing directly with the man who represented all that great latent power that was sleepy provincial America which if only it could be stirred into mortal action just like during the Great War then their salvation was assured in the long term. This was one of the biggest challenges currently occupying the efforts of Churchill. ENGAGE AMERICA.

He muttered more to himself than to anyone on reading and re-reading the telegram.

- How on Earth can we draw in bit by bit that enormous potentate and put it to smiting the multitude of evil intent that assails us and civilization from all sides - Churchill tended to talk to himself in full-on speech mode.
- Pardon sir you spoke? - The valet leaned forward to listen better as Churchill looked up from the paper.

- Yes indeed by God. Tell my private secretary there's to be a meeting of the intelligence chiefs here in one hour, one hour mind - As the factotum quietly glided from the room in a manner perfected over half a lifetime of personal service, his gentleman again looked down at the page in his hand, scarce believing his eyes he began speechifying out loud again - Dark days look to be getting darker and the day of deliverance yet further from our feeble grasp – he liked the phrase and mentally noted it for later as he turned to refill his glass.

Cabinet War Rooms, Whitehall, London, the same day

- How close are they to a workable prototype? - Churchill directed his comment to Admiral Johnston, head of naval intelligence.
- At this stage, we have very little firm facts to go on PM. We do know that Hitler has fast-tracked the development of what they call 'strategic weapons' mainly rocket technology and propulsion aircraft but at this juncture, nothing much has come of their work.
- What about our efforts in this area? – PM Churchill.
- Again like the Germans, we have concentrated our resources into areas that will produce tangible results over a shorter period, such as radar stations covering the entire coast, anti-submarine weaponry and our jet engine program going on in Wales but I must stress Prime Minister that no one is even sure if this type of weapon will ever work, not even the experts in the field know or will hazard a guess.
- What about it then Maurice, what do you think of all this high science? - the war leader asked the head of Q Branch, the quasi department charged with keeping Britain free of Axis spies and occupied Europe full of Allied ones.
- We do know that top German scientists in this area have sounded out opinions among their fraternity, worse is that they have access now to some of the finest physicists in some of the finest universities throughout the countries they have overrun. We have recently received reports through resistance channels that this has led to some work going on in occupied Norway. Trying to change in some way the properties of water needed to proceed with other avenues. Evidently, it's a tricky business making the raw materials for this weapon, which after a huge effort might not work after all – The Q branch's summary on the latest goings-on.

The small group shared preoccupied glances and edged even closer to the speaker as the head spook continued.

- We've also had reports from Jewish academics smuggled out of Denmark that Heisenberg the renowned German physicist and discoverer of the principle which bears his name travelled to Copenhagen and met with Niels Bohr, the Dane credited with being the father of modern atom physics. They talked for several hours. We don't know what about but we are certain this subject was discussed.
- What if they get a working weapon - asked the PM - you know about these things Arnold?

Another man gathered at the table, Professor A.N. Gibbs, head of the government's secret research programs replied as he'd been prompted to.

- It's checkmate if they have just one, they can have two or three or as many as they have the radioactive material for but it will only take one used on London to knock us right out of the war.

- Good God above. Knock us out of the war. Surely it can't wipe out a nation, two thousand years of achievement gone in a minute.

- No prime minister, not a nation but a city yes, a witness to the energy unleashed by a minuscule quantity of uranium during tests in a Cambridge lab said the results were ferocious. We can't imagine exactly what will happen if we harness this power. They speculate that it could cause gigantic tidal waves, earthquakes, huge sonic aftershocks shattering everything manmade for hundreds of miles, blinding light causing raging fires. Truly we must fear the power of the atom and we can't resist those who have mastered it. The age of the atomic weapon is close and our only hope is to be the ones with those weapons.

- I've been down the East End after a raid and the destruction struck me as Biblical, how those brave fearless people stood it I don't know. But to do that to the entire city with one bomb, Gentlemen we must as you say have that bomb before the Germans, the broken shattered city must be Berlin not London. For those of you present who don't know, I must tell you that the Americans have proposed a joint research group to be set up. Roosevelt has ordered it at the behest of Einstein and other leading scientists. A secret venture codenamed the Manhattan project, why Manhattan I don't know.

- That's where the meeting of the scientists took place PM, Oppenheimer's heading it up - answered the stickler for details John Grant, head of the army's intelligence division.

- I want you to set up a joint committee to identify the top people we need in this esoteric pursuit, identify them and recruit them. They must be made to understand the critical importance. The fate of the civilised world, the world we love, is ever more in peril as if it was not fighting for its very life as it is. And I need not remind you that not a word of this must ever get out, it would be catastrophic if the German were to get wind of what was going on but even worse would be if the American isolationists ever found out.

Palace of Whitehall, London April 1941

- Schrödinger's in Dublin – said the fixer.
- Dublin!! What's he doing there? – said the sailor.
- Physics being a physicist I'd imagine – said the scholar.
- Quite. I mean how he ended up there of all places. Do the Irish have an atomic program too! – the ocean goer queried.

The last statement was made in mock-serious surprise and concern. The banter continued between the three men in the room located halfway down a long corridor in the war ministry's imposing Regency building. Of the three only one had worked for the government before the current crisis, Osborne of the Blue. Currently ship less he sometimes wished he was back commanding a destroyer, steaming across the Atlantic with a convoy, as he had spent most of the last war doing or clashing with the German high fleet as he had done in sixteen at Jutland. It was all so much simpler then. Now he dealt with duplicity and deceit, double-cross and guesswork. Dealings he found to his considerable discomfort he had a God-given talent for. If he couldn't command a fleet in action the next best thing was finding out where to send that fleet to fight.

- What can do the most damage? – the fixer asked the scholar.

Across the teacup strewn table sat Professor More O'Farrell of Imperial College London. He had become the government's primary source of likely bodies to be shipped over to America for Manhattan, now just the "project". Any physicist he didn't know hadn't done anything to merit a blip on the international scene. The other man completing the trio answered the Admiral.

- De Valera's a bit of a mathematics aficionado, seems he saw an opportunity to get a first-class mind working in the Free State. Even set up a special institute dedicated to advanced physics to house the great man, eminent scientist and fugitive on the run from Nazi Germany - Colonel Hugo Coburn said.

Coburn was one of those military types who flourish during an all-out war and stagnates under the dull routine of peacetime parades and regimental dinners sat beside prattling COs daughters. Small talk with the COs female relatives was worse than being under sniper fire but Coburn had a justifiable reputation as 'someone who gets things done'. He was the 'fetcher' in this operation. He didn't know why he was looking for a Belgian named Remark who worked in Gothenburg before the war but all the same, he'd find out what Remark was doing and whether he was available for the Allied cause and if he wasn't game well it was a dirty war and dirty things happened all the time. Now that the heads had come up with a name, a place and a time, it was his turn to make a suggestion.

- I don't think the phone will be the thing for such a delicate mission and I don't think he'll come running after a few telegrams sent from a mysterious contact.
- Dublin's not far by any stretch, used to go fox hunting there in the twenties. Hard to think it isn't still with the rest of us, politically that is. Place was full of charming lads and lassies just down from Oxford or Trinity and the high teas in Bewleys with my maiden aunties takes me right back   Osborne waxed lyrical.

Coburn never one to miss an opportunity when it lands in front of him gift wrapped in navy blue and white with postage paid across the Irish sea, looked at the admiral in a way that made Osborne glance quickly away at the windows with the big paper X's taped on the panes.

- Hmm, contacts, local knowledge, familiarity with the situation on the ground – Coburn surmised.

His thinking out loud making the Admiral reach for his cold cup of tea with the kettle scale forming a nice flower pattern on the surface. Coburn's next sortie caused him to gag on the vile tasting remains.

- Admiral, how do you fancy another weekend of high teas in bonnie wee Ireland, all expenses paid by her majesties government?

21

Spring, Dublin, 1941

Dermott Mulligan, Dermo to his friends of which he had a wide selection, entered the bar through a side door from the street. Unhurried and deliberate he had, any neutral observer would swear in court, the look of a man who wasn't pleased to be in a bar. An unusual Irishman hence would be another note in the observer's testimony. But there is no observer, neutral or otherwise, watching, luckily for Mulligan, his reluctance being understandable as when a twenty years old secret steps out of the shadows and taps you on the shoulder giving you the fright of your life. Dermo to his credit was uncomfortable because he was technically committing treason. Betrayal of his fellow Irishmen and woman, of his country, of all he outwardly professed but times had been hard and money harder to come by and the ease with which the Brits parted with readies, for the most widely known tattle had been the reason he had become ensnared in the British espionage cloak all those years before. It had set him up grandly at the time and his innate caution had him avoiding the fate of many an informer during the tan war. Namely a single-way trip to a roadside culvert up the Wicklow Mountains to be left with a small-calibre bullet hole in the back of the head and a sign 'Death to all informers' hung around the neck.

Mulligan the retired informer sat down, he thought he had heard the last from his paymasters in 1922; the avaricious part of him had been sad to see them go, the realist relieved however. So the phone call, he wasn't in the book, with his old code name had shocked him to his tricolour waving Free State core. Unfortunately, he had not hung up immediately, he blamed a rabbit-like freeze, they'd made it plain it was in his best interests, a small roll of Irish banknotes, a matter of no interest to the Irish authorities, no harm promised, sure he'd heard that one before. And so now he found himself in a nice comfortable snug, 'perfect' he thought 'to return to the loving embrace of his majesties service', his old spy craft coming back to him, the snug obscure and private yet with views of the doors and anyone who entered it. He nursed his pint of stout a while, musing on business matters and more importantly what he was doing, why had he come, what could he gain, what could he lose and what the hell did they want from him after twenty years?

The rustle of a nearby newspaper by a gentleman at the bar counter diverted his attention; the gent holding it up was reading the death notices on the back page. Cheery old soul thought Dermot, probably seeing whom he had outlasted. He subconsciously absorbed the headlines, not exactly reading rather his eyes sweeping the titles and relaying all of it back to the brain, raw and undigested. A bit like what they said these new Radars did, saved Britain once already they had, 'U-Boats wreak havoc on north Atlantic convoy' his brain unjumbled. 'Oh God and James Oliver Plunkett! Did the Brits intent marching back into the 26 counties?' Like Norway but before the Germans this time. Was this the historic prelude, the meeting to decide the fate of a nation, as Dermott fanciful notions became even more lurid, Gaelic Quislings, blue shirts and whatnot, a movement at the door saw his contact walk in.

A man in his early fifties, clean-shaven, a shock of grey-white hair noted the balding Mulligan sourly, well combed, rich and nearly luxurious in its extent, long sideburns, still with a dash of dark colour in them. The new arrival had a small attaché case in one hand and a shoe hornpipe clasped in his mouth, this along with the farmers' journal he held in his other was the prearranged meeting signal. Dermott raised his arm to beckon the man over, 'Oh well I could have slipped out the other door but I'm in it now' thought Mulligan mournfully but with a fizz of excitement in his belly, just like the old days. The man shook hands and sat down without saying a word, politeness and the rules of hospitality held court, drinks were petitioned and arranged in front. Mulligan didn't know if he drank stout but that was the best thing they had in the bar so stout it was! Anyway, Mulligan's mother swore by it, 'has eatin' and drinkin' in it' she'd say and told him that after his birth the midwife had made her drink a glass, 'good for the blood' she said 'and after a twelve-hour labour you'd left me with little enough you scut'. The two men sat quietly and tried to sum up the other.

Outside half an hour later the city was quiet, a low cloud of smoke hung over the tenement areas towards the north of the city, trams rattled around St. Stephens Green and groups of same-sex friends passed by to get to the local dance hall. The Admiral was struck by two things as the tram car passed through the streets. Girls still wore stockings, the Admiral like many a navy man had an eye for a stocking calf, that and that the shops had laden front windows, full of mouth-watering hanging joints of meats and sausages, eggs, cakes, packets of butter, tins of biscuits, chocolate, coffees, teas. It had him frothing at the mouth coming as he was from a drab land of rationing to this well-provisioned paradise.

23

- Will we have time to do some shopping? You know to bring the wife back something nice.
- Sorry Admiral, we'll need to keep your visit here under wraps as much as possible, we can't risk being seen in the street for the sake of some jam tarts and cream buns. Jerry's got eyes all over this place.

Osborne felt his stomach lurch with avowed disappointment.

- Don't you worry we won't send you home empty-handed; we'll send somebody out to get you some ration bursting goodies later.

The incongruous pair jumped off the tram on the main city thoroughfare of O'Connell Street dominated by the imposing General Post Office. The GPO only 25 years earlier had been pulverized by British artillery during the abortive uprising of 1916. Barely had it been put back in some sort of order before it was smashed apart again by the same artillery, this time the culprits being the Irish army, who'd borrowed the heavy weapons from the departing British. Oh, the ironies of history.

- You'd never believe this was the hottest part of the Western front for a week, would you?
- Quite - snorted the Admiral whose cousin had commanded a troop of Hussars which had been pinned down for six hours by a handful of snipers as they had attempted to relieve Dublin Castle, the snipers they'd found out later had been a shopkeeper, his delivery boy and two tram drivers.

He still remembered his cousin's letters describing the sheer ordinary savagery of it all. Horses slipping and dying in a crimson melange of their own blood and innards, shops stalls under bullet-ridden canopies, old women in black and children standing barely yards from front line positions urging on his brave boys, even pointing out snipers positions. 'He's up there in widow Turner's front room, tore down her lovely lace curtains like a Sibereen vandal the fecker, third window on the left Luv'.

- I'm going to make you look very good, we're going to go up and knock on the great man's door itself. I called my contacts and he is at the institute till nine this evening, let's go.

Mulligan's grandiloquently named 'contacts' were his char ladies husbands' nephew who worked as a porter at the school. For the price of a few pints, he would leave open a side door for an hour or so. Still, it's a confidence game Mulligan mused, a confidence game.

- What! Go there ourselves now! Surely we can wait and not rush things, there's a chap at the embassy who's much better up on this sort of thing than I am, why don't we go and get him - gasped the admiral sounding more like a midshipman taking his first command.
- Ye'll have me escortin' the band of the Welsh guards around Dublin next for the love of Jaysus, it's bad enough with you, now come on, left right left right left - Mulligan was having the best time he'd had in years.
- Alright but I'll tell you one thing my young man, there's absolutely no reason to take the Lord's name in vain. None at all and I'd kindly like you to refrain from doing so.
- Weren't you in the navy? I thought sailors swore as much as nuns pray.
- That would be the lower ratings you'd be referring to.
- That's all right so. I would have been a lower rating. But here there's no reason to get your knickers in a twist sure I didn't mean any harm. And wasn't it only a wee quiet 'Jaysus' that escaped. Sure the poor man himself, suffering the agony of agonies on the cross, wouldn't have minded.

London May 1941

'It was the best of times, it was the worst of times' a line worthy of Shakespeare but the boy wonder from Stafford couldn't blag all the good lines, this one was coined by another of the immortals, Dickens when describing the tumultuous events on both sides of the Channel during the French Revolution. Now nearly 150 years later the enemy once again had the whole of Europe ranged against England, glaring rabidly at her from across the self-same waterway. And those dozen words summed up it exactly, the good mixed with the bad, the insufferable with the bizarre and the madness with the surreal. One minute you were taking a bus, something so ordinary it would be uncommented upon, next minute you would find yourself crammed in by the hundreds into a shelter during an air raid. Life wasn't normal; it was cheap and as exciting as hell.

Of course, everybody by that summer had had a year to get used to the situation, abnormal became the norm. This was Britain's' great moment, herself and her dominion allies standing alone against the might of the Nazi Hitler's' hordes, that funny German with the funny moustache parodied in Chaplin's film didn't seem so funny now he was Europe's new ruler. This titanic struggle had been a lonely one since

25

the French had capitulated, who'd have foreseen that, the proud French who'd fought four long years last time now throwing in the towel this time after little more than four weeks. The French misfortune was to share a land border with Germany, it wasn´t the RAF that had saved Britain, though they had helped, it was her geography. Tanks didn´t float as well as they cruised through Flanders.

So Britain waited, got thinner and shabbier and copulated more often. The food was bland and tasteless no matter how inventive the Ministry of Agriculture's recipes were, but wasn't it like that before the war but just more plentiful, gastronomy had never been a noted talent of the British, the culinary French were far worse hit by the shortage of truffles, foie and the like. One of the unexpected positive side effects of the subsistence diet of meatless meat pie and vegetables boiled to a uniform pulp was the gout rout, it had all but disappeared. It was the only rout the British had managed. The gluttons and the nation had never eaten so sensibly.

Ranged against this garden party was the whole of German occupied Europe. The latest daring German operation in Greece and Crete had temporarily ended British interest on mainland Europe. Abject millions had only one source of hope and that was the BBC World service, a tenuous insubstantial undulating link that if discovered tuned in on your wireless dial could have you shot. Only the invisible radio signals could travel with impunity and without a Reich's pass. Imagine it then sitting in the best room of the house as invariably the wireless was given pride of place and rarely found itself in the kitchen. Outside their safe domain was a nightmare of Nazis, identify papers, endless forms, restrictions, rationing, resistance (on a very small scale) and its evil twin, reprisals at ten to one. Worst even to all good free liberal minds was the hopelessness; there seemed no end in sight. The Germans appeared invincible with no one to stop them and only the British miraculously holding out. Imagine then the hush that came upon the rooms full of people aching for news, good or bad but any news at all; imagine the voice with its British clarity, its British clipped vowels, and its British freedom- 'This is London calling'. A firm voice from hundreds of miles away in a land that was at once battered but unbowed. That stood alone but stood undefeated, that seemed cornered but was fiercely defiant. BBC broadcasts were the most visible signs of British intransigence, that and sorting out the Italians in Africa. But at this stage and most of Europe agreed, just staying in the war was in itself a glorious act. England's finest hour indeed.

Amidst all this in another quiet office along another quiet corridor in Whitehall, it being full of them, two senior civil servants of a division of an unlisted section of government considered the problem Osborne's Dublin report had given them. A problem that would have to be solved somehow.

- So that's what the Admiral found out, snooping around Dublin in his best tweed suit – said the first.
- Yes, we know where one of the science chaps we need is, have to have him it says here. And even more curiously the chap who can get him for us was mentioned as being known here and there as well – his senior colleague said, two weeks only but he loved pointing it out.
- Two birds. Happens now and then. You know the German idea of a concentration camp is a bit different to ours; they seem to have refined it. Damn it, it's just like the tank all over again, our military chaps think of something really spiffing, the pen pushers bury us under triplicate forms for each blasted nut and bolt and before you know it Johnny foreigner has nabbed the idea without so much as a thank you, improves it no end and is using it against you. Lot to be said for how they do things. 'Camp' makes it seem outdoorsy, smell the fresh air, Boy Scout lark but according to reports, the conditions are brutal. Knew Baden Powell myself incidentally, met him at...hmm...it's on the tip of my tongue; dash it now I can't remember where still a charming man. And those bloody Germans robbed that idea as well, Hitler Youth be damned. Returning to the subject at hand, what about this scientist chap then? – Junior, he might be but he loved to drop a name when he could.
- The Americans are keen as mustard too; they see him as being a key man on the project we are working on together – said senior in a knowing way.
- We and the Americans! But they are a neutral power, mores' the pity. What project? How can we be working with a neutral power? – Need to know stopped short of this colleague.
- There's neutral and there's neutral, the Americans know they will have to come in someday and so they're leaning towards us in a heavily neutral fashion – said in a let me put you a bitwise manner.
- Can't come a day too soon and the project? – pleading do tell
- Some sort of wonder weapon, 'fraid can't say any more but Churchill's very in favour and without this Kessler who knows.

27

That's where the other chap from Dublin comes in, Malone, Dagan Malone. - telling.

- What sort of name is that? DAGAN MALONE. Sounds more pagan than Christian – COE sensitivity offended.
- Well apart from that, Malone's the man that can get to Kessler and without Kessler the project will be delayed months they reckon. So we must have him.
- Malone?
- Yes. And hence Kessler.
- He's in confinement as well actually – junior has his own choice tibbits - sort of a coincidental, thief catch set.
- Really, banged up to? Another camp perchance?
- Not exactly. Bit worse, a prison.
- How's Malone going to help us then?
- That is why they come to us, we're specialists in extractions. This time it's double the work. A pre-extraction extraction so to speak.
- Speak less – senior finished on.

Chapter II

Havana Central Jail, Cuba, early summer, 1941

When the shotgun totting guards high up on the ledges around the prison common area started turning their backs that was the first sign something sinister was going to happen. A faint hum started making itself heard from one corner as inmates started gathering. Prisons worldwide are tough miserable places with few bright moments and not known for having an extensive evening time repertoire of entertainments so when news went around of an impending 'navajazo' most of the prison population not in solitary confinement could be depended upon to show up.

Opposite the rapidly growing noise, in the far corner of the prison common area sat the prisons non-Hispanic inmates, mostly white and black apart from one old Chinese man. He had been locked up for drug smuggling, his crime not being the smuggling but his lack of largesse when it came to paying off sufficient members of the police force. The rest of the group was a mixture of drunken sailors, not so sharp card sharps, a mixed bag of assorted losers and finally to one side was a broad-shouldered dark-haired man of medium height, his hair, slickened by naturally produced oils, was thick and swept back over to beyond his ears exposing a small pale skinned forehead bookended by thick eyebrows and a pair of cobalt blue eyes which marked him out to both men and women for different reasons.

This man, from the blighted periphery of old Europe, would not have looked out of place in a sacred forest grove with a Druids sickle and hazel rod. This Celt of the ages was wearing a middling to full beard, an expression of bemused puzzlement and what appeared to be a tuxedo. The tuxedo, barely recognisable from its former glory was currently enjoying the hospitality of the Cuban state just like its porter. The bemused expression was not the look of a man overwhelmed to find himself in the worst jail in Havana, or the look of a man writhing against the injustice of his incarceration, more than the faint smirk at the corner of his mouth was the end product of a complex neuronal reaction that could be summed up in the word "hubris", what goes round comes round.

What had brought him here was decades of devil take the hind bit blatant tomfoolery, intense and effusing it had been, much better than cutting turf on the bog of Kilterran, helping on the family farm or with his father the local GP. That rural idyll had been left behind to study medicine in Dublin. He'd found himself two years later via the Rising and the rise of Sinn Fein on the run from the British. A nasty ambush in the Vale of Limerick had left Black and Tans dead, creameries destroyed, bridges blown and a village burnt out as the British dealt out biblical levels of retaliation. He'd been on the run since then, legally and illegally, starting with the British then his ex-comrades on both sides, from his homeland, from Russian communists and Italian fascists. He had dodged amorous Charlestown dancers, social queens of Fifth Avenue, double-crossing Hollywood movie producers, French policemen, Wall Street bankers, Spanish Guardias Civiles, Albanian drogues and any number of tax, customs and excise officials. The Scarlett Pimpernel life he lived since dreamy flying squad days bivouacked in roofless famine era cottages had its downsides and as he surveyed a cockroach scurrying across the dirt strewn floor he was left in no doubt that here he was smack bang in the middle of one of the darker periods. Life was like that, just as the splendours and glories of the imperial Rome gave way without too much of a fuss to the bearskin clad hoards from the German forests ushering in a millennium of regression, ignorance and darkness. Then before you could say Black Plague along came the Renaissance.

Not quite on that time scale but the length of this man's current reverse could be measured by the twenty-one lines grouped in three sets he'd scrapped on the cell wall, an age-old form of chronometry engaged in by endless legions of inmates. Three weeks since he'd been led straight from the casino to the jail, the writ of habeas corpus crossing the road in the process so as not to trouble itself making his acquaintance. The necessary paperwork which had finally been done the following day made some side swipe reference to casino chips that arrived with the accused and had not gone to the trouble of being purchased at the cashier's desk. At the standard rate of twenty dollars American discretely passed was the standard reset but this time the police captain had coughed politely, shrug his shoulders and mention some misunderstanding with the current amour of the casino's boss. So here he was, sitting in his progressively deteriorating smoking jacket still impressive even in its present setting. The thought 'there's worse things than jail' arose in Dagan Malone's head but he was forced to admit that at the moment he was totally at a loss to name any of them.

- Nope can't think of a single God damn thing, plague, Viking raids, volcano eruptions maybe - and turning to the Chinaman he added - and that's from someone who used to make his living in politics.

His lip curled up at the edge forming a faint smile the Chinaman would have said smacked of resignation if the Chinaman had been paying attention. Instead, it was directed at the crowd ghosting its way towards and around them, Dagan followed his line of vision, you can never allow yourself to totally relax in prison, it's too dangerous, you have to be alert at all times which made the non-receptive soporific state he'd sunk into during the brief self-pitying stock take so dangerous.

Suddenly it was as if he'd touched a live element, a jolt lashed its way across his consciousness, all his senses crackled into a state of hypervigilance, sight, hearing, smell, taste and touch, all his stimuli frantically taking in the surroundings with the voracity of a black hole desperately compensating the time lost. The Chinaman stepped aside and behind as from the crowd came an expectant hum and from its tight embrace his challenger stepped forward. *Hubris, Nemesis,* whatever. Today Cuba was all Greek. The crowd instinctively backed away so the two adversaries faced each other alone but surrounded on all sides.

- *Hey Irish tienes problemas* - somebody shouted from the edge.

'Big problems was right' Dagan thought facing his opponent who had a half-grin fixed on his face

- *Oye Irish hoy vas a morir* - the man said then switching to English - I'm gonna cut you good gringo *hijo de puta* so not the mother who shat you wonna know you - Carlos he was called, a diminutive pox marked jailhouse fixer and enforcer. He was barely up to Dagan's shoulder, but bulk didn't matter so much in the tight confines of a ring hemmed in by the crowd where you were as likely to receive a quick jab to your kidneys with a stiletto knife as to have the luxury of dying while actually facing your adversary.
- *Apestas Carlos y tu inglés también, smelly Charlie* - Dagan replied, appreciative laughter came from parts of the crowd, they knew Carlos stank, everyone did but they didn't know his pigeon English did too.

Dagan took heart from the reaction, not everyone was on Carlos's side, at least half were neutral, and it meant Carlos was probably working for himself or one of the lesser prison bosses and not Paco, the acknowledged prison big man, someone Dagan had managed to keep on side by the simple artifice of not annoying him. His curiosity value as an ex-freedom fighter had won him many admirers; substitute Cuba for Ireland and the US for Britain and you had a fairly similar emotive makeup.

Carlos was small and wiry, his taut muscles covered with tattoos of 'chicas' visible through the tears in his singlet as several inmates egged him on. The pair circled each other; Dagan quickly removed the dinner jacket and wrapped it around his left arm, being a leftie or *ciotóg* as they still said in his home town. Mind you they also made the sign of the cross at the same time, left-handedness seen as perverse and even sinister. Still being sinister was the only thing keeping Carlos from closing in for the kill as Dagan kept the jacket buffered forearm right opposite him closing the stance, meant Dagan's torso was harder to reach.

The jailhouse knife, really a pair of old shaving blades artfully set in a long piece of wood, was a slasher weapon only. It could do terrible damage especially as the rusty blades would carry all sorts of bacteria, shit rubbed in as a sort of homely prison version of chemical warfare, the wounds would be superficial so Carlos must have another somewhere to deliver the *coup de grace*.

Carlos thrust right before turning like lightening to slash from the left. Dagan just got out of the way.

- You fight like a *neñaza* – Carlos said with an edge in his voice.

By now the crowd was getting restless. Carlos could sense time was running out, the guards were throwing back glances ever more frequently, as Dagan barely had time to react as Carlos swung in a high arc while in a flash the real knife appeared in the palm of his left hand, blade carefully concealed up to now behind his wrist. The sharp edge just missed his arm as Dagan drew back and the sleeve of the now defunct tuxedo was slashed to the core.

Carlos now glancing to his left and gave an almost indiscernible nod to somebody there, and one or two in the crowd started moving to Dagan's rear blind side. Dagan stayed away until now from the parts of the crowd where Carlos cohorts and jail dependents were but it was time to do something and fast. Dagan eyed a small stool to his right, he needed Carlos to talk who duly obliged, a look of triumph edged on to the mans face, all he had to do was corral Dagan back between his amigos and his two knives. Checkmate. He couldn't resist gloating about the impending victory, death assured, he was the macho, *dos cojones*, but it wasn't half as enjoyable unless the opponent knew, the glory was brief and needed to be savoured, the hapless victim had to be taunted. Carlos was no stranger to these situations and having always come out on top his confidence was overbearing and was going to prove fatal.

- I can smell the *mierda* in your *pantalones* from here.

This was the opportunity Dagan had been waiting for, he let his tux jacket unravel slightly, just enough so when Carlos was distracting himself by mouthing off instead of coldly going for the kill, Dagan prepared and aimed. Carlos got to the part of his speech where he glanced at his now in position allies right behind Dagan, this was when Dagan fired off his jacket from his hand like a whip, the button ended edge of the coat reached Carlos smack in the face as he wasn't looking, just where Dagan hoped, in the most delicate part the eye, the whiplash was vicious and a loud cracking sound sliced through the open air as it blasted its way into Carlos's left socket. Dagan felt the crunch as the small stone at the bottom of the lining he added thranked against the eyeball. The next seconds witnessed the end, Carlos screaming in agony brought his hands up to the face as Dagan flung his jacket at the first of the advancing thugs now hesitant and shocked at the stricken Carlos, Dagan took advantage of this grabbed the stool by the leg and swinging it viciously across the other side of Carlos's face, slamming it into the temple with such brutal force that the leg shattered as it met the head full on. The blow instantly cut off Carlos's screams as he dropped to the floor like a sack of potatoes.

-   Strike one! – Someone shouted out in an American accent, one of the black sailors.

Even before that happened Dagan swung around and launched the now two-legged stool at the first approaching body. The hesitation gave the battered stool sufficient impetus as it flew towards its second victim who had no time to react as the stool made another crisp clean contact, squarely connecting from forehead to chin.

-   Strike two – Dagan heard another one of the black American sailors shout out.

The remaining assailants stopped dead in their tracks suddenly uncertain, the near-certain easy kill of less than a minute ago had turned into a slaughter. The biggest in such a rage at his fellow imamates sprawled unconscious or poleaxed around him was spurred on to avenge them. Dagan backed away as the enormous shaved-headed giant came roaring at him.

-   'Mudarfocker!'

Dagan skipped over Carlos and tried to grab the knife from his inert hand but the prone man somehow retained enough grip to thwart this attempt, Dagan cursed as the bull bore down as without a weapon to hand the giant was likely to crush him flat. His earlier luck got set to desert him when suddenly the second black American stepped out of the crowd and slashed the onrushing attacker with a lightening like jab in the kidneys with another prison-made weapon. The enraged giant screamed and crashed into Dagan who quickly turned to deflect the crushing mass to one side where the giant slammed into several of the onlookers. The brush by left Dagan winded while the full force had more that one of the spectators needing to be helped away in extremis. Fight over, hushed silence in the amassed crowd apart from the bundle of screaming bodies the inert giant was on top of.

-   Strike THREE brother – the other black shouted triumphantly.

This brother turned to the other coloured gent and they started hand dancing was all that Dagan could make of it. Where he might have shook hands they raised their arms and smacked one palm against each then lowering them they gripped each other by the fingers, bumped fists like two judges gravels before punching fist on fist.

33

At this stage, all hell had broken loose the crowd streamed around the broad Negros as they fled the advancing cordon of guards. Dagan stepped over the twitching body of the last casualty and started away from the charging wardens as their batons crashed down indiscriminately on all sides.

- *Hijos de la gran puta!* – He heard screaming just before a sickening crunch of a nose being smashed.

The stairs to the upper cells was rammed with desperate inmates rapidly trying to escape the blows. Soon them who hadn't moved from their cells were raining down mattresses, urine-filled bides, tables and chairs and anything that could be thrown was being hurled at the massed guards.

That rules out plan A though Dagan as inmates savagely fought each other to get up the stairs. Spying the two Negros climbing up on the table he gingerly edged his way closer. The tallest of them cupped his hands and launched the other up the first landing, once safety over the second Negro hauled up the first. Dagan didn't think twice, he ran towards the table jumped in mid-step and in some variation of the triple jump landed a foot on the table then a second and continued the upwards vault catching the railing on the first landing. The clatter drew the attention of the two blacks who looked down.

- Man, this cat has more than nine lives – said the first looking impassively as Dagan hung on.
- Just wanted to thank you in person, if you'd just lend a hand gents I'd be much obliged – Dagan stretched out a free hand and was now barely hanging on.
- You'll be wanting us to save your bony white ass for the second time then?

Dagan swung his leg up and caught the rail and bounced off. A shotgun went off close by as the raucous below reached biblical proportions.

- As one Samaritan to another you could put it - Dagan swung his legs up to avoid a baton. No time like now – he said through gritted teeth. The two 'Samaritans' looked at each other, nodded and hauled him up in one brisk movement so fast that Dagan felt weightless for a second - Dagan Malone pleased to meet your acquaintance. You boys are certainly in good shape.
- Cornelius Murphy – said one.

- Aloysius Brown and sure the navy likes to keeps the coloured man busy – said the other more reluctantly.
- Not too busy now are we to hear a proposition? – Dagan started at them before they turned away, time to make his pitch - If a man was decided that his present lifestyle wasn't to his liking it could occur to him to do something about it.
- Bro you talking like my officer, all highfalutin waffle, one who never says it straight out what he wants to say – said Brown more aggressively.
- The one you hit? – elaborated his friend.
- Ok, the ex-officer but I didn't do it out of no disrespect.
- Excuse me – interrupted Dagan - minor tiffs with authority figures aside why did you sideswipe that big guy on his way to flatten me into a pancake? – Dagan felt he had the right to ask.
- I didn't just hit the mother. I stiffed him and it wasn't cause I felt sorry for you or nuttin or cause in here you is a white nigger and damn if I don't know how they can gang up on a man and do him an injustice.
- So it wasn't out of the goodness of your heart.
- Shit no and shit yes. I wouldn't have saved you if I'd known you were going drop all this explanation bullshit on me. Hell no my preacher told me a lifetime of badness can be redeemed in an instant. Maybe the Lord made me do it cos I just did it, I felt inspired – Murphy said this to Brown.
- It wasn't cos we like ya – Aloysius affirmed.
- Cos we don't – Murphy backed up the common sentiment.
- It was cause growing up in the south marks a man. I hate a lynch mob stringing up an innocent brother, nothing personal.
- And the spics hate us as much, if they're still after you we're safer – added Aloysius.
- Amen to that brother. STRA-TE-GY they be calling it. You should have let that Carlos dude can his ass altogether – Murphy the second half of the dark destroyers had no truck with whitey it seemed.
- Well listen 'the why' doesn't matter, you did it, you dropped the man and that is enough for me – Dagan spelt out - So I'd like to show my appreciation by repaying you in the best manner possible.
- What could you do dude, rustle us up a couple of sugars! – the two struggled to feign even half interest.
- You boys are righteous but very cynical, but as I hinted at earlier it's time to go without saying goodbye – Dagan left the cheese in the trap

35

- As if it's that easy – Aloysius didn't bite.
- You with me or not, I've got a plan and you've got the ways of making it happen.
- Oh yeah – Murphy sounded more than a bit sceptical
- What's up brother listen to the man, after all what's we got to lose
- Only three more years in this dump – Murphy snorted.
- Shoot! That long – Aloysius added his own snort - Now what were you saying about 'lifestyle changes' – Dagan had their attention.
- I like the sound of that brother – Murphy admitted - Are we talking unscheduled parole?
- Self-granted early release my man.
- And who can help us with that? – they asked.
- I think it's time we paid a visit to the warden, *el grand commandante* – Dagan announced.

José Bardos had been blessed at birth with a myriad of qualities. None of them, however, conspired to obtain him any great advantage in life. Neither ugly nor handsome, short nor tall, fat nor thin, he was medium in all his statistics. It was most annoying. His greatest ambition was to be happy and hope all those around him were too. If he'd been asked at school for his ideal job working as a prison guard wouldn't have been it. However not being predisposed to launch upon any other endeavour unaided and having an uncle as the warden of Havana's main prison that was where he had ended up. Still, if you held your nose up at some of the more nefarious acts of your colleagues and turned a blind eye to the nastier behaviour of the psychotic inmates you could almost convince yourself you were somewhere else. While morally corrupting if you let it, the office had abundant opportunities of self-enrichment. Earning a bit on the side to subsidize a miserable salary wasn't deemed morally wrong or even counted as corruption.

The most common services conducted by the prison staff was alcohol and drugs. Legends abounded of a special room where the richest inmates could buy the services of a woman but José had never actually been part of any such exchange. If the inmates weren't half doped up they'd be much more trouble for us was the self-justification most often uttered and not without veracity. Hence when José saw two of his most lucrative customers approaching his mind was on other things than the potential danger playing with seemingly innocuous inmates can entail. His thoughts ran slipshod over his prudence as the two black Americans approached accompanied by a third. That man was a trouble maker according to the commandant but José had always found him to be solicitous and polite, a gentleman on his uppers, *sin plata*, passing a misfortune but whose good breeding couldn't be slapped down so easily.

According to the whispered asides of the commandant, asides loaded with sour onion breath, the Irish prisoner was the son of a papal Count and knew Carmen Miranda biblically. The rancid smell of sour onions was torture, a strategy of the commandant's wife to load his food with it to make it all the harder for her philandering husband. As the men approached Jose didn't feel any cause for alarm, the excitement of earlier had died down completely. A few heads cracked, the dead men hauled away, 'In the sewer, two less rats to feed' the commandant had said and the usual simple innocents caught in the middle now passing some weeks in solitary. A typical week in the jail but now back to business and here came business. Jose motioned the men to a niche out of the overhead guard's line of vision; those guards would later receive an obsequy to keep them happy. Everyone's a winner.

- How much of the weed do....

That was as far as José got before a hand clasped him from behind and another hand clamped over his mouth before he could utter a warning sound. Pinned by overwhelming force and completely defenceless José felt his bladder loosen. A warm gush filled his underclothes and flash flooded down his legs.

- Damn, he's gone and pissed himself - a harsh whisper behind in his ear as the hold on him tightened even more. Jose heard a whimpering sound and realized it came from himself.
- Let me talk to him. Jose, nothing's going to happen to you, we're not going to hurt you in any way if you do as we say nobody's going to get hurt. Do you understand? Nod if you do – Dagan started whispering into José's ear, sweet embellishments to encourage him to let himself be manipulated, they needed his active co-operation or the plan became wobblier than a crème Brulee. Jose nodded, his cheeks burning with shame as his urine started to cool – Will you do as we say? – José nodded again, anything to buy some time, why wasn't anybody becoming suspicious – and what's the first thing we're going to do, well let's get you a change of trousers, no need for your colleagues to know about this accident. a

He felt dizzy and couldn't believe he wasn't going to be harmed, of course, Counts' son would behave in such a way, else all honour cast aside killing a defenceless man. A surge of brotherliness welled up in

37

José, almost like love, Latin machismo was the code Cuban males lived by and anything else could only pale in comparison to the mortification of childlike sodden pants.

- So what the fuck do we do now? - Cornelius asked five minutes later – and why did I have to give him my trousers
- It's simple. None of us can pass for Cubans, so we can't get far without him, we'd be rumbled straight away. You cover him as he shackles you. I have his gun, we march over to the main gate, he says he's taking us to isolation and on the way we pay a visit to his uncle.
- Then what?
- *El commandante* leaves for home every evening doesn't he? In his big Chrysler, so we'll just hitch a lift with him. Okay let's go – The grip loosened – Jose do your thing.
- *Tres para el zulu* – shouted José at the gate and to his colleague Miguelo behind.

Jose was having second thoughts but as long as the big black hombre *montaña* stood a foot away from him he didn't have the luxury of acting on his doubts and screaming for help. He involuntarily touched his gun holster flap, a tic he had when under pressure. The heavy metallic reassurance was missing; instead, a lighter wooden decoy replaced the pistol butt. A drop of sweat rolled down. The gate guard paused with his key ring only long enough to sow heart-stopping fear in Dagan, Aloysius and Murphy and an uplift of hope in Jose but before that could register the guard slipped the key in the lock. He missed the first time, cursed and got it the second time. He seemed drunk.

- *Si este condado tenia pelos no me costaria tanto metermela* – the guard stammered and gave a lecherous laugh winking at José. Dagan felt the panic rise in José's body, so gave him a dig in the ribs as the other guard looked away while opening the gate. Jose took the hint and in a quivery voice attempted to return the ribaldry – *Muy bueno Miguelo muy bueno, con pelos y no olvides uno bien lubricado* – They passed through as Miguelo burst into genuine laughter.
- *José! No me esperaba algo así de ti, muy bueno por cierto. Buenas noches* - the guard hiccupped and sat down again.
- What did he say? – Aloysius whispered out of earshot once through and along the corridor.

- That if the keyhole had hair he wouldn't have so much trouble finding where to stick the key in – Dagan had managed in his time to pick up enough Spanish to get around.
- Damn, that's a good line for a spic – Murphy expressed his appreciation for a good line.
- And José's come back about the keyhole being well lubricated was worthy of note. Now sssssch. We're coming up to the last gate, get through this and the coast is clear to the warden's office. Jose keep calm – Dagan knew the fine line they trod between outright success and outright disaster.
- How are you so sure he's here? – Aloysius asked. Dagan jabbed Jose in the ribs again but harder this time.
- He is here I swear by the blessed virgin of Guadalupe and all the saints – Jose affirmed.
- There you have it, no higher authority than that, besides Wednesday night is check up night. Nurse Rosa gives the warden a good going over. *'A solos'* of course. Anyone in the office that happens to be still in is told to look for jobs to do away from the boss's door. The *commandante* doesn't like an audience around for his revisions.
- The man's got it sorted that's for sure, that nurse is one hot mama – Aloysius voiced the general consensus of the prison population.
- I'm beginning to see how this could work whitey – Murphy grudgingly admitted.
- Gotha give you credit man, you're got all the angles figured out – Aloysius had always been more on side.
- Hey, it's just luck that today's Wednesday and not a Tuesday – even Dagan marvelled at how well things tended to turn out for him. He wasn't counting being thrown in jail obviously but so far the plan to get out was.
- Every day except Tuesday. The commandant is a worried man when it comes to his health and well being – Jose pointed out.
- Damn but that's good – Murphy.
- More wellbeing than anything else – Cornelius chuckled.

They crossed the interior patio to the administration building and went in and down the last airless corridor where the wall paint was peeling in the oldest places. As Dagan had promised the normal office staff was noticeable in their absence. They went on turning left and quietly up two flights of stairs to a short corridor of offices where at the end a half glass door led to the warden's suite outside of which old Pepe was slumped on a chair. Pepe as a nod to his venerable status was given the easiest jobs, like sleeping outside the warden's office on revision nights. His deafness made him eminently suitable for the task as Rosa always let the warden know in sonorously and stridently appreciative ways that his efforts at thrusting forward were not in vain. Old Pepe gave a snorting sound as the three prisoners and their foil reached the door.

- What do we do with him? – Cornelius whispered.
- Much as I hate to drag someone out of a good restorative sleep we've have to make an expectation. Make sure you impress on him the need to silently meet the waking hour.

Aloysius put his massive shovel of a hand over old Pepe's mouth as he promptly awoke with a start, jabbing from behind the meaty stopper his arms about. Aloysius whispered in his ear, old Pepe's eyes widened to such an alarming degree you'd expected them to fall out like glass lens that no longer fits securely in the glasses rim. Aloysius said something else and old Pepe nodded vigorously and finally whispered 'Vale Vale Vale' when Aloysius let him talk. The septuagenarian reluctantly stood up, his lack of haste evident in the embarrassment on his face and the bulge in his trousers, old he might be but he obviously entertained carnal thoughts of Rosa during his naps at the door.

The girls down the port will count on one more customer if Pepe made it out of his present predicament alive. God owed him that much after six months of listening to the Latin love beat from five meters and through two thin walls, hardness of hearing notwithstanding. Chuckling Aloysius pushed the old-timer through the door after first carefully checking to make sure no one was inside the outer office. A husky female voice was heard coming from the inner office.

- *Ah mi amor, ah, sí, eso mi Amor, soy tuyo mi máquina de amor* – said a sultry voice that could only be Rosa.

Cornelius motioned at the two captive guards to sit before he started to tie their hands.

- *Ahí va ahí va* – came Rosa's theatrical exclamations from the next room.
- *Me pones chiquilla! Me pones* – a deeper male voice gravelly with lust replied.

Even given the seriousness of their predicament, Old Pepe and Jose exchanged smirks as they were being tied up.

- *Esta Rosa, madre mía* – José said in a whisper.

- Sssh – Dagan put a finger over his lips, as much to Jose as to Aloysius as he began to turn the knob of the inner office door silently.

The scene revealed a tastefully decorated office with a large desk in front of a picture of the Cuban president opposite a book-lined wall of stands and shelves with a leather sofa. The books looked mostly like legal texts, dusty and neglected, their primary role of gravitas lending accounted for.

- Who'd have thought there were so many statutes of law in Cuba? – thought Dagan taking in the leather spine filled view.

Turning towards the table, a Dionysian image of venal debauchery could be made out. The rise and fall of the pale white buttocks, broad in expanse and hairy in a way that marked them inerrably as male and belonging to a prosperous middle-aged vigorous man about town. This primordial sight was framed by a pair of heavy linen trousers; brown leather suspenders dropped to one side currently being gripped by a petite pair of immaculately manicured hands with red varnished nails that inexorably drew the eye.

The hands disappeared to be replaced by shapely legs into small white heeled shoes as Rosa's legs clenched the back of the male's legs between them, the quivering male's behind gave a substantial shiver.

- *Si si mi pequeño señor*
- *Ahaaa siiii si,*

A crescendo appeared to be approached as the flushed face of Rosa came into view to one side of the commandants head swaddled in her arms and hands.

- *Oh!* – Rosa said in meek surprise as she spied her audience wearing wry smiles of those knowing another's most intimate affairs.
- *OHH* - said Rosa, louder this time in confusion and bewilderment.
- *Si mi amour si* – came her partners reply failing to grasp the reason for Rosas marked change in tone.
- *NOO ERNESTO NOOO* - Rosa now tried to shrug off Ernesto.
- *Pero estoy estooooy esperaaa* – Ernesto had reached a critical point of almost total frustration, close to the summit but out of oxygen.
- *NOS ESTÁN MIRANDO.*
- *Mirandonos, quien, HIJOS DE PUTA.*

Ernesto in a filthy rage brought on by his unreleased libido turned to murder the first person he could find who happened to be a six foot four inch solid wall of black muscle. As Ernesto swung his fist the rage on his face turned to shock and then fast became the beginnings of a call for help. Ernesto's whimpering cry went no further than a shrill blip before it was muffled by Brown who neutralised the face down whimpering warden. His paramour was another story. Aloysius was busy so Dagan dashed to cut off Rosa as she athletically swung her legs to the other side of the table while at the same time grabbing the phone and dialling the operator

- *Ayudanos ayudanos hay hombres...*

Dagan reached around and pushed the hook down while grabbing Rosa's wrist. Rosa took a deep breath as she prepared to scream but wisely stopped as Dagan shook his head and squeezed her wrist as a warning of futility. A look of pure hate from Rosa cut Dagan to the quick.

- What's the point of screaming? People will only think you're pretending too much to be enjoying Ernesto's attention – he said intending to hurt.
- *CERDO* – Rosa fairly spat out the words, her look one of sheer loathing.
- Quite! You are as brave as you are beautiful if you promise to behave we won't tie you up I promise – Rosa not mollified by the old world charm one bit nodded curtly.
- Okay gringo PIG – what a pair she had and then in a show of sheer pizzazz she stood up from the table, flattened her shirt modestly and walked over to the sofa to sit down, all the while feeling five sets of eyes on her hips which seemed to sway to such an extent it seemed like a drunk. On the way for good measure she stepped on and over the back of her lover in a blatant show of contempt.
- *No lloras como un niño, comportas como un hombre* – with a sweep of her hair she sat down, crossing her legs and folded her arms.

Such a combination of strength and vulnerability, the female of the species, deadly in the art, facing a situation from a position of serenity and cunning, she'd see how the new power balance worked out before attempting any move.

'What *cojones'* Dagan thought again, Aloysius took his gaze away from Rosa with difficulty and met Dagan's glance, a raised eyebrow showed that he too knew a class act when he saw one.

- Now what – he said - We got them or they got us?
- I don't feel to free neither – Murphy said passing his eyes over the prostrate warden, tied up guards and one praying mantis ignoring all before her as she filed her nails.
- We'll be out of here in ten minutes I promise.
- There are three gates, two perimeter fences, twenty guards and God know how many rabid mutts between us and outside – Murphy summed up the situation in its worst possible light.
- Seems like a toughie I know – Dagan said with brimming confidence – Now who wants to drive?

American Embassy, Habana, 10:30 pm

The embassy major demo knocked fussily.

- Ambassador, you are wanted in the communications room.
- What in the cotton-picking world are you on about? Can't a man have ten minutes to himself to dine with his family without mindless fuss pots dragging him away for no rightful justifiable God damn reason known to man - the US ambassador to Cuba JC Holden wasn't accustomed to state department niceties having been during thirty years one of the most successful sugar tycoons in the south and one of the biggest donors to the Democratic party in his blessed state of Alabama. His reward, a destination any sugar man would appreciate, had been Cuba. His wife wanted Paris but he wasn't that big a donor, she dutifully made the most of a posting in an even steamier climate than the one they left behind. She now motioned to her husband of thirty five happy years.
- Now honey, don't get so worked up, Uncle Sam needs you so run along and do what you have to sugar plum. I'll stay up waiting till you get back so we're both frazzled at the drinks reception tomorrow.

In the face of such emotive mixture of tenderness, devotion and patriotism John C's gruffness melted away as it had every time during their long and happy marriage. Besides saying 'don't you dream of staying up' as he pushed back from the dining table he then added in a barely audible voice 'you're still the belle of the ball'.

Passing the embassy factotum with a 'pretend you didn't hear all that and pretend real hard sonny' scowl on his face JC strode down the corridor and changed gear with the single-mindedness that had served him well all his adult life. He wondered what was waiting for him in the inner sanctum of the communications room, the only one guarded by two of the marines attached to the embassy. Why even his quarters only merited one of the ceremonially dressed ramrod straight dazzling spit and polished young marines. The reason, of course, was the code room; in any sudden attack on this small sovereign part of the United States, the state department codebooks represented an infinitely greater prize than the mere flesh and blood of its envoy.

Once inside JC encountered Macy, Simmons and Sam Culvert, the three next in line to him in the embassy pecking order so something big was up. Macy was his political officer, Simmons the military attaché and Culvert, well JC tried not to take too much interest in Culverts activities, diplomatically labelled 'trade attaché'. But how many trade delegates went around armed to the teeth and knew nothing about sugar and in Cuba for Christ's sake. JC nodded to each and knew it was really serious when it was Culvert who spoke up first.

- Ambassador, we've had a class one communication from Washington – he said in a southern drawl.
- Class one? We're not at war with anyone I hope – Class one! Maybe he wasn't going to be back to his dinner that soon after all.
- Washington has cabled us the following urgent protocol. Immediate release of one Mr Dagan Malone stop American citizen born in Ireland stop from jail Havana central stop once in Americans hands return subject to Washington without delay stop.
- State wants us to spring some guy from the clincher, is that what all this fuss is about?
- Not State sir, the cable came directly from the White House, its signed FDR.

John C would have done anything for the president, his president; the man he believed had saved the very soul of the nation when it was at its lowest ebb. Why people had even started emigrating to the Soviet Union! Ordinary decent working Americans had arrived at such desperate straits as that and FDR had almost single handily restored the pride of the nation JC believed was God's own. A Republican all his life till the depression now he was neither Republican nor Democrat, he was a Roosevelt man through and through.

- Well jump to it son, start making calls, get me the president of this damn country on the line, then the head of United Sugar.

Let's start banging heads together - JC's voice rose to a crescendo – Why if I have to go the damn jail myself and drag him out with my hands I will. If Franklin Delano Roosevelt wants this then I won't rest till he is damn well satisfied.

Havana Central Jail

Forty minutes later Culvert and two burly men from 'services' were on the road to the jail. If the collective noun for a group of rapid calls was a flurry then no better word could describe the frantic telephonic activity that had gone on to some of the islands most illustrious personages. Thanks to that Culvert was armed with righteousness and a pardon signed by the head of the Cuban supreme court. That eminent jurist had been yet another person ripped from the embrace of dulcet sleep by the cacophony of events bigger than he. Culvert remembered the bemused gent trying to sign the release warrant with the pen upside down. Why do so many successful men become so somnolent Culvert hoped to rise in his profession but continue to view the world as it happened in all its vividness in the hours past ten o'clock at night.

The Oldsmobile cruiser arrived at the outer gate of the prison as fast as it could through the empty night along unpaved unlit roads that had kept the driver in a state of constant alertness.

- *Pasad ustedes* - said the ranking guard who shot to attention as he spotted the miniature states and stripes flag on top of the right-hand front bumper.

As they passed the opening gates Culvert leaned forward to speak to the front pillion passenger who spoke the best Spanish of them all.

- That guy addressed us in the formal manner right?
- He did sir.
- Good. Don't want any disrespect shown to the flag by any two-bit spic gatekeeper – Culvert saw red if his flag was even slightly besmirched.
- He also said 'sons of bitches' when his back was turned and something about the wardens medical check-up being interrupted. At this time of night? – The linguists face was a quizzical picture.

-    Why that son of......- before Culvert could vent his pique on the defamers of his sacred star-spangled banner events happened in quick succession.

As they moved off from the front gate of the jail an alarm bell went off at the same time as from around the corner another car came roaring along at top speed. A car roughly on the same level of prestige as the Oldsmobile, big, powerful, modern and with several emblems, flags, lights and what not to testify to the importance, imagined or otherwise of the dignitary it belonged to. Upon seeing the Oldsmobile its driver swerved to avoid it while blaring his horn. From the front passenger seat a head emerged shouting at the gate guards.

-    *Fuego fuego! Dajad pasar el comandante, dajad pasar!!*

The horn blared to good effect, the gate opened as the passengers screamed *'Fuego! Fuego!'* while motioning to a window up in the administration block. The new arrival flashed by the Oldsmobile, momentarily giving Culvert a glance of two un-Cuban men in guards uniforms, one very black and tall, the other very white and pale, along with a grey-haired man in his fifties in the back seat with a dark suit on, his eyes clenched shut as if petrified, his mouth moving as if he was muttering or praying. The brief scene was completed by the vision, and Culvert didn't use the word lightly, of an extraordinary handsome woman, garbed in white, her face for one instance towards Culvert and in a moment he'd never forget, smiled at him. Culvert a keen Pentecostal Baptist in his youth who looked amused upon Cuban Catholic fervour for plaster cast saints dressed up and paraded around on feast days. For one moment his contempt for colourful idolatry slipped as he felt as if he had witnessed an apparition. Then the car was gone, flying through the hastily opened gates and into the night. Before they had time to take a breath the long howl of the prisons general siren broke through the night.

-    What the Dickens is going on, the place is on FIRE – Culvert recovered his sense of the situation.
-    Doesn't look much, just smoke mostly – his driver pointed out.
-    Get the car started, we have work to do, fire or not. What's all that racket going on? – Bells and engines jangled from all around.
-    That sounds like the general alarm to me sir – one of the passengers said.
-    Oh Christ – the driver forgetting his bosses prissiness when it came to blasphemy.

- Oh Sweet Jesus! – Culvert himself in the moment threw propriety to the four winds.

That was when the Oldsmobile, treated so infamously by all comers that night, was smashed into sideways by a siren blasting chase vehicle packed with heavily armed guards which was in turn rammed by another similar vehicle from behind while the occupants to man shouted the same mantra.

- *Han fugado han fugado!*

US Embassy conference room, 3 am

JC had already downed three coffees at this stage but Culvert's report had him jumping around in disbelief. A simple prisoner handover had gone over like Dodge City.

- So who else was in the car then, this Malone character and the warden, who else? You counted six – JC's incredulity was manifest.
- According to the deputy governor, the car contained Malone, two more American prisoners, the warden, the warden's medical advisor and one guard they'd tied up.
- And the fire? They set fire to the building to cover their escape! Simple and clever, fiendishly clever. But to put so many lives at risk if it had spread out of control, my God what kind of people are we dealing with, what could the President possibly want with this boundless ruffian.
- It was more smoke than fire Mr Ambassador, they put a bin close to the window and soaked it with the warden's best rum. It would have burnt out very shortly any way even if it hadn't been extinguished by the fire brigade – Culvert continued his report.
- Who raised the alarm?
- Another guard left tied up managed to slip out of his bonds.
- And they might have been thwarted if you hadn't been in the way of the chasing prison guards.
- Back luck sir and we'll need to request another Oldsmobile, ours is a total write off, we're lucky no one was hurt in the collision – Culvert sounded rueful, he loved the Oldsmobile.
- Ah yes the collision. That could have led to a huge diplomatic incident, a shootout in Havana jail involving US embassy staff as if the situation wasn't bad enough.

- It was tense Sir, they thought we were part of the 'jailbreak' and the guards even fired some rounds in the air.

Culvert remembered the confusion vividly, the impact of the crash, the aftershock. One of the embassy staff had suffered a concussion; the rest pistols out while shotguns were pointed at them. A lot of panicky shouting eventually cleared the air – AMERICANOS - but it was a minor miracle that no shots had been fired. Sweat broke out on his forehead just thinking about it.

- What about the flown birds? – After that debacle, the ambassador was ready for a boost.
- We're confident that they'll be apprehended soon. The warden and the other guard were dropped on the side of the road a mile outside Havana.

At that point, a messenger arrived with another cable from Washington. Short and blunt.

- Addressed to 'My dear Cal', who could that be? There's no 'Cal' or 'Mr. Cal' on the embassy registry - The messenger waved the paper around with a puzzled look.
- Never mind that sonny, I'll take it – the Ambassador grabbed the note from the messenger's hand.

Cal was the private name the president used when they were alone. The 'C' in JC stood Calhoun, a favourite of JC's mother back in the days when the south lived it's golden (depending on your colour of course) autumn before being overwhelmed by the swarming blue coats. He read the message to himself – 'Hope we have that fellow in our hands by now, it's of vital importance, I wouldn't have asked you otherwise, please don't let the side down. I'm relying on you Cal. Send package post prepaid whenever you can. All our best to Mary. FDR'.

Cal felt the weight of presidential expectation on his shoulders. He was keenly aware of the impending sense of failure despite what his staff said. How could he break the bad news to his president? JC figured this Malone to be one smart operator who wouldn't be picked up that easily or quickly? His friend the president, the shame of it but just sitting around and waiting was never his style. JC turned to his staff.

- Get my car ready! – He barked.
- But ambassador it's way too early for your daily round of golf – the messenger was excelling himself today.

-     Golf! You're talking about frigging goddamn golf. Listen here sonny boy, all leave is now suspended forthwith; call in every Tom Dick and Harry we have. I want everybody working the phones, the newspapers, the police, the bars, the casinos, the hotels. No one is to have more than four hours off till we find this son of a bitch – JC who had never sworn in front of his staff, was known for his refined southern manners faced an audience of shocked staffers - Well get to it, don't just stand there with your stupid mouths open so flies can get in, now go get my car ready. If I have to case every saloon, cat house, roadhouse and canteen in order to get this guy I will and the sooner I get started the better.

The melee of diplomatic and domestic staff in the room was electrified by the force field of iron will the ambassador gave off. The heaving room emptied rapidly as people raced to begin the hunt, teams were formed and reformed, destination assigned, contacts given, addresses shared. Just as the ambassador began to feel on top of the situation a figure appeared at the door, his major-domo.

-     What is it now? Don't get in the way, can't you see we're putting everything into finding this guy.
-     Sir? – the man's pallid features stuck out even more after spending a night attending to his hyperactive principal, but there was also a sheen of excitement in his manner that added a tint of colour to the cheeks – there is no need.
-     For what? – JC felt close to losing his cool again.
-     To look for Mr. Malone.
-     Why the hell not? – Despite trying his hardest his tone increased substantially.
-     The commotion downstairs?
-     It's damn noisy there. Now, what's this about not needing to look for Malone?
-     That was the noise, Sir, Mr. Malone and a some others just rang the doorbell, took the lobby marine guard hostage and is right now entrenched between the rest of our Marines and a lot of angry Cuban police right behind.

New York City, summer, 1941

Dagan knew where they were going. He'd asked twice only to be met by stony glances from the fedora hat dark suit white shirt narrow tie types who had been escorting him since his return to the continental United States of America. Government goons was how he thought of them who they could be working for any of many shadowy federal agencies. The exact one being a major step forward in helping to identify your principal adversary.

The roomy back seat of the Buick sedan would have been a fine way to travel if it hadn't been for two bulky agents sandwiching Dagan between them. The car stopped at some lights somewhere in mid-Manhattan, a group of girls with swept-up hair and breezy early summer pleated dresses with broad shoulders crossed in front of them lifting Dagan's spirits no end.

- So that's the fashion this fall, green seems to be popular. Thanks guys, you've been great, I'll hop out here, Cleary's on 47th and 8th is just around the corner – Dagan reached over to the handle.

The first reaction of the goons was to smother him under their bodies, blocking not just his exit but daylight and even breathing became difficult.

Okay – Dagan said in a strained voice as 500 lbs of meat sat on top of him – lighten up there, I can't breathe - the pressure lessened as the heavies eased off - What is this. Am I under arrest or what? What gives you the right to hold me against my will? And zero for observation, the door is locked from outside remember so you didn't have to do anything and your reaction time was a mere pass.

Would you like us to drop you at the Cuban consulate? – The front seat passenger turned around – We heard they're very anxious to talk to you - Young and smart looking, his suit fitted him and was obviously the person detailed to deliver the 'merchandise'. Despite the veneer of government respectability, he was someone who wouldn't have any qualms about having Dagan worked over if told to do so - Don't make this harder for yourself Mr Malone; we have orders to escort you from your hotel to our destination. That's all, if you cause trouble we'll deal with that don't you worry so it's up to you if you want to get there in one piece. You can walk in or we can carry you in but you're going in.

- Okay fine, I won't try and wriggle out of the box – The man stared at Dagan some seconds before he nodded at the two bookends and the tight hold loosened.
- Last time I was here was at a Jean Harlow party – Dagan said apropos nothing, a habit his Mother also had of thinking out loud.

- We know – front seat man said without turning around – it was in your file, one of your files.
- You seem to know a lot about me but what do you want from me?

The car turned off 5th and pulled into an underground car park of the Rockefeller Centre.

- We don't know what they want with you, we're just the mailmen but you can relax, considering the way you entered US territory I think you've been treated very well. All I do know is that some important people want to see you.

Malone couldn't but agree about the 'being treated well' bit. Ever since the tense standoff at the embassy had been interrupted and relieved by the ambassador things had taken a strange turn. While not the author of his own destiny he'd still been attended to by the finest doctors for the accumulated minor ailments and nutritional deficiencies endemic in Cuban prisons.   He'd been housed in comfortable quarters, his wardrobe had expanded at the rate of a suit a week as his vitality returned and his chest filled out. All the while under the watchful eyes but all the same he had been magnanimously treated.   Just as the ambassador had promised.

- Two months tops on easy street courtesy of Uncle Sam if you all just put down your weapons, release my marine who was only doing his duty and give yourselves up. – This had been said to Malone by a distinguished gentleman in a white suit and Panama hat, southern in his graces if he placed his accent right. Someone with the gumption and balls to stand up in the middle of the carnage in the reception hall of the embassy and call for calm. Dagan could still see him now.
- No need for panic, everybody just take it easy – He had said as unarmed he had approached the makeshift barricade.
- And who are you – Dagan had asked – the wizard of Oz?
- Better than that, I'm the ambassador. I've been looking for you all night and sure do appreciate you turning up on my doorstep, saves me the trouble of looking any further.
- You going to hand us back to the Cubans? – The Cuban police could be heard banging on the door and shouting - 'Cabrones, hijos de puta, os vais a morir' and other such endearments.
- No way brother, don't trust the whitey – shouted Murphy as the ambassador held up his hand.
- I can assure you that you'll be treated with the utmost respect, fed, clothed, I'll send for my personal doctor and then back to the

States, free men, all of you - with that he turned and issued orders to Culvert - Tell the Cubans to scoot and fast. This is the sovereign territory of the United States of America and if they don't back the hell off we'll start shooting.

JC knew he'd exceeded his remit, it was only the Irishman his good friends in the White House were interested in but he was a man of his word and if he wasn't going to return Malone to the Cubans he damn sure wasn't going to do so with the spare parts. Dagan looked over the well-dressed gent in his three-piece white linen suit and gold fob watch and chain dangling from his waistcoat. He could have been returning from a track meeting except for the huge black bags under his clear blue eyes. Something about his demeanour, his poise, his utter self believe that had carried him unarmed to parley with what could only be described upon seeing as a desperate bunch of marauders and cutthroats.

- Come on son, it's the best offer you're going to get tonight – his comfortable patrician tones of yesteryear reached out as did the bone china whiteness of his hand, the only flash of colour being the gold ring. Dagan knew the game was up but somehow, he didn't quite understand how, it had worked out, Dagan reached over to the proffered hand shook it first and then deposited his revolver in it. It was the handmade shoes that did it for Malone, anybody wearing Ferragamos of Sunset was a class act.
- I'm all yours – he said placing his gun in the outstretched hand and there-in ended the 1941 Cuban embassy siege, one of the State department's least known and most mysterious chronicles.

A special convoy of diplomatic cars had taken the four of them to the airport a couple of days later. Where surrounded by embassy security staff they had been loaded on to a DC-10 and flown straight to Miami. The Cuban police witnessing this with sour looks had been kept at bay, their rage evident at seeing Malone and the rest get away, it had been tense and at one point it looked like turning into a diplomatic incident but common sense and the big stick of the Americans had seen off the doubly offended locals.

Miami was where Dadan bade farewell to Rosa, Aloysius and Murphy. Murphy, delighted to have his slate swept clean, had requested a transfer to the Pacific fleet which was duly granted and had set off for Hawaii that same day. Aloysius, on the other hand, was finished with the white man's navy and took advantage of the generous discharge granted him to enrol in a black college in his home state of Mississippi.

- Going to shake up this world brother. The black man has to learn the tricks, learn the law to advance his race. You ain't heard the last of me brother – he had said.

The parting with his jailbreak buddy's was full of embraces and back-slapping bonhomie. No one could quite explain the wholly positive outcome.

- God damn but it's the first time I EVER got mixed up with a whitey and something GOOD happened – Aloysius joked.
- Somehow the Lords light shined down upon us – was Murphy's answer on the subject.
- And may His providence shine down all day long. Praise the Lord – Aloysius added.
- Amen to that brother – Murphy.

And with a nod to Culvert who had accompanied them the two formidable black men strode off down Collins Avenue as if they owned it. Dagan turned to the embassy officer to offer his gratitude and his farewells but got stopped in mid-sentence.

- Just a minute Mr Malone, we have to arrange a meeting for you with those agents who so determinedly sought you out. These 'men of state' cannot be identified for security reasons. We are not in on the purposes, intents or designs but they mean you no harm and would only like to speak to you – Culvert broke the not so unexpected news to Dagan.
- Have them call me; I'll leave you a number – Dagan knew what was what but he wasn't going to go along quietly. Not in his nature.
- They would like to have the meeting in the next day or so. After that you are free to go where you like – Culvert knew the type and played along.
- You mean I am not free now?
- Your liberty stretches as far as going northwards with my colleagues to New York City as a guest of the nation. A nation we might add who just saved your hide. It's not much to ask, you'll travel first class on the train leaving in 50 minutes and be housed and dined in the best hotels. Bear with us please – the embassy fixer secretly envied this Irishman, he was obviously deeply involved in something big.
- How can I refuse?
- It would be ungrateful of you to do so and it's not really an option. Please lend us some of your time and that's it.

The fact is Dagan didn't feel any danger or menace; he knew the four men around him were armed and would prevent him from leaving but they didn't seem to represent any other threat apart from being broad-shouldered babysitters.

- New York is my kinda town. Lead on McDuff – Dagan raised his hands up in resignation.

All that remained before catching the train was to wish Rosa well. She'd taken up the offer of passage to the west coast. The humiliation of such an influential man as the jail commandant was likely to rebound on her and it was a good time to take leave of her native island and see what America had to offer. 'The gringos love Latinas with big hair, big behinds and big fronts and I have all three' she had told him on route all the while fending off men with practised ease.

- So Rosa how are the gringos coping with you?
- Gringos, all I am meeting yet is people like me everybody is speaking the Spanish to me. More Cuba than Cuba. I can't understand it.
- Ditch them and come see the big apple with me. I'll show you how well they live in the five boroughs. I'll show you what snow looks like!
- You a crazy man, far too cold up there for my fiery temperament. Snow I only want to be seeing in the postcards you send me – and with that she blew him a kiss and left for her train.

And so it was Dagan alone except for his keepers who hit Manhattan. He was an honoured 'guest' and would be at liberty shortly but for a couple of routine meetings, they wanted him at. The result was delays and more promises, experiences they would like him to share, advice he could give, Uncle Sam would certainly be appreciative and they would forward a considerable sum to his account as soon as these minor matters were sorted. To Dagan with 28 dollars and 59 cents in his checking account that last pledge couldn't fail but to awaken some interest. The real reason why Dagan hadn't skipped away was simple. Although the heavies thought they had him under control at all times Dagan was used to close confinement and could have slipped the net on more than one occasion. Nor was it the money or any of the other gilded cage enticements dangled in front but a promise he'd made. Made under trying circumstances but made all the same. He'd given his word to the ambassador for this post-dated liberty, he pledged to listen to what they wanted and then he'd be off. Simple sweet and for once his conscience wouldn't trouble him. Dagan had seen many promises broken and the tragedies that ensue. He'd hear them out because he'd promised and was sick of the hypocrisy he lived among. One oath was to be honoured this day. The car turned.

- Radio city music hall! I am about to enter the Rockefeller centre - the front seat man said, all of a sudden less heavy enforcer than giddy with childlike delight - That's where the famous photo was from. The one of the construction crew on their lunch break sitting on the girder iron, New York in the background like they were suspended in the air or something. Well, that photo was taken right about our heads, 500 feet above our heads. Would you believe it – Grunts of acknowledgement from some of the other car occupants.
- I seem to remember that. Quite something – Dagan gave up some wow factor too.

Dagan remembered the day it was published. Amazed, the next day he'd gone down to the worksite and by bluff and a set of architects prints he'd lifted from the works office he'd sat with the same crew on the same girder. Half of them seemed to be from County Galway and had been more than willing to share their tack boxes, talk about their newfound fame and argue their counties chances in the football championships going on back home.

From the Rockefeller parking lot a private lift took them up 30 floors, they exited to a plush hallway like a high powered lawyers firm. All red velvet wallpaper, polished wood panelling, heavy oak furniture and silk lampshades, very swish. They were met and led to a suite of offices at the far end. Security was heavy and most curious was the British accents of the men they had to show their papers to. The lettering on the door explained it all. *British American Corporation Inc.*

Dagan was immediately on the defensive, were the Yanks going to hand him over? What did the British want with him? His relationship with them was more troughs than peaks. Especially 1916 to 1922 and he had clashed with several elements of the British establishment after only to end up working together occasionally to attain common goals. A convoluted and strained relationship, Dagan still considered them an unwelcome presence on one-fifth of the island of Ireland and the condescending airs they gave themselves being one of their more positive attributes, all added up to a self-mutual disdain and loathing. Had it really been the Brits who'd pulled the strings to get him sprung? Banging him up was more their style.

Dagan was lead to a door with 3306 on the plate that opened to another large badly lit room, smoke hung in the semi-darkness, stark lights gave a harsh glare to lit sections of the room leaving you to guess what was in the gloom beyond, Dagan guessing would place it alongside that of a tennis court. It was huge. So this was the big friendly welcome.

In the centre, a half-dozen men were sat at a large mahogany table of exquisite quality but now pockmarked with burns and coffee cup marks. Piles of paper were held down by paperweights and brimming ashtrays that spilt grey ash over folders labelled 'CONFIDENCIAL'. But not labelled 'Treat with Caution' thought Dagan, as he approached the men stood to greet him, one stubbed his cigarette into the closest ashtray displacing yet more grey powder on to paper and table.

Introductions came thin and fast, hands shook, some with intent and purpose and others mere perfunctory. Half were American blue blood Ivy League types, it was all over their sense of dress, club ties, Harvard's cuff links, Yale pins. The other half were British, plumy voiced public school tweed suited ones.

- Would you like to sit down Mr...?
- Malone - Dagan finished the sentence and pulled a seat over to himself.

Dagan knew he was dealing with amateurs, the man had just been introduced to him, but was making a play at not remembering when he probably had been studying his file the time it had taken him to get from Cuba to 5th Avenue.

- Yes quite – said his closely shaved interlocutor, pink in parts and rashy red in others. Dagan could see the skull and bones signet of one of the most exclusive Yale students clubs, the man continued in a Boston nasally drawl - You probably are quite curious to as why we brought you here?
- No more than you as to why I came – Dagan looked around the room and into the shadows, this comedy couldn't go on much longer.
- Well – the man said clearing his throat rather nervously for a Yale man – we represent elements of the US government.
- Just elements, not the whole. Which elements?
- Does that matter? – The man exhibited the first signs of a more robust command.
- I like to know who I'm jumping into bed with, prevents nasty surprises later – Dagan said.
- Which elements exactly I'm not at liberty to reveal at the moment.

- Liberty! Just as I thought. Does Congress know?
- Know what? – The man sounded even more uncomfortable.
- That unidentified elements most likely the executive branch, i.e. the White House, are consorting with agents of an overseas power presently at war with another friendly government. A type of behaviour so poorly thought of by Congress that they'd outlawed it in at least three acts I can name now and more I can't – Let's wait for a reaction.
- Okay Mac enough with joking around, this guy's got us over a barrel and knows it - a voice boomed out from the shadows. Finally thought Dagan - Playing with us like carneys at the fair duck shoot so we're going to come good – Out of gloom stepped two men and the first bounded straight over to Dagan took both his hand and his shoulder – William P Donovan – he said in a voice full of life, used to command and with a hint of impatience to be noted. A man in a tearing hurry to get things done and done well, the type that if some rear end had to be encouraged with the big boot being in contact with it well so be it, no malice intended. Dagan took to him straight away and shook Donovan's hand vigorously who adding – as one Irishman to another I'm damn glad to meet you, between you and me it sweetens the pill of having to work with the Brits – grinning he shouted over to the other figure in a tweed suited – only joking Admiral - turning back to Dagan – Son this is one of those perfidious Albion types, fresh from kicking us around from one end of Eire to another and now they need our help, can you go figure that?

Donavan's lilt put him firmly in the Irish-America second / third generation bracket as clearly as his name and demeanour did. 'Kicking us', Dagan took that comment with a grain of salt. The tweed suited gentlemen reached over and extended his hand.

- James Osborne, perfidious Brit and ardent anti-Nazi, at your service, if you'll put eight hundred years of occupation to one side for a minute – the man had intelligent eyes and a military manner even in the civilian suit. The accent was pure public school vowels - We're all facing something even worse and it would be a good idea to see what we can do about it together, the past is the past. If Jerry can bomb London he can bomb Dublin.
- Delighted and all as I am to meet new people, don't be upset if I seem a little less than overwhelmed – Dagan was determined to enjoy himself.
- I understand entirely and am a bit surprised you're still here, I read your file and even though my colleagues assured me that

57

you were tied up like a cat in a sack I know that you could have slipped off dozens of times – Donovan took over.

- Let's say I'm curious and anyway I was well looked after, a bit of R&R was just what I needed.
- You're an interesting fella as your file and my friend Ozzy can testify – here Donovan nodded at the Brit who looked a bit surprised to be referred to in such a familiar way.
- I've had my moments – Dagan said modestly, he generally was whether it was warranted or not. His mother could never get over it – 'You're as good as anyone but the way you carry on only God knows it'. 'Sure Mam, you, me and God are a good start and the rest can find out to their loss' – he'd replied.
- I'll grant you that, which is why you're going to listen to what we have to say – Donovan sounded sure of himself but probably always did.
- I'm all ears – and eyes and brain, Dagan was taking it all in.
- Born in Cork at the start of the century – Donovan acted like he was warming up a crowd for the main event.
- That's right boyo
- Lost that accent though – Donovan continued
- I wasn't Lee side for long – Dagan loved Cork and wished he spent more time there.
- Terenure College Dublin and schoolboy runner in the 1916 rising. I'm sure your teacher was a bit put out by that.
- Youthful exuberance, who doesn't want to be a rebel when they're young, I didn't miss a day of school either as it was Easters holidays and my teacher wasn't put out as he with me the whole time.
- Released from his majesties custody in 1917.
- I was a minor but I got off fairly lightly for high treason even I have to admit – Dagan said tongue in cheek.
- You then started Medicine while at night continuing your political activities.
- Irelands moment had arrived it seemed and I was on hand to witness it happen.
- Make it happen too, you were on the run full time from around the end of 1919.
- Hard to lead a settled life with an arrest warrant out for you, makes you a bit tetchy in lectures wondering whose outside.
- Three years of medicine, so how did that give rise to a nasty habit of blowing things up?

- Not ordinary things, police things, stations, boxes, telephones, lorries and trains. Anything involving the police really. I wasn't fussy.
- 24 local stations, 8 barracks, 2 derailed trains and 6 armoured convoys attacked.
- The small chemistry course we had in first year I really took on and developed it – Tongue to other cheek.
- All you have is destruction to your name – Donovan came in hard-hitting.
- The construction was to come after and it did – Dagan said in his defence.
- After the truce you left Ireland why?
- Revolutions devour their children, ours was no different. I didn't want to be around for that, brother against brother. I could see it coming, could see the long fellow and the big fellow and Griffiths fellow and that entire shower of fellows at each other's throats. I needed to leave, call me a sentimentalist but I prefer happy families. Anyway, all this is ancient history; I feel a yawn coming up – he wasn't joking, he felt very sleepy all of a sudden.
- Just setting the scene, colouring in the background.
- Setting the scene, you sound like a Hollywood producer.
- Hollywood glad you mentioned it, you passed through there as well, putting your demolitions experience to good use.
- What of it, the best place to be in the world in the mid 20's. I wrote, acted, did stunts, downed many a bottle of whiskey with John Ford and not to mention the girls. You never did anything else apart from quote people's lives back to them in smoky dark rooms rented to foreign powers?
- That foreign power is standing between us and the gates of hell. And if I was a betting man we'll be sending them more than destroyers and material before long. As for me, I was a soldier, a lawyer, now I'm helping out my country and boy does it need it. And not only my country but the world, theirs – here a nod to Osborne – mine and even yours. There no fence-sitting now, unless we stop the Krauts somehow like we did in 1918 the whole world's down the crapper, forgives the crudeness. And that is where you come in, you could help us just like you helped the Spanish by organizing food and medicine, like the guns you ran to the Ethiopians and like the rest. I admire the hell out of you I do and I know why you're here. You decided to help no matter what we ask – Donovan didn't grandstand just said it out matter of factly.

- Woe, steady on their cowboy, what a pitch. Europe survived Napoleon; it will survive the Germans, the most civilized nation in Europe by all accounts.
- Napoleon had nothing on this guy. The only thing they have in common is being uppity corporals. But this latest guy is far far worse.
- God knows I'm no fan of the current leading light in the Rhine and master of the bits of Europe that count. I even tried in my misguided manner to stop the belligerence. As you've mentioned Spain, I saw some bullets wizz over the *Casa del Campo*, saw planes over the *Meseta* bombing and strafing everyone and their mule and yes I did try and help out. Call it a heady mix of sangria and sun and señoritas in distress but before you could say 'No pasarán' it all turned ugly, the Russians moved in, not helping out, more like practice and manoeuvres for their pilots and gunners. Chekists squads around every corner. I'd gone to help and barely escaped with my life. And don't have me crying for the poor Brits and their Empire, for me the Russians are just as bad as the Germans. Let them fight it out among themselves with the Brits watching on the side-lines. Do what you did against Napoleon, fend them off till you find allies, then let them do the fighting and most of the dying, feed them, supply them just enough so they can keep going. And when it's all over bar the shouting nip in and enjoy the fruits of victory. How's that plan Admiral?
- Dagan, you got the smarts, you read situations well, which is why you survived so many. Moscow in 1923, Alger's in 1927 I could go on and your reading of Germany's adventure in Russia is quite interesting. But don't you feel this is a bit different than say 1805 or 1915. Don't you get the feeling that Hitler is the worst we've encountered in thousands of years? You can't stick your head in the sand – Donovan was leading somewhere but wouldn't come with it yet.
- Why not? I'll be at the beach at the very least
- So you're not going to help us – Donovan sounded disappointed and Dagan actually feel like he was letting him down. What a salesman but I see through your tricks.
- Doing what? Why? I've personal motives, the Germans can spent a few years eating ' foie gras' and then it will be back to normal. You haven't sold me on the deal. If you were a second-hand car dealer you'd be looking at a lean year.

- You're a tough sale but I haven't yet used up all my snake oil vendors tricks – Donovan levelled with Dagan. It was a sales pitch boiling down to the gravy.
- Snake oil I would buy but what you are selling I ain't buying.
- We'll see, I'm not known in the business for my smooth-talking lawyer shyster patter, I let an argument convince the doubting Thomas's.
- You've more arguments lined up? I hope they're better than the ones you've tried out so far. Like the one about helping out poor beleaguered Blighty.
- I think our hosts have been a bit mean with the refreshments – Donovan changed tack, no pipe smoking but a tea party always helped coalesce a group - Hey Admiral there are two Irishmen spitting feathers here, how about something wet please seeing as our guest will be staying a bit longer.
- You mean I'm free to go? - Dagan didn't think so but no harm asking.
- Figuratively speaking of course – they both knew what that meant.
- Figured as much – And Dagan told him.
- I'll level with you, you could walk out of that door any time you like, I'd even escort you to the lift but I'm begging you to listen some more and I don't see you moving on your own. So technically yes but for practical purposes no - Donovan laid it out like it was.
- How reassuring - Dagan knew a pro when he saw one.
- Your German pals wouldn't be so accommodating – Donovan pointed out.
- I'm not so sure, they seem quite fond of me on occasion. Admittedly not since 1938 and the treaty ports but I'm sure that's all blown over – The last time Dagan had been mixed up at home with the Brits the result had been very gratifying except nobody gave him any credit for it. Three naval bases handed over to Irish control. Plus la chance.

A door opened to one side and in came a middle-aged charwomen dressed for the heat in woollen tights and dark lace-up shoes. She struggled to place a tray stacked with cups, saucers, milk, teapots, biscuits and whatnot on a low table. Dagan jumped up to help to extract a low wattage smile in return.

- They should get you an assistant – Dagan said to her in a soft Celtic lilt.

- You could do with two assistants Jenny – Donovan said – these limeys don't stop with the tea all day.
- Shall I open the curtains - the Admiral said collecting himself?
- By the way, the Germans haven't got to Russia yet they're tied up in the Ukraine – Donovan backtracked - How exactly are they doing Admiral?
- I'm not at liberty to say but if I could I'd be telling of advances of seventy miles daily. Basically as far as their tanks can drive in 24 hours.
- Invaders of Russia don't get stopped on the borders but the steppes, thousands of miles from home – Dagan pointed out.
- They'll be close to Moscow soon – Donovan added.
- All valid and with a bit of luck it will happen the way you think it will, Hitler will go the way of Napoleon and it will be the commissars taking up all the best seats in the Parisian cafes
- Dagan took a different slant on things - You see, you are backing my argument, so why bother getting involved, either way, the snotty French waiters will be as rude to one and all.
- You noticed that too – interrupted the Admiral - They are quite appallingly rude at times – in his case his schoolboy French had met derisory snorts and condescending replies in near-perfect English. He'd even gloated briefly after the fall of France thinking of the garcons new clientele before realizing that insufferable Allies were a small price to pay than facing the whole of Europe alone. Thinking of just that temporary unpatriotic posture he added – thought the coffee is out of this world, nothing can beat it.
- Part of it boils down to the old slap in the face they gave to the conscientious objectors. Would you fight to prevent somebody killing your family, they said no, knowing full well it won't come to that but this time it might, that's why I wouldn't want anybody swaggering around my country telling me what to do and shooting me if I don't unless I tried to stop it – Donovan raised an eyebrow.
- I don't see the Germans swaggering down Pall Mall and photos of Adolf with Big Ben in the background. The RAF saw off the Luftwaffe last year – Dagan reminded them.
- Twenty seven – Interrupted the Admiral.
- Twenty seven what?
- The number of raids this month to date, people think the Luftwaffe's too busy in Russia but it didn't just stop last year with the glorious few bloodying Goering's nose.

- You know how they fought off the numerically superior German air force Malone? Well before you get all impassioned I tell you – here Donovan paused.
- I'm all ears – Dagan – Really, I don't have any answers.

Here Donovan paused, everybody, downed tea as the showman took position right in front of the Irishman. In a soft confident voice he began.

- The unexpected, the unknown, the about to be unleashed. Like when an equal number of warriors armed with stone meet and equal number armed with bronze. Outcome stone dead, long live bronze. Until one day the bronze guys have to tackle iron totting arrivals. The outcome is again more than predictable – Interest was piqued as all lent closer.

Donovan prepared to continue intending to inject a sense of breathless urgency but before he could Malone interrupted.

- Does your script go through the entire history of warfare?

Momentarily dumb struck Donovan managed to come back with.

- Almost, we decided to leave out the bit about chariots.
- Shame because it would be highly relevant – Dagan said sarcastically.
- Tracks for wheels, horsepower for horses - piped in a young man with pale eager eyes.

The Admirals assistant couldn't get over being in New York, exciting pulsating shameless New York while back at home people had marmite as the closest thing to a fun night out.

- Thank you – said Donovan politely
- I'll skip the rest but the adage of how generals always fight the last war – Dagan stated the obvious. He'd commanded flying columns and knew about military evolution - Tell that to the French, sitting behind their shiny new Maginot Line, 1930's take on 1918's trenches, formidable and 200km away from here it was needed. Ironic that the Germans who couldn't put a decent tank together twenty years ago are running rings around the Brits who invented the damn things.
- It's true, the Prime Minister's very proud of that invention – Osborne said.
- Never mind that, the English Channel is still the most effective opposing force the English have but getting away from Dover's

cliffs, Vera Lynn and barrage balloons you wanted to tell me something about Germans and iron swords.

- Iron beats bronze every time, hands down – Donovan said simply.
- Reading the heavy hints you're giving out. Have the Germans got something really iron-like, new and shiny and better than our best-polished bronze – Dagan hazarded a guess.
- Maybe? – Donovan's head tilted toward Dagan.
- Oh come on – Dagan saw the gesture and didn't buy it - To knock out the Brits and the Soviets the Germans need to knock out the industries and destroy the cities, could England carry on without London or the Tyne shipyards or the Soviets without Moscow, Leningrad or the factories around the Urals. Doubtful but at the present rate it would take them hundreds of years and thousands of aircraft.
- So what about one plane and one bomb – Donovan suggested.
- Even the plane mightn't be needed – the assistant interrupted again – I'm sorry I should introduce myself, James Silver, of the strategic weapons office.
- How would the bomb get there James, on the bus!
- On a rocket bus maybe, the Germans have been pioneering rocket science since the twenties and now under a genius called Von Brun, they're getting close to developing rockets capable of reaching over five hundred miles.

Silver spoke with a look of intense excitation as if the Germans have disappointed him by only five hundred miles. His admiration was evident.

- And if five hundred miles is possible they'll quickly reach one thousand, two and then the east coast of the States will be in range – The Americans in the room shifted uncomfortably and looked at each other.
- And there's no defence against a rocket – Silver added the killer punch - Five minutes warning but you wouldn't even see it, it will be a whoosh and if you hear that you are toast.
- But I still don't see how one or even a hundred rockets could reduce a city the size of London. What's their nose cone capacity, they'd have to be big or use chemicals or rags dipped in the armpits of plague victims.
- They're calling the capacity *waffenutzlast* or weapon load in English, they have it at three hundred pounds, a medium-sized bomb – Silver pushed his round glasses back up to the top of the bridge of his nose and coughed as if suddenly realizing how much of the meeting he'd take over and from such a junior position –

Beg your pardon for the interruption – he sat back to nurse his tea.

- Don't apologize my lad, that's why we brought you in on this meeting.   Matter of fact I'd be more annoyed if you didn't interrupt – the Admiral showing how to handle men the navy way.
- My turn to interrupt if you don't mind and it's been more interesting than many centuries but I still don't see what has me here in this august company. America's super spy, England's ear to the president plus the wonder kid of the new military age so as I've finished my tea it's time to get to the point.

Dagan could feel a drop in temperature, the two main players, British and American espionage circles, overlapping secrets only imagined within their reach, exchanged glances.   Osborne nodded and as Donovan assented in return and he began to speak.

- Go ahead give it to him straight.
- What you're about to hear how is so secret that you could count on one hand the number of British cabinet members who know.
- Same goes for us, the president, and two others – Donovan added.
- Hence we can only tell if you tacitly agree to help us.
- Even if it means agreeing to well just about anything? – Dagan paused mid-sentence - How could any right-minded bunch expect an answer in those circumstances.
- Well yes. A tall order. If it will help any, you'll be saving the lives of two old friends. Nothing more nothing less – Donovan was giving it his all.
- Sounds like a choice I've got to make which is no choice – Dagan said seriously but truth was he hadn't agreed to anything and didn't intend to.
- You're an idealist; I firmly believe you will want to do what we ask.   On the other hand, if we tell you now what you want to know and you DON'T go along with us we'll have to put you up in more secure locations till the end of the conflict.   And America isn't even in it yet. You are fond of quoting Acts of Congress and this would violate a basket full but we'll lock you up somewhere. The risk of you letting slip even innocently what we're about to tell you is too great. We're playing for keeps here – Donovan was jabbing and jabbing. Final rounds here. Dagan rang the bell.
- I know things about people and events over the last twenty years that would make your hair stand up and never once not once have I let slip. The British and most certainly Winston Churchill can testify to that - Dagan spoke directly and bluntly – and if you

don't believe me ask him yourself – directed at Osborne who moved awkwardly in his seat.

- He said you'd be a tough nut to crack but...- left hanging.
- But what? – Dagan asked annoyed.
- But nothing, Uncle Sam is mighty paranoid now, say yes, we can't tell you why but you'll want to say yes.
- This would give Confucius a headache – Dagan said exasperatedly - Gentlemen if you can't tell me then I can't say yes, so if there's nothing else to be said I'll be toddling along. New York in the summer is a fun town. It's been interesting, instructive even, but I'll be on my way.

With that Dagan rose, no one stopped him which surprised him. Maybe they'd be waiting outside. Sure that's it; the heavies would be waiting out there. Still, he'd go down fighting; midwesterner would be first for a kick in the gonads and wouldn't forget this assignment in a hurry. Still no reaction from the men at the table, Donovan just looked at him with an expression of regret almost pity that made Dagan wonder. He'd formed the opinion that the spy supremo was a straight talker, honourable in so much as his acquired profession allowed him to be and capable of a strange compassion. His look said as much as Dagan started towards the door. Not a sound could he hear except his own breathing as he threw his coat over his shoulder and put his hat back on. All the while thinking vaguely of what they wanted. Something valuable needed to be stolen or blown up or maybe eliminate a certain person. Something big real big that in their minds would help the Allied war effort.

Crikey they weren't even allies yet and were already working elbow to leather patched elbow. The Germans were right to feel aggrieved although few people saw it that way, the Americans said trade with the Germans was permitted but unless the Germans took delivery by U-boats up the Hudson there was no way American goods could get through the blockade even via Portugal or Spain. The still mighty Royal Navy might have problems with convoys in the mid-Atlantic but they had Europe sewn up tighter than a maiden aunts cross stitch.

Not that Dagan was overtly aggrieved by the stitch-up of the Germans nor did he feel like rushing to aid their distress. A collective madness has taken over the world which Dagan had witnessed happening in slow motion a long way back. Aghast and horrified at the succession of calamities inflicted by one power-hungry cabal of monsters on another and those in turn biding their time till they had an opportunity to add their savagery to the annals of human depravity and always sold to the neutral bystander as ideals wrapped glitzily in soaring lofty slogans, stirring declarations and vociferous proclamations.

Turning your back on the sickening madness while it played itself out seemed the only sane course of action in an increasingly insane world. So the Germans were having the wool pulled over their eyes by the Anglo Saxon Atlantic friendship cabal of convenience. So what! They had the rest of Europe as a consolation and were halfway to Moscow. Dagan had seen the Germans in action on more than one occasion. Spain is a case in point. There they had perfected the art of terrifying innocent civilians with aerial warfare to new dimensions. Attacking towns on market day, one wave opening the assault by bombing the centre, the second arriving shortly after to strafe the fleeing people in the open fields. As warfare, you couldn't fault it but it had killed off any lingering admiration and comradeship leftover from the time when Germany was Eire's ally in the struggle for freedom. While his feelings now towards Germany were neutral that didn't translate into a positive for the British. Sod the lot of them better said.

- Mr Malone – Donovan broke the tension as Dagan almost reached the door, most golf putts were longer than the distance covering that stretch but it felt like it was taking longer than most golf rounds. Something they had said was nagging at him- just a short question before you leave if you don't mind. I think you owe us that at least that after extracting you from a Cuban hellhole – Donovan called out in a raised voice to Malone's back who turned around.
- I knew I wouldn't make it to the door and I got out of the Cuban hellhole myself.
- But you would never have got off the island.
- Maybe yes maybe no, remember I was with two sailors. I'll take a question and answer it as long as it doesn't slur the honour of any woman, nation or the knights of Columbus. And while we're at it I have a question for you as well. Which friend's lives would I be saving?
- I couldn't believe you haven't asked that yet and would you believe that it ties in with my question, so bear with me. A simple one for you. What do you think of the German government's behaviour towards Jewish people? – Donovan shrugged his shoulders challenging his adversary to come up with an answer.

A pause, Dagan took two steps back to the table and pushed up his hat uncovering his forehead at the same time.

- I wasn't expecting a question like that – he said quietly.
- As I said a simple one – Donovan flourished a wide smile.
- Simple he says! Put it this way, I won't wish on my worst enemy the fate awaiting the Russian Jews recently 'liberated' by the advancing Germans.
- Can you be more specific?
- Everybody knows Hitler got off on blaming the Jews for everything. From the war, the crash, the runaway inflation to the morning paper being late and the milk gone sour. But he was also blaming the communists and the Allies at the same time. An electioneering platform was thus built. But give him credit, he's delivered on his word, German Jews have to be some of the most forlorn, unlucky, stricken, bedevilled people caught up in the mess we call a civilized world – Dagan summed it up the way he saw it.
- That's all you want to say – Donovan acted shortchanged.
- What else can I say on the subject? The man's mad, he's proven it again and again but he'll not be there forever, Jews have always been convenient scapegoats for chancier politicians on the rise. It's been happening for thousands of years but they're still here. Hell, the Irish can't exactly throw the first stone; an uncle of mine told me how in Limerick at the turn of the century things turned pretty ugly for a while. A small scale ' kristallnacht ' you could say. So the Irish have no right to be giving sermons on the subject to others based on recent events.
- I didn't know about Limerick, seems out of character – Donovan looked around for confirmation and got several nods.
- Sure we don't advertise it. We like to make out we're the good guys, friends to all so we've swept that sort of stuff under the carpet. But getting back to your question. No, I don't like what the Germans have done, but they're only doing what dozens of governments have done over the ages. And the Jews are doing what they've done over those self-same ages, grin and bear it, clean up the damage, sweep up the glass and wait for the whole thing to blow over. Till they have their own country that's what will continue to happen.
- And if you had any Jewish friends or acquaintances in German-occupied territories what would be your advice – Donovan pressed Dagan on the question.
- That's a second question and you haven't answered mine.
- We kind of just did, please indulge me, I'm not getting any younger – Donovan said but he looked like he could wrestle a horse.

- What would I tell them, beg, borrow or steal enough money to get the hell out of there.
- And if they can't – Donovan lingered on the word 'they'
- WHO exactly are they? - Dagan heart froze – I don't play games like this, its bad manners - he said through gritted teeth, a hint of menace in his soft voice.
- I'm sorry to break this to you son like this, why don't you sit down for a second.
- Why don't you go jump of a cliff. – Sniggers from some - You'll be getting me a restorative glass of sherry next. I'm not going to keel over like some maiden aunt. You said 'they' now stop jerking my chain and tell me who do you mean?

Dagan had dozens of Jewish and non-Jewish friends all over occupied Europe. Some he knew were in hiding or had fled, others he hoped had but it was very difficult to get reliable information out, sometimes you heard bad things and the next minute you bump into the person out at Coney Island. But that was the exception.

- You remember your Czech physicist friend and his daughter?

Dagan had by now inched his way back to the seat he'd only just vacated. On hearing that confirmation he omitted a pained grunt and sank back into the still-warm chair, winded for all intents and purposes.

- Jaysus fucking Christ! - Came out almost involuntarily as Dagan swept away everything in his reach onto the floor.

The profanity and the sudden violent reaction shocked the normally moral straight-laced Americans and their Episcopalian outrage at blasphemy. Donovan felt wretched watching the anguished reaction. The mass of paper and cigarettes stubs and ash on the floor lost import.

- We want to get them out and we want you to help us – Donovan laid it on the line, the sparing was over.
- So that is what this has been all about - Dagan had demanded the truth and now had it.
- Yep son and sorry I had to break it to you by hitting you over the head with it

Dagan by now had unclenched his fists and was breathing easy. The rage had passed from the Irishman.

- I'm sorry about the mess, I'll clean it up – and with that Dagan in a daze got up and started to retrieve papers from the floor.

- Leave it son we're more important matters to go over. This came almost as a relief, Dagan slumped back in the chair, feeling almost as if he been poleaxed by a blow to the solar plexus. Exhaustion suddenly overtook him. The underlying tension of the last weeks hit him by surprise full-on like a footpad lurking around a dark corner. The effect was devastation. He heard himself mumble nonsensical replies to Donovan solicitous inquiries. Grunts and incoherent intonations was a more accurate description. His mind was swamped with memories of magical times he and Maria Kessler had shared. From when he'd met and befriended a curious awkward girlish visitor to Dublin, daughter of a prominent lecturer in physics, the friendship deepening over a space of weeks before one day they'd held hands almost by accident. On a tram both trying to maintain their balance, giddy from jars of creamy porter after a meeting of the university science club. The giddiness gave way to hungry looks, furtive smiles before Dagan was overwhelmed by the desire to discover the texture of her lips. Pulling down her clamped hand, drawing her closer, eyes locked until lips in slow motion met eliciting puritanical outrage on the Dublin tram.
- Would you look at the state of them eating the faces of each udder – said one lady?
- Shockin truly shockin – said another.
- Young hussy and he's could be her father - a Gertie said.
- Gertie, fathers pushing it, her uncle anyroads.
- Indecent I've never seen nothing like it in me life except that time at the RDS me fella pulled me into....

But before long Dublin's ribald wit couldn't turn down the opportunity of a bit of fun, a bit of 'slagging'.

- Hey mister, save a bit of that for me – a white-haired old one, head to foot in black, whistles started going round.
- If you could bottle it it'll sell like hotcakes – said another.

Maria pulled away from him at that moment laughing as her hand covered her mouth in the mock outrage. Barely twenty, dimples in her cheeks when she smiled which she did often, Dagan remembered the first time; it had nearly knocked him off his feet. Dazzling, full of life and mischief, all innocence and childlike, eyes twinkling while at the same time a hint of knowing sensuality, the art of being present and desirable, passed down the female line through millenniums. From that day they'd begun a dizzy affair, walks along Killarney head and picnics in Blessington to begin with, Maria's old fashioned middle European

70

sense of propriety much more in keeping with the Ireland they found themselves in than Dagan, ostracized in spirit if not deed as he was from the land of his forefathers.

Wet misty summer months passed, Dagan found Maria every bit as fascinating and captivating as the day they'd met but something was wrong. No matter how much he tried to deepen their relationship, bring it into the open, Maria resisted. So they kept to the shadows while in public resentment boiled up in Dagan as he struggled to remain friendly without inadvertently giving the game away. When he asked why they couldn't behave like a normal courting couple all Maria would say was 'Her father meant everything to her and she couldn't leave him'.

- And your own happiness? – Dagan countered. 'She had promised her mother on her death bed she would look after him'.
- You're not helping by being his devoted housekeeper and lab assistant, mending his socks and darning his jacket elbows. He'll never get over your mother that way – Dagan pleaded with Maria.
- But he's like a lost boy, he even forgets to shave unless I tell him – was how she responded to that.
- That's an absent-minded professor rather than a poor lost soul. He can manage to give research papers at conferences across half of Europe, teach classes to hundreds of students, meet your mother and have a family. He sounds capable of boiling an egg to me – Dagan certainly could, cooking being a speciality of his, same as chemistry in his eyes. Just mix the right ingredients in the right proportions at the right time and success was guaranteed.
- I promised and a promise is a promise – neither Maria nor her father knew that three minutes in boiling water was all it took but they had a cook who did.
- So if I knock down your dad by accident in my car you'll be free of your promise – Dagan believed earnestly in accidents, some of the best things in his life had come about that way. Not that he was going to run over Professor Kessler.
- I hope this is Irish humour you are talking to me with – Maria wasn't so sure.

Maria and her father moved back to Prague, Dagan made sporadic visits but the arguments went on until Dagan was invited to London by associates for a weekend. He ended up staying nearly six months something he told Maria by letter, not even telephoning, he mentioned in his letter that he needed to get away for a while to see the wood for the trees or some such phrase. Their time had ended; back in his loggings, several letters from Maria arrived for him. He opened one but dropped it on the floor, the tear stains visible on the headed notepaper, a stinging reproach for his offhand shameless behaviour, had he seen the woods yet she asked, the writing smudged in places and barely legible. She'd wished him well, the last and most excruciating personal reproof. Maria had despaired. And so the bright lights of London held his gaze for long enough to crush a venerable girls heart as Dagan quickly found companions amongst the hordes of London town. Deep down he had known in the places you hardy feel able to let in the light that Maria had been something refreshing in his life after years spent on the move in a life transitory and ephemeral, the people especially the women he'd met during all that time were similar to him, adventurers living life outside most social dictates. The nine to six Monday to Saturday routine as alien as the social concept called a home, that underpinned that sort of life. Dagan didn't destain it in the least, he was full of admiration for people he saw as holding society together. And Dagan had seen enough societies where its absence had blighted generations as he saw it. But his paramours had been a means to mutually fore fill physical desires that couldn't be ignored and in certain cases had had a veneer of being something more but it hadn't worked out for a variety of reasons. Hence the appearance of Maria Kessler in his life had awakened hopes of an escape from the vapidness of his personal interactions, young, bright, bursting with vitality without a hint of cynicism or world-weariness. Someone worth giving one's self over to settled life, roots and family and a more conventionally respectable existence. Bourgeoisie here we come. As such the final failure of the relationship had been his fault entirely. His inner self knew he'd bring heartache and desperation to Maria in the long term. His natural nomadic instincts couldn't be overcome by any short domestic interlude while he'd fooled himself into believing that he could change and be worthy of the love of this vivacious youg woman.

He'd hated himself for the way he acted but knew that by being himself he was in effect saving Maria. Or was he? One never knew until you did something whether it was right or wrong. That was the problem and if you didn't do it you'd never know either way and worse could spend years brooding on the imagined outcomes of action's not taken and now lost forever. One could go mad but fortunately for Dagan, the world seemed to be beating him to it and that gave him plenty to do. Within months Dagan was too busy dodging triad's bullets and smugglers vendettas to have much time to think of Maria. He did occasionally spent quiet moments recollecting tender sweet times and became an avid follower of Czech life and keeping up with his scientific journals when the occasion arose and so a distant forlorn witness to Maria 's startling progress under her father's tutelage.

- They say a man's life can flash before his eyes in the instance before death and I believe them – said Dagan to the gathered people in front of him.
- Brought back memories right? – Donovan could imagine, he'd been young once too.
- You bet and most of them very sweet ones. How did you put me and Maria together if you don't mind me asking? I thought it's something known only to a hand full of people.
- Young girl falls in love with older dashing world-wise man. Young girls seeks advice from her best friend back in Prague young girl does her talking on a phone line monitored by friends of ours – here Donovan looked over at the admiral and his group.
- She rang from my phone? Why the cheeky young minx, I always wondered why my bill was so big. Thought it was the transatlantic calls – Dagan was surprised to have missed that but his suspicions had also been confirmed for the funny clicks he occasionally heard.

Dagan knew the British kept tabs on him, they liked to know if he was up to anything especially if it ran contrary to the interests of King and Empire. And maybe there were others too at various times, that why he'd always told his 'lady' visitors not to make calls from his line but as he couldn't really go into details as to why, well, when it boils down to it women hate being told what to do.

- I'm sold, what do I have to do, tell me and I'll do it – Dagan just came out with it, instant decision.
- Forgive me for being cynical, it's the business I'm in you understand. But how does the mere mention of an ex-girlfriend of long ago and God knows you've had a few of those, make you change volt face and suddenly forget all the high handed neutrality, the 'it's nothing to do with me' you're been spouting. I mean I've ex-girlfriends too and believe me I'd do anything not to see them – Donovan pressed Dagan on his spectacular instantaneous 360 negative to positive.
- I presume it's the father your more interested in – Dagan countered.
- You presume correctly
- For his scientific knowledge?

- A certain field of it. We need to be the ones who benefit from his wealth of knowledge and ongoing research. For various projects being considered, I might add – and Donovan did.
- And if it's a choice between the daughter and the father? – Dagan was getting to the nexus of his choice.
- We naturally would prefer the return to safety of them both, we know she won't leave him but the father is vital. The White House itself is asking.
- That why me and why all the effort. It's my turn to be cynical, you get anyone else and I know they'll leave her and take him.
- Nobody ever said you haven't got the smarts, I'll entrust all the rest to our new friends. My part is done, it's time I was back where I can be seen. Just to let you know I'm damn proud of you - Donovan rose and shook hands with Dagan - I knew you come down on the side of the good guys because that what it boils down to now – with that Donovan left the room but not before turning and asking – Are you sure about this? Not to wait. Wouldn't be fair not to warn you that me and the admiral discussed the possibilities of success and survival, given the factors involved being behind enemy lines, in action, detection and flight. We came up with a rough estimate of 15% - Donovan said it as positively as he could, it took a lot of sugar to sweetly coat those odds.
- Nice try bud but I'm all yours, after all the effort you put into talking me into this I ain't letting you talk me out of it that easily – Donovan smiled, he know and admired who he was dealing with, with a salute to forehead he closed the door - I'm all yours gentlemen – Dagan said to the Brits left behind – and I never thought I'd see the day I'd say that. Lead on Mac Duff!

Shortly afterwards Dagan found himself in the same lift that had brought him up and in what seemed to have hours had been been less than 40 minutes, tea break included. With him were the Admiral, his brainy box sidekick and two others, the driver and bodyguard respectively. Sam and Nick they'd been introduced as. Like a game of the pass the parcel this is thought Dagan.

- I've about a zillion questions, like where are the Kesslers now? How do I get in? How do we get out? I could probably get to Berlin myself using old contacts but from there where do I go? – Dagan zeroed in on the practicalities.

- Answers will be forthcoming – was the reply – we can't be too sure who's listening and who's watching, the eyes of the enemy are restless. The biggest concentration of Axis intelligence services are here in New York. Just keeping an eye on the convoy sailings alone would justify it. Damn their hides – Nick and Sam shuffled on their feet – And if it isn't the Hun it's the Portuguese or the Spanish currying favor with fellow travelers ill-got - by this stage they reached the underground parking - Tank full Nick? – asked the Admiral.
- Aye aye that it is Sir – Nick was a Margate boy born and bred, a glass of water was enough to make him queasy but he liked to play the able seaman with the old salty dog. Dagan overheard the comment and understood.
- At least let's pass by Carneys and have that pint I've been after and then the hotel to collect my razor – Dagan wasn't worried about leaving the clothes he'd been given, it was the idea of just going along 'quietly' that wasn't in his nature.
- All your stuff is in the boot or truck as they call it around here. We took the liberty of counting on our support and especially with Donovan on side. Sorry old man but I swear on the mast of my first command that you are on the right side in this – Osborne couldn't put is more solemnly.
- And where is my support taking me and my razor? – Cheek of them thought Dagan.
- To a nice pint of Canadian ale – answered Osborne.
- Ah! – makes sense Dagan recognized.
- And now if you'll pardon me I'll take a nap. Not the youngster I used to be in the last war when I'd be awake days on end in command of my cruiser. Now I can't function without a catnap. Age catches up with us all. If it hadn't been for Mr Hitler I'd be in my Hampshire garden overlooking the Solent, damn his eyes, the geraniums are just coming into bloom as well.

And with that the weary sea salt put his hat over his head and moved into the corner of the car as it sped through and out of Manhattan, looking for the interstate highway and the Canadian border. Within seconds snoring was coming from the Hampshire gardener, Vice Admiral of the blue RN retired, crack geranium grower, active pursuer of tyrannies downfall, and living exponent of the sailor's knack of catching up on their sleep where ever and whenever they could.

Chapter III

Chichely Hall, Buckinghamshire, England, July 1941

From the small garret room he'd been assigned high up in a wing, Dagan looked down upon the elegant gardens of the enormous late Regency house he'd been calling home the last two weeks. The garden showed the neglect of recent years with untrimmed verges, irregular flowering beds, and hairy topiary where manicured hedges of rigid elephants and swan reverted to a less defined outline. It was still impressive and Dagan liked nothing better than to walk along the gravelled paths between hedgerows, old lawns, and newly dug vegetable gardens. This wasn't the only grand country pile he'd been in since his trans-Atlantic crossing. The organization looking after him, the Special Operations Executive or SOE, set up by Churchill to set Europe ablaze, had been nicknamed stately homes of England by some sharper wags. Not without a grain of truth mused Dagan? If the Germans were serious about espionage in England all they had to do was pick up a copy of Debrits, check out the home addresses of its listed members and presto they'd have uncovered grand part of the network spy arranged against them.

But for some strange reason, the Germans seemed determined to keep winning the real war while losing the secret one. Their attempts at infiltration had so far been derisory. Not for those involved, of course, they either cooperated to the full if deemed useful or were quickly handed over to the hangman.

Dagan didn't know any of this but he did know that Germany's attempts at establishing a network in a supposedly friendly nation like the Irish Free State had been singularly ineffective. But if the Fatherland was making a mess of things generally that didn't mean they were completely blind, few North Atlantic sailings slipped away unnoticed and unreported to the waiting U-boat packs.

Below the ancient rheumatic head gardener, Wainright shuffled into view pushing a barrow erratically. As a distraction from the routine Dagan had sought out the faithful retainer and had insisted on helping out.

- But I can't have that sir – protested Wainwright.
- Why ever not? You'll be doing me a big favour – Dagan wasn't kidding either.
- Fifty years man and lad I've worked here, barrow boy then gardener then head gardener and never in all that time has

anyone from the big house offered to 'helped out' as you put it - the old ways were strong in Wainwright.

- I'm not from the big house; it's my workplace just like you.
- It's not right it's not – Wainwright continued.
- My bedroom if you can call it that was where they exiled the scullery maids!
- Well in that case – reason prevailed.
- What do you have to plant this season? – Dagan asked.
- Well, I'd like to put some life back in the flower beds, fruit and vegetables is all very good, don't think I'm complaining and right welcome but the beds make the place. Where do I find the time, the hedges never stop, the lake needs attention, the drainage gets clogged. The old bones ain't up for it – Wainwright needed more help than he let on and outlined out just what Dagan now offered to get stuck into.
- Listen I'll start on the hedges you tell me what to cut and that will free you up for those beds of yours.
- Well, we really ought not, don't know what the lady would say if she know – Wainwright finally weakened and gave in, resigned and relieved.

Dagan's encounters with big houses hadn't been that frequent but they had been memorable. The first had been like lots of Irish Catholics growing up in the early 20th century, you normally were near a big house and would see the Anglo Irish ascendency going about their swansong with great gusto. Curious, charming, and antiquated, their lands had been taken and resold to the tenants and the former owners were going about spending the windfall with alarming alacrity and forethoughtlessness. Spending themselves out of existence but leaving a marked cultural legacy in doing it. Later he saw more big houses during the arms raids at the beginning of the war of independence.

Their occupants tended to be great enthusiasts of hunting and hence lots of guns were available, more than once Dagan had calmly deprived the choleric tied up house owners of the gunroom keys. All in the name of the Republic mind, a comment guaranteed to elicit further spluttering from behind the mouth gags. Innocent days then gave over to more savage warfare. Towards the end and in the following civil war big houses were frequently burnt down. Centuries of history represented by furniture, books, and collections would go up at the same time. Dagan thought it a huge sad loss. His Ireland was to be the ideal for all creeds and backgrounds where the old aristocracy would be welcomed to form a part, the class of Wolf Tone, Emmet, and Parnell. Big house Protestants to a man. But those lofty utopian aspirations had

77

evaporated by the blinding hate generated by death and mayhem. What seemed to him an integral part of the common heritage was a 'collection of objects pillaged during centuries of repression, paid for by the sweat of innocent Catholics forced into indentured slavery by a protestant over-class'. Heady stuff and mostly on the mark but to wipe it from the earth was to lose the fruits of the hard work of generations which had little else to show for its back-breaking labours. Class and religion made a potent cocktail of prejudice and hate. It was these extremes that had driven Dagan back to Dublin disillusioned with the course of events.

Dagan looked around his sparse garret room and saw an iron bed frame with a saggy mattress on saggy springs, honestly more hammock than fixed frame, to its left a non-descript tall elmwood wardrobe, more than half empty, a rickety table accompanied by an even more rickety chair, try as you might no way was there to achieve a stable balance. Finally the fireplace underneath an anodyne print of a day's hunting, all spread leg horses jumping over hedges. The fire in it was dying a slow sooty death against the cold as the barely heated corners wilted and the chills crept back to reunite in one frosty kingdom. There was a knock on the door and Dagan's mood changed for the better.

- Come in if you dare – he said with a grin.

The door opened to reveal a young fresh-faced female, carrying a tray with a pot of tea, a cup, a covered plate, a knife and fork, side plate with two slices of bread and a dob of grey butter.

- Good afternoon – the wren said cheerfully – I've got some lovely hot soup for you love – she said in a broad accent pinpointing her childhood in the vicinity of Saint Martin in the fields.
- Not that hungry thanks, why don't you have it – Dagan said less than enthused by the meal.
- What eat this? I wouldn't give it to my dog! – came the mock shock reply as Emily (after the suffragette, her mom was an eternally grateful female voter) put down the tray and jumped on the bed which groaned in a springingly angry manner.
- I'll end up sleeping on the floor if you keep that up.
- Well, you'll have to do without my company in that case, come here and give a girl a kiss like a good gentleman - Dagan did just that.
- I haven't had to undo a tie on a girl since Marlene Dietrich made tuxedos all the rage – Dagan said with a wolverine look as he

worked his way through the wrens khaki green clothing - A girl wearing a tie and in uniform, the world backwards.

- Marlene who? I'm only 18, just gone ducky - the wren giggled as she pulled Dagan down on top of her.
- Hey, I'm only on the third button!

Emily would never admit it openly but she was secretly thrilled by the war. The drudgery of shop assistants' life that had been the most enticing option open to her before had given way to a never-ending adventure that had led her from one end of the country to the other. She was far from being the only girl who thought so.

06:45 AM

Reveille and shave at nightstand in water provided by batman.

07:15 AM

Breakfast, on a tray in the bedroom, powdered eggs, fried potatoes, and a streak of very streaky bacon alternating with porridge. Followed by two slices of toast cut diagonally and 2 g of butter enough to cover one third and thinly at that. All washed down with a pot of tea that got weaker as the week went on.

08:30 AM

Five mile run around estate parameter directed by Sergeant Major in the company of several other apprentice agents. Fraternization strictly frowned upon. Gasping panting stuttering comradeship at the culmination of jolly outing positively encouraged. Cigarette exchanges between same sufferings out of shape espionage acolytes tolerated. Presence of females among an eclectic bunch of aspiring cloak and dagger specialists an eye-raising curiosity. Females just as prone to gasping panting post-exertion smoking.

10:30 AM

French / Czech language lessons; given by crusty old émigré arrivées longing to hone you into their personal instrument of vengeance on all things German. Example phrases are given in homework 'I had to kill the German swine, it was him or me, 'take out the German sentries one by one', 'blow up the commandants car as it passes' heavily outweighed more innocuous but far more useful lingo franc 'where is the bakery', what time does the train for Prague leave at?'

12:00 Noon

Tea and a digestive biscuit.

12:30 PM

Unarmed combat. The self-defense and offense class given by an ex-army NCO Bill Jenkins who had served in the Far East, mostly in Hong Kong – Until malaria said it was time to head back to Blighty and enjoy my retirement. Starting in July 1939, perfect timing - he joked. Trim and dapper with a dainty pencil mustache a la William Powell the former staff sergeant had taken a new slant on the usual techniques, introducing elements of unarmed combat well known in Asia but still a mystery to the average European.

- And it's the average European you will be trying to kill hence you regain the initiative - explained the instructor - the aim is not to prolong the duration of the struggle but to keep it as short as possible. You must be the person on the offensive even if it began with you being attacked. You will become familiar with throws and falls, how to slip out of one, and project the assailant into another. Jujitsu will be a boon to you as it has been to eastern peoples since we were living in muddy huts. You will learn to direct force within the usual boundaries and with the edge of the extended hand, fist, knee, and elbow. Elbows are harder to break. Ka-ra-te as it is known applied to the correct susceptible points of the body will render the opponent defenseless.
- How harmless? – asked a shrill-voiced man pushing bottle-nosed glasses back up the bridge of a crooked nose.
- On a scale of one to ten, let's say between dead and dying – said the eastern ex-pat returnee obviously frustrated.
- Sounds rough – said one.
- I'm just a wireless operator – said another.
- Me too.
- Will I break a nail – whined Jenkins and changing tack called out to the class in a stronger clearer voice - Now listen up. We isn't, pardon, aren't doing this by halves, if you're rendered helpless and captured you await certain slow and painful torture before a hopefully swift dispatch. Each and every one of us knows, no matter how naturally talented at the spy game they are, it is a matter of luck once set loose behind enemy lines. The risk of detection is ever-present, that's why you have to play to win, no

other outcome is conceivable, and this is not the playing fields of Harrow we're at here.

- Thank God for that - another class member ventured, attempting to lighten the mood of the group because if you really thought of the odds involved and the risks faced no one in their right minds would go. It was as simple as that - Those Harrows boys really do fight dirty – the tension eased, a few grunts at the inane wisecrack, appreciating it for what it wanted to achieve. Gallows humor.

Dagan's turn came about. He stood facing the back of Jenkins with the task of 'taking the target out for good'. Dagan waited. 'Any time you like Sir' the ex-police inspector invited him on. As he did Dagan leaped on him, grabbed his neck and in one disorientating flash found himself flat on his back with the mustached faced instructor's shiny polished boot pinning him down by the neck.

- Anticipation and counterweight, you did half the work for me with that reckless lunge – Jenkins's boot receded.
- How did you manage that – Dagan gasped holding his sore throat?
- Here let me help you and I'll show you – Dagan had thought himself well versed in the down and dirty street fighting black arts but the two instructors had shown him that 'believe to be' was boarding on the foolhardy and fatally to the wrong side of ingenuousness.

1:30 PM

Still limping slightly Dagan and the rest went to their mess hut on the grounds. The dinner lady in charge was busy cutting slices of bread carefully measuring the thickness of each against a Ministry of Food chart on the wall. The thickness being more like thinness which didn't make slicing easy but the loaf would have to do the whole mess. Europe was on a diet. At least the meal wasn't Woolton pie again and the potatoes were plentiful. They weren't rationed and any Irishman worth his salt could go a long time on tatties alone. The diet served out wasn't that bad by the standards of the day. Game from the surrounding estate kept up the protein levels while fish from the local river also helped liven up the monotonous wartime fare. You'd think secret agents wouldn't have ration cards for security reasons but most of them in training were ordinary normal run of the mill types who led normal run of the mill lives and had ration cards to prove it. Except run of the mill was a description which could never apply to the volunteers here as they learned to blow up trains, code and decode, fix and maintain radios, send in Morse, to parachute at night in the dark, to camouflage and disguise themselves. They were individuals prepared to fly into enemy territory and live clandestinely until victory or discovery, being hunted by the most rapacious vicious secret service in the world which would be merciless in its treatment of them.

Would be a safer bet given the survival rate in the field where every contact could be friendly or could be a sell-out. Worse was making radio contact with England, literally you were in a field. Never were you so exposed. The Gestapo had huge resources plowed into radio detection. Interceptor vans were constantly crawling major urban areas trawling through lower frequencies, experts at detecting and vectoring signals in a matter of minutes.

This was upward in agents minds, typing code as quickly as possible, in isolated locations, receiving instructions also in code, one ear out for the tell-tale signs of approaching vehicles and once received the agent had to hurry away with a suitcase, a dead giveaway, leaving the area as fast as possible all the while avoiding even the most minimum contact with the local authorities or God forbid any Germans.

Dagan sat and listened as the instructor explained the drill, 20 minutes was the maximum time, not a second longer. 'Again' said the instructor a Czech word Dagan had by now come to recognize and the whole class took to the fields around the grand house. It was like hide and seek for grownups. Every once and a while a shout of sssshh or hands up in German/Czech resounded through the grounds. Dagan lugged the five-kilo suitcase to the southern area of the estate, looked around him and crouched down behind a bush, opening the case he took out a small seat with a stake in the end and stuck it in the grass. Crouching was too hard on his knees after too many Hurley knocks and strains not to mention the bang times he didn't like to recall. He took out of his pocket the message he was to send along with the King James Bible to be used as the code template and set to cooking the message.

Between the lines of the message, he should have connected the radio to the battery but he didn't want to start emitting yet. Finally finished the finicky job of coding Dagan connected the live wire, switched the knob to transmit, and rapidly converted the message into dots and dashes. Once that was done the reply came swiftly, HWHA WTQM QRKM, what the dickens did that mean? Riffling quickly through the

Bible, all one thousand pages plus of it, made decoding grim work. W.E.

E.R. Y.. Dagan stopped before the end guessing the rest and not caring if he was wrong doing it, wasn't my sort of clear instruction. Who cared where he was? He quickly coded *'Reply with orders'* and his personal tag. The reply was swift and he decoded with a dexterity that surprised himself as the sweat under his armpits added to the verisimilitude. If this was a drill what the Christ was it like in the field. AWAI TARD RSST AXON UNE

Dagan was amazed to see fifteen minutes gone on his watch he'd left down beside the Morse transmitter, he decoded of a - 2MORO- before he disconnected and without even pausing to follow the shutdown procedure he closed the case and started moving in a back-breaking crouch through the bushes as silently as he could. He'd barely gone thirty meters before the heard crashing behind him. Dagan veered to the right and put distance between him and his pursuers – *Fuck* – he thought to himself – *I forgot the seat!*

A whistle blew signaling the end of the exercise, Dagan stopped his pell-mell flight through the undergrowth, pulled him upright, groaning at the shooting pain that went up his back and brushed himself down. He headed back along the country lane, an altogether more convivial manner of getting around and passed his pursuers in a side hedge. These even more disheveled than he was, twigs in hair, leafs stuck to sleeves, muddy knees and hands, on seeing him the smaller more rapine looking of the two called out - *nearly had you there mate* - while at the same time making a gun shape with his hands cocking the thumb and making a clicking sound.

- Nearly caught is still better than nearly escaped, better luck next time and you can keep the seat – Dagan gave them the finger. All well and good joking about with the hounds but that was damn close thought Dagan. Just what the instructor fairly spat in disgust at him later in the post-exercise review.
- At least you got away even if your aftershave was still wafting around behind you – he said pointing directly at Dagan.

The finger then pointed at a cowering small thin man with thin slicked back hair and big round glasses.

- Unlike you or you or you...

The deadly finger-pointing continued around a room covered with large scale maps, newspaper cuttings, and pictures of recent cultural events

83

in Central Eastern Europe. Many were from newspapers forced to close by heavy-handed German censorship, others their supine regime approved mouth pieces replacements, full of happy content German loving Czechs and detailed tributes to the successful military campaigns that kept following. The instructor continued.

- If that had been for real I'd have been left with a couple of agents for the whole country and wouldn't give tuppence for their chances the next either. Right we take it as if you've never done it before and start from the beginning – A collective groan met that statement – You'll thank me later but before we start a late bit of news for you, tonight after supper there'll be a meeting up in the big house, in the ballroom, some sort of get together. A sherry reception no less it says. So everybody scrub up, very much needed after today's exercise, and put your best foot forward.

A hand shot up.

- Err, yes what is it?
- A question about the foot, left, right or does it matter? – asked the man with the arm up in the air.
- Does this mean there'll be dancing? – piped in another.
- Hells bells - thought the instructor - give me patience Lord I beseech you.

Back up in his garret Dagan looked away from the window set in the overhanging roof and towards the young wren beside him in the bed, she was laying on her side and supporting herself with her elbow, blonde hair, loose and crumpled from being hidden under berets formed in turn a wavy self-curtain to one side of her face.

- You'll behave yourself tonight won't you? – she said sternly as her pretty half hid face made what Dagan considered a pout.
- You're pouting. Makes you look lovely by the way but what for? It's only a silly meeting. I'll be counting away the minutes till it's over and thinking of you at the same time, I do that a lot to be honest. Very distracted in class they tell me.
- Really! – Coo's in the air.
- Of course – Dagan knew women liked that, not to be told they were ravishing and beautiful and the like, they did to be sure look favorably on such flattery but when they're with you. Women like you to be thinking of them when you aren't with them. It reassures them that you're not checking out the eye candy but instead fervently willing time to move on till the object of your thoughts can be with you.

- Anyways why are you worried? It's hardly the Viceroy's spring ball is it?
- Remember your training that all.
- Now you've piqued my interest, what exactly is this all about, you obviously know something, start spilling. Tickle check - Dagan jumped over and started tickling her tummy and sides, she squealed and squawked.
- STOP!

Dagan did as he took her leg in his hand and started to massage her thigh, Emily flipped over.

- Ah not so fast – she said.
- Don't you like that?
- Do and don't, you know I won't – her hair played like so many marionettes dancing on Dagan's chest.
- Do you like that I like the way your hair tickles me like mad. Okay you do and you don't, how very mysterious.
- I can do other nice things too. I've learned a bit about life this war. I've heard things about tonight that's all, you think it's an innocent drinks reception to celebrate something or other but it's more than that, it's some sort of exam.
- A test?
- Well, it's odd, last time there was one of these nights a couple of lorry loads of people turned up just before. Full of young gals in makeup and boys bathed in eau de cologne. Hurray Henrys with gelled back hair and pencil mustaches and the girls were wearing REAL nylons. How unfair!! – Emily was indignant.
- I like your legs just as they are, natural like – Dagan gallantry rode over verbally.
- And milky white, you can see my veins – Emily responded.
- Only up close – Dagan couldn't help himself.
- Hey, cheeky bugger! I talked to one of the girls in the kitchen about the nylons before I was shooed away. All she said when I asked was 'that it was the least they could give her for serving her country the way they'd asked her too' and with that off she went laughing. Silly cow.

6 pm, Main Reception room, Chichely Hall

At six o'clock sharp the soiree started, the main function room of the grand house was decked out with bunting, Union Jacks mixed with V for victory along with the flags of the Allied and Empire nations. No tricolor insight thought Dagan. The curtains were drawn, chairs placed in front of a small raised podium upon which a piano was found. A local concert in aid of the war effort, well attended by local dignitaries, the great and the good to be found in the neighboring counties. By no means all of the 'alumni' on the estate were present but a fair sprinkling.

- We'd been told to enjoy ourselves but not to give anything of use away – giggled one colleague close by. Hmm quite a delicate task. Was his name to any use to the enemy, probably. His reasons for being here, definitely. What he was actually doing, most certainly. So that left the weather, thankfully the English were genetically disposed to comment on the climate with great gusto and at great length.

"Might clear up late into the week...."

"Expecting a good/wet/dry summer...."

"Shocking the amount of rain recently...."

"Rum punch anyone?"

Some of these comments he overheard from the respectable matronly women and gruff no fuss gentlemen, all middle-aged, well able to remember the relief of Mafeking. Still, Emily was right on about the younger men and women who jarred conspicuously with the home country set. "Rum punch isn't it?" Dagan found himself up at the refreshments table elbow to elbow with a young man in a well-cut ill fitting suit, borrowed he supposed, freshly shaven, aftershave French pre-war expensive, the male pleasant looking with an open smile which never faltered.

- Punch is it but there's very little rum in it I'll say – Dagan always answered polite people. A habit that caused no end of trouble.
- Irish aren't you, one of our Hibernian visitors – asked the man as Dagan assented with a small nod of the head.
- A few of us around but not enough to warrant a flag – Dagan tilled his head and nodded at the bunting.
- My aunty lived in Cork, must visit sometime, maybe you could help me with some sightseeing tips – politely put so a joke was in order thought Dagan.

- They do say that the best thing in Cork is the road to Dublin.
- The road to Dublin! Ah yes, oh I say that's a riot, the road to Dublin, must remember that. Speaking of visitors to our shores, there's quite a hodgepodge here tonight, Poles, Czechs, French, I mean what gives, not that I mind, all welcome except the Germans of course.
- How do you mean 'what gives'? – queried Dagan.
- I don't want to be nosey but it's all rather intriguing, hush hush and all that, just refugees, lucky to have escaped the Boche – Dagan was tight-lipped - What about all the talk in the village, they say it's very interesting up here – the man came back.
- What village, what's the name – posed Dagan, he'd know unless he was a plant.
- Just of the main road, can't place the name, stopped in the village pub on the way – he replied. Dagan thought it was a fair answer in normal circumstances, showed talent at this.

More fishing along those lines went on but Dagan wasn't varying from his 'just refugees' cover.

- I notice you're not in uniform – Dagan said to change the subject – looking around for somebody he knew to escape to.
- Flat feet. Couldn't believe it when they told me. Like a man in uniform do you? – the man changed tact abruptly and with an arched eyebrow, a half-smile on his lips, his hand gently resting on Dagan forearm who thought 'what the hell' before deftly shaking loose the offending arm.
- Shame - the man said with resignation - you really have lovely eyes.

Dagan pointed out an elderly French émigré with a small potbelly and thick glasses on an angled bearded face.

- That gentleman over by the bandstand has nice eyes as well if you get my drift – Dagan informed the younger man.

His conversational partner looked over and muttered 'just my luck' under his breath and clenching his teeth took leave. These plants are so obvious and so amateur it made him fear for the quality of the rest of the training he was receiving but there's no point thinking about that now. Dagan made a beeline towards a young lady he'd seen earlier but hadn't approached because of the promises he'd made earlier to Emily. More aloof than some of the other attractive young women, she held herself with an elegant poise, one leg standing straight while the other was swept back at an angle creating a curious visual effect, as if she

87

was about to step away. She wore an elegant but simple green dress fashionably cut accompanied by a belt that accentuated a slim midriff, as Dagan got closer he made out the blonde hair clasped by a butterfly clip at the back, a face finely proportioned and lightly made up, the sort of face that needed a touch to distance itself from an unbecoming paleness yet rebelled against a heavy hand with the powder brush, the result of that being a garish over slash of color on marble. A girl uncertain of her beauty, unsure how to show it off, unused to events like this. The color of the dress matched her eyes was the last thing he noticed as the man who she was talking to excused himself and Dagan arrived to lay a hand on an exquisite arm. His turn at man handing he thought wryly.

- You won't get anything out of me without a struggle I'm warning you – the surprise and humor that showed on her face lit it up and reflected back to Dagan. His spirits soared.
- Pardon? I beg your....- the accent clipped, the tone imperious yet impish, the voice divine, Dagan cut her off.
- The rose garden is this way - Dagan gestured toward the open double doors leading out to the gravel patio and the gardens beyond.
- And why on earth should I accompany you to the garden – the woman asked in such a way that Dagan knew she would even just for entertainment.
- Because I arranged for them to flower today just for you – Dagan felt a bit bad for Emily but she'd understand, it was his duty.
- What a charmer you are – she laughed despite herself.
- And I'm sure we'll find one with the same name as you. Dagan Malone, secret agent and avid admirer, your arm please.
- You're already made its acquaintance, Daphne Armstrong and there are three types of rose with my name. I'll come with you not because the notion particularly appeals to me but because it's hot in here. Don't get any ideas; all three rosal Daphne's are renowned for the sharpness of their thorns.

11 am, following morning, Chichely Hall

- What do you mean spending half the night alone with the lord lieutenant of the counties' daughter? – The centre's chief administrative officer Basil Holden asked Dagan cholerically.
- I thought she was a plant – Dagan replied innocently.
- A plant! The flower of England and you demean her as such, the worst bounder in the shire would not stoup so low.
- I beg your pardon. A plant as in a plant, a stage, a put on or put up, somebody infiltrated – said Dagan exasperated by this inexplicable lack of US jargon, the Masai know more about the world – to get people to incriminate themselves – he'd intended to assuage the ire of the unit head bod but it had the adverse effect.
- Infiltrator, Daphne! I mean Ms Cavendish, she is nothing of the sort, I can assure you, I've known her since she was a toddler, invited her myself to the party, England's finest.
- Exactly but once I saw she was wearing real nylons – ventured Dagan.
- Nylons! What's that got to do with the price of bread apart from further lowering you in my estimations if that were possible. A couple of classes of code and you start talking gibberish – Dagan cut the chief short.
- Has Ms Cavendish made some sort of complaint? – Dagan wondered about those middle-aged bureaucrats who ended up in positions of power and influence in the realm of INTELLIGENCE, it never ceased to amaze him of their essential colourlessness, he could be talking to his draper.
- Err that is beside the point, talk of the county it will be.

Drab rule book lovers, back coverers and invertible killjoys. Dagan had thought to find a bit more laissez-faire among the pen pushers but his overwhelming impression so far had been middle England lace doilies pipe smoking Church of England Times of London types. They were well-meaning to give them some credit but he hoped the people who planned the operations were waiting in the wings. He was worried about what they'd told him so far, an airdrop and a rendezvous with emergent Czech resistance, emergent! That didn't sound very promising or at worst shivers down the spine. Look it up, developing, innocent early stages. Did that sound like the type of organization that could carry the mission off?

Earlier that week plans had been outlined involving the jump from a long-distance bomber flying over half of Europe, hideout in Prague and the surrounding hills, an armed assault on the concentration camp by a dozen fighters with getaway cars gunning their motors. It all sounded bad Hollywood to Dagan, they didn't know the jargon but they'd seen the flicks. Too much depended on chance, too little was hard fact, how many guards were to be on duty? How many machine guns? In how many towers? Did they have access to heavier weaponry? Where were the local Wehrmacht troops stationed? Nearby? How safe were the safe houses? How good was the local Gestapo at wireless detection and infiltration of the resistance networks? Of the groups where did their loyalties lie? Moscow? Or London? The answers to those questions conditioned everything.

- Do you know why I'm here? – Dagan asked the now calm centre chief.
- A vague idea hmm yes – faintly embarrassed cough, how many more knew?
- Then what do you think of the plan for insertion?
- I think we can get in – Holden said emphatically this time, the last voice many an agent heard before their missions, the voice of supreme confidence and way off beam of course; one must transmit hope above all.
- Well, I know someone else who can definitely get me in – Dagan countered.
- Who! – Total surprise. Holden.
- The Germans – Total honestly. Malone.
- And why would they do that – Total incredulation. Holden.
- Because we're going to ask them – Total conviction. Malone.

London, 1 week later

The three men sat around the chilly room on packing boxes, steaming cups of tea to hand.

- Pass the sugar.

Dagan said this to the youngest, a dapper smiling meticulously dressed youth in his early twenties bubbling over with good humor and goodwill who Dagan knew well as he'd given him classes in Czech at Chichely Hall. He'd come down from London, Jamey was his name. He'd explained how the war had cut short his time in Oxford, how his Slavic language skills and a bad case of asthma had put paid to his pass through his majesties forces, but his George IV had plenty of other organizations at work all needing conscientious hard-working Nazi hating people to do it. Jamey as he'd introduced himself had a special reason to loathe all things Nazi, having family in southern Germany, family he hadn't heard from in a long time, so Jamey loved the war and what he was doing and he deeply loved London. Dagan got the impression when talking to Jamey that he was reveling in this exciting life a bombed-out capital offered, Dagan understood, he'd gone through the same in Dublin as a young rebel tear about sucking in life and love as if he hadn't five minutes left on the planet. It was exhilarating. Jamey was the duty officer at the observation point when Dagan and another man arrived.

- Here you are – Jamey said in a cheery put on East End voice as he passed the sugar – and it never saw a ration card in its life – one eye winking.
- We deserve it - said the third man taking the sweet sand, he was taller and dressed soberly in a dark suit with a trilby overcoat tied by a belt.

Jamey, on the other hand, wore a jumper and some sort of woolly over garment to keep himself warm.

- Specially me guv, stuck here all day, staring till I'm half blind at the house across the street, all the time wondering if the place is going to fall down on my ears - the room they were in was reached by stairs exposed to the elements, the wall beside them showing the effect of the blast it received months before.
- German approved housing ventilation scheme – said Jamey.
- At least you're not being shot at – said the other - Did you see her enter? - pointing to the photo of a young woman, staring straight at the camera, confidence, head held high, blonde hair tied back, full lips, a very handsome woman.
- She certainly did, a pleasure to have to look out for such an attractive lady – Jamey said openly.
- Ok - and turning back to Dagan the other man said - looks like your lady friend can help us.
- She can, risky it isn't, the worst they can do to her is sack her – replied Dagan.
- But you'll be right exposed once you're there – the other tellingly said – This operation is highly irregular, she's not a trained agent, she's no experience in intelligence and covert missions.
- Oh, she's more than capable – Dagan affirmed his endless belief in Daphne's abilities.

91

He remembered the moonlight garden, the way she brushed aside his smooth practised advances with practised evasions. At first, she rebuffed him with sharp clever ripostes before they just ended up talking about this and that. Conversed minutes turned into hours as the dawning of day surprised them as it stealthily arrived to their amazement. 'I like you even though I think you're naughty' she'd said, 'And I like you even though you're not a bit naughty' he replied during this genesis of mutual admiration and attraction. It was during that heart to heart amid laughter and swapped anecdotes that he learned of Daphne's work in the Red Cross, an organization which straddling both sides of a brutal conflict. Dagan had figuratively given two fingers to operational security and had told her about the camps and what they needed to do. To his surprise, Daphne knew about it and suspected they were worse than the Germans let on and that then gave Dagan a glimpse of an idea, an audacious plan to get into the camp as an invited guest.

- I've met her as well and there's no denying it, she's a game girl - Detective Pinner, the third man in the room, had met Dagan and Daphne in a back street boozer in Lambeth, far off the beaten track.

Not so much as to avoid the prying eyes of diplomatic staff friendly to the axis powers but so as not to be seen by fellow Red Cross staff. The organization jealously guarded its neutrality; any taint of partiality would be seized upon by either side to severely curtail the humanitarian mission of the Red Cross which was to alleviate the suffering of the victims of the conflict.

Hence the run down out of the way pub, all Victorian brass and cigarette marked oak counters and ochre walls covered with pictures of music hall stars.

- So this is what a licensed premise looks like from the inside, I'd always wondered – Daphne cooed.
- Is this the first time you've been in a pub? – Pinner asked.
- Good heavens yes, no one I know would go to one except daring Marge and I can see why she liked it now. Agog with colorful characters – it was Daphne who was agog.
- Charley Chaplin used to drink in the snug over there with his dad – Dagan added.

She gapped around at the assorted men and women huddled in corners or up at the bar.

- Do you think they will sing I hear the people are very jolly and there's a piano in the corner? – Daphne said wide-eyed.
- It's a bit early but you never know, Yeats was curious about pubs too so he went into one day, had a sherry and left saying to Gogarty that they were 'ghastly' and he never went to one again - Dagan did not say that he'd come along with Gogarty and had even been the instigator of the fleeting visit. The sherry had been shocking it was true.
- Perhaps it offended his artistic sensibilities – added Daphne.
- Who's this Yeats Fellow? – Pinner asked.
- The poet and sage of Ireland – Dagan told him.
- Ah. Right you are. Well leaving the esteemed versifier to one side for the moment and before the Cockneys start singing or the Germans start bombing, tell me again about this plan you concocted behinds our backs – Pinner was no fan of the plan. Very much off-piste.
- Well – started Daphne - you know where I work or should I say, volunteer, I don't need to work and would never have if the frightful Hun hadn't started this ghastly business. Everyone has to do their bit but at least I didn't take a salaried job some other girl might have missed out on.
- How does volunteering for the Red Cross count as helping the war effort? – interrupted Pinner.
- Because as we speak there are over forty thousand British and Allied POWs spread over Europe and Africa which only the Red Cross has access to and let it be said to Axis prisoners too. Third parties, of course, Americans, Swiss, Swedes, anyone neutral not the Germans or us. That means there are more than forty thousand Allied families, sweethearts, mothers, sisters, daughters who know their loved ones are alive and being treated well. Tell them we're not helping the men; tell me we're not keeping up morale on the home front - The tone was exasperation and something more.
- Looking at it in that light – Pinner reflected – I'm inclined to agree but if that's all true and you stand convinced of the need for the Red Cross and the work it does why are you putting it in jeopardy by helping us. If you do what you say you'll do and it works the Germans will know about the switch and there's a mole in London. How they'll react is anyone's guess but we know how nasty the Gestapo can be.
- It's not necessarily traceable to her, it could be the Red Cross offices in Washington or Sweden and if I.....

- Wait! – Dagan said – I've thought of all that but the risks are still better than the alternatives – Dagan knew the other man couldn't argue that point in front of Daphne without revealing what the alternatives were – and I have an idea about our American friend that will leave the Red Cross free of all suspicion. A trick I picked up from some Atlantic City racketeers.

Neither Pinner nor Daphne looked very convinced and even Dagan betrayed himself slightly by sounding less than his normal cocksure self but better this than creeping around the Czech countryside prey to all sorts of misadventures, conflicts, and exposure. Let the enemy do all the hard work, bring him right to the mission goal, let them house him in nice hotels, bring him to swanky receptions, give him free access to the target to enable him to seize up the surrounds before committing to an eventual operation. Then either undertake the mission and vanish from the visiting party or just continue with the Red Cross back to neutral territory after its tour was completed. It sounded crazy and it was on a lunatic scale but it was just so crazy it could work, again Dagan's duel Irish-American nationality afforded him double protection.

- Look, I'm Irish, American, very anti-British, known to the Germans due to the flowering of previous mutual interests - not finding a polite way to drop 'the defeat of the British empire' into the conversation Dagan glossed over it – they know I'm close to certain senior figures in the Roosevelt administration, hell they'll be delighted to see me, pardon my French - Dagan looked at Daphne but she seemed to take blasphemy very much in her stride just like back street boozers – my adventures in Spain I can pass off as humanitarian, ergo my interest in the Red Cross and Ethiopia as a business opportunity.
- And supposing this all miraculously works out how do you propose to get in touch with Czech resistance while not alerting the Germans to your sudden disappearance?
- Any ideas Daf - Dagan asked Daphne as she giggled.
- Harry Houdini himself would have trouble with this one – she answered more seriously.
- Nothing for it so - Dagan winking at Daphne turned and asked Pinner - What's the maximum range of a Wellington bomber then?

Before Pinner could reply the dash tangle of piano keys rang and a Cockney voice sang out – 'Everybody now, the Lambeth walk'.

- Oh goody – cried Daphne I've heard of this one, let's all sing along, Madge will be raging she missed this!
- We can't tell her Daf – said Dagan.
- Oh, spot and bother.

Charleston, South Carolina, July 1941

Bryant Jenner had a lot to be thankful for in life; youth, health, good looks, an expensive education, and most importantly, a doting grandfather who was one of the wealthiest men in the south-east part of the US. But sometimes even the most worldly blessed encounter forces bigger than themselves. For Bryant it was the sweet-faced ingénue he met at his favorite bar in Charlestown. Not a bar any self-respecting southern belle would expect to be in either. Still and all one could relax with liked-minded souls apt to put aside accepted social conventions and that applied equally to the women and the men. Her name was Molly she said, a typist in a local office, new to the town and tired of her pokey bedroom shared in her boarding house. Bryant had caught a whiff of perfume and the sight of a shapely leg closely aligned to a prominent chest was captivated. The pretty summer dress fitted her figure to perfection. The doll-like face, full lips smeared generously with ruby red lipstick and heavily shaded eyes made her stand out. Bryant hadn't wasted time, he paid for two drinks while edging closer, had touched her arm several times and was now dropping all sorts of indiscretions to impress. Did she know that Bryant was off to Germany, the Wolfs lair itself in a short time?

- Really! I do declare how interesting. A holiday destination for the bravest - Molly gasped.
- A holiday is what we could go on one of these days but Germany is a special mission.......for the same US government. They have asked me to go – Bryant let slip winking.
- Why this is the most daring thing ever, tell me more – Molly took hold of his arm over a rum Dakarai, the latest craze was for rum cocktails - now what's this about that there Germany and perhaps excusing a poor gals ignorance of politics, a fine man of the world like you could explain why they were being so nastily and all to the English who seem very gentlemanly folk with civilized airs. That Ashley fella in Gone with the Wind being a fine example.
- I don't like to brag about my grandpappy but he is philanthropically minded and the Red Cross has been on the receiving end of some mighty cheques on his part.

- Your grandpappy? Why he's not the Jenner of Jenner coal and gas?
- Why yes he is – Bryant answered in good-natured surprise.

Bryant as ever was well pleased the effect the family name had on another impressionable young gal. Always makes them more inclined to get reclined as he joked with his cronies. The script was played out, the fore runner to any serious foreplay, tales of subsequent shortfalls in the rent and bothersome landladies enlists sympathetic comments from Bryant along with gallants offers of short term help, any friend would do likewise, look upon it as a long term loan. Once the initial reticence was overcome the final details were coquettishly arrived at. Five o'clock that afternoon in the lobby of a downtown hotel. But the script was not his entirely, poor Bryant, little did he know that Molly was not exactly what she professed. Starting with her name, Molly she got from a book, her real one the more prosaic Mary Jane Kapaloviz who seeing little difference in 12 hours shifts in a factory or domestic service had opted for a less onerous day job as a courtesan. One or two select gentlemen at a time and most of the day free to herself for occasion work like the opportunity that had arrived out of the blue the week before. Five hundred dollars to entice a young gentleman to a certain hotel suite at a certain time entertain him and collect another five after for doing so. One thousand dollars was enough to live off for three months, she'd been understandably keen to start and within a week her opportunity had arrived. She wondered who was behind the sting, his wife or ex-wife or her family but didn't dwell on it not for long; she had a job to do so she did it. She'd 'leave the nought smack bang in the middle' the rest of the noughts and crosses she'd leave to 'interested parties'.

The hotel Dubois, slightly off and away from the best part of the town had seen better days, it wore the air of faded glory as one does an ill-fitting school blazer handed down from an older relative. Chipped paintwork, lampshades pallid imitations of their original glory, carpets spent and threadbare in places, dust encrusted in corners overhung by photos of high society balls held before the Great War. The unkempt receptionist with his luncheon serviette still tucked into his dark and shiny with age high buttoned livery jacket couldn't suppress a knowing smile as Bryant paid.

- How many nights will that be sir? – The word 'nights' came after a leery pause.
- Two please – Bryant didn't like the man's oily tone boarding on insolence.

- Two sir? Very good, will I ring for a bellhop to carry your...wife's luggage – another pause, the receptionist poked his head out of the counter and looked left then right before repeating the question – Luggage?
- It's arriving later? – Bryant had had enough.
- Very good that's 2 nights at 20 dollars a night, 40 in total paid in advance.
- I truly apologize for that man's presumption, rarely had one seen the like – Bryant said as Molly and he approached the lift.
- That's very gentlemanly and neighbourly of you - Molly looked over her shoulder and winked at the receptionist an acquaintance of long standing – That man is truly a bore and God knows I loathe a bore. You, on the other hand, are a gentleman to the core. The very definition I'd say - these were the last words as the lift doors closed and it rose to the third floor.

There in room 337 Bryant passed some of his most pleasurable and painful moments, physical and mental. Molly, a pro to her manicured long pink fingernails soon dropped her coy persona and taking him by the tie led him to the bed. Her instructions were clear and the honey trap was closing but at least she could sweeten the pill, she'd even began to feel a little sorry for the man, he wasn't the worst by a long shot.

Ten minutes later agents Kevlar and Monroe of the FBI burst into the room with a photographer who captured what was later described by Edgar j Hoover as 'complete and utter surprise' on the faces of the two entwined figures. Molly might have known what was coming but it still caught her on the hop, Bryant had no such luck. Two dark-suited men with badges and guns stood over the bed as the photographers flash popped from various angles.

- Can you kindly stop that sir – Molly said covering her chest with the sheet. Hoover would also remark that it was the very definition of a fine American chest, 'and he'd know' joked one of his cohorts.
- Who the frigates are you? – Bryant's low baritone voice, of which he was very proud of, had risen several notes and now came out as a shrill cry laced with fear and understandable indignation.
- Agents Kevlar and Monroe of the FBI sir. Did you know that it is illegal to have intercourse with a minor in the state of South Carolina?

- A minor? What! But how old are you sweetie – Bryant asked his bedding partner regaining a little composure and voice - Tell the man it's all been a terrible misunderstanding – he pleaded.
- You age madam – Monroe prompted Molly.
- Why I'll be turning sweet 17 next month. On the 14th to be exact – she said pleasantly.

Chapter IV

Baltic Sea, autumn, 1941

The cargo ship SV King Harwich was a modest tramp steamer in service since the start of the century but still well able for the Baltic routes after retiring from the north Atlantic. Her bunkers normally carried iron ore from Swedish mines to the hungry German war machine and this voyage was no exception. Her destination was Hamburg and the only difference this time was she also shipped her full complement of passengers. Since the start of the war that hadn't been much call for her staterooms, apart from an occasional businessman traveling back and forth along with diplomatic staff. The German embassy in Stockholm being one of its largest, not that German diplomats had much of a choice these days, finding countries not occupied or not at war with the fatherland or just plain reachable was difficult. This time however the occupants of the cabins weren't diplomats or businessmen on the make but an international Red Cross party invited to visit Germany and inspect prisoner of war camps, installations etc.

This was not an unusual event but was notable as a civilian work camp had also been included, something not normally done. Each side still played lip service to the sensibilities of the still neutral states around the world and wanted organizations like the Red Cross to give them respectability or a veneer of it. The staterooms were on the upper deck near the bridge and the captain's quarters. As well as eating with the officers the passengers enjoyed the run of the day room in the morning which contained the library, deep warm brown leather chairs, a large dining table and a sideboard set up with a cistern of hot water to make tea and cocoa. Around this, the members of the Red Cross committee were making friends and small talk.

- This is all a sham you know – opened the Brazilian Dr D'Silva, a small set jolly man, wide of girth with a lightweight tropical suit, cream coloured, at odds with the rest of the group as it was October after all and sombre greys or blacks predominated.
- A sham! What do you mean please - Dr Takenaka the Japanese member of the party sounded indignant, medium-sized whippet-thin figure in a neat morning suite, a small moustache very popular among the elite Japanese and thick black spectacle gave evidence to considerable myopia - Do you mean not true, false, a

trick to be played? If you do I hope you are making, how do you say, a jest – he continued.

His English, the common language among the group and agreed upon as the lingo Franca, was a bit rusty. Dr Takenaka as he insisted in being addressed hadn't spoken it since a 1920s posting in Washington, he preferred German and had tried to have French used instead but had been overruled mostly because of the South Americans, D'Silva and Mendes the Argentinean. It was common to find substantial representation on Red Cross groups from that part of the globe as the South Americans were benign and confused onlookers while the rest of the world went at each other like wild cats.

- I agree with Dr Takenaka we must strive to maintain an impartial outlook, it will be no good to go with the impression already formed – the Argentine came from a country very taken with the Fuhrer and his ways and means, an open ally like Japan in all but name. The impression is and will remain positive despite all evidence to the contrary in the coming tour thought Dagan, so far a distant member of the party who had joined the ship at its stop in Sweden walking on board with the Swedish member, the fifth of them, Neilson, who chose that moment to intervene.
- Please, we must refrain from all comment, influence, or diatribe, we are not here to judge, our mission is to see, look, been seen, be shown, listen and then report. No more, but be seen is vital – his English was impeccable if convoluted.
- *Esta es el problema, nos enseñen lo que ellos quieren, no cree usted* – Dagan said this to D'Silva. They show us want they want us to see basically was his drift.
- I'm from Brazil, we speak Portuguese there but I understand sufficient Spanish to understand you.
- How true, I'd forgotten that – Dagan conceded although he had known it.
- Yes they show us what they want and we see what they want us to see - Neilson summed it up.
- We can hardly have free run of the place, there's war on, anyone out on their own would be considered a spy and shot - D'Silva said. Dagan didn't like the way the conversation was developing, especially the shooting spy's part.
- You were not in the original group – Takenaka spoke for the first time to Dagan, who despite the Japanese's short polite bow sensed danger, it had been too shallow. Speaking to Takenaka was practically the same as speaking to a German. I'll have to be candid thought Dagan.

- A last-minute change so they told me, I was asked to substitute somebody who couldn't go.
- Last-minute, war going on, you decide Germany ok, cross submarine swimming seas ok, visit disease invested camps ok – the man from the land of the rising sun wasn't making it easy.
- Steady on with 'invested'.   They're not leper colonies – Neilson interjected.
- Germany is an old good friend of Ireland.   While I was initially going to refuse I thought why not, this will be a way to help them and thank them for their help in our struggle against the British. I hope to run into several acquaintances while we're here, we might even see Hitler I believe.
- Ireland is not with the British Empire in this war? – Takenaka sounded amazed.
- Damn, right we're not. For what reason? What did Germany do to us by God? - Dagan bristled, strong feelings on the matter greatly helped
- Before you keep going Takenaka remember Japan was with the Empire AGAINST Germany in the last hostilities and did quite well out of it – Neilson added in timely fashion.
- Good and we did. Emperor's shining wisdom - Takenaka was pleased with the Great War and saw lots of opportunities in this before he shined to the subject of where he was and where he was going – Hitler, yes, a great man, to meet him would please the emperor greatly – Good tic to notice, 'mention the H' man and Takenaka gets distracted. Needed as too much scrutiny too soon was burning up his luck. Dagan was sure he was going to need lady luck, the phrase made him think of Daphne, an association made with her and the word lady. He'd read about the theories on associations we make for loved ones or things of significance especially our mothers and fathers. At a party in Vienna, years before a distinguished man called Freud with cropped grey hair and goatee had spent a good part of the time explaining the concepts to him. By the end, Dagan had had to excuse himself because of the cigar smoke and the turn of the conversation to the role of mothers and desires in general. The whole thing had left Dagan a bit queasy though he noticed in the press later that the good doctor had managed to leave Vienna after the *Anschluss* and had been glad of it. Not like Georg Pick or others who'd refused to leave and now where were they, in another camp at best.

A stocky Viking of a steward popped his considerable head in the door to say 'Docking in 30 minutes, nobody allowed on deck during docking. All photography strictly forbidden' and promptly left. D'Silva reacted first.

- Why don't we make all our cases ready and re-join here to leave the ship - D'Silva the amiable figure had taken on the role of group organizer, his conciliatory nature a boon from the more strident Japanese and Argentinian - Don't worry they know their way through the minefields and even if they don't only a short swim now - he added as a joke.
- Minefields! - Mendes had a nervous disposition, he'd spent the voyage prophetizing their imminent doom, a British submarine just waiting to send them to the bottom. Even Dagan who normally asleep as soon as the light was off had his slumbers disturbed. Mendes was about to forget about floating mines and switch to his next worry, British air raids. It promised to try the patience of the rest of the group but perversely it had brought the others together. Takenaka made a stern face, in Japan one didn't roll one's eyes Dagan supposed and told Mendes 'that all was under control, no need to worry, great German Reich taking all consideration'. Reich came out with the characteristic Asian sound that had Dagan suppressing a smile, should find it amusing, and own ascent caused mirth and bewilderment in equal orders of magnitude. The Swede seemed to have had a similar internal struggle and intervened with a bit of local knowledge 'the crew tell me a pilot will be on board for the docking'.
- *Vale está bien* - said Mendes somewhat more relaxed.

Dagan had his luggage packed and ready and so remained while the others left, the portholes here larger and higher up than his cabin. Looking out he could see the harbour as they approached along a mine free corridor. Most of the wharf cranes lying idle except for one or two unloading big grey rocks. The precious iron ore needed by the German war machine. Further into the early morning, some vessels of the German Kriegsmarine could be seen, mostly small inshore craft, minesweepers and dredgers and other such. Dagan couldn't see far out in the distance. Finally to one side of the port lay the huge U-boat pens looming large and grey, dwarfing the area around them. A favourite of the RAF as a target and as a pathfinder for deeper inland raids they seemed relatively unscathed however. German engineering at its finest. They'll be mostly empty thought Dagan, their need now lessened by the manifold opportunities offered by Norwegian and

French ports. U boat crews rarely saw the Fatherland these days Dagan didn't see any more as right then Takenaka entered followed by the rest, Dagan hung back from the window so as not to look overtly curious still Takenaka gave him a guarded look.

- What you look at? – He asked – but he was drowned out by the voluble South Americans arriving in animated discussion, Spanish and Portuguese pouring from their mouths and neither paying the slightest bit of attention to what the other was saying. Takenaka came right up to Dagan - Why you look? - in an accusative tone
- Why not look? – Dagan said staring defiantly straight into the eyes of the Japanese.
- Spies look – Takenaka's words got the attention of the rest.
- *Cuidaaaado* - D'Silva said alarmed.
- *Por Dios* – Mendes added blessing himself.
- The RAF could fly over here, take photos and see ten times more than I can see through this porthole - Dagan snorted, his back was up, spooked by the speed of the Japanese using a word like 'spy' as they were about to dock in port. He hadn't even set foot in Germany yet.
- You going to see places where RAF not photographing – Takenaka insinuated.
- We all are – Mendes lightening the atmosphere.
- I was looking from my cabin window – D'Silva chipped in trying much the same.

Dagan turned back to the Japanese and headed to the dispenser

- Tea anyone? – behind his back Takenaka fumed, looked around for support, found the South Americans shuffling and looking at their shoes while the Swede pointed out to him 'our work is hard enough' with his hand on Takenaka's shoulder who shrugged it off before storming away.

The three remaining members all looked at Dagan whose turn it was to shrug his shoulders.

- He's a couple of geishas short of a pleasant personality – Mendes was the first to smile.
- A geisha might be difficult to obtain but some sake we could find.

At that moment the boom of the ships horn sounded as a decided bump could be felt while the ship met the buffering of the wharf. Gangways could be heard being hoisted up, voices mixed in German and Swedish shouted at each other as unloading was being prepared but first the prized Red Cross delegation was to be greeted with all the garlands it was due. Three German officers entered the stateroom followed by two civilians and a photographer.

- Good evening to you all – I'm Colonel Von Bitterlich and this is my assistant Lt. Muller - Muller clicked his heels - and introducing Herr Voller of the foreign ministry, Herr Rehder of the German Red Cross and Captain Hoffman of the SS. All of you are very welcome to the Fatherland, in the name of our glorious Fuhrer of the Third Reich, which even in these dangerous times knows how to treat her good friends. Now please we will film your arrival on German soil as you go down the gangway and we will be taking photos to record this occasion.

They didn't even wait that long as the photographer had started working away, he was obviously going to be busy, the Fatherland was short of prestigious visitors and the Red Cross group fitted the bill. They were big news hence with the whirl of film cameras and the pops of flashing bulbs still before their eyes the delegation was led away.

- My luggage, I must get my suitcase - D'Silva asked as they went.
- Please not be worrying about your suitcase, we have arranged everything, you will all get your luggage back after the reception. Please follow me now, we are running behind the schedule.
- Already – murmured Dagan under his breath while Takenaka spoke of German efficiency as praiseworthy and an example to the whole world.

Down the gangplank, they all went and into the waiting Daimler cars for the short journey to the *Rothaus*, the seat of the local government and town council. Dagan squashed in with the South Americans, Muller and the Foreign Affairs official made small talk on the way. Dagan noticed the streets were nearly devoid of traffic but otherwise everything seemed normal, families and workers mingled on their way back from work and on the way to shops. No sign of bomb damage could be seen except for the odd pile of rubble being cleared by gaunt figures of men and women wearing long overcoats against the autumn cold, the yellow Star of David visible on their sleeves. Dagan shuddered involuntarily, that and many other vile actions was why I was much better off in the US thought Dagan. Muller noticed the shiver but mistook it for something else.

- Shall I turn up the heating sir – he suggested.

- That won't be necessary but thank you all the same – Dagan said this in German, Muller was delighted
- Ah very good, you speak some German. Always appreciated, our English is rusty and for obvious reasons we feel reluctant to speak it, it seems somehow unpatriotic – Muller gave a short laugh - Ah now we are arriving.

Hamburg Rathaus

And with that the car pulled up in front of the red-bricked Rothaus, the awaiting brass band, their second, in Wehrmacht uniforms stuck up as soon as their cars stopped and the doors opened. As they gathered and were ushered in it was busy working its way through its merry per war repertoire they didn't need musicians on the Eastern front yet thought Dagan. Arranged behind, beside and in front were cheering groups of school children dressed in Hitler youth garb, the pigtailed blond girls and boys cropped in the style of Himmler's near-flat Mohawk, both boys and girls wore their red neck scarves toggle out and over their overcoats, they all carried small swastikas mixed with Red Crosses on sticks waving from side to side.

The youth student's proud teachers, all females, made straightened Heil Hitler's salutes, amid the clamour photographers captured the adulating crowd as a backdrop to the impassive faces of the Red Cross delegation. All except Takenaka who arrived in the following car seconds after, his face shone with uncharacteristic delight and open admiration, walked up to the children and put a hand on some heads and arms he turned to Muller and said something which Dagan didn't hear but was complementary as Muller smiled at the Japanese. They were all ushered inside and upstairs into the main reception room to be met by the town council, mayor and leading citizens. Dagan noted very few clergy, normally assiduous attendees of this type of event in practically the entire western world. Odd that but you'd have to have a pretty hard neck to be able to lump in the message of Jesus Christ with support for a brutal police state the Nazis had created with Teutonic mysticism thrown in.

The Red Cross group were led to the podium and seated facing the gathered Hamburg grandees. The Colonel also sat on stage gave way to a figure dressed in the blackest of uniforms, glistened high boots, a peaked black cap, all sinister in the extreme, its main reason d'être. A general of the SS no less, the crack military-political arm of the Nazis, once just Hitler's praetorian guard but after its Abel like ascent over the truncated SA it had become a mini-state inside a state, charged with what people call 'the dirty work' of Hitler's Aryan dream. Along with the Gestapo, it had become the twin pillars of the fear-inducing fascist state. In the eyes of right-minded Germans of whom there existed quite a few, as recent attempts by the military at assassinating Hitler demonstrated along with the deliberate absence of men of God at the reception. They existed in a nationalist socialist nightmare of atheist calumny where they had every reason to fear whatever contact with the Gestapo as their first was likely to be their last. Any opposition to the regime resulting in being sent to brutal labour camps run by the SS. Word got about especially in circles lukewarm on the regime which with characteristic duplicity and cowardliness didn't publicize the existence of forced work camps or camps located in the more remote east. What went on there could only be guessed at. Still, the regime felt completely justified in imprisoning without trail German citizens but didn't like the rest of the population knowing about it. Ever such were brutal dictatorships shrinking violets when it came to freedom of information. But people knew and they knew people knew, in this panorama overseas visitors meant a lot, it was the propaganda frontline, this visit was to show the world the camps as re-education centres, tough yes but necessarily so was how the sales patter went.

- *Kameraden* - boomed the voice of the General in the microphone, the use of that word reminiscent of Bolshevik commissars, polar opposites to the Nazis and their dogmas anathemas to them but whose brutal control amounted to much the same – our great Reich, gloriously led by our beloved Fuhrer welcomes to its shores this group of friends – a chubby arm was briefly swung in the direction of Dagan and his cohorts - Germany has always openly welcomed visitors to its peace-loving lands. But now due to British aggression on the seas has had her trade and commerce brutally cut off. And who suffers as a result? Children, the old, the sick even as the state is striving to help. These are criminal acts the Red Cross must condemn. The Fuhrer has instructed me to hand over a list of the barbarous crimes being committed by British forces every day. We expect the Red Cross to bring this document to the eyes of the world, then the British will be revealed as their true selves and the world will finally know who is really responsible for this unfortunate war.

Dagan sat listening impassively as it was time to button down his emotions, the compassionate human in him to go on a short vacation while this topsy turvy version of the world was anointed. Whatever the

Brits were doing this General was spouting a pack of lies. Other members struggled to comprehend the sheer grandiloquence of the welcoming speech meanwhile Goebbels's cameras kept on silently filming the whole spectacle for the later Pathé newsreel type diffusion, especially the expected part where the Red Cross had to take sides and denounce the 'true aggressors' on the world stage. That wasn't what the Red Cross was about though; Dagan did feel a twinge of guilt on the dirty deeds they'd done to get him this far and how they were using the nominally neutral aid organization for their own ends. Both sides overlooked any transgressions involving the Red Cross as long as they were minor because it suited their interests. Red Cross members in Germany were card-carrying Nazi party Germans without exception, it was a useful way to exchange opinions and sound out the stance of the armed opponents, things still weren't at the stage where a compromise couldn't be reached so it was always good to keep some channels of communication open.

Applause blubs flashing, shouts of Heil Hitler. Now it was the turn of the delegation. D'Silva rose, approached the podium stand with evident hesitation and took out a sheet of paper. After first clearing his throat a burst of sound resonated in the microphone causing a high pitched shriek and feedback to whip around the hall. Dagan like most grimaced nice start.

- Good evening ladies and gentlemen - D'Silva's opener.

He started in passable German, foreign-sounding of course, softer, less stated, the Latin musicality lending it a velvety texture. A noticeable change from the German the general spoke, of whom D'Silva thanked as well as a large list of civic authorities, the other military big hitters present, the local business community and a reduced diplomatic corps of Hamburg consuls. As Dagan surmised, the great and the good of Hamburg society weren't going to miss out on a show with brass bands and canapés to boot. D'Silva thanked the German state for facilitating their visit and it was here Dagan began to lose the thread of the discourse. His German had never been more entertaining, jay picking and extensive vocabulary. Learning grammar was his problem not remembering words. Putting words together with an odd verb, usually the infinitive and mashing it all up with subject pronouns and liberal sprinklings of Latin, English, some French and hand signals generally got him understood, fed and laid while at the same time bringing out the sense of humour in even the most German of Germans. Hence his descriptive use of the word 'entertaining'.

But over the course of the summer, in between code-breaking and making, pistol shooting, self-defence, Morse, knife work, evasion and wireless classes and a long list of others Dagan had suffered through several classes of German. What struck him as strange was a nation so rigorous and organized as the Germans should have such a rigorously disorganized language, there seemed to be a case for every eventually and the least useless dative the only one that stuck in his head. Words were put together like so many train wagon cars that ended up train crashing.

Only by applying himself to Jesuit levels had Dagan been able to make the great leap from barely understood to rarely misunderstanding. D'Silva now stated or so Dagan thought that all parties in the present conflict claimed right was on their side and whether this was the case or not was not his concern, what mattered was that all sides undertook to respect international agreements about captured troops and non-belligerents. Braver words had seldom been said in front of a Nazi SS General and with good reason, the Waffen SS man with his skull and crossbones collar badge looked furious at being harangued in this way, his face contorting and muttered oaths emanated from his mouth. He looked close to an open breach of protocol. As D'Silva evoked the tolerance of Erasmus the gathered Brahmins, taking their cue from the visibly and openly snorting high ranking Nazi, began to put on a collective hostile cloak. Seat shifting, coughing, murmurs and open shouts swept through the rows of seated guests. Erasmus and his high ideals getting short shift from people who expected to be in the frontline of the imminent world domination by Germany and weren't going to be told how they should behave by anyone. Dagan hoped D'Silva didn't have much more of this or any other humanist subject as it just wouldn't wash with this crowd so full of themselves after years of near bloodless victories.

But D'Silva had sensed the loud enmity of his audience. He glanced down at the remaining pages of his carefully worded speech, specially crafted to showcase all the best of human endeavour and achievement and the concepts and notions of the Red Cross and came to the rapid conclusion as Dagan had that this wasn't a venue deserving for such elevated principles. He quietly removed two pages and put them away. Dagan had been away from Germany since the early thirties and so had no great point of reference either way to the regime in power since 1933 but a gut feeling gathering ever since he landed was crystallizing into a certain God awful acknowledgement that the Nazi's were way off any normal moral compass. D'Silva gathered the rest of his papers together with resigned dignity and facing the rabid audience and loudly into the microphone above the crackling din said clearly.

- Civilization is not a right it is an obligation, civilized behaviour is not expected but demanded, you measure your success by the number of people you help to fulfil their lives, and no one is the master to another. Quoting Goethe 'Every day we should hear at least one little song, read one good poem, see one exquisite picture, and, if possible, speak a few sensible words.' Thank you – and he sat down abruptly.

Dagan rather admired the old duffer, who'd shrunk visibly during the speech but he'd spat at the devil in the devil's own living room and that took guts. Dagan sensed a kindred spirit, an ally perhaps even should he ever need one. Dagan's goodwill towards the Brazilian was in direct contrast to the feelings in the hall but as they were visitors and friendly ones at that and canapés were in short supply these woe begotten days, the Germans put away their fangs and put on masks of amiability. After all the imminent fall of Moscow will herald the end of this temporary situation while restoring them to their role of undisputed overlords of Europe. Meanwhile, five diverse members of a Red Cross committee and several tables of nibbles were an acceptance stopgap.

- We'll have the Bolshoi back as soon as the army sweeps away the ragged remains of the Russians just like in spring of 1918 - Dagan was told this by a Bolshoi loving Russian hating notary.

The lawman was corpulent and jolly, his jowls shaking as he recounted the previous summer's setbacks to the mighty Red Army, six hundred thousand prisoners in the Kiev pocket alone, red-faced he paused to grab another glass and canapé from a passing waiter, Dagan noticed that the guests were taking full advantage of the state provided nibbles and finger food, Rheinische Bratwurst, Thüringer Leberwurst, Bavarian Landjäger, Berlin Sülzwurst and so on. It was as if the elite provincials were suffering acute shortages of life's culinary pleasures. The shirt collar of his conversational companion now had a size or two on its wearer. A jowl or two was a small sacrifice to make for pan European domination the rotund but reduced lawyer confirmed.

- What the Bolsheviks need is Trotsky back but the ice pick in his head would make it hard to concentrate on battlefield strategy don't you think?

Again the lawyer indulged his own humour by chuckling merrily and his appetite by liberating another canapé as it passed by. Herr Kolst

109

was his name, Dagan saw a petty fogging provincial lawyer who had hit the big time by hoisting his pennant fate to the Nazi firmament, honoree captaincy in the SS included, by the time Kolst turned back he got the feeling that the Irishman, with the limited but serviceable German, was a bit distant, weren't the Green boys famous for a good sense of humour. Dagan stared back at him but concealed his frustration and fury. More frustration than anything, what got to Dagan in these social situations was the glad handling, the people generally were the same the world over, self-fulfilled, self-centred, moneyed mollycoddled elites that Dagan wasn't drawn to and that made chitchat a drudge. Dagan turned away to conceal his feelings, can't let unctuous fat cats like this affect him so much. Worse because what he said was true, what would the Red Army be doing now if Trotsky was its head, a darn sight better to start with. How life's ironies made a case for God's existence, a creator, the hidden hand, how else could you explain the death of Trotsky months before a German invasion? Stalin would have been in the NKVD's dungeons and Trotsky, who was Jewish to boot, would have been in the Kremlin if he'd been alive in June 1941. Vagaries of fate and fortune aside what had riled Dagan so much was the raw pain of it, he'd been there, he'd seen the corpse, he could have prevented the murder with a bit more luck if he had arrived when he had planned to and not been delayed by a derailed train. Derailed history perhaps. The whole episode was what had sent Dagan into a spiral of self-destruction arriving with every swig of whiskey and had finally led to a Cuban jail. And here he was 15 months later talking to an ardent Nazi about it. Poor old Leonski, a ruthless fucker when he needed to be but there was less blackness at the centre of his soul than in that of his politburo comrade. Dagan decided to take his leave of the lawyer, downing his drink in one go, he excused himself politely with an *'Ein schuldenking bitte'* and went to circulate. He needed another drink though he knew he shouldn't go too heavy on the liquid nectar. Over at the reception table, he spotted Valencia oranges, Danish hams, Bordeaux labelled wines. Europe under the heel was certainly doing its best to keep the Fatherland in fine victuals. As Dagan contemplated Belgium cheese on Polish cracker bread or so he imagined, a uniformed figure appeared at his shoulder waiting for him to turn around before starting to speak.

-   Ahem, excuse me for bothering you Herr Malone – Hoffmann, the SS officer from earlier. Was this good or bad and what a moment.

Hoffmann was quiet mannered, taller than Dagan and fairly well built. His head was close shaved at the sides and back, the features of the face were pleasant with pale blue eyes and a broad forehead.

Bespectacled, his glasses, haircut and uniform were practically the same as Himmler but the effect wasn't as sinister.

- May I introduce myself – he continued as Dagan turned and without waiting for any permission began – I am Captain Hoffman of State Security.

Here he stopped, obviously the mere mention of the words 'state security' was sufficient to produce instant acquiescence in the citizenry, Dagan could sense that even the people nearest to them, ardent regime supporters all, subtly backed off somewhat and behaved themselves, leaving behind a bubble that Dagan and Hoffman inhabited alone. Dagan had a bad feeling but that was nothing new, his poker face on as his guard went up, what could state security, the friendly name of the Gestapo, want with him?

- Dear Captain Hoffman a pleasure – Dagan extended his hand and his fullest smile - how can I be of service?
- We would like to ask if you are enjoying your visit to Germany – Hoffman acted and sounded polite.
- Of course, without a doubt very interesting I can say, I feel, we all do, very welcome. I have been here on many previous occasions though.
- Yes we are aware of your long association with our country that goes back a long way and we are honoured to count on your presence again – a curt nod which Dagan acknowledged by returning the compliment, maybe these state security people weren't as bad as the millions for corpses implied. Maybe he was just bored and was practising his English, excellent as it was. Or were on to him already, maybe Takenaka had had words.
- Excellent English, I wish my German was half as good.
- Thank you, a not totally wasted year in Hampstead London, do you know the area? – Why was he asking about London where Dagan had just come from?
- Few Irishmen don't know it, forced as we were to leave our shores – Dagan played the downtrodden Celt card.
- Ah yes, the English have a lot to answer for – and Hoffman showed it working again.

Even Dagan unashamedly pro all things Irish baulked at comparing the occupation of a small neighbouring island with the occupation of most of Europe. If the envisaged one thousand year Reich managed to reach that grand old age that would still be two hundred more than the Irish had to put up with. Hoffman continued.

111

- The area must have changed a lot since I was last there – here he made another pause, Dagan waited as well, the silence continued – wouldn't you think so? – The German insisted while Dagan smiled broadly.
- Everything changes with time I'd imagine - Time combined with Luftwaffe stick bombs did tend to vary the urban landscape he could have said.
- Yes things change and people too, I've seen a lot of Germans who were thought good citizens and then – a pause, an expert in pauses this guy – and then well I won't go any further, a shame, one never ceases to be amazed, such changes – the tut-tutting SS man seemed positively shocked that anyone could oppose the Government or any rational person even think it would do any good but Dagan took the hint about people changing and the danger present in such innocuous words. Some sort of palpable reply was needed.
- People should always remember from where they're from and where they are going – Dagan said po-faced, nodding at the same time and looking directly in Hoffman's eyes who lapped it up.
- How true, wise words, thank you, Mr. Malone. I noticed that you weren't among the original members of the delegation – Here it comes thought Dagan involuntarily tensing while Hoffmann continued - A last-minute substitute. Very curious – Dagan felt like shrugging his shoulders but wisely didn't.
- I happened to be on hand and that was it. I couldn't resist the opportunity to visit Germany, a nation I esteem highly, a true friend of ours and see the changes that have taken place. Who wouldn't have done it? And as you said it has been a while for me
- And how did you come to be in Sweden?

Good question and one that had exercised the finest minds in US, British and Malonian intelligence for a considerable time, the only likely reason to visit Sweden during a war, an expensive and hazardous trip, was because you were Swedish or wanted to get to Germany. So that is what they had decided. But then why go to Germany when Dagan had long ceased to have any active involvement with his revolutionary friends and comrades. Because the revolutionary motto that went 'England's enemy is Ireland's friend' was as true today as it was then.

- I was in Sweden because it was the fastest way to get from the States to Germany – Dagan stated.
- You were already planning to come here? – Hoffmann didn't look convinced.
- That is correct.

- To what aim?
- More or less the same as when I was here in 1919 and after.
- But your Ireland is free now – Hoffman pointed out.
- Not all of it – Dagan said through gritted teeth, the mere existence of the North galled him in the extreme.
- I see, so when you were asked to become part of the delegation, it was how we shall say, fortuitous.
- Decidedly yes and decidedly no, as a member of the Red Cross committee I must remain strictly within the confines imposed on the delegation and I must not engage in any activities not in keeping with my role here. So whatever reason I might have travelled with is now secondary. I hope I have explained myself as I don't want to cause any awkward moments.
- A shame, we are always interested in our friends with whom we can work with for mutual beneficial aims. I would have passed you on to my colleagues in the overseas affairs department but if I read you correctly that must wait till current activities are tied up.
- You read me correctly. Thus with your permission, I will change the direction of the conversation. May I be so bold as to ask which department you are involved with? – Dagan wished he hadn't asked the question as soon as he had, an instinctive Irish trait if people talked to you about holidays you ask them about holidays in return.
- My area is precisely counter-espionage – 'Saints preserve us' thought Dagan, that's what you get for polite conversation, making chit chat with your friendly local secret service policeman. Still, this obviously wasn't an innocent encounter, all visitors were potential spies after all, sure wasn't he one himself although he preferred the modish words secret agent. Dagan had to say something.
- Very interesting job. Always asking yourself is everything as it seems? Constantly on alert. Caught anyone recently? Are you here socially or professionally?

Dagan loved skating on thin ice, don't act suspicious and you won't be suspected was his credo. No point pricking around, you're on their turf Dagan me boy, they can pick you up any time they like. One thing you learn on a flying squad is to trust your instinct, this fellow was used to people shaking in their boots in his presence and his instinct told him that this man enjoyed that almost as much as everything else. Don't pander to that side.

- We're always on duty whether we like it or not but today not to any great extent. Why should I be? – Hoffman sounded amused thankfully.
- You tell me but between the two of us, our Japanese friend is not above suspicion – Christ he couldn't believe he said it, crashing through the ice he must be going.
- Dr Takenaka, you surprise me and what makes you think that our estimable friend and representative of the empire of the rising sun is suspect.
- Amateur radio ham, he is an avid fan – It was the one fact he knew about the Oriental.
- Radio, surely he wouldn't need to bother. He will be seeing his ambassador, he won't need a radio – Well it was worth a shot thought Dagan - Adding two and two and getting four hundred, you are joking perhaps – Hoffman joked, this was a surreal situation thought Dagan.
- You did ask! – He said innocently, never admit to joking with Germans especially state security ones.
- You mention radios, let me tell you a secret, I am full of praise for our radio detector teams, they usually locate the transmission sites on the second occasion, impressive don't you admit.
- The Germans have always excelled technically – Dagan had to admit.

Dagan drew an absenting nod off the German's head. Apart from the obvious pride in such expertise, Dagan was being given a hint, broadcast loud and clear to use a pun. Besides that it was invaluable information, 'located on the second attempt', sweet suffering Jesus! That would go a long way to explaining the near-suicidal loss rates for agents. You could never transmit from the same place. The solution sounds easy, keep moving around but lugging a suitcase weighing ten kilos around was asking to be stopped. Did the Germans think they'd find strange parts in his luggage, which Dagan knew for sure was presently being meticulously picked apart while its owner was at the reception. Two transmissions he could hardly believe it, back in Blighty he had been told between six and ten, this they had to know back on the other side of the channel but he was forgetting he wasn't an agent he was a personal one-man rescue party. If he made it back he might let it slip in casual conversation. What if the German was bluffing? Put the fear of God into the agents who might be easier to spot as they moved around from one safe spot to another with their giveaway suitcases. Dagan didn't have a radio or need to but he knew where he could get one. Everything he needed was in his head, including that.

By now the party was thinning out as the food finished, the schnapps was only starting though, and boisterous shouts could be heard. Packed groups of mostly male members of the elite, armbands with swastikas moved around from one group to another, like polar bears swimming from floe to floe. Across the way one of the groups rearranged itself for a brief instance and Dagan had the plain view of the face of one black-garbed man ecstatically smiling and about to burst into laughter as the man beside him was bent over thigh-slapping. Dagan took this in and more and reacted by grabbing two schnapps glasses from a passing waiter. The harsh guttural laughter and symphonic braying on flushed pallid faces did it, the two shots disappeared; the satisfactory fiery sensation gripped his throat as the schnapps slid by his gullet.

- You're not in Kansas anymore Dagan old boy – he said to himself as he headed out the door after a hell of a first day in Germany.

Later that evening Dagan looked in the enormous mirror in his well-appointed hotel suite. They all had good rooms, not many visitors were passing by these days added to their hosts desire to impress meant they could do so at no great effort or expense. Three-room suites for each member, the mirror was new and built into the wall and he wondered if there was possibly a camera behind it, why renovate during a war. Their rooms were non-adjoining so it was also perfectly feasible that the empty suites on each side were occupied by watchers and listeners. D'Silva had told him the Germans put them in non-adjoining rooms so no one overheard any snoring, made as much sense as anything in this crazy world.

Dagan put the radio on to some ghastly German channel, all triumphant bomb blast and wall to wall Ring cycle while he searched the room in an innocent curious way to dissimulate what he was actually looking for. Lamps and flower vases he lifted and admired, wall painting he un-hung and put them again on other walls looking for the perfect spot but really checking behind the painting and the wall it was hung on. Hands he gracefully ran behind radiators, under tables, on top of mirrors, no dust at all. Within minutes he had identified several suspicious wires and while ringing reception to ask for a wakeup call he'd hadn't hung up immediately and had heard an extra click after a couple of seconds. The request for a wakeup call met with incredulous head-scratching from the other end, Germans, it seemed didn't rely on third parties to raise them from their slumbers. Finally taking his case to unpack, he noticed infinitesimal differences in how he had packed his luggage. The hair he'd left between two shirts was no longer there, the eau de toilette was the other way round. Granted a hair might shake loose but it was unlikely that the scent bottle would have turned around of its own accord. Usually counter-espionage teams take photographs beforehand to facilitate the exact repacking later so this was careless or maybe deliberate. The mind games in intelligence were a headache, everything could be read and re-read endlessly. Did they want him to know they had been through his private belongings? What had they found out apart from his shirts size and the name of his New York tailor? Well, nothing incriminating, the same Red Cross credentials the rest had. Dagan changed into his pyjamas, hung up his suit neatly in the wardrobe something he did usually but not so early, 10 pm and he had nothing to do, nowhere to go, no one to see. He'd briefly considered a stroll around the area but he'd been met by two burly types with a brainy one to direct. Brains had said in excellent English that evening strolls were a bad idea if there was an air raid he wouldn't know which air-raid shelter to go to, everyone had their own. Hence the Red Cross group had to be kept together. In a smooth salesman voice, he added that the Red Cross had an extremely tight and busy schedule of activities and the members needed to rest at all opportunities.

Dagan countered by asking in his smoothest politest supplicants' manner if one of Brain's braver colleagues could accompany him, he felt tip-top, had his papers and was a guest of the nation, surely it would be possible.

Brains an officious young man with pleasant features who worked in protocol was well used to escorting visitors and corralling them at the same time. He smiled unctuously, it was a game they were playing and both knew it.

- Unfortunately, we can't spare a man, minimum escort detail, and even if we could we are powerless to act in this case as they had strict instructions to keep the group together in case of emergency – Brains continued congenially.

Manpower shortages! Dagan couldn't imagine this lot at the front and for state control if the end came they'd be the last ones in the firing line, old folks, women and children first. Dagan tried one last gambit.

- And if I decided to go on my own responsibility – Dagan pushed.
- I'm sorry but I have my orders, you understand - Dagan did – I would get in big trouble if I permitted that, truth is I can't and my

colleagues know it even if I were to say yes they would intervene, so you see...- Again the urbane smile the hands open side up a slight shrug.

- Orders are orders – Dagan helped him out.
- Yes, our superiors know what's for the best even if we find it hard to understand why – said with faux resignation, satisfied, another sticky moment smoothed over.
- We sure do hope so, don't we?

Dagan returned to his room, paced around it a bit, smoking some before deciding to pay a visit to D'Sliva. The delegates had bid each other good night earlier before the next morning. Dagan said to brawn – 'Not going far' – and knocked in D'Sliva's door which opened on the second attempt.

- Still up? – Dagan ventured.
- Yes, not very sleepy.
- Me neither, I could use some company before turning in.

Across the hall the door of the Tanakana's room opened a crack quickly and quietly. Brains, the German who had just been speaking to Dagan, slipped out right in front of them, saw he was being observed nearly did a turnaround before deciding to brazened it out. With a curt nod and a Heil Hitler in their direction Brains continued towards the lift.

- Seems we're integrating well with the locals – said Dagan turning to his colleague.
- Some of us maybe, I for one haven't had any private visits – D'Silva said sadly closing the door.
- Nor likely to after your performance at the reception.
- Better all-round, we're here for a job – D'Silva didn't sound put out.
- Fancy a walk, a stroll, 'um passelo'- Dagan suggested in Portuguese to see what D'Silva would say.
- No walks my friend, they won't let you.
- I know I tried.
- Knew you would, this isn't my first time here in these circumstances, they don't want you wandering about, you might see something they don't want you to see, talk to someone they don't want you to talk to or simply get mistaken for a spy or get caught in a raid. It would look bad if a guest of the nation got splat, very bad especially as they don't even like admitting that air raids happen. Summing it up you get minded 24 hours a day.
- What's next besides idle dreams of idle strolls in the park?

117

- The itinerary is in your documentation, it's the same for all of us – D'Sliva looked at him quizzically – or maybe you don't have the documentation being a late addition – Dagan's smile stuck rigidly to his face, that swine who was supposed to have been on the delegation obviously held some things back, like the detailed itinerary - It's very embarrassing to admit old age but I only just found my glasses, I can't read that well without – Dagan recurred to an old stratagem, as old as reading glasses themselves, he took out his pair as D'Silva pushed over his copy. Relief soared over Dagan as he was delighted to read and confirm that Terzinstat was one of the scheduled camps to visit along with an inordinate number of public acts sandwiched in between the prison camps, POW camps and at the end the Czech work camp - Keeping us busy by all accounts, what do we hope to achieve with all this? – Dagan asked casually.
- What do we hope to achieve, neither of us is under any illusions about our generous hosts, we will achieve almost nothing in itself, it is my opinion that they are beyond pity, beyond feeling. Don't worry – D'Silva said as Dagan raised his eyebrows and make cupped ear signals alerting him to possible listeners – they know my thoughts, not the first time I have voiced them, we provide a diversion, a welcome day off during our visits, that and the parcels and post we deliver but our real achievement is just being here, a beacon of hope, a reminder that the world does not end outside Germany, a visible sign that civilization has not disappeared, that even the Nazis bow to a higher ideal – the South American was getting worked up again if his colour was a guide. Dagan not wishing to stage a repeat of the Rothaus diatribe for the listening state security agents cut the rising colic before the dam broke.
- Where are you from? What part of Brazil? I know Rio fairly well, sambaed with some fine ladies – Dagan asked in an evident change of subject.
- Aaaaah - visible deflation in the man - I was how do you say running away with myself no? Well, you know how I feel, how important I think our presence here is, a bit light in a dark world. And I'm from the southern regions of my country, not pampas but close, my family made their money in beef – D'Silva told him.
- Beef, a mighty good steak is something I'd like right now – Dagan went off subject.
- Wouldn't we all, it's been weeks of rationed slop till today, I'd kill for a good rib-eye steak as well. I live in Rio, it's easier for business and I have also danced with agile young ladies on many

an occasion. It was on one such night that I was introduced to the Brazilian Red Cross chairman. Something we had difficulty explaining to our respective wives later on. And here I am a pain in the side to Germany as much as I am to my own country's authorities. You could say that samba is the fault I am here.

- Samba has a lot to be blamed for – isn't it the truth though Dagan wryly.
- But not all of it is bad. And what brings you to this place, this time; you don't seem the type if you'll pardon me the presumption.
- Pardoned but why do you say that?
- Please don't misunderstand me but you give off a different air, maybe a bit cynical, a loner. Not that I think you a bad person or unfriendly on the contrary you mix well but at times when you think no one is looking you seem to be far away. I sense decency, a morality at odds with how we have to behave. You didn't enjoy the reception as much as some, you mixed less and then had a big chat with that tall SS man, strange as I noticed you haven't been chummy with the Germans even though you were here before. You don't like what you see perhaps.
- This Germany is very different from the one I knew, that is evident – Dagan vowed to get pally and fast, he realized from what he was being told that he'd been standoffish, he needed to integrate, it would be better cover and create less suspicion – I'm here because I was asked (true), because I was available (true'ish) and because I wanted to come (out and out lie) and without a doubt, a historic time to visit (massively true) and I thought it could be entertaining (a whopper) at the same time.
- Entertaining! You think this is some sort of excursion – D'Silva bridled?
- Sorry wrong word, interesting is closer to what I wanted to say or better challenging. Half the world is engaged in an inexplicable and savage war while I was sitting around, so this is my way of seeing up close what the hell is going on and to make sense of it all – Dagan reversed in full.
- To whom? – D'Silva openly sceptical.
- To myself, I feel the need to get involved without fighting or taking sides, it seems to be the defining moment of the century, of history. And I didn't want to have to say years later when asked where was I to have to say sipping rum Collins in the Florida Keys or sunning myself beside a Los Angeles swimming pool.

Truth was Dagan had been quite happy to sip rum Collins' beside any pool with any number of bathing costumed lovelies until he'd been told of what was happening and what was really at stake. That and twenty-two hours in the wartime Reich had turned him into an avowed anti-Nazi. The fires in his soul that had raged against empire and injustice but which had been slowly but surely dimming as the cynicism of the world and its people crept in, well that fire was stoking up furiously. How could he have been so blind?

Later as Dagan returned to his room, the excellent Scotch provided by room service still tingling its way through his innards, the smell of the South American's tobacco heavy on his woollen jacket, certain thoughts and ideas pinged around his slightly uncertain spongy grey matter, firstly the whisky, most had gone down the Irishman's gullet whereas the rum ended up being consumed by D'Sliva. Much to his relief, the next day would transpire on a train, an in-between day, a 'don't ask too much of me day'. Rum was far too easy to drink; a tot or two could go down nearly involuntarily. No wonder sailors loved it, as hard as a sailor's life is we're not here to mull over the sailors lot. Too many people were dying innocently to get distracted by keelhauling dry flogged rum totting lemon eating pigtailed wearing sons of the seven seas.

Maybe my perception is a bit antiquated anyway, Dagan continued his mind spieling, the women, the wars, his life, this day, that day, the triumphs, the defeats, being at histories big table or its elbow, watching it happen as it happened not reading about it in the newspapers. The women, every one special, Elsa, Karen, Melanie, Aisling, sweet creatures all, the lamentable state of hotel corridors, better off leaving them bare, than hanging the fourth rate landscapes of mystified alpine mountains and meadows. *'Pass me the bucket Heidi'*, by that time Dagan sank into the big bed head still a buzzing, did I brush my teeth? Yes of course I did, there's even been some tepid water. He thought about shaving, taking advantage of the warm water and he preferred shaving at night because it gave time for the rashness to dissipate. But he changed his mind, the morning will be fine. What was he was doing? His mission, his life in peril, do or die Herculean task, was it going to help end the madness? Could one person make a difference, really help turn the course of momentous events or was it all futile. He could kill a few Germans and better if they're secret police but shorten the war, he could save his scientific mentor from a certain death and maybe his contribution would be decisive. Only a committed unified body could achieve the unachievable. One only had to look at the Germans with most of Europe under their boot. How did that happen and how the hell could anyone break the stranglehold. What can you do with a lost course, a last desperate roll of the dice perhaps?

Out of the whiskey mist of his mind, Dagan began to see a face appearing slowly, the eyes first staring and bloodshot, intense light blue irises with one streak of green, the cheeks high and focused, the forehead slightly too large, placid and fevered, a small lock of dark black hair, lank and flaccid, cutting across the centre falling eastwards from a swept fringe, the nose and the small neat dark moustache laid at its feet. Him, could it all be laid at the Austrian corporal's door? Dagan had faced the same problem, in 1921 the cabinet divided but Collins in favour and it was Collins who had the men in place to do it. By early summer that year Irish resistance was down to its last bullets, its last weapons, its last men, they didn't know how long they could continue, the fight was over, only bitter defeat and exile or death and prison awaited, the reaping of an acerbic harvest.

But they could go down fighting and taking as many as they could with them. The ballads writ would be mighty and be sung till the next time rebellion reared its head. Desperate times called for equal measures, no point rushing out and plugging a few poor Tommy's or the detested Auxiliaries or Black and Tans. What was the point, why not aim as high as you could and wipe the smile off those who were about to glory in your defeat and probable demise, no more internments in the chill of the Welsh mountains; it was the last roll and why not make it one for the highest stakes.

So that's what they'd started to plan, wipe out the whole bloody damn British cabinet was the audacious plan drawn up. You can't cope with all the pawns but in chess no matter how bad our position was or how many pieces were arrayed against you if you did for the king you won; being realistic it wasn't going to happen that way even if the plan had succeeded. Look what happened with General Smyth, his shooting has been a fiasco and his two assassins ended up being hung themselves. Who sends a lame man on such a mission I ask you. God love him and forgive him but they must have been desperate. Asking the London IRA to organize the elimination of the whole cabinet was asking the impossible and then to repeat it seven times. The plan had been abandoned but it had been considered and even put into preplanning but in the end their cause hadn't been as lost as they thought, barely weeks later a truce was called and not a year along the line the same men who had plotted to kill each other or had been searching for them as traitors, sat down and signed a peace treaty like the gentlemen diplomats and statesmen they'd always thought of themselves as.

They'd been luckier than the Confederates, Wilkes Booth idea's had been to wipe out Lincoln and his entire cabinet and in the confusion, the South would get off its prostrated knees and rise again. Only the Lincoln part of the plan had resulted in a fatality but even the death of that political giant didn't derail the victory or the reconstruction.

Dagan didn't think for a minute that he could get a clean shot at Goebbels, Himmler, Goering and Hitler all in one go but he didn't have to. Adolf would be enough, it was he who had mesmerized the masses with his vitriolic rhetoric, had taken over the barely formed Nazi party and had moulded it into the political expression of his will, then came the SA, the SS, the Chancellery, the Reichstag fire, the night of the long knives, the Olympics, the Nuremberg Laws, the Rhineland, Czechoslovakia, Poland, France and now Russia. HE was making it all happen, HE would be enough, those after him would lack credibility, would fight among themselves, would be picked off by Himmler who would, in turn, be picked off by the army. The secret police chief never got the top job; the last thing Dagan remembered as he drifted off was the friendly cyanide pill, the nice sweet almond taste before being ripped to shreds. Hell why had they given him one anyway?

The next morning with curtains open and blinds up he awoke with the grey filter of light limping in, Dagan always liked to let the new day announce itself softly on his senses, arising he padded over to the mirror to check himself, there to his own self staring back he said.

- Dagan Malone reporting for duty.

And quite pleased with himself strolled over to the window door and went out to the small balcony. Below he could see the early birds busily going about their business, office workers, delivery vans, street sweepers and uniformed soldiers, clearly on their way back to barracks after a night's revelry, linked arm in arm and singing. He'd been thinking about his revelation the night before, his one man one-way ticket to the pantheon of (in)famous assassins, Brutus, Booth or Princip. Princip with his assassination had started the Great War, hastily renamed the First World War by shocked commentators confronted by the present even GREATER conflagration. If all that could be started by one man committing one murder (no posthumous offence to the Archduke's wife who died also that day) maybe this one could be the reverse, ending with a murder. The phone rang startling Dagan as if they were reading his mind, he let it ring a while, the call was from reception and the polite voice on the other end registered relief upon hearing him. Nothing of great note, details of breakfast, to be brought up or in the breakfast room?

- Breakfast room please - location given.
- A newspaper Herr Malone perhaps?
- All of them thanks - it would help his German and might even have a grain of truth in them.

Though that might be asking too much. He was also provided with the organization details of the day which in typical German fashion had been measured off hour by hour. If he didn't die by being shot against a post he might just keel over with boredom.

Chapter V

Soltau POW Camp, October 19th, 1941

The prisoners were mostly British, some downed aircrews but mostly the left behinds from Dunkirk. The rear-guard, 'somebody had to hold off the Germans while the rest got away' as one bitter Scots Guard told him.

- Better off out of it - Dagan replied - sit it out safe and sound while it all sorts itself out. Your family as least can rest assured you'll be returning.

- If only, aye, that's ma plan but they're never stopping with the escape plans and tunnels and committees and meetings. A man can hardly get any peace and the pressure to get out is terrible man. And I can hardly speak English never mind Hun laddie.

- Tell them you're agoraphobic – Dagan suggested.

- Spending half ma time underground I am. Agra what? Come on for heaven's sake?

- Fear of small spaces – Dagan told the man.

- Aye, I've a touch of that man; what else can you expect aft a life spent down the mines – said with resignation.

Dagan gave up, he actually had a very gratifying afternoon, they been greeted by a band playing God save the King, which normally grated but not in these strange days and the whole of the prisoner collective arrayed in neat lines like recently sprouted vegetables. Neat military lines at the front while towards the back the ensemble was more laissez-faire, ad-hoc, the uniforms less decipherable, legs bandied, salutes a tug at the forloch.

- Merchant seamen sir – Came the reply in explanation, mostly north Atlantic.
- And how are the conditions here? – Dagan asked for the umpteenth time.
- The foods scarce and bad at that, the barracks is cold so just like before except they're not shooting at us – said one old sea salt, a comment greeted by looks of horror from the officers alongside.

Quedlinburg POW Camp, October 21st, 1941

The camp was organized in barrack huts which the Germans pointed out were built originally for Hitler youth so had been used by Germans civilians. And so the guards are using the same barracks now.

- Are the guards are in bunks stacked six high like the POWs? I'd like to see that – D'Silva never gave up his quixotic quest, the German took him literally.
- Sorry you can't, the guards' quarters are off-limits but I will answer your question, they don't sleep in bunks stacked six high. They are after all guards and they are the victors, they don't have to suffer the same privations as the defeated. This makes sense – as the German spoke Takenaka nodded in full agreement.
- Those with no honour should expect nothing less – he said.

Not enough to stack them straight, the berths were less than two meters long. Meaning the taller prisoners spent their sleeping hours bent, a British officer detailed with escorting the party explained that the men huddled together to keep warm at night, the Japanese Takenaka looked disgusted, as he had all week, the man looked upon the entire prisoner concept with utter contempt and disdain boarding on loathing. 'Wouldn't want to be in their hands' thought Dagan. The Triple Axis included Japan but only Italy and Germany were at war with GB. Would it be too tempting to join in and claim the spoils on offer? Since all the western countries had fallen in two crazy months the year before their colonial processions, Dutch Indonesia and France Indochina were ripe for the taking whereas even though the British remained undefeated their Asian jewels were vulnerable because they were so overstretched.

Would the Japanese be able to resist such prime opportunities? Or an attack North on the Russians in Siberia what was going to happen next, Dagan couldn't even begin to guess but he knew it would be soon, this year or the next, something was going to give. It was lightning before a storm, sparks and flashes could be seen and heard across eastern Asia and the Pacific, the temperature was rising and when least expected the torment would break. It was then that Dagan felt a chill, he had packed his Irish passport as a contingent. He'd travelled on an American passport because he was replacing an American Red Cross delegate but unbeknownst to his handlers, he'd brought the Irish one just in case. They would have been dead set against it but he had dual nationality. Why shouldn't he travel with both? Hitler was Austrian after all. Not sure that argument would work and not sure pulling out an Irish passport would work on the oft chance the USA one was suddenly a liability. Still, he was glad he had sown it into the jacket that he was careful never to be it without.

- The bunks seem very close together, is there any way to give the men more space? - D'Silva asked.
- You will excuse a little joke but we are not the Ritz - the German smiled, uncharacteristic of them, the joke and the smile – your liaison Lt. Blatter will explain.
- It's a camp joke which only our senior officer doesn't get – Lt. Blatter explained.
- Fleas surely it prompts fleas – Dagan had seen some of the prisoners scratching furtively.
- We keep on top of the problem – answered the young British officer – all prisoners are instructed to report any outbreak immediately – the crisp vocals denoted a public schoolboy. Public when it's private, it's up to them how they organize themselves! – The clothes are removed and boiled and the affected prisoner is showered and deloused.
- Hot showers? – Dagan interrupted.
- Pardon! Ah of course if available – came the doubtful reply.

No chance then and a less likely bunch you'd find volunteering for a cold shower with the cold biting your bum. No wonder he'd seen some figures itching. All in all, captivity was way better than being shot at but it was grim all the same. Dagan and his colleagues made some more small talk, asked and answered some more desultory questions mainly about those coveted blessed sainted mammon from heaven Red

Cross packages. Neat little labels of Red Crosses on a white background stuck on small cardboard boxes filled with treats like chocolate and cigarettes and also with dietary staples like potted meats, canned vegetables and dried fruit that padded out the nutrient light diet the prisoners were receiving. It was indeed all they thought of the whole time the inspection lasted. When were the parcels to be handed out? They were saintly and salvation all at once, a flash of light in the long dark days of incarceration. So far they'd born up well with the visit routine but bit by bit the Christmassy hilarity was being supplanted by a nagging sensation that the visit had come but not the parcels even though both Dagan and his fellow members along with the camp authorities had repeatedly told the POWs that the anxiously awaited lifelines would be putting in an appearance. The session was brought to a close shortly after as the German officer indicated light refreshments would be served before a small concert. So back towards the canteen barracks and wafting siren-like aromas, Dagan's stomach lurched involuntarily.

Spangenberg POW Camp, October 24th, 1941

Only senior Allied officers were invited and you could see the herculean effort the pallid drawn tired men in their loose-fitting faded patch worn uniforms put in to appear dignified and not fall on the proffered food, laid temptingly out on trays. Bread, sausages, gherkins, pickled onions, cheeses and coffee, delicious aromatic liquid that recalled far of lands to the mind and was a reminder of better times before the conflict and the trammelling of so many lives. Where did they get it, via Spain perhaps or Turkey, they certainly needed it, it seemed to be their demonstration of power, half the world starving and they had coffee, it couldn't be Ethiopian though, the British had overrun that the year before.

- Please be seated gentlemen, the spectacle is about to take place
– The German liaison officer called out.

Dagan sidled up to a mid-ranking British officer close. The sort of rank involved in planning escapes. Seniors under orders to behave, anyone below Colonel to misbehave.

- Who's your escape officer if not you? – Dagan side mouthed in a whisper.

- I beg your pardon; I don't know what you're talking about – This Captain in the Welsh guards nervously replied looking side to side to make sure no Germans were near.

- Good man, just what I would have said, tell them so that the tunnel from hut six is under the latrine and that they should be careful with the air currents, it makes patterns in the dirt above – the officer's colour rose on a severe worried looking face, hair cropped back, thick black round glasses on strange honey gold-coloured eyes which were looking suspiciously at Dagan.
- Why are you telling me instead of the Germans? – He asked.
- No need to tell them at all, they'll find out for themselves if you don't take more care. I have some personal experience in this having been detained against my will. Call it common courtesy to a fellow traveller - with that Dagan went off.

The lights dimmed, the curtain went up and the show started and what a show, the last thing Dagan had been expecting was a spectacle on a par with the London hippodrome but that's practically what they got. The chorus gals might have two day stubble, the singers off-key and the dancers more left footed than you expect but these were minor quibbles, the sheer energy and palatable enthusiasm of all concerned made it a wonderful enjoyable scene. At the end of the romp, the audience gave up forthright exhalations which the thin cast lapped up during successive curtain calls. There was even an encore.

Dagan later asked where the band had got all their instruments. "Confiscations" had been the mysterious answer. Confiscations. Depriving sweet innocent musical lovers of their instruments, tut tut, their only consolation in these difficult times.

- How they arrive is not my concern - the German thought a bit before continuing - as a good music lover I can only appreciate the music when I hear it. As to whom they belonged to before well we are all making sacrifices – he added a shrug by way of justification.
- Is there anything you can't for? A shortage of harps or French bassoons for example just out of curiosity.
- We can have a concert piano or two or three if we would so wish and request it – came the proud reply.

Dagan thanked the German and started wondering about the strange tides that ebbed and flowed during the war. Imagining a veritable sea of musical instruments washing across Europe, taken from some poor unfortunate and given to others only marginally better off. If they took

127

musical instruments and the like what else did they take, the very clothes off their back no doubt. Grand pianos by the truckload had to be from Jews judging on what they told me. Just then the British officer alerted to the flagable tunnel came back as Dagan conversed with some German Red Cross officials, he walked pass giving Dagan a sideways look.

Kessler had a grand piano, a beauty, turn of the century, double toed, beech and maple wood outer rim, spruce wood keys, some chips in the ivory covered white ones due to much usage, it was a monster, weighing in a 500 kilos. It was along with Maria the pride of his life and both came together as she passed long hours sat learning the classics at it. In her teens, the well-behaved girl had rebelled against this and much else but when Dagan met her she'd come to terms with her father's insistence and tinkled the ivories daily to please him and herself. Good at it too, like most things.

Why did Dagan talk about their piano in the past tense? It disturbed him but the nagging truth was that Kessler's piano was sitting in some big depository of European wide pillage or had already reached some well-connected party member's front room. Kessler's grand wasn't the type handed out to scrawny itch hungry shabby POW. Dagan excused himself by knocking back the rather good coffee and indicating that he'd go for another.

- *Nach eines bitter.*

He went over to the table with the coffee urn on top and handed his cup over to one of the German army lance corporals and while he was filling it Dagan turned to the officer.

- Wonderful performance don't you think – Dagan said with gusto to make it obvious it's not a clandestine conversation.
- Yes I thought so too, the preamble was a surprise but greatly appreciated now, so much so we're singing the same over in hut six, was just there and you're advice on the hidden depths of the piece was well learned, we owe you a debt of gratitude – the lean officer said cryptically, by now the two men were some way removed over by empty orchestra area.
- Major, if you to meet with Hitler which I might be doing, what would be your first reaction, what would you do? – Dagan had been dying to sound out someone, he surprised himself by just coming out with it.
- Throttle him slowly with my own hands but as they'd be all over me in seconds, I'd settle for ripping his heart out and holding it

up as the lights fade out of his eyes – The officer has also been surprised by the question but taking Dagan a bit more seriously he turned and asked – You're really going to meet the spawn of Satan himself?

- Perhaps, perhaps, but please excuse me I shouldn't have brought up the subject. You take care and stay safe. This will all end one day - Dagan bid the major farewell and rejoined the main group.

He realized surrounded again by black uniforms what a mess he was making, one that could get him strung up by piano wire, ironically making yet more use of pianos being as it was a favourite method of the Nazi's for dealing with their enemies. He could only blame the lavish amounts of alcohol nights before. Damn, what am I doing if this guy is a German plant? There's been more than one case of English speaking Germans or turncoats Brits, Mosley had been quite popular, being inserted in camps. Once there getting to know as much as they could before being transferred to other camps before they could be uncovered. It didn't seem likely, Dagan was good at reading people but he had to admit that it was a subjective talent rather than scientifically proven, it had served him so far in life. Except look where life had got him! Alone, penniless, near destitute, no hat stand to hang his hat on, no hearth to sit in front of on a cold winters night in his twilight years. It's a hard life and then you die, that's what my granddad used to say and Dagan thought that about summed it up.

A twilight's hearth: Didn't expect to live that long.

Alone on his own: Never for long and someday he'd find his great love.

Money: He had enough to get by and if he could ever get back into Russia for half a day he knew where there was a good stash Romanov's gems to be pocketed. And no pockets in shrouds, you can't take it with you when your time is up as the Romanovs themselves could testify.

No fixed address? The world was his to peruse and enjoy.

He wouldn't change a thing. He'd been at coronations, premieres, summits and treaty signings, he'd witnessed and survived shootings, bombings, arson, treason, earthquakes, monsoons, deserts, tigers, prisons, mountain summits, rats, revolutions, castles he stormed more than one. He wooed and caressed starlets, shop girls, bluebloods, firebrands, nurses, cabaret singers, pianists and flappers. It definably had been interesting and much more so than if he'd followed his dad's advice and entered the postal service. 'Have to think of the pension my boy' the man swore by the public pension, nearly as well as government gilts. He'd been right and wrong, Collins had been in the post-service and so can't be all that bad. Dagan had been in the service of several states apart from his own, some in danger of disappearing, some coming into their own, some fading into the background, states he hated, states he loved and not once had he been free of adversity, calamity or danger or all three at the same time. And here he was again putting life and limb in dangers way for one he had a personal animosity against but which had persuaded him to pit his wits against another he had a much more favourable opinion of. Go figure as his buddy's in New York said. Why was he doing this again?

Eichstatt POW Camp, October 27th, 1941

- Excuse me. Russians - asked Nielson - Are there any here? – a question he asked at each camp.
- There are some in the adjoining camp – Blatter said pointing over his shoulder.
- So why can't we just pop over and have a quick visit – the Swede followed up.
- No harm in that, ten minutes more on the schedule, sure St Peter wouldn't even notice ten minutes – Dagan backed him up.
- That is impossible! – Blater said to them both.
- Now that you say it I can see them clearly in the distance now – Mendes joined in and it was true, a disorderly brown uniformed shaven-headed mass was clearly evident in the distance, gathered against the wire fence and looking in their direction. Dagan had assumed it was just another part of the camp they didn't have time to visit. The Red Cross had explained to him the sheer mind-numbing number of POW camps, work camps, concentration camps the Germans had operating. They were pretty sure they didn't have the full list either and there were camps hidden from them or camps within camps or camps they weren't permitted to visit, like this Russian one.

Dagan saw D'Silva speaking animatedly with a German officer, the South American gesturing wildly with his hands with typical Latin feeling. The German stood impassively just in front, typical Germanic sangfroid, hands behind his back holding a ridding crop with which he tapped the back of the knee boots, the only outwardly signal of any inner annoyance. Dagan went to investigate; his opinion of his colleague D'Silva was rising.

- *Kann ich helfam bitte* – Dagan asked the German as the South American fell silent, his face flushed from the evident frustration.
- We can speak in English if you like, I speak it perfectly Herr Malone.
- When in Rome you know, so what seems to be the matter?
- You must ask your fellow Red Cross colleague, he doesn't seem to know the Geneva Convention.
- The Geneva Convention, even I've heard of that – Dagan said light-heartedly.
- I admire you can make jokes about something so serious – the German replied while even Dagan had to admit it wasn't the time or place, Germans tended to rub the wrong way- But if you couldn't laugh at the absurdities of life what could you do, the Americans called it wisecracking, the Americans did it all the time, Dagan got on great with Americans, Dagan loved it in America
- True, please excuse, don't know what came over me. But even so can you please tell me what is the problem exactly – Dagan tried again?
- You would like to see the Russians – the German started to explain slowly – But the Russian government has not signed the Geneva Convention therefore the convention's rules are not applied to Russians prisoners of war. You do not need to trouble yourself about them in any case, they are treated in accordance with the rules for captured enemy combatants.
- Do you mean to say they have adequate food, medical attention, clothing and heating – said D'Silva - If this is true then there should not be any problem visiting the camp, it is beside us after all.
- That is just not possible, we have orders that permit us this visit and this visit alone. And we follow orders, otherwise, chaos and anarchy will follow.
- Because of an unscheduled visit? – D'Silva said nonplussed.
- No, because of a breakdown in the established order and your place in it.
- Just because the Russians haven't signed the pact doesn't mean you have to stop visits, its common decency. Those men have families that should be aware they are safe.
- I understand the Russians are refusing access to German prisoners. Why should we do something the enemy doesn't do?

Can't be that many Germans in Russian hands, the Germans on the other hand with the ebb and flow of war over the vast front line had taken hundreds and hundreds of thousands of Russians prisoners in huge encirclements. It was only months after the start of the war on the eastern front that Stalin realised the futility of no retreat under any circumstances which only led to encirclements by the fast-moving motorized Germans? These pockets could be picked off at will leading to scenes of huge straggly lines of prisoners stretching across the steppe as far as the eye could see. Better to lose ground, not armies, the ground was being lost anyway. However, that still left the safety and welfare of the thousands of combatants taken early in the onslaught.

- In the name of human decency are you going to let us visit the Russians and confirm their supposed well-being – the Swede putting it the simplest non-ideological terms possible didn't give up easily.
- We would exceed your remit. I suggest you take up the matter with my superiors in Berlin. Good day – a quick clicking of boot heels, a neat 180 turn and the German was gone.
- I'd take that as a no then, will we take it up with his superiors in Berlin? When are we going to Berlin? – Dagan knew who could be found in the German capital.
- His superiors are worse if you could believe that – Neilson said wryly.
- Come my friends, let us get on with the visit to hand but not forget what has happened or those poor unfortunates behind us. Witnesses who can not be silenced – in brotherly fashion Dagan took the Swede and the Brazilian arm in arm and ushered them onward with a last wistful look at the multitude massed against the wire fence. The guards belatedly started trying to disperse them, shouting and the fearsome barking of Alsatians, the best-fed species Dagan had seen so far, clearly audible as were the pleas in a multitude of Slavic languages. The scene was pitiable as Dagan and his fellow travellers turned away, the laminations and cries for help battling against harsh guttural German equally busy shouting them down.

Wetzlar POW Camp, October 28th, 1941

A tour of one of the prisoner huts was next. The forty-meter long wooden building was warmish counting the oncoming deep winter. Dagan imagined the blood-chilling cold that would arrive soon contrasting with the sweltering heat of high summer. All along the length of the hut were bunk beds piled high from the roof to floor with the space between them minimal. Dagan and the committee had seen it all before and again here it was laid depressingly in front of their eyes.

- Christ! – Dagan muttered to himself as they looked around. But not quietly enough.
- Shut up –D'Silva hissed elbowing him in the ribs – Never let them see us without hope. Never. You would be a piteous thief if you did – this passion and commitment was a direct reproach to the Irishman who ashamed and mortified turned to the South American
- Your attitude is an example and I have shamed myself, forgive my behaviour, totally out of place. This the fourth hole we've visited today and it got to me. Unforgivable. Let's continue and I will give this my best you wait and see - With that, he turned and with a ready smile on his face launched himself into cheery conversations with the nearest group of POWs.

6 am Hotel Arnou dining rooms, October 30th, 1941

Dagan went down to the breakfast room set aside for the visiting committee members, on display on a cloth-covered side table laden with cold meats, apples, bread, rye and wheat, juice, anything you could do to an egg had been done, fried, scrambled, hard-boiled, this country didn't do 'soft' so that had to be asked for specially. Beside egg central were the hams, bacon, mackerel and toast. Dagan didn't stint, the condemned man might as well have a decent last meal and so he loaded up a plate of food, booze usually gave him a ravishing appctite the following day. He and his wobbly plate sat down as the round table with his colleagues who all looked fresher that he did and all but the Brazilian were finishing.

- The early bird gets the worm, is it not in your language – the Swede asked him.
- Faigheann an t-éan go luath ithe - Dagan said to blank looks all round - English isn't my language, I just use it because it's faster for me to speak English than for you to learn Irish.
- Typical nonsense - muttered the Japanese.
- What did you say, it sounded very different to English, what are the origins – at least the Swede was game?
- I said that the early bird gets eaten – Dagan enlightened him.

- Ah very original - he said after a pause - Are you packed and ready to go?
- Will be after a bracing breakfast – Dagan tucked in with gusto.
- You certainly have a lot on your plate if you'll forgive the pun.

Neilson must be on the axioms chapter of his English primer but with his evident good humour, Dagan couldn't help but warm to the rustic Northerner and his hail heartiness. How did he cope with what he was seeing Dagan could only guess? Looking down at his plate Dagan noticed he had piled it up with cold meats, eggs, kippers, Sauer kraut, tomatoes and a slice of toast perched precariously on top of some potato dumplings.

- Quite a bit of a smorgasbord I'm afraid – Dagan said using one of the few Swedish words he knew - I have overdone it, I don't normally breakfast as much.

Might be the munchies or some sort of physical reaction to circumstances he found himself in. Surrounded as he was by a sea of grey and black uniforms, skull and crossbones adorned lapels, Jew baiters and hater's, belligerent and bellicose, full of themselves and fixated on death. Each and every one of them would fall on him like a pack of hounds and tear him limb from limb if they knew half of what he'd been sent here for. Just thinking of that and his new half-baked plan to kill their demi-god wasn't enough to give you an appetite what was? Wasn't the first time this behaviour had happened, on the outside the tension didn't manifest itself as fear or nervousness but as secondary symptoms such as hunger, bravado and brimming energy. Dagan hadn't felt this alive, this minute to minute existence since the spring of 1921 when the war of independence was at its apogee. It was a pattern that repeated itself again and again afterwards. I must be addicted to these situations. I'd never last in an office day to day, paper clipping each binding folder another nail in his lead-lined box. Bury me upside down so if I come back from the dead I'll live in Australia.

- What are we doing today? A spot of cabaret, that's what I liked most when I was last in Germany and the museums and art galleries of course – Dagan opened with.
- I meet many English and Americans, not so many Irish but I have come to be able to distinguish when you are joking and when you are talking in earnest – Neilson said smiling – And I believe the museums are closed so its a bit of cabaret today – his eyes twinkled as he said this.
- Now, who is the funny man!!

But both knew that with the Germans the day was measured out millimetrically, nothing was unaccounted for or left to chance and save a direct hit from a Lancaster bomber they knew where they'd be during the whole day and even a 1200lbs bomb made in Bradford and delivered by the RAF might not put the plan off by all that much. The Germans puzzled Dagan, so organized it took a lot to beat them, so civil and polite it was a pleasure to be in their clean cities among educated people. Why did they go around invading other countries, prosecuting their Jews, fellow Germans citizens after all and how had they ended up with the government and leader they had, Dagan couldn't figure it out but what was inexplicable regarding Germany was a tragedy for the rest of Europe.

- You slept well I hope? – Hoffman yet again on hand and solicitous. Friendly SS officers. A sure sign to be on maximum guard
- Better than expected – Dagan said to the questioner.
- You didn't sleep well then? Was there something wrong with the room – inquired Hoffmann perplexed.
- Deary me, 'room' is much too much a modest description for it, I thought it was for all of us at the start – True. One hundred and fifty square meters all for little old him. Dagan was still felt lost in the immenseness of it.
- The state, the party always tries its utmost to make its treasured guests comfortable – Hoffman's evident pride showed from ear to ear, he seemed so less sinister. Dagan was warming to the man. But behind the man were the gates to hell. Dagan was stuck by one turn of phrase.
- Pardon my question but are the state and the party one and the same thing presently? I'm confused.

The look of temporary bewilderment was enough for Dagan; he loved the how the literal Germans looked lost, like talking to a child, throw in a few misnomers and nonsensical answers and they genuinely felt that logic had been waylaid on route to them. He was not here for fun he had to remind himself.

- Can you recommend some of the delicious food on display? We are spoilt by our hosts – Dagan went easy on him.
- Ah yes of course, we do our best – Hoffman's relief was marked and his pride again swelled. As for the party-state dichotomy, Hoffman was probably just old enough to be put out by the question, remembering a time when the relationship of one to the other was separate and how other parties used to exist. How

135

quaint. The tall SS man turned to the buffet and pointed out some hams that came from his region.

- Have you been escorted overseas Red Cross visitors before? – Dagan was fishing. If Hoffman was normally assigned to this task that would be fine. If it was an exception that could only be bad because the single reason Dagan could think of for that would be that they were suspicious of someone.
- Yes I have had that pleasure – Hoffman glowed – Sometimes the onerous duty to the state is not so onerous – here he looked around the sumptuous room slowly smiling. Far too early to be so amiable.
- You seem to be a morning person. If you don't mind me asking, if we go to Berlin, sorry but its in the air. Will we have to attend more public functions with leading members of the government – Dagan tilted it as smoothly as he could. All pally. Not more receptions. More foie 'Mon Dieu!'.
- Tongues are always wagging. I don't approve personally or professionally but even I admit it happens. And they say Germany is very strict! – With a conspiratorial nod to Dagan – Berlin. Well, we'll see, not all the secrets are out yet. Why do you ask? – in lightening volte-face fashion Hoffman went from joker to deadly serious.
- Just curious?
- You are referring to some Fuhrer perhaps? – once again the tone and posture of the German changed as if conjoined with an invisible force, Hoffman shined with the mere utterance of the word.
- It would be something of major note as things stand in the world. Sure you understand - was Dagan being too forward but on he pressed - you see once I met Herr Hitler although he wouldn't remember it and the changes in both our fortunes since have been dramatic.
- So you know the Fuehrer, have met him and have spoken to him? – Dagan now basked in the reflected glory.
- I have had that... – here Dagan paused looking for the correct phrase, he had to be careful, on the actual day back in the twenties he'd been an amused onlooker, the latest upstart noisy politician, an Austrian country bumpkin. Was supposed to have been better than a cabaret but not a chance, within minutes the whole event had made his skin crawl. A window on the horror what the world would later witness via blitzkriegs and Stukas. Dagan had been so put out he had paid for company that night, a rarity but amorous comfort couldn't be left to chance.

- Privilege? – Hoffmann suggested bringing him back.
- Yes yes of course but I was also looking for another more fitting word for the occasion. It was after a political meeting in the late twenties, several of us were introduced to Herr Hitler – a mere limp hand brush – But it does not do it justice, mesmeric or some such, words fail me.
- Yes I see, words do there best bit leave us wanting. I once had the occasion to be standard-bearer on a nighttime parade, the Fuhrer podium light up by our torches as we filed past. It was the happiest day of my life as the Fuehrer saluted us – Hoffman took up the clarion call.
- Incredible – was all Dagan could manage, he understood the hysteria more clearly. For this fellow, it hadn't been his first beer or smoke or kiss or his cup team winning or any of the thousand things that constitutes a coming of age wonderment. No, it was passing under the lantern-lit spellbound gaze of a viperous bile-filled hate-spewing Aryan supremacist rabid demagogue. That was the young man's happiest moment. What the frigging hell has happened to this grand nation, why have the Gods and sane men abandoned it, why has it taken the left-sided path and travelled so far down it. If one man could cause such a swing of the helm could another start the swing back? - You must excuse my emotion please, it must have been some spectacle – Dagan managed to get out.
- It was and you are excused entirely understandable reaction. And now it is my turn to be excused as I have to leave you – Hoffman withdrew with an amiable nod of the head and was gone, not even a click of the heels or the hint of a Heil Hitler. Very atypical Nazi this one. Curious. More like Kessler funnily enough. Dagan was heartily sick of Heils, the countries favourite salutation said the louder the better and at every possible occasion. Members of a visiting delegation were excused this incessant gesture to a large extent but was expected on formal occasions usually with a photographer on hand to capture you doing it. Dagan found it galling but had to keep up the pretence.

Holzminden POW Camp, October 30th, 1941

Looking around he supposed the POW camps the Allies had looked much the same. What difference was there between the sides, the Germans controlled Europe á la Napoleon while their opponents ranged

137

from the British whose flag was on a quarter of the globe to their new erstwhile friends, Russian revolutionaries who had started out by mercilessly shooting down the former ruling family, innocent children included and had recently been on supping terms with the devil and indeed partners in dismemberment and absorption of several countries, the same diabolic former associate now ripping out its entrails. What a panorama.

Why do this? He'd been living an exciting adventurous life without a care, the war seemed so distant, even in the hell hole of a Cuban prison but that stop was always going to be temporary, he'd been in worse scrapes than that and had effected a brisk return to civilian life without undue distress or incident one way or the other. Why was the distant echo of a long-gone romance enough of a pull to bring him out of retirement so to speak to use his diffusely acquired mayhem skills from delicate international missions. This made him sound IN his own mind supercilious, 'international mission' and how's your father, Dick Tracy he wasn't someone who got involved just because of someone he knew, or for plain old money, hey it made the world go round, it certainly made his world go round and in the early 30's money had become noticeable by its absence. He could have joined the chorus of Gold-diggers of '31 and had it on a sash around his neck no problem. But he'd always at least tried to keep his moral compass pointed in the direction of the common good, in the direction of Saint Peters in Rome. Trying to do things that improved the lives of others in some way and trying to remain true to the ideals of his revolutionary mentors.

He stood if backed into a corner and forced to drop his joker facade, for equality, freedom, justice for all, woman's votes, secularity (though he was himself a good catholic boy at heart), the right to unionize, strike, protest, primary education, social assistance and wealth distribution for those less able, the sick, old, infirm, young, minorities, womenfolk. Those who had too much had to give some of it up if you had more give more. Those who had little or nothing should be given the skills, training, loans to contribute to society. Give a man a fish and you feed him for a day, teach him how to fish and you feed him for the rest of his life he was fond of saying. That's how he summed it up, it's seemed fair to all elements in society. The Russian revolution had cured him of any desire to see a more widespread reorganization of society. So it all boiled down to him riding to the rescue of one old Jew and his beloved daughter, like some knight errant of yesteryear except that if his plan change came to fruition he'd be detained in Munich and if the war continued the British, slightly put out I'm sure but they'd have plans to do away with the German chancellor as well, would send someone else on the mission or the war ends. Either way, it should see Maria and Kessler released. Dagan came back to practical matters as he always did, the goal and how to get at it, it didn't matter why, he was here now, fait de compli, and had things to do. The officer British was at his elbow suddenly and broke into Dagan's reverie.

- We're very grateful, now that we out of earshot of Jerry. Two years since I saw my little girl or my big girl for that matter, that's the hardest. And things hotting up in Africa and this lot on the rampage out Eastwards means we are not getting out of here any time soon – he said to Dagan.
- It seems set for the long haul alright; I was in a place like this myself – Dagan told him looking around.
- You'll be back in Blighty before me won't you Sir? – the man asked.
- I don't know where I'll end up after this stint - Dagan hoped he'd be somewhere than 'Blighty'.
- Well if you do get back there can you pass on a message to my girls, I have the address on a piece of paper.
- Better just tell me, I'll remember it don't worry.
- The Vicarage, Canning Court, Suffolk. Tell them you've seen me and I'm fine, bucking up and safe from harm's way, tell them to keep safe and I'll see them as soon as this is all over.
- Will do I promise – Dagan told the officer who put out his hand.
- Be careful, don't do anything too heroic – with that the officer turned and marched off.

At that moment the guards started shouting at the POWs who responded with cheers, jeers, cat whistles and hurrahs as unrefined merriment broke out. What else could it be but the Red Cross parcels had arrived. In came two lorries with Red Crosses covering the green canvas tarpaulin, the members of the committee were escorted over to the distribution area by back-slapping Germans officers and civilian suited officials who were effusive in their praise of the German branch of the Red Cross and the Fuhrer ensuring that POWs in German hands were accorded the highest standards of care regardless of how badly Germans were treated by other counties. An area in front of the rear end of the now parking trucks was roped off and set up with tables and chairs staffed by civilians and their lists and stamps to check off the fortunate recipients as they came forward to collect their parcels. Honestly, they were overegging it a bit thought Dagan, no one was completely blameless for the current state of shambles. Boy scouts they weren't, each man called out came forward to one of the desks, the package, neatly parcelled in brown paper with a white cross stuck on it was handed over and the man signed as the civil servant ticked them off. Those returned to the ranks brimming from ear to ear as the next was called and as the end neared even those not about to receive anything this time looked in good form. Dagan overheard a German explain it to the watching Red Cross committee.

- The men with parcels only keep some cigarettes and personal items from family, the rest of the food, canned meats, pate, vegetables, suet, jams, sugar, powdered eggs, it was quite a culinary mix - he heard the German say - I would like for my wife! All goes to the camps cooks who use it to how would you say, to enlighten or enliven, Ach, to improve the variety at mealtimes. So everyone is gaining from the parcels, even we Germans, as our guests are happier so our job of looking after them is easier.

Too true – thought Dagan – now the POWs had cigarettes, chocolate and coffee they had goods that could be traded easily for other merchandise as the internal market that always operated in these situations would swing into hyper-action. The guards would be supplying the contraband, clothes, shoes, tools and radio parts. It was a dangerous game as the guards were risking their necks and later they spent a good part of their time looking for the selfsame parts they brought in and gave over. It was worth it for the guards because they had precious hard to get goods to enjoy, make the humdrum rigours of wartime easier, impress their girlfriends or trade on the wider black market. As the German said 'Everybody wins'. The ceremony finished, the empty trucks left, the Germans cleared up, the prisoners mingled and milled around.

- You all look happy – he said to a group of NCO's, tough wizened looking grey-haired POWs, odd to see, even the majors and colonels tended to be in their mid-thirties.
- We love your visits Sir – said one Regimental Sargeant Major.
- Oh yes – said another.

NCO's were the backbone of Great Briton's unrequited love with her army and would have started on the Western front. The ones that survived, staying on after instead of civil street, life as a footman, docker or labourer seemed to hold no attraction after the trenches. Some had loved the trenches, thrived in them and missed them even. The majority had been shitting themselves, Dagan remembered dumbstruck teenagers under orders from revolutionary superiors to enlist and receive invaluable military training, medical corps, flying, artillery, signalling, everything the proto republic's army lacked and needed and all to be supplied free of charge by his Majesty's training corps. Don't worry lads it will be all over by Christmas, you won't even arrive in time to hear shots fired in anger. Ha! Even the rebels misread the situation; the poor buggers packed off were soon up to their necks in blood and muck. The few who made it back told Dagan about the horror, the rats, the cold, the fleas, the incessant gunfire and artillery. And those were good days, the bad ones gas attacks and up over the top.

- How's life here? – Dagan asked – career soldiers are you?
- Signed up for life and proud of it Sir, here it's deadly dull but at least we're not being shot at.
- And much better than the trenches – Dagan ventured.
- No comparison really. Know anything about it yourself Sir?
- No need to call me Sir, trenches I was told about and was glad to have missed that show.
- But you have the look of someone who's held a rifle if you don't mind me saying so, rebel laddie were we?

Dagan didn't want to talk about that, once he'd been walking down the Stand in tails when a voice behind him had called out. 'Oye ain't you that runny-nosed kid we picked up out of the GPO, Malloy or some it, you done well gov, spare us a schilling', Dagan had politely said we're all friends now and had handed over a pound – 'Cor blimey Sir, who'd credit it, God bless you, rebel boy'.

- I was more ordnance but I'm glad we got it all sorted – Dagan said.
- Don't mean any disrespect or trouble begging your pardon, I'm well glad too, my old gran was from the royal county – the NGO didn't want to offend.
- I'll be damned, they're a bit peeved with me, blew up a bridge over the Nore, five-mile detour to get to the market they had. Take care now and keep your nose clean, better off here I can tell you things are going from bad to worse everywhere else – Dagan gave hints of the most precious commodity, news.
- Bit of information sir would be most welcome – it was something they were strictly told not to do but Dagan occasionally let slip some gems.
- Same old same old, bombs on London, Italians on the run, Germans winning everywhere else, pray for the Russians.
- And there was me trying to bollocks up their revolution in Archangel and now they are our biggest hope, could you credit it,

sir? Oy watch out here comes trouble – just then the officer who nixed the Russian side visit came up.

- I hoped you have enjoyed your time here – the officer interrupted.
- Most enjoyable, it is not what one expects, the level of care and attention is excellent - Despite their discrepancies Dagan gave it wellie, he was singing from the same sheet. Meanwhile, the NCO shook his head and looked at him funnily.
- Really – the German glowed with pride – this is, of course, the way we do things, properly and with all the details taken care off.
- Talking to the POWs I was also pleasantly surprised to have them tell me how it is more than they expected themselves, they're bored but happy.
- We really should look at workshops or some more activities, I will look into to it – the German was all sweetness and light and such was Blatter's mollified state that he mentioned what had happened before – I am sorry about earlier, the rules are the rules you understand.   Not be worthy of a mention in your report – said in a tone that implied acting as a team. Very positive for Dagan.
- Not to worry, my input will reflect the 'relevant' events without any personal opinion or otherwise, what we have done, the good state of the POWs, the successful checkups. Basically, the facts and nothing more – Dagan signed off on a positive note. German content. 'Gut' he said and Dagan was glad because he had other things on his mind and didn't want to stand out, upsetting his hosts in any way or form, under the radar they were saying now. Radar, no one had heard of it a year ago and now it had entered the lexicon all over the place. Dagan didn't want attention, to be noticed, it would only invite more scrutiny and that was only bad, especially the particular 'shortcut' to the war's end he was considering. So Dagan was keeping his head down, his nose clean, his opinions to himself and going on the big charm offensive. In Dagan they had a man close to their hearts - The prisoners seem well cared for given the circumstances we find ourselves in. Fed, sheltered and given opportunities to improve their levels of culture.
- Yes, we set great store in the higher disciplines, I have greatly improved my English, is it not so, yes?
- Not Russian though - Dagan joked.
- No that would be a waste of time, they will be learning German in any case if they mean to survive but thank you for the concern – Blatter laughed, Dagan laughed, it was chummy. Boy was Dagan integrating.

He was learning how to be a cold-hearted bastard, mixing aloofness and mushy romantic longings for music and culture. It was as if they functioned in a schism framework, the left hand kept from the right hand and neither cared or bothered about what the other did. Duality coexisting, higher and lower, Jekyll and Hyde, but that was a book, this was real and it was worthy of study. Dagan had heard something similar in a public lecture which he was fond of attending, along the lines of those of the Royal Society, he loved advances in music, culture and technology. It led him to think how different his life was from that of his grandfathers, astounding, and Dagan's grandfathers would have thought the same of their own grandfathers, Dagan's great-great grandfather. Those gents would be like visitors from the Middle Ages or to be fairer and to give our visitors their due, the Age of Enlightenment. Even so. Astonishing.

Chapter IV

Berg Els, 30th October 1941

That night after the long week of visits the Red Cross committee was brought to a Schuss a few miles away by the crow from the last POW camp but millions of miles in terms of human comfort levels. The Count in residence of the imposing twin turreted castle overlooking the small town even apologized for the sad state of the accommodation. 'The damned war' was how he put it, to Dagan eyes the room he was allotted seemed sumptuous, especially compared to banks and banks of bunks he'd seen all week. From his window he could see the inner courtyard and the cars of the delegation down in the parking area, black sleek Mercedes, powerful engines housed in long bonnets with rows of cylinders showing over big wheels with white inner tubes and glistening silver-coloured hubcaps with red swastikas in the centre. The drivers, guards and staff milling around were in for a long cold night poor buggers. The Germans certainly knew engineering and excelled at it, it was a treat to behold, what other marvels of the mechanic art were they capable of creating, it was going to need the Allies on top of their game if they were going to compete with the Germans in battlefield hardware. America should start now before events overtook her.

A car came through the castle gates and parked, the driver got out and opened the door, Captain Hoffman alighted and brushed himself down as a figure approached him. It was Takenaka, they greeted each other warmly and Hoffman took the arm of the Japanese as they went in talking animatedly together. Dagan felt a chill to see them, Takenaka had hardly spoken a word to Dagan since they met and who knows what he was up to with Hoffman. A knock on the door recalled Dagan.

- *Komen Sie* - he answered.
- Herr Malone excuse please – a small sprite man of middling to advanced years wearing the livery of the house, all billowing plumb coloured trousers, white knee stockings, Lilliputian buckled shoes finished off by a side buttoned high hunting green coloured jacket. The enchanting figure escaped from a fairy tale entered carrying a formal dining suit which was deftly laid down on the double poster bed.
- When is dinner being served, please? – Dagan asked eying the suit.

- 8:30 sharp Herr Malone, in the grand hunting hall. You are kindly requested by the Count to put on the suit and tie.
- Looks like a good fit - said Dagan taking up the suit and putting against himself - How did you know my size?
- The Count gives a lot of dinners and so we have a lot of suits, you are a bit more than the average size and broader in the shoulder – the footman answered wearily.
- Good to know, what's the occasion?
- The occasion Sir?
- The reason for the dinner? – Dagan couldn't believe all this trouble was for a normal day to day meal.
- No reason the Count always dines and he likes to entertain his guests and treat them like this was their home, not a hotel – the note was one of vexation, another plebeian to be pandered to, servants could be snobbier than the lords they served - Meanwhile please refresh and be at your ease. Would you like a valet to shave you? Most of the male guests being pleased to have this.
- Some of the females as well – Dagan muttered.

He couldn't get over the armpits he'd seen of the fairer sex, no self-respecting gal stateside put that sort of show on anymore. Irish girls he wasn't sure about, only their husbands saw their bare arms never mind the armpits.

- Beg pardon! – The taken aback valet wasn't sure he'd heard correctly.
- Come down in tails like a swell – Dagan 'repeat', the valet looked hard at his charge as if to say he didn't get paid enough for this sort of leg-pulling – Not to worry I'm fine, I'll shave myself thanks.

Dagan almost felt like tipping, about to grope in his pocket he stopped himself. He knew it would be ill-advised and inappropriate and likely to be badly received but he also hadn't any money that could be used. He hadn't any money at all except for American dollars, Swedish krona and some gold hidden in everyday items like his drinks flask that might be needed during the mission, except that he changed the mission. Eliminate Hitler was the order of the day given half a chance, the film kept playing over in his mind, put him in your sights, pop, bug-eyed Austrian drops, crunch on cyanide, almonds in the air. Yummy cyanide pill, convivial whisperer of eternal rest, the curtain falls. Exit of D. Malone Esquire.

Dagan went through his *décolleté*, the bath had to be drawn for him, six times young strapping female members of the housekeeping staff entered with large tin churns full of hot water. The six went into the bath and once the parade had stopped Dagan then followed suit in the inviting steamy liquid. 'Glory be' he thought as he soaked up the comfort proved by the water salts and soap. The massive cast iron bath stood on four supports shaped like lions feet and made of silver as far as Dagan could see in the middle of the room adjacent to the bedroom, at one time it had been a large closet or some such before being converted into a white-tiled salle de bain, with a washstand and commode and turn of the century plumbing that made a cacophony of gurgling rumbling and rattling when called upon to perform its waste disposal duties and even when not, Dagan reclined and looked up at the impossibility high ceiling and listened to the tubular symphony as he slowly soaked.

Quite a contrast to the sanitary arrangements of the POW's. Dagan waited till the water reached a temperature that caused more discomfort than relief before reluctantly stepping out and wrapping himself in a large white bathrobe emblazoned with the coats of arms of the Count's family. The emblem suitably Holy Roman Empireish, all four quarters of the heraldic shield holding some fierce imaginary animal or some serious old-time weaponry. Two of the quads depicted bears, one of which wore the same livery colours, another quad was diagonally striped green and black and the fourth held a crossbow, helmet and mace.

Dagan shaved with the open razor blade he found on the washstand, the cream already prepared in its bowl with the brush to one side. Is a man at his most honest when looking into a mirror shaving? Does he ever see himself more truly, face to face, pouring over contours, eyes meeting again and again, an inner monologue exchanged between real and reflected self, unsaid words in a decidedly upbeat form. We have got this far haven't we, damn right we have and now we go down to the enemies den. To find what? Find? Keep our eye on what we are here for, Red Cross, Red Cross, forget anything else, kill, need to make like it's for real, easier if we really believe what we're doing. Red Cross committee all the way. And tomorrow all over again, one day further in, one day nearer the end of the mission. Go team Dagan GO.

When the time came a knock on the door announced pre-dinner cocktails about to be served in the library, he was to follow if he was ready, he saw the South Americans standing behind the household staff, ready to be towed down to the pre-arranged meeting. Dagan joined them. GO.

- You look very smart - D'Silva said.
- Don't we all – Dagan replied and wasn't it the truth, evening suits for half the world.

The three looked ready for a ball, the suits were tailored, fitted well and made of the finest cloth, old style but fine tailoring never ages. The button tied collars were most uncomfortable as they'd got his shirt a size too small, it felt his head was on top one of those conical collars dogs wore to stop them scratching. It was going to be a long night and he imagined the Count wouldn't be one to let the collars down until after dinner when the cigars and coffee and brandy went round. Hot baths, coffee, cigars, clean sheets in a room with a view, he certainly wasn't suffering – 'Into the lion's den' – D'Silva said as they approached the door, Dagan looked at him, it seemed an odd comment from the Brazilian at the time.

They entered the library to be met by the amazing sight of the high ceilinged long space occupied by row after row of books, so many that there was a gallery above running around the whole of the room reached by a spiral staircase in the corner.

- You are admiring my library my dear old friend- Dagan turned as he was being greeted by a man of medium height, close-cropped hair, glasses and a duelling scar on the right cheek of a weather-beaten face, small dark blue eyes filled with intelligence and it seemed good humour.
- Our esteemed host, it's a pleasure to meet you here today – Dagan smiled a knowing smile back.
- A long way from the last time and place and so much changed, we shall not mention that though, a gentleman would never – Old acquaintances.
- And you are a gentleman to your core; Dagan Malone at your service now and always. Might I say your hospitality is astounding – Dagan raised his eyebrows as he said this.
- I was asked to accommodate, provide light entertainment so I did, we live in a country where one does his duty whether one wants to or not - a note of discord thought Dagan – I have a long standing relationship however with the Red Cross and was delighted to oblige.
- Your duty has made my life very comfortable and your library's a marvel to the eyes.

147

- I'm glad you like it, we have an original Guttenberg Bible, tracts from Luther, Matheus, Hans Christian Neilson and many more.
- You must spend a lot of time in here – Dagan would in similar circumstances.
- I do, I've even read a book or two – the Count whose ancestors went back to the early middle ages, laughed merrily to himself – a joke you don't mind humour.
- I find it more appealing every day, the world is so serious – this was certainly not what I had expected.
- So how are our POW camps, are we up to scratch Dagan? – the Count asked.
- Better. As ever Germans doing things well – Dagan kept up the upbeat message.
- How very diplomatic, you can speak freely here. What do you see if you look up above?
- A carving of a rose and a jester, an odd combination – Dagan called out what he saw as he craned his neck.
- Fool's freedom, jesters could say anything in front of the king and you can in front of the Count, the rose is my vow, the rose of silence.
- I've never heard that, how original. As I was saying it will all be in our report but the POWs are fine. They are safe and out of it, a bit hungry but who isn't.
- Ah, I feel embarrassed by what you say because your dinner is the best we have, our table was always famous for its hospitality but I can tell you it's not normal now, we emptied the larders, wine cellars and most of the meats are game from the estate. I'll sure it will be a wonder, maybe the last I will be able to host till this struggle is over. It seems criminal given what's going on but the State asked me to put a good show on so enjoy my hospitality and tomorrow return to the real world. As for your report, I could have a copy for my library. the fiction section of course.

Another self-satisfied laugh, Dagan didn't know what to make of this. He hadn't heard anyone talk like this since he'd arrived but even before the Count had always been his own man. Maybe social rank conferred its privileges but the way this country was set up he doubted it. And to cap it all, his host was the very picture of Aryan Prussianess imaginable. Duelling scar and all.

- I've always been very curious about the scars I've seen on people's faces, very Prussian and very proud of their facial markings – Dagan thought he could field the question.

- I'm not! - Again the laugh – it spoils my looks for the ladies - he really had a very highly developed sense of humour thought Dagan.
- I must admit and please don't take offence but you have a great sense of humour, better than I remembered although we weren't playing it laughs back then.
- For a German you mean, my mother was English, that might explain it and I spent a bit of time there and the US, with my cousins – The Count had a very different outlook on things, would the Nazis trust him completely? Dagan though not or maybe they were sufficiently star stuck by the titles, the castle and the paraphernalia of aristocracy to care or notice. Nazis loved a lord and now the Count putting a hand to his face the man continued – it was expected, the duelling but the scars are more a sign of bad swordsmanship and I can't be proud of that can I? – The man spoke in a world-weary tone.
- Again you'd be surprised; there are people among our escort who would love to be similarly disfigured, what a world – Dagan noted.
- I think I can guess who you mean – the Count glanced over at a group of guests which included Hoffman.
- Come. I am keeping you from the rest of the guests, we must mingle as you say.

Dagan saw the usual collection of high Nazis chiefs and their wives, most had the look of prosperous assemblage who always went with the dominant power, whatever clique that held sway and so survived and thrived through the generations. The women were thrilled to be here, to be part of the conviviality, make-up overdone, laden down with jewellery they were still a jolly bunch if you avoided talking about the war or politics and no doubt helped along by the Counts' superlative wine cellar, opened with veritable aplomb and no thought for tomorrow.

- We get the best French wine for nearly nothing now, no Americans or British buying it all up, what a war eh!

Dagan was told this by the mayor of a local town whose name he didn't catch, another surprising element and again it must have been the Count's work, was the presence of a scattering of people who could only be described as Avant-garde, earthly, colourful, standouts in the crowd. Plush saris mixed with monocles, cigarette holders, boa feathers, tilted wide hats with birds and fruits on them, spats and pearls, capes and slinky shiny clingy silver dresses Jean Harlow would have worn. Dagan talked to poets, singers, gardeners, artists. All of them spoke of pre-war events, travels, friendships and very little about the present situation

149

except to say that they hoped it would be all over soon and they could see their pals in Monte Carlo, London or New York again.

Beside them, the well-dressed Nazi coterie looked frumpy and staid and didn't mix too much but there wasn't any tension in the air. Dagan had hardly seen his fellow Red Cross committee members the whole night; he was having such a great time that he had to remind himself this wasn't a normal party at a normal time. Battles were raging about them, nations rising and falling but it all seemed very remote at that moment, the uniforms more glamorous than sinister the drinks faster than a speakeasy with Gillespie in house, the music by a quartet of evening dressed ladies soothing and melodic. Then it all came crashing down.

- Herr Malone, good evening - was how it started.

There by his shoulder was Hoffman of the SS, joining without further ado a nice intimate conversation Dagan had been having with a well-known sculptress, statuesque in height, blond crimps escaping from green silk scarf worn head, eyes heavily made up bring out the deep liquid blue of the iris's, Egyptian and highly original. They'd had just been comparing French lovers how possessive the females were in comparison to the males when interpreted – Pardon me – Irene the artist retired into the waiting throng.

- Good evening – Dagan replied after they had been left alone – enjoying the party?
- The Count is famous for the wide extent of his social circle, there are certainly people here you would never meet in a normal public setting, it is truly a good party.
- Have you tried the French wines, they really are superb, 1940 was a vintage year.
- For French wine and German arms, it was a historic year I would say but I am on duty unfortunately and cannot drink.
- A shame – Dagan almost meant it - in that case, are you talking to me officially or socially.
- Officially I'm afraid but nothing to be worried about, just a small matter, paperwork, some information. We are working to clear up the matter as fast as possible – Hoffmann sounded almost apologetic.
- 'Paperwork' I don't understand, all that was looked after by the American and Swedish Red Cross I was led to believe.

Dagan clearly did understand, had there been a cock-up or a mistake somewhere in the documents or had someone inadvertently said something. A chill presented itself as a small eruption of sweat along the small of his back despite the friendly tone and the admirable chummy way Hoffmann addressed him his steely eyes looked at him talking in every detail, looking for any weakness, flinch was to invite suspicion, a secret policemen but a policemen all the same.

- Yes, of course, anomalies can't be placed at your door that is why you are being allowed to proceed as part of the visiting committee and not have to leave it. We will keep you informed – Hoffmann acknowledged.
- Yes, please keep me informed and if there is anything I can do you just have to ask, I would hate to have to abandon the group, such important work it is doing.
- Yes of course - Dagan didn't know if he was referring to the important work or keeping him informed-
- I appreciate being allowed to continue with the task at hand, firmly believe what we are doing is vital to all sides, we are the difference between civilised war and brutal savagery of before, the fact that we have access to captured combatants is massively reassuring to family members and in easing their anguish – Dagan larded it on, any attempt to put up a smokescreen.
- I see you firmly believe in what you are doing – Hoffmann took note.
- And all credit of your governments that allow us to undertake our visits, facilitates our access and our distribution of parcels – Dagan pro-German, pro-Red Cross, pro-team player.
- One more matter, as you said you are the last-minute replacement for Bryant? – The name being given was important; Dagan's guard was up as he clocked Hoffmann using a standard technique to trip up suspects.
- I was just contacted, asked if I was interested told it was short notice and that was all. I've never met this Bryant.
- We are trying to contact him but he's been unavailable for some time, the consul has tried many times, it's like the world has swallowed him up.
- I don't know the man as I've said, perhaps he's gone fishing or hunting, the Americans are very fond of those solitary pursuits – Dagan ventured.
- Even the ones from New York – again Hoffmann was letting drop specific details and wrong ones
- A New Yorker! Upstate New York has lots of good hunting but I'm sure you'll locate him soon, it's only a matter of time – Dagan knew Bryant was a Southerner; Hoffman knew too but obviously

151

didn't know if Dagan did.   Was he hunting or just natural behaviour.   That subtle difference was vital.   Dagan's life depended on it.

- Yes, a matter of time, we'll get our hands on him.   Ah but I do have some good news, it will be your host who will make the announcement, all I can say is that you are to be greatly honoured – Hoffman changed tack.   Dagan's tension lessened.
- Honoured you say, that sounds very intriguing, a medal perhaps, some sort of citation.   Truly we are already highly honoured just being here and the wonderful reception we have been given by our hosts.
- I can't say anymore but it is a much bigger honour than any mere bauble I can assure you – Hoffmann smiled.
- Personally, I like a nice bauble but I'm intrigued.

Dagan felt his colour rising and his heart beating faster than after the veiled threats he'd just been receiving, there was only one thing these devoted blind idiots could remotely consider as the highest honour short of slapping a helpless Jew in the face or pushing over Polish market stalls or burning a book and that was a good old flag-waving goose-step marching torch-bearing jamboree.   An invite to Nuremberg perhaps, a Speer directed fire and light show to enthral and enslave the masses expectantly lined up row after row.   If Hitler was there then his plan could still go ahead.

- Ladies and gentlemen your attention please – The head steward of the household announced over the throng.

Hushing sounds went around the room, people stopped laughing, sobered up and turned to listen.   Hoffman at his elbow commented to the effect that his curiosity would now be satisfied.

- Gather around please, His Grand Excellency Count Karl von Eltz, Lord of Vukovar, Rübenach and Knight of St Malta will make an important announcement.

The Count looking sheepishly embarrassed by the litany of heraldic legacy stepped over in front of the huge fireplace that occupied the middle section of the left wall of the library, reticent maybe but hugely proud, a Prussians Prussian when all comes down to it.

- Thank you for your attention, I will be brief, we are here to enjoy the gathering and not to listen to me - and here Dagan's German went on temporary leave but he got the impression that he said

lots related to the fire biting his backside or along those lines the Germans in the audience found it wildly amusing.
- He is such a cad, as you Americans, excuse me, Irish Americans, say - Hoffman adding during the brief lull, the smile was still evident on his face.

Proud of his English it seems and my German, how much studying would I have to do to get to that level, if I laid off the dames and the booze and saving the world I'd free up some time but it wasn't German vocabulary Dagan wanted to remember when he was older. Assuming he got to reach a venerable age, still okay today unless Hoffman was a better actor than anyone in Hollywood there was no great reason for concern, the Gestapo was curious but not that suspicious. Although having the Gestapo on your trail even at half steam and chasing shadows was enough to keep a man awake at night listening for footsteps outside and knocks on the door. How long did he reasonably have? They might get a break at any time, Dagan had no illusions on that score, he could be traded like a pawn on the great big chess game going on or sold out or found out or take a wrong step himself. Talk in his sleep or reach the tightly held frat boy Bryant or any one of a thousand things might happen to land him in big and almost certainly fatal trouble, might just start having those sleepless ear to door nights. He decided there and then to have several more drinks as soon as he could and go looking for Irene, the Count continued as the laughter died away.

- I have been asked, commanded, obliged to tell that the great Fuhrer, beloved of all Germans, whose attention is everywhere, has been following the esteemed work of this Red Cross mission, he wishes this known, next eighth of November in Munich the Fuhrer will address the faithful at the annual commemoration marking the uprising of 1923. And you will be there.

This last part caused a furore in the room, gasps, outright screams, applause, shouts before a huge cheer ran around the room as everyone got to their feet and clapped. The ardent Nazis peeled of several Heil Hitler's, the officers hooped *Deutschland uber alles*, Dagan experienced flashes of terror and delight, 'Serendipity' he thought 'We're going to be in the same hall as the spawn of Satan but how close would they be? Close enough for a clean shot; the range of his only firearm was 10 meters, point-blank range. The Count made signals, there was more.

- And you might be invited to a private room afterwards with the Fuhrer and surviving 1923 veterans – again widespread applause

153

and cheering - As I said a great honour, you will see and meet the man who has singlehandedly put Germany back in the glorious position she was meant to occupy.

- I envy you – Hoffman said in his ear.
- You won't be there? – Dagan assumed he'd be seeing a lot of his secret police spectre
- Unlikely, I have much work to do – Dagan didn't doubt that like the Reichstag fire - It would mean so much more to you – Dagan thought and said.
- We are mere worker bees, you are honoured guests – came the glib reply, yes Mister Bee buzzing around Europe stinging everything that moves.
- Is this usual to invite groups like ours? – Dagan was decided and so kept on the subject.
- Before yes but now with the war on. Our leader is much occupied – Hoffmann's leader was up to his neck in brown stuff to be sure.
- You paraded in front of him but have you met the leader i person? - Dagan asked curiously
- Oh yes. On three occasions, I remember the time and date of each. At a 1934 Hitler youth gathering where I was a policeman on duty and presented to him, my 1938 SS graduation ceremony and again in December 1938 in Munich at a beer hall.

Hoffman eyes shone with delight and remembrance but there was something else, it didn't add up with Hoffman, so much like all the others but somehow not. Still he couldn't get over the slavish big devotion for someone who Dagan considered a cruel, aloof, unimposing, hysterical, warmongering, Jew-baiting non-entity. Must be the moustache. If I could follow what he was saying instead of seeing the evident passion as mega hyperbole wrapped up in histrionic gesturing I might get it. Dagan had to give credit where credit was due, as a Jew tormenter Hitler far surpassed everyone from the Pharaohs through Herald and on down the line. He also had half of Europe at war you couldn't fault the man for mayhem either. With Hoffman Dagan expressed himself in a suitably refined manner. He didn't have to go too overboard, referring to the opportunity of meeting a major European historic figure as welcomed, he didn't appear over-enthusiastic, Hitler wasn't his Fuhrer after all. They drifted apart eventually as Dagan used the excuse to refill his glass to celebrate the good news.

The reception continued in good order for sometime after, till they were called to dinner. The women filed out escorted by the men, vividly enjoying the sumptuous surrounding, the luxurious trappings of accumulated wealth and power, gilded panes of ancient title bearers hung on immense walls, suits of armour stood tall at the double doors, arms both ornamental and functional filled the eye overhead. Dozens of liveried staff ushered the guests along the richly carpeted halls, till they came to the grand hall and were led to their assigned chairs if the library was big the hall was huge with an immense ceiling, flags and lances formed an overhead canopy on each side, wood panels dark and richly roasted brown adorned with highly polished intricately carved woodwork. Chandeliers hung along the room blazing light, miniature solar objects dazzling to the eye, the table formed the greatest part of the visible furniture, apart from sideboards and chests of drawers and the odd mismatching upholstered chair of varying providence, 17th, 18th, 19th century. The enormous table nearly filling the room was covered by crisp white linen table cloths, boarded with the crest of the condal house motif, the centerline was set with huge vases of flowers spaced at regular intervals, everything existed at regular intervals, crystal glasses, knives, forks, spoons, more knives, more forks, more spoons, more crystal all together surrounded the piled high crockery sets at the centre of each setting. Ooohs and aaahhs and yaaaas were heard all around. Here was he contemplating regicide and all the while having the time of his life at a cracking party full of despicable villains, spineless facilitators and avant-garde glitterati all proving to be excellent fun. I wonder what dark thoughts other people had behind the cheery exterior. Dagan sat beside the D'Silva and another gent whom he hadn't met but whom he'd seen talking to the Count. They took their seats, his voluptuous sculptress friend, unfortunately, was far down the other side of the table, so Dagan just nodded to D'Silva turned towards his dining companion and introduced himself, the reply left him shocked.

-   Albert Goering, pleased to meet you – said the man.

A large powerful frame running towards fleshiness, small round black glasses, was there a different style in all Europe, framed a round face of general ordinariness, a small pencil moustache in Taylor Powell Thin Man style. Brother? Cousin? Or just someone who happened to bask in the glow of an illustrious compatriot. The people in the world with the surname Hitler must be extremely pleased or completely annoyed at having to share it with the main driving force of the Third Reich.

-   Goering did you say, I don't have to tell you share a surname with one of Germany's leaders – Dagan decided to smoke out the exact relationship.
-   Such an honour, one of Germany's biggest leaders is it not so, a fulsome figure – laughter ensued – Yes I think it's safe to say that

155

the Reichs Fuhrer is a good eater, enjoys his food.   Herman certainty does, he is the one who shares the surname, I came first and we not only share a surname but a mother and father as well! - further peals of laughter and patting of the stomach.

- Truly! – was the best Dagan could manage. Was this a good a bad thing, this was believe it or not Herman Goering's elder brother, the man who's Luftwaffe was bombing half of Europe, the henchman and acknowledged number two of Hitler and here right beside him was his brother – your brother is quite a personality, quite a leading figure in the government - Dagan added.

- Yes, you know I didn't even vote for him - again an explosion of merriment before coming more serious - when we use to do old fashioned things like vote.

- A minority voice I believe in the country at the moment, I don't mean to be rude but it might not be best to express it too loudly, given the people we're dining with.

- Well yes, why ruin a perfectly excellent night with such comments, it's true, one has to be careful, too careful, being a good German isn't enough nowadays, you have to be a good Aryan, untainted by Jewish blood and in good standing with the party.   It's barbaric and my views are well known.   It gives Herman no end of trouble I know; if it weren't for him I would be somewhere else a lot less comfortable sharing slops for dinner.

- You don't appear to be the number one fan of your brother's party.

- The rakings off the street; they have sullied and dishonoured the country, the people and the army.

- Strong words and very risky ones especially saying them to a relative stranger, you had only met.

- I have, how do you say, a good nose, I rarely misjudge a person, it's been my saving on many occasions.   My friend the Count vouched for you, who do you think sat us together. Besides from what we've spoken about and your tone you're not very impressed I can tell. You don't buy it. Edgar our host knows you well, you have quite a reputation in many fields, a capable resourceful man with many deeds to his name, I can't quite understand what you are doing here with this – an airy gesture of his arm indicating the room, contents of - propaganda circus - At that moment in between the soup and the fish Irene approached.

- Dear Albert, dear Dagan, how delighted I am you two are sitting together - profuse kisses to Albert's brow, if only I could be here squeezed in between the both of you, that would be so nice, I'm stuck over there between some very serious types, you have to be

156

so careful darling, minding my p's and q's, if it wasn't for the champagne I would scream.

- Why don't you pull up a chair with us, one of those job lots against the wall, we certainly have enough cutlery to go round. To hell with the protocol of the thing, a damsel in distress and all that – Dagan suggested.
- Such a sweet boy – Irene said stroking his chin with her gloved hand – Maybe later, my dinner partners will be upset if I abandon them, they've taken a shine to me. Goodness! What one has to do to get along in our new Germany.

She glided off back to the other side of the long immaculately set table, to her place between two uniformed rotund figures flushed with fine living, uniforms adorned with ribbons and medals who reacted to her return by lighting up like a pair of roman candles, effuse in their extortions to find Irene's chair. The comical pair acclaimed their dinner partner with operatic guffaws, knee and back-slapping, a sight to behold for any of their soldiers for sure. Irene glanced over briefly with a bemused look and promptly was enveloped by their attention.

- What a show woman.
- Yes – Albert said - despite what she says she loves the attention from you, from them, from the patrons, the Germans and before the Jewish ones, who were also Germans.
- It seems to be the worse time ever to be a Jew in Germany – Dagan still didn't know how to read this, he hadn't heard any dissenting voices against the regime, so it was doubly stunning to hear it so vocally put and by such a highly placed source, was it a put up by Nazis to smoke out real or imagined opposition? A ruse? The British used to do this a lot in the cells of Fogonach, was this guy on the level, either way, it was remarkable and one had to be extremely cautious in whatever one did.
- Was there ever a good time to be a Jew, since the crucifixion anyway – Dagan countered.
- Some people I didn't even know were Jewish, doctors, lawyers, artists, intellectuals were suddenly overnight social outcasts. It's a truly civilized society that lets that happen. What can one do, one person?
- Not a lot
- No, not a lot but sometimes we can surprise ourselves and them by well taking some small risks – Albert said mysteriously.
- There's no small risks these days, we have a saying, *hanged for a penny as for a pound.* The amount stolen is unimportant to the judges, they string you up you either way – Dagan advised.

157

- True for most, not true for me, for better or for worse, my brother is my brother, he seems to take it personally if Himmler's boys show me too much interest and I can also call upon the family name to get things done that mightn't otherwise be done.

Dagan felt the time pass by; the courses came and went while Albert Goering, brother of the Reich's deputy and he became as thick as thieves. Dagan left his new Red Cross team a million miles away. Far from what he expected the brother of a top Nazi to be, he was engaging, critical, witty company, self-aware and above all human, he described himself as a patriot to Germany which is why he could never openly oppose the regime but one could be pro-German and not pro-Nazi. The two were indivisible in his mind. He, therefore, counted himself as the ad hoc resistance, especially concerning Jews in general and German ones in particular, his upbringing had been heavily influence by a Jewish friend of the family and he knew many personally. Albert just couldn't agree with the propaganda the Nazis had flooded the airwaves, print and billboards with. Dagan couldn't agree with him more, the biggest blot on modern Ireland's history had been the Limerick anti-Semitic riot of the early 1900s. Jews were just your convenient target to deflect criticism and heap blame.

- You mentioned some minor acts of resistance. No act of resistance is minor, I'm sure you're being too modest. During our struggle against the British, we used to turn up at prisons or police barracks dressed as British soldiers with cars and trucks and all the appearances of a bona fide British army cavalcade. Usually, somebody could be relied upon to put on a good British accent or even better was a British army deserter of Irish parentage raised in London or Glasgow or Liverpool. The trick was to get inside in force and release the lot and get all the guns, it worked a couple of times but then you have to leave well alone months, till troop rotation provided enough military amnesia to get going again. What's your secret, then?
- I use headed notepaper - Albert mentioned his more prosaic method, based on his family ties and the German general acquiescence to the former Prussian ruling class.
- That's enough, just headed notepaper!
- With the family crest from the family's country estate and castle, Goering printed all over it, that and with some sympathetic or overly trusting agent miracles do and have happened.
- And it's never questioned.
- Sometimes, that is when Herman finds out and being a good brother claims the letter comes from him and the prisoners are

released, what's one less Jew he told me, he isn't even very anti-Jewish, more a total cynic and as such a brilliant politician.

- How often? Who are the people you try and get released?
- Friends, acquaintances, good people who shouldn't be in this situation. But you could say that for all of them. I can't save them all or even close, it's a pinprick but at least I feel I'm doing something – he shrugged his shoulders – I'm not so brave, I don't even sign it, just show headed notepaper.
- I like it, it's simple, the best plans are always simple, less can go wrong and not signing it is a masterstroke, its iron cast deniable. After all, who's going to question the Deputy Reich's Fuhrer, I like it a lot – Dagan admired the ruse.
- You surprise me, such enthusiasm; you are supposed to be the Red Cross, po-faced, neutral, Swiss.
- I surprise myself sometimes, I'll let you in on a secret I'm not really what I appear to be.
- No – Albert looked around and drew closer.
- No, I was a last-minute replacement on this delegation, it's my first time and I'm not sure I'm the right man, the kind they're after for this job – Dagan admitted.
- It's a very strange time to come to Germany if you've been before you will find it very changed.
- It's very strange everywhere. I thought the '30s couldn't be beaten but I was very wrong, I'm not sure future generations will be kind to us.
- Germany mightn't have the luxury. Unless we knock out the Russians quickly we are done for. The Russians can put up with a lot of suffering, more than us and they're very well organized, they've never been this well-led it's incredible. The further we go to the East, the more we destroy, the less clear the outcome. They just keep coming. If we don't take Moscow now my bet is overwhelming numbers will win out. We can't afford to die as fast as they can.
- But I thought everything was going well, Leningrad surrounded, Moscow practically yours, Ukraine 'liberated'. If I was Stalin I'd be wondering if killing Trotsky has been such a good idea. Damn good general Trotsky was.
- If I was Stalin I'd just try and get through this year. Germany was made for quick wars or walkovers over our small unfortunate neighbours, not for 15 round bruisers. The Russians are built for thirty rounds, you won't believe it - Albert said in a quiet voice although the conversation couldn't be heard in the slightest as vibrant gaity reigned all around.

159

Their conversation took a turn less treasonous and more prosaic and the participants even engaged their neighbours. When the marathon dinner finally broke up near midnight Dagan and Albert took leave of each other in most cordial terms.

- A pleasure - Albert nodded and clicked his heels, still the Prussian coming to the fore despite the dissidence or because of it. Dagan noted the genuine feeling behind what to others would seem a perfunctory parting.
- The pleasure has been all mine I can assure you.

Dagan was more effusive after all he was a Gael of long-standing verbosity, he nodded in return but heel-clicking was something he was averse to, that and his brogues didn't have the necessary hard heel either instead soft leather, good for quietly padding along in the dark, something he had done more than once. Guests moved and milled around, he nodded several times or raised his glass, Takenaka he passed without acknowledging, it'd be a waste of energy, Takenaka felt the same and made no effort either. Dagan did stop however to talk to the South Americans.

- *Gott in himmel! Dios mio!* Oh my God, can you believe the news, off to see the caudillo, the head honcho himself – Dagan's brimming excitement came gushing upwards.
- We have indeed been honoured - the Argentine's comment was laced with irony.
- You seem very excited by the news – D'Silva looked him straight in the face just as he had done when the news had been announced, odd thought Dagan at the time and again. He felt observed.
- This sort of thing you can't keep bottled up – Dagan realised he'd better calm down, the rich food, fulsome alcohol flowing, high spirits, the refreshing encounter with Albert Goering had left him mildly euphoric.
- We still have plenty of work to do before then.
- We'll take it day by day so till our prize for good behaviour.
- Oddly, I've never heard of any of our Red Cross groups meeting the 'head of state' before - D'Silva added.
- Did you enjoy the dinner? Smashing occasion – Mendes.
- It made me angry, so much food in front of me, so much hunger outside – The Swede joining them injected indignant.
- Let me tell you I was once walking down a street in dear old Dublin when I saw a fella I knew, he was down on his luck and it was obvious he hadn't had a square meal in quite a while. Did I

mention fish and chips, I had just bought steaming vinegary and salty ones from Burdocks. You could smell the briny sea-i-ness of it. And mushy peas to boot, well I gave him the whole lot. Oh he was delighted and so was I to give it to him. The upshot was that I went to bed hungry and the next night so did he. Where am I going with this sermon and you're very polite all of you for listening this far. Basically, your own dinner will do little to solve the world's problems but getting out and working every day to eradicate injustice and make sure of a fair distribution of a nation's wealth is the only thing you can do. And that's in part what we are doing on this itinerary. There we go, end of sermon, enjoy your dinner as the hungry will still be hungry.

- You might just possibly be correct, that I concede - the Argentinean doctor agreed.
- I did enjoy it no point not to! It would be insulting to the host – D'Silva.
- I find your attitudes perplexing – Nordic gripes.
- Perhaps, but we're not here to fall out over the egg mayonnaise – Dagan closed the subject.
- Delicious I must admit – Mendes said.
- Did you enjoy the company at least?
- Yes, some very interesting people present, we had a lot of opinions in common - Dagan could only speculate what type of people that would include.
- Gentleman – Irene gracefully approached and joined the group. The Latin in the Latin Americans came rushing up, their sap visibly rose. They stood upright, flashed smiles, kissed hands, bowed heads, educated gallantry and eternal servitude as her loyal vassals. It was an impressive performance even more so when disguising their disappointment once it became clear that her interest focused mainly on Dagan and any attention remaining was strictly the product of good breeding and a rigorous Alpine finishing school for girls.
- Madam, Señor – both intoned, more nods in the direction of the Dagan and Irene and they moved off. Not before one last parting shot from D'Silva.
- We must talk about your future plans – he said enigmatically.
- What plans are these? Am I included? – Irene gave him a coquettish look once they were alone.
- My plans were that the four of us would have a long conversation, where did they run off to?

Dagan kept a wry and knowing smile on his face, two adults playing cat and mouse. It was thrilling for both when the rules were well established. Unattached consenting mutually attracted and attracting, Dagan took a good look at Irene as they raised their glasses and toasted each other with rare as curates eggs vintage champagne. Tall, blonde, athletically limbed, proportioned, hourglass figure, languid poise, beautiful blue eyes pale pearly complexion, high cheekbones, pale rosy cheeks, a cute snubbed nose being the only element off range, her lips were fuller on the lower end and were freshly painted, even her teeth were almost totally even and white, one incisor hadn't obeyed the dictates of nature and had strayed out and over its neighbour. But overall she was a picture-perfect German maiden and better still she was attracted to him. Dagan had never taken his looks for granted, he was as God had made him with few earthy embellishments, he knew a fair number of females found him attractive, the devilish lightly teased Celtic dark air he gave off but he'd never played on it, he wasn't a natural seducer he enjoyed the company of women and felt blessed, slightly under six foot in his socks, he had a slight stoop at times but basically it was to put less tall people more at ease. Broadly built, he'd played second row on the school senior XV and sometimes centre back due to his speed, something that had saved him on more than one occasion. Slim, long legs or long enough to reach the ground as he liked to joke, dark brown hair, blue-green eyes, his lips fuller than normal, his imperial roman nose, strange as that might seem seeing as the Romans never settled in Ireland, it adored not detracted as so often a nose can, his curly hair was rich and full and could take on a life of its own and was ruled by swirling cows licks, it had almost as much character as he did, well that's what he'd been told. It looked better without hair cream so he used that lightly or not at all or only when the moment called for it. During the 30's it had been slicked down more often than not but he hoped that fashion was on the way out. As he'd got older the various scars and abrasions inherent in being shot at had accentuated rather than taken away from his charms. Women were curious and intrigued and it made for easy pillow talk, Dagan thought his eyes were too big but again the opinion of the opposite sex seemed to be different, doe-eyed not bug-eyed was the consensus. His face gained by cragginess, the inevitable passage of time had left wrinkles on his visage but what helped Dagan was his smile, it lit up a pleasant face and made it angelic and as Dagan was wont to, being one of those natural optimists, always been inclined to look on the bright side, a sunny disposition, he couldn't help smile, people would ask him, 'why was he so happy' and he'd just shrug and say 'why not'. They'd respond giving him a litany of reasons why but he just kind of felt sorry for people who lived under the black shadows of the facts. He'd be no prisoner of the situation; his mind was always free to give solace.

He never took women for granted or their attention, he genuinely loved their company, women spoke about completely different things, he enjoyed the conversation as much as anything, interested in all his fellow human beings as he was. So it was natural that beautiful accomplished women came and went in his life. Each affair being the star at the centre of his universe until some reason or event brought the omen of closure. Be it a jealous husband, a revolution, a pressing creditor closing in or the affair had naturally reached its denouement and each part went their separate ways. Dagan rarely broke badly from his trysts as there was usually a good reason for it and they knew he'd been sincere and not just chasing skirt. And so it happened again in the midst of a brutal war, a dangerous espionage mission and a half-baked idea about springing at the most guarded man in Europe with his lunch fork Dagan fell into the comforting arms of an intelligent mature world wisely woman who like him was not looking for more than a brief charming amorous respite from the general horror of the world and from their own personal circumstances, unattached people leading full interesting lives but still needing to share personal intimacies. Winners Only, no loser's, give and take on both sides.

Hours later they lay in the bed mutually exhausted mutually satisfied.

- You will forget me in two days – Irene said to him.
- Two days never, a week at least.
- Ach, so you are a swine – Irene playfully hit him on the head.
- You should take...ouch stop.

They grappled, rolled over, knocking the empty Bollinger bottle they'd pilfered from the party along with some cigars and a small bottle of brandy. They sprung at each other as they rolled against the headboard of the four-poster bed. Irene laughed, Dagan smiled as they held each other.

- You have the nicest laugh.
- You have the nicest smile.

They kissed, they sought each other out, they buried themselves in the other, the heat from the ceramic stove kept the cold at bay but the other side of the bed, away from the heat it was obviously November. Dagan, always the gent occupied that position.

- Let's get right under the blankets – Irene wisely suggested.

163

- My goosebumps are not going to argue with that.
- What expressions do you have for brass monkeys?
- In German its *nachterkalttot*.
- Goosebumps is very English.

They wrapped themselves up in each other under the fulsome eiderdowns and crisp white linen sheets. They began rubbing each other warm.

- I'm so cold in this war, last year was ok but this year...birr I can't tell you what I do to keep warm – Irene owned up.
- Will it raise my eyebrows?
- Noooo, ack you are doing it, well I know what is being implied but I tell you there was a lot more going on before the war. Now your hot water bottle is your best friend and a full ration card.
- But aren't you winning the war, Spanish oranges and Russian wheat and every French grape and Greek sponge in between at your command.
- At somebody's command maybe but very little of this comes to the people, the Ethiopian coffee didn't last long either.
- This is fighting talk.
- Dangerous talk, if one of those black vultures overheard me I'd be kaput.
- Do a lot of people feel that way – Dagan inquired?
- I think so but you can't be sure, you can't share these thoughts with anyone. Most people don't like the war, wars are dangerous even when you were winning, all that time it felt wrong, I mean all of France, Poland, Denmark and so on, who gave Germany the right to take all that.
- Why are you telling me all this, I mean it's so dangerous to speak the truth.
- You are a good man and you are not German, I'm jolly and light and happy, I laugh a lot. The black beetles see me as one of them. I even laugh at those stupid Jewish jokes. I hate myself for that at least, I don't make jokes of Jews, I don't wish misery on anyone. Everyone should live in peace. If that old fool Hindenburg hadn't let the little corporal in, Ach, everything would be much better without him, he has the nation hypnotized. I saw you during the dinner and before the way you spoke to Albert, he is such a dear but if it wasn't for his brother he wouldn't even be allowed in the party. You got on very well with him and with the other officer, Hoffman, he frightens me but it is the way we have to treat them. You however almost at a distance, not fawning,

almost as an equal as least. We have to be so careful, be false, be oh so pleasant and sycophantic and laugh at all of their jokes.

There was a small knock at the door.

- Did you hear that? – Dagan whispered.

The whole night having alternated between dulcet tones of coquettishness, base sounds of lovemaking and the intimacies whispered in each other's ears under the blankets far from any door decked quickened listener or any intrusive microphone. Irene looked at Dagan, it was an hour before dawn, a knock at the door could only be trouble she visibly blanched before recovering her composure as her recent transgressions against the state weighed on her mind. Better to put a lid on all honest emotions till it was safe not to have to do so. No further sound was heard as they waited with bated breath.

- Look there's something under the door – Irene's eyesight reached across the dimly lit room.

Dagan put on a bathrobe and padded over, a cream envelope was indeed squarely visible on the floor beside the door. He picked it up, 'what is this? '. Dagan opened it and took out the single sheet. The first thing he noticed was the epigram, the watermark of an imposing Schluss. Dagan recognised it immediately, the writing on the paper was brief and to the point, if Dagan was making out the German as well as he hoped. The bearer of the letter has been assigned a vital task for the German nation and was acting under the direct responsibility of the Reich's deputy. The bearer was to be allowed to proceed with the business of the Reich's deputy; all assistance requested was to be given forthwith. He who failed to do so, who failed to obey was guilty of failing the state, the party, the German people and the Führer and would pay the highest price.

The written penmanship was bold and unwavering. Large loops and trailing y's. Dagan had never seen a sample of the supposed authors' handwriting but he was sure it was a close match. The signature at the end one word. Goering. Dagan read the letter again; it was his ace in the hole. The strangest things happen, when least expecting them. Cuba, then the divine Daphne, the visit to Munich and now this.

- What does it say? – Irene asked following up with - get back into bed you'll freeze – as sweet as his Daphne.

He put back the letter back in the envelope and into the small night table which he promptly locked. He thought about another letter of

165

similar purpose, fictitious but famous and the only reference he had, the all for France letter Cardinal Richelieu wrote and which Dumas used as the saving of the musketeers. Double justice too on the original owner of the letter, Milady, one of the greatest female villains in literature up there at the top of the pantheon with Lady Macbeth. Both came to a bad end finally. These types of letters were just as likely to hinder you as help you Dagan thought as he climbed back in bed beside Irene.

-   Well? How mysterious – she persisted.
-   I could tell you a lie but I never want to start lying to you – Irene looked at him sadly.
-   I'm intrigued but I've learnt when to talk and when to stay quiet, the romantic in me hopes that some damsel in distress will be helped by what just happened – she said wistfully.
-   You are a romantic, I like that and maybe you are closer to the truth than you think.
-   So many secrets these days. God how I long for the days when it was just who was screwing who.
-   I'm all for that, the worlds a better happier place when we're all screwing each other mad and not fighting. Hitler seems a cold fish, if there was a Mrs Hitler things might be different - Dagan doubted it though.
-   There's been a few Mrs Stalin's' and he's just as bad and I've heard there is a sort of Mrs Hitler on the books – Irene had all the latest gossip on the highest Nazi's, Dagan already had a ton of stuff Hedda Hopper would die for.
-   Really. I thought he was married to the German nation? – Dagan couldn't wait to hear what was coming.
-   The German nation doesn't keep you warm at night, it's a good bit of propaganda but I believe there is an unofficial and unacknowledged paramour.
-   Interesting, so Hitler has an orgasm coming like a train face.

Irene burst out laughing, breaking the whispered silence; she muffled it on the pillow. Dagan always liked to demystify the powerful, make them less intimidating. His aunt always said 'The Queen of England farts too you know' and so he imagined them doing what everyone else, mere mortals do. Churchill straining on the crapper face, Mussolini picking his nose and eating it while he thinks nobodies near. And on it had served him in stressful situations, at times less successfully, remembering the face on the Hungarian foreign minister after Dagan had burst out laughing in front of him because the mental image he'd conjured of the minister washing skid marks out of his underwear. It had been worth it but best not to go too far.

- When I meet him next month it is going to be very difficult to keep a straight face – Dagan ventured.
- Of course, the announcement, how lucky you will meet the great man – Irene said in mocking tones.
- What would you say to him?
- Hmm, maybe I will ask him how's Eve, his photographers assistant.
- Really, fine I'll ask him how Eve is doing.
- Can she cook strudel?
- Does she like the mountains?
- Is she a party member?
- Any Jewish friends? - They laughed like fools under the covers.
- Seriously what would you say? – Dagan started again - What would you like to say?
- If I could say what I liked I'd ask him when the next elections are, when can I vote again? I'd ask where are all my Jewish friends, I'd ask him when is he going to stop the war, I'd ask him when is he going to go to hell, the bastard.
- What! Get it off your lovely chest why don't you.
- I use to ignore politics and just live my life, have fun, see friends. I ignored it and didn't realize its importance until one day it was gone. No squabbling political heads anymore just Hitler. The rest of them and my friends started disappearing, journalists, Jews, effeminate men, journalists, artists, communists, you have to be very careful and toady up to the most odious low bred riff-raff. It's the world upside down, kiss me damn it.

They stopped talking, later they stopped making love, then they drifted off to sleep as a thin streak of predawn light made its way in through the clink in the heavy curtains. Dagan pondered on the situation he found himself in for a man on a one-way mission to stop the course of history he was certainly savouring the best life had to offer. He briefly imagined the pendulum would have to swing back but that was tomorrow's problem.

Chapter VI

Munich, November 5th 1941

Dagan sat in the dark of his bathroom reassembling the gun he had smuggled into Germany. Shear madness but he had done it. One of many secretive stops around London one of the days he gave his escorts the slip had been to visit an old republican comrade who was a gunsmith. There he picked up a true one-off item meant for a single one-off job. Blank range one shot and all hell breaks loose. The gun was disguised as two steal pens that fit together as the barrel, a cigarette lighter was the handgrip, a tie clip the trigger and various other innocuous pieces of personal accoutrements became moving parts. Bullethead, for example, were double studded pea-sized gold cuff links, four in total, Hitler was to be done down with 14-carat bullets as Churchill had been destined to be before, being Secretary to the Colonies during the Irish struggle for independence had put him high up on the assassination list. Truly bizarre if a weapon originally designed to do away with Churchill was to be used on his fearsome foe years later. Even in the dark of the bathroom, his hand was in his pocket. Animals could see in the dark and if they could humans would get around to discovering how. Devilishly clever people were at work and a way may have found. What they told him in New York was surely only a small part of the scientific advances going full pelt on each side. Hence the gun parts never left his pocket, never visible even in a dark room, the bullets casing inside the pens had chemically altered gunpowder packed tightly so as not to flow out like sand.

Dagan wondered, as he dexterously fitted the cuff link bullet head on the bullet casing and saw it clip on ever so lightly into place if this contraption had ever been fired in anger. The world would soon know if the dammed thing worked he was thinking just as a knock came at the door. Damn! Something fell on the floor, one of the cuff links? He turned on the light and frantically looked around. Nothing. Shit! More knocking on the door, harder this time. Dagan hoped it wasn't the heavies, he'd a loaded gun in his pocket, quite an incriminating item to be caught with but at least I'll plug one before they get me.

- Coming! – he called out.
- It is I D'Silva – from the door, Dagan's closest companion on the tour apart from the singular entanglement with Hoffman.

They'd often sat up late into the night discussing everything and anything. The POW camp visits had flown by with constants such as disease, misery, humanity, cruelty, survival, hunger and surprising doses of laughter and frivolity. The prisoners were happy to see them, the Germans were happy to see them, the committee were happy to be there and each camp got them closer to home. The journey south had been accompanied by the gradual appearance of early winter with shorter days and colder nights. If the POW camps were starting to feel the approaching winter what of the labour camps. Those people were expected to work, further sapping their strength which must rely on a diet substantially worse than the Geneva protected POWs buttressed also by the number of Axis prisoners the Allies had counterbalancing their own.

Kessler thought Dagan was in his mid 60's, not much physical labour could be extracted from him before he'd buckle. He'd been there since the summer, it all depended on how hard he had been worked, Germans seemed to work hard so it goes without reason that the 'campers' would have the privilege of being doubly engaged. The pace of the Red Cross's own unstinting work schedule had included very little free time. The Germans had thrown themselves unflaggingly into their roles as had all the members of the committee and it must be said too Dagan hadn't let up or wavered, he'd buried himself in the routine to avoid thinking about what was coming up and the real dangers involved. He slept better that way.

He still felt jaded though, it was proving to be mind-numbing hard work, 'never killed anyone hard work' his Granddad said but he hadn't been a great example, he'd worked very hard and didn't see his 60th birthday. D'Silva was at the door, Dagan smiled and let him in.

- Back in a minute – and with that Dagan went to the bathroom and hung up his jacket. He'd dismantle the gun later, should be safe this once. The Germans hadn't been too inquisitive since the first days.

If he made it back his handlers would be appalled at that spycraft and even more appalled at him having a weapon in the first place. But they'd approve of the final result if it comes off. He undid the pen/barrel from the handle/lighter put his cufflinks/bullets back together, re-hid the bullets and re-joined the Brazilian. It took no time at all as his recent practice was paying off.

- *Guten abend* as they say in these parts of the world – D'Silva said cheerily.

- I agree but just to be amiable, my official position is that of total bleakness, the world is about to end. What could be good about that? - Dagan played up the black Celtic soul - Here are the glasses for the whisky. Looks like a malt – he said holding up the bottle.

- *De acuerdo*, maybe the bleakness is not total, yes, I'll pour - D'Silva took back the whisky - I got it off the barman, a few American dollars can work wonders. What shall we drink to – he said raising his glass after passing one to the Irishman.

- Exactly what we have here, good company, good whiskey and being alive to enjoy both. Can't think of anything better at the minute – Dagan screwed up his face as if 'searching'.

- I like that, *me gusto*, so true, we have good whisky and someone to drink it with, no small thing in these days. Munich – D'Silva said looking out the window – And this is where we go to the beer hall and a ceremony with you know who.

- See and meet you know who? – Dagan asked, D'Silva as the senior should be in the know.

- Nothing firm yet despite what we were told. I think it unlikely. You know he is a very busy man however you seem very keen to meet the head of the Reich and that surprises me - D'Silva looked hard at Dagan.

- Why? I am doing my best to establish and maintain excellent relations with our hosts – Malone countered. If it's not sure a personal presentation Dagan would have to try somehow somewhere when an opportunity presented itself.

- I know and that also is surprising. Lots of people want to be close to Hitler and not all for good reasons – D'Silva noted looking straight at the Celt.

- I'll keep inside what I think and the Red Cross wins, that's the important thing – Dagan argued back holding the stare.

- At the start, I would have put you in the bracket of those wanting to be far away from here. Then well you changed tack, publically at least, you are more pro-German than Takenaka and get on better with our hosts than him.

- Serves him right for having no personality – said Dagan nastily.

- But when we talk you are different, less poised and staged, I see the real opinion you have.

- We have to put on an act, otherwise, if we told the truth well you can imagine you are also right in not counting me as the greatest follower of the person in question but after this is all over I'll be able to say I've met all the principal leaders involved, a minor whim, a fleeting capricious desire but why not. These are the people who are shaping the lives of millions of people.

- And ending lives too, so all you want to do is say you've met Hitler – D'Silva said sadly – And you have met Stalin?

- And Churchill, Chiang Kai-shek, Petain, Roosevelt. Just that, call me a shallow flibbertigibbet but that's about it.

- A flibberti...what?

- A flibbertigibbet, love that word, full of b's, a person who flits between inconsequentialities.

- An interesting sounding word but I would never look at you in that way. You are not that word with all the b's I have forgotten already, more serious, much more; your eyes say it even if you are doing something else.

- Ah, I feel unmasked and here's me just trying to put the best foot forward – before the perplexed look on his friends face Dagan added – *mejor cara*.

- Ah *entiendo*, I understand, reading Yeats prepared me for chats with you as you bring me away with the fairies it seems "to the waters and the wild". – D'Silva was then strangely silent, he'd never been this tongue-tied on any previous occasion - Maybe, maybe not, maybe it's the whisky, mine is a bit bitter, are you thinking what I'm thinking – Before Dagan had a chance to reply there was a loud banging on the door. Something serious given the impressive clamour.

- Open please now! – came an insistent authoritarian voice through the door.

Dagan and D'Silva looked at each other; D'Silva shrugged his shoulders and indicated that Dagan open. Another hammer blow hit it

- *Raus bitte*!
- Coming. Wait a second - Dagan shouted and undid the latch.

In the open door, a German officer introduced himself quickly and then politely but firmly insisted that Dagan come along with him. Behind him, the whole corridor was alive with movement and people. The whole floor was being cleared. Danger.

- What's going on, it is very late – said Dagan to buy time as he thought of the disassembled gun weighing down his jacket in the bathroom.
- We have a drill and you will please come with me – the officer politely insisted.
- I don't have my documentation – Dagan said, a perfectly reasonable statement, not having your papers was on a par with not breathing, you only last moments - I'll just get them – As Dagan went to turn back into the room the German tensed.
- Stop! – He ordered in a voice which left no room for doubt - With me please now, you will not need your papers, I will vouch for you and be with you the whole time. – He placed a hand on Dagan's elbow.

Dagan shrugged it off immediately, somewhat too brusquely. The German was incensed, his hand straight over his holster but just before he managed to get his pistol out D'Silva appeared at the door.

- I have his papers and mine – D'Silva said to the German and to Dagan - You left yours on the table. Please remember we are honoured guests of the nation and are invited to see the Fuhrer – this addressed to the infuriated German. Who switching attention to the Brazilian started to relax a notch.
- *Ja aufpassen* – the German said at last – be careful - he added in English to Dagan before a more laconic– now you have your precious papers come with me, please.
- My jacket? Is that too much to ask for – Dagan requested more in hope than expectation. He was desperately trying to think of how he'd left the pen fire weapon, dismantled he prayed but it was still all in one place. The inconspicuous cuffs were at least back on the ends of his shirt sleeves.
- You wouldn't need your jacket, this way please – said in the brook no arguments tone again.

There was nothing for it, Dagan and D'Silva followed the German and the rest of the people to the ballroom where with laughter all round they were congratulated on a successful fire drill. Asked why they were still in the hotel if the hotel was theoretically on fire, the answer came '*it was mere pro-forma. The fire exits were right beside them so although they were still theoretically in danger the reality was they could pass through and wait outside if they liked but low temperatures and bad weather meant accepting a partial result.'* More laughter, Dagan didn't know German fire drills were so jocular, who'd have guessed. The officer continued *'Better than the resulting colds that would have certainly manifested themselves later'*, people had been surprised in bed, in the bath, in all sorts of situations and stages of undress. Dagan could see he wasn't the only one jacketless, many more fared worse, men in dressing gowns, shirt sleeves, overcoats with bare legs and slippers. One pretty blond lady was half made up, another wore little more than a military overcoat and a heavy scowl. Dagan and D'Silva gathered around their fellow Red Cross team, each in his own way a bit put out by the fire drill.

- A bit strange to be having a fire drill, just before the big meeting – said Mendes in a dressing gown and slacks, the eyes blinds still around his neck.
- Lots of aerial aggression from their enemies, firebombs and high explosives, good to practice fire alarm – the Japanese was the most dishevelled, missing his webbing belt, hat and tie. Dagan hadn't been the only one rushed from his conveniences.
- I heard the party is nervous, the war isn't finished yet, there's talk of army opposition - the Swede ventured - I heard rumours before I left home – he added realising who he was with.
- Nonsense – Takenaka said - maybe they're looking for a Jew or maybe it is a fire drill!
- "Looking for a Jew" is a very strange thing to be seen as a normal statement in any place or country – Hurrah D'Silva.
- We are not here to judge our hosts - the Japanese replied stiffly.
- Sure is hot in here – Dagan wanted to change the subject, he had his reasons for not wanting Jews to be a conversational topic, best keep off the issue. The Argentine looked at him and said – I dare say that lady ventures to differ – he nodded in the direction of the pretty blond, her bare legs covered in goosebumps and beside her a shirts out braces hanging florid high ranking military 'friend'.
- Hot – the Japanese snorted.
- So I'm in a minority, I think I'll go stand near the window - before he even got that far an announcement proclaimed the success of the drill and that all guests could return to their rooms.

Dagan light-headedly walked over to the lift and seeing a huge throng of people blocking the way circled the nearest corridor to the service lift which was unfortunately out of service.

173

Nothing for it but take to the stairs. He climbed up the first flight easily enough but had to use the handrails to drag himself up the next four whereas he normally took steps two at a time. Christ he felt tired even contemplating the lift was out of character, he took them when he was obliged. Dagan reached his floor sweating and dog tired, he entered his room and quickly looked around, all seemed in order. He went to the bathroom, where he found his jacket and he put his hand in the pocket. The lighter was missing, everything else was there. A surge of adrenaline shot through him, that sensation you get in the worst of circumstances, lost money, or women or health, his heart was thumping loudly in this chest he had to sit down. Did he drop it, lose it or put it somewhere else? He tried to kick start his mental processes, 'unfreeze Mr Rabbit man, get out of the light's glare', he thought 'think head damn it think'. Did he take it; did he have it going downstairs or up? God, he couldn't think, he desperately tried to recall the last half hour, the bottle of whiskey still sat on the table along with two empty glasses and to boot he had to change for the function quickly. 'Sorry I'll be done in five, looking for my gun to shoot the man' he thought giddily of a very honest if unsuitable reply if he was called.

He checked the pen in the pocket which could still be fired without the cigarette holder only it was a damn sight harder as you had to buttress the back to put the trigger and that required both hands. Which mean he'd have to take it out of his pocket to fire and that meant exposure to witnesses, a minuscule window that still substantially shortened the odds. Dagan sat on the bed, half in his trousers and half out. The whole thing was an effort. A knock on the door, curtain call in five minutes, Christ he was still in his vest. He splashed water on his face, washed his armpits and lashed on some aftershave to smell good at the end, it wasn't easy but he finally got ready just before another bang on the door. He looked around the room one last time, everything in it stood out, sharper, cleared, more fragrant, effused with colour, always happened to him before a battle or a fight and he'd survived those he might even survive this. He opened the door to the simultaneously sharp and blurry world; he was sweating as he walked out of the room and into history. The front page kind, not the footnotes, assiduous scholars could find him already if they were bothered to look up behind the scenes characters. Now he was going to be headline news.

The trip to the beer hall venue passed without incident the Argentine and the Japanese more than excited while the Swede and D'Silva were more sedate and contained. Quite something to be more circumspect than the Oriental gentleman, he sat next to the Swede but it was the only thing he recalled apart from feeling faint, weak and thirsty. Was

174

he coming down with something he'd got in the camps? Easily enough done even if you took all the precautions in the world, the camps were perfect breeding grounds for epidemics as there was some nasty stuff going around, typhus, diphtheria and the rest. Sod the microbes, he wouldn't be around the day after for them to drink their fill. The car arrived close to the Munich opera, they'd have to walk through the jammed back streets to the beer hall, blocked with people of all hues, ordinary citizens mostly women, children, old men and those in uniform thronging the narrow old town's streets and squares hoping to catch a glimpse of their leader. Closer in the group were shown the spot where the police had fired on the putsch march, a secular shrine under permanent guard and obligatory to all the passers-by to show proper homage and diffidence whether they wanted to or not thought Dagan. Albert Goering had told him there was a side road around the spot which avoided having to bow their heads at the eternal flame but the Nazis suspected it and regularly placed guards on the shortcut. If you were caught more than once you were likely to end up in a camp Albert stated, such was the level of oppositions tolerated by the Nazis to their regime.

Dagan could feel the blast of warm air hit him as the doors of the beer hall opened, he nearly retched, till now the cold autumn-winter air had had a bracing effect, enough to keep him walking under his own steam. Now he felt his legs were like rubber, reluctant rubber at that, he wanted to go one way they wanted to go another, just then a voice behind him and a hand holding his elbow.

- *No estas bien* – he heard – *debes irte* – D'Silva whispered.
- *Estoy bieeeeen* – Dagan said even though it nearly killed him saying it. They were brought to one side and quickly searched. The SS Stormtrooper assigned to him was proficient and quick.
- *Du ist schmall* – he said.
- *Alles clar*, all okay – Dagan said as the guard pointed to the pen / gun barrel in his jacket pocket.
- Was ist los? – He gabbed again at Dagan.
- *Fur fuehrer autographen* – Dagan wished the guard would look closer and end it there.
- *Ja ja* – laughed the soldier and gestured him onward.

They entered the main hall, the place was heaving with late-night diners, practically in their entirety party members, military high rankers and their lady friends. In one corner sat some serious looking gentlemen in tradition leather Hossein, high white socks in mountain boots and capped to a man by Bavarian hats with feathers in them. All

175

had elaborate drinking mugs with ornate figures painted on the sides, fancy handles and a closable metal lid, hardly any of the men were clean-shaven, whiskers and sideburns, full curling skyward moustaches and beards abounded, fecundate and verdant and some were even plaited with scout-like woggles tying them at the end. They were the members of the beer hall; present every night of their lives, happily stuck here, away from their families who probably didn't mind. They looked a serious lot.

- They say the lids are to stop people poisoning your beer – Captain Hoffman appeared beside him again, hey it had been a while, all of what? A day or two! Dagan jumped and he tried to say something and sounded drunk even to himself.
- Are you alright? You look a bit peaky, indisposed, infirm.
- You've been nipping at the thesaurus again – Dagan smiled lopsidedly.
- I like to show off I admit it and also very useful when we beat the British, for a London assignment! – The German answered good-humouredly.
- Or when they beat you. Ha! – the 'Ha' escaped at the end of its own accord, Dagan felt a fatal desire to be whimsical. Talk about bad timing.
- You Irish, come on now, they are on their knees. If the Fuhrer so wanted we could be in London for Christmas – Thankfully Hoffmann took it well, he was in an excellent mood, after all, he was to see his idol presently. Didn't he say he wouldn't be here Dagan vaguely remembered.
- Why doesn't he? I think the Fuhrer has a secret admiration for his British opposite part, a special fondness for Churchill.
- That degenerate glutton, a sorry excuse for a leader! He is lucky we are busy pushing for Moscow – said Hoffmann sourly, Churchill didn't play so well with him.
- How is your Russian, that could be very useful too either way.
- The famous Irish wit. Easy to be funny when there's no bombs falling on you – Hoffman's sense of humour was being taxed to its limit.
- The famous German straight talking. I think we are lucky not to share a land border with the 3rd Reich and as well I seem to remember some bombs dropping on Dublin recently, my aunty Pauline fell off her bicycle she told to me in a letter. She told me – Dagan repeated for no great reason but it just happened, he truly felt at odds with his body, his speech.

- Please pass on my apologies. You seem less pro-German today. Years ago you were prepared to blow up lots of things for your cause. What is the difference now? We are doing it from above, your explosions were from below.
- I sense hostility, that was pure fantasy, the most fantastic plan we could be think of, to attract the fantastic help we were going to receive, we were desperate, we were up for anything.
-

Dagan remembered the time vividly, defeated Germany on one side, bitter and hate-filled elements of the still massive army, Irish rebels with goal pallor still evident, desperate for arms, making wild promises ever more fanciful at each turn. A re-run of Guy Fawkes you're after your honours? Sure if that's what you want that's what we'll promise. Those were the days alright.

- Are you still up for anything? You got our arms and the money and we never got anything in return. We could certainly be interested in that project now – was he serious? He should have known, the Germans would be mad for assets on the ground in England, just like last time.
- You wanted us to kill Brits and we did our best, our debt is paid, not all our plans were feasible – Dagan's head was double-sized it seemed.
- Still, we shouldn't be averse to the rekindling of old friendships for mutual benefit, after all, you were in Sweden planning to visit us – Hoffmann said while Dagan paused trying to think quickly, not easy when your head is throbbing and thumping like the piston engines on the Titanic. And those he knew were HUGE so they were. His Uncle Paddy McFaul who worked in the Belfast shipyard engineering team had shown Dagan and his father the mint fresh engine room shortly before the sea trials began. Dagan would never forget the majestic piston heads and shafts and screws, shiny metal gleaming new and how months just later it had all gone down under the semi-frozen North Atlantic waters never to be seen again.
- You honour me too much but I must request that we talk about it later, as you noticed I'm not one hundred per cent and would like to conserve my energy for the coming occasion.
- Of course, as you wish we will talk later – Hoffmann withdrew.

Dagan didn't think he'd be as keen after but that was hardly a priority now, Dagan re-joined the rest of his colleagues as they were led through the multitude to the doors leading to the back stairs, Dagan noticed the swastikas painted on the bevels on the ceiling mixed in with Bavarian blue and white pennants and flags, a striking clash, up the stairs they went and were shown to their seats, fairly decent ones in the middle of the hall, facing a raised stage at one end of a high banquet hall adorned with more painted ceilings, this time scenes from Teutonic mythology, Wagner operas and was everyday Bavarian activities and from which hung huge candelabras all ablaze to join forces with the fading winter light.

What happened next is part of historical record noted by several participants, attendees and organizers. If you asked Dagan what he saw, he'd mention stirring music, myriad fanfares of thumping trumpeters choreographed entrances and exits of flag-waving guardians and emblem bearers. It was a small scale Nuremberg rally in an enclosed smoky as hell place. Great if you like that sort of thing, headache-inducing if you didn't. Hitler and his closest cohorts made their entrance from the side of the dais; the place erupted in pure and utter adulation. Dagan had seen some political rallies in his time, Lenin in his prime, Churchill in the house in his wilderness years, impassioned anti-Nazi tirades washing over near-empty green leather benches, Roosevelt placating and cajoling his nation through its darkest years. But all this paled in comparison with the frenzy inducing antics of this leader. If Dagan had doubts about how Hitler came to the summit, he could see now how an Austrian of humble background, the chancellor just before him had been a general, unpretentious appearance, serious in aspect, hampered by a strange at the best of times moustache that even in his political prime never caught on. How could he do it, just stick him in front of an audience and watch how things turn out. Dagan looked on, dispassionately studying the performance, remaining unengaged, he wasn't German or a Nazi sympathizer and he couldn't speak German well enough to keep up all that well plus the blinding headache and general nausea kept him on the sidelines as an observer but he was fascinated by the show if not the content.

Pure theatre, politics as a spectacle, the beginning was orthodox enough but soon left the paths that most orators would recognize to blast into the orbit of demagoguery. Arms began swinging and flaying, fists banging, legs stamped, the chest was thumped, clenched hands moved up and down like sledgehammers. And that was just the body, the metallic voice swerved widely between loud, very loud, shouting and quite some out and out screaming. It never adopted a normal tone, crescendo after crashing crescendo; tirades and rants seemed the whole content. Germany and Germans struggling against everyone for its rightful place, conspiracies, plots, backstabbing and open conflict flung at the Allies, the British Empire and the Russians, the crowd went wild, lapping it up. No one interrupted unless prompted and then people outdid themselves trying to be more Hitlerian more National Socialistic, more rabidly anti-Semitic than their neighbours. Whipped into a frenzy they'd have ripped apart the first Jew / Russian / Briton available if they could have found one in the least Jewish / Russian / British friendly place in the world. Dagan imagined the reaction of the strapping well-fed, flushed Germans after he'd fired and hopefully killed their deity and began to feel fear, began to doubt himself. His will to live overcoming his wanting to do what he thought was needed, let me just slink off into the night. All around the relatively stoic committee members were being jostled in the back and sides by their neighbours incensed at their placid unaffected controlled non-reaction to the inflammatory speech. Dagan remembered the cyanide tooth and it gave him the necessary renewed impetus, he started to assemble the gun casually placing his hand in his jacket pocket, dexterity and nimble fingers were sorely absent and he keenly felt the missing lighter while the constant eddying and flowing of the audience around him made the task even harder but the practice he had put in paid off. Even so, he didn't know if he was going to have the firearm ready in time, he began to sweat heavily as Hitler was now reaching the end of his speech. The whole room was on its feet in ecstasy, even the committee members had been ushered to a standing position by Hoffman, Takenaka didn't need any prompting and was smiling broadly a most disconcerting facial appearance, D'Silva nodded to the rest to follow suit more for their own safety, which plainly couldn't be guaranteed if they remained seated. Dagan felt tension in his every nerve and fibre as he rose as if the universe was trying to fit into his head. Hitler stepped down from the podium, Dagan could see him clearly, the supreme leader nodded curtly to his immediate entourage and moved towards the first lines of the audience, Dagan put his hand in his pocket and charged the gun pen. It was ready to fire, Hitler was receiving flowers from children clad in Bavarian attire. The little girls and boys looked hideously adorable giving the Hitler salute, such corruption of innocence bemoaned D'Silva who was beside the centre aisle. Would Hitler continue on the floor, would he come this way? Yes, he was after handing the flowers to one of his secretaries Hitler started shaking hands with the party bigwigs in the front row, continuing till he finished the other side, glad-handling like the practised vote-getter he was. He started up the aisle, perfect thought Dagan, all he had to do was reach across D'Silva for a point-blank shot, this just might work he thought. The noise, the smoke as people kept smoking one after the other, the flames of the torches, the heat and the crush of bodies, Dagan felt like a cork floating on a storm-tossed sea. Hitler bathed in the multitudes and slowly, agonizingly slowly for Dagan, approached, ten meters now then five, progress to a crawl, arms reaching out, bodies crowding in, now just feet away. Dagan felt his leg wobble and go from under him but he caught himself.

- You okay? – D'Silva mouth moved, Dagan didn't hear any sound but read his lip as he hit his leg a few times.
- Fine – he replied through gritted teeth.

A huge pain in the chest, difficulties in breathing, D'Silva's hot breath burning in Dagan's ear though Dagan could hardly make him out.

- You....something something....ery unwell, please sit down, terrible pallor must sit down – along those lines, certain urgency – MUST SIT DOWN – D'Silva pulling at him his voice came in slower as if it was a 78 record played at 33rpm.

Hitler was a matter of meters away lapping up the adulation, stiff and stern in general, an occasional rigid half-smile for particular acquaintances and the odd hand on the face of a young woman, those of obvious German hue, blond and blue-eyed. It crossed Dagan's addled mind what Irene had told him about Hitler having a lover could very well be true. His face and body were much more relaxed and open when confronted by the *Mädchens*, the things you think about when you are seconds away from the big sleep, eternal ill-gotten fame and zero fortune. At which quick limed common burial plot would they come to venerate him? Hitler moved closer, his assassin began to slowly raise his arm with the weapon half in the hand and half still hidden under the cuff, another meter and by the time he moved again, he would be in dead centre. Dagan ran his tongue over for his death tooth and kept raising his arm higher, so many were heiling and heiling Hitler their messiah that it looked like he was doing the same. Just had to bring his left arm over to yank the trigger protruding under his sleeve. His waivered, he couldn't do this, a cheap cowardly blow, unworthy of a gentleman to his oblivious foe, his arm continued to waiver, his eyes started to water, his eye left now on Hitler and then a corpulent German in front twisted around to see his idol, camera in his hand eyes ablaze with zeal. Dagan sickened turned back to Hitler in front, here now was a man full of hatred for his fellow beings, if even his most ardent followers had been tossed to the flames what could his enemies expect. Emotion surged up in Dagan, now or never, his stopped arm started to rise to point straight at the imaginary X in the chest.

Death was close for both, delirious joy overcame him, he smiled broadly at the devil in front and to the devil waiting just behind, Hitler started to turn towards his end at Dagan's hands, Dagan's smile locked, it hurt, he was present and absent, the noise receded from his mind, his head began to tingle, images of his mother drifted to his head, the version who is everything to a four year old boy, the centre of all happiness, her face smiling down at him long ago, she was here, she had come to help bring him over, she held out her hand, he was four and forty at the same time, he wore shorts and long trousers, her scent, lilies of the valley, he was overwhelmed with happiness as she gently stroked his face.   He began to bring his other hand across to pull the firing mechanism. Behind the haze he saw another figure behind his mother 'Father' he said tears streamed from his eyes, he blinked rapidly to clear them away, he didn't want to shoot the adjutant, Hitler was just in front. This was the moment; he aimed at the spot just above the ear lobe Lincoln like. A small breath and just pull.....Suddenly two bear like arms came around and crushed him in their hold, the pressure broke the spell that had kept him upright, mists came rolling in before his eyes, his body drained in a second, he slumped over and the last thing he remembered before blacking out was a distinct German voice, heard and feared all over Europe.

- This happens all the time, the emotion! This man looks terrible – in German, every word crystal clear and then D'Silva saying 'I am a Doctor' before the darkness.

Munich, 12th November 1941

Dagan came to and rose up to a milder form of consciousness and half-opened his eyes, the room was white and very bright, shadows moved before his vision, voices in German. So he was alive he thought, joy swelled up in him before it crashed down. He must have failed and was now in a German prison. Somebody came close and examined his eye, subtracting the lower lid.

- Coming around slowly – she said in a whisper, her touch gentle, her perfume discreet but delightful. Maybe he wasn't in a prison after all he wondered as he drifted on off back down.

Again noise and light, vague, blurriness in patches, a thin light opaque veil between one and the clatter and chatter around him in the white room. He could hear Portuguese then Brazilian accented German, a

181

manly aftershave not too much, not too little, a contrast to the delicate wafted aromas from the nurse. Where is she today? Is smell the first sense back?

- *Amigo mio, ¿Qué has hecho?* – Light in his eyes slid away again - *Duermete bien* – and as if summoned sleep came and took him away again.

Next time he felt air on his skin and warm water brushing down his sides, torso, legs, he was being given a wash, he felt like a horse, somewhere in his mind he neighed. The nurse opened his legs while passing the sponge over his thighs, scrotum and penis which gallantly responded to the attention even though they were purely therapeutically. The nurse with the same perfume as before giggled as she turned Dagan over to the other side and both he and his member rapidly lost interest falling back into the warm abyss of sleep.

He awoke just as the train crashed, what had he been doing on a train and where had he been going he couldn't remember. Just as he had turned to his partner and clinked glasses of champagne, ah it was New Year's Eve 1927, as they tilted the glasses bells clanged, stream whistles and brakes screamed through the atmosphere and with a massive jolt everyone fell forward. Precisely at that moment, Dagan came fully to. His eyes blew open, his body gave an involuntary shudder, he jerked upwards and fell directly back as his head throbbed cannons.

His mouth was parched, tongue glued to his palate, he detached it with difficulty and nearly wept with the pain as it came back off. After a second and a grimace he took in his surroundings, the white room of his semi-dreams, he spied a carafe of water and a glass beside him on a high white metal side table, he pulled himself towards the edge of the bed and took hold of it, to start with his hand opened reluctantly as if it wasn't even his own hand, he held the carafe like he wore oven gloves. Both hands-on he drank it dry, sipping slowly at first, then in gulps and finally in a torment that end up half in his mouth and half over his chin and chest. It caused him to cough, a good deep rumble, it felt good, like the machinery was moving again and then settling back.

He felt like a five-day drinking bout and this was the hangover. But while his head throbbed like bejeesus he had no fever, his battered abused mind gingerly peeked out from behind the piercing pain, 'I'm here if you need me but what the hell happened'. The last moments before the blackout were hazy in the extreme but he wasn't handcuffed to the bed, actually he seemed to be in a normal if exceptionally white hospital room as far as he could see.

Dagan moved off the bed at snail's pace and took a step over to the window through which he could see the city around him, the cathedral bell tower *Alt Maria* as they called it wasn't far off and he could hear the regular comings and goings of the hospital ward outside his door. He finished exploring the room by finding his clothes in the corner wardrobe, cleaned, pressed, hung and folded, Dagan checked his pockets and as he expected the lighter and pen and cuffs were all gone. 'Think you dumb mick think' Dagan started to feel dizzy and a light sweat seeped through the armpits though, not the torrents of before. His head was a scene of wild Atlantic waves crashing against the foot of *Dun Aengus* on Aran Mor.

This is bad but it doesn't figure, the gun is gone but I'm not under guard or in prison *ERGO* the Germans can't have it. Watertight? Yes but, always a but, who does have it? Friend or foe, did it matter? If they hadn't said or done anything so far they were more likely to be friendly and by not doing anything they were complicit in what he did. As long as they come to me first. Watertight? Not by a long shot. Dagan's biggest fear, have the German secret services discovered subtly?

Dagan noticed his clothes had been dry cleaned, maybe the cleaners had kept everything, his wallet, German ID papers, Red Cross pass, handkerchief, watch and signet ring were all gone even his St. Christopher's medal. Dagan was uncomfortable prepped for the shroud. No point getting dressed and walking out, he'd only been given one name in Germany and it wasn't even a name, it was a church and hundreds of miles from here in Berlin. He didn't think he'd make it, best to stay put, till scheduled to part company. He went slowly back to bed and made himself comfortable. A nurse walked in, their eyes meet, she let out a squeal of surprise and shouted to outside out of the room – He's awake Doctor he's awake he's awake – she rapidly came over, fussing, chattering and that, feeling his head, his pulse, talking non-stop in a sing-song voice.

- Good day sir, you are feeling good *Ja*, you look fine, stick out your tongue, DOCTOR! Let me take your pulse – she flustered around him.

For the pulse, she calmed down, put on a face of deep concentration as she looked at her watch pinned to her chest and counted. Her mouth moved as she did so, it was a nice face to look at, Dagan made to say

183

something but she schh'd him with a tut-tut, lost count, swore, put her hand to her mouth, giggled and started again. 'You is definitely not in prison brother!' as Murphy might have said.

The Doctor arrived just as she finished, he entered expectant, curious, she reported his vital signs with evident pride *'Gut Hansa gut'* he replied – *Danke Docktor* – she nearly curtsied. The doctor, middle-aged, tired looking, cropped head, tall and thin, party badge on the white doctor's coat he wore, smiled at Dagan, his voice warm and soothing, great bedside manner and serviceable English.

- Good to have you back, how are you feeling? – he asked, Dagan found his mouth dry, hard to swallow but managed a *'Danke'* and then took flight.

- What happened to me, what day is it? – He grabbed some water.

- Don't worry about that, just rest, drink lots of water but slowly, you had us very confused till your colleague who had been in the Amazon with Humboldt identified dengue fever, very strange, have you been to the tropics recently.

- Cuba, Mexico, Dominican Republic, Brazil, all in the last year, I get around a bit – it all came out in awkward pauses, some in German some in English and one word in Gaelic which Dagan repeated in English.

- Okay – the doctor said slowly after Dagan's performance - I see that you still need some time to recover fully – Dagan took another swig of the water and said in a clear voice.
- I'm fine thank you, sorry about that stuttering start, some oil in the engine as we say, I'd like to thank you for your fine care and attention during my illness and to ask for help in organizing my discharge – in German without any pauses, hiccups, stuttering, English or Irish for that matter. He even nailed the grammar.
- That was much better, like Goethe himself. You still have to remain in the hospital three weeks no matter how good your German is – Doctors orders were orders.
- Three weeks! Isn't that taking precautions to its extremes?
- With dengue fever there are no extremes to extreme – the doctor said sternly, Dagan did some rapid calculations, there was time, he'd rejoin the group just before the camp visit, the doctor continued - the general health of the German nation is paramount - out came the marionette - no precaution is too much – the speech over back came the bedside manner – but

come now, this is for your own good as well, you are in the hands of the best doctors - the older ones, the young ones in uniform visiting the steppes learning all there is to know about bullet and shrapnel wounds - The best of care the German nation can provide and the best carers. The Fuhrer himself has ordered it, these are from the Reich's chancellor's office.

The doctor beamed and indicated the exuberant fresh bouquet of flowers beside the bed, Dagan thought he had misheard. What does the Fuhrer have to do with him, he tried to shoot him and now he's sending me flowers, talk about no hard feelings. What the blue blazes, from what he knew of Hitler this could only mean they hadn't rumbled him. The doctor proudly proffered the card with boasted the emblem of the chancellery along with some official-looking text and then a small handwritten note 'for rapid recovery and a rapid return to work, *Der Fuhrer* - Dagan reread it disbelievingly, holy sweet Jesus, what a turn up for the books. The word incongruity didn't come close to covering the situation. If I get through this I'll keep the message for the laugh. He looked up at the doctor then the flowers again, all the tulips they want, six day invasion.

- When you leave I would consider it an honour to be given the card if you don't want it of course – the Doctor nodded.

Dagan momentarily faltered, was he some kind of Nazi hero, maybe he could play it in his favour, get him out of here earlier? Who wanted a signed card of Hitler in their possession anyway and even stranger a get well card from your intended murder victim.

- Certainly. A small trifle to express my gratitude for all the excellent care shown to me. All yours — Dagan handed it over.

And so it was done, the faces of the nurse and doctor lit up, effusively the doctor replied.

- The honour had been all ours, I thank you – and changing tone – Ah but this is not all, I have another surprise, Nurse Muller please the newspapers.
- Ah yes! - Nurse Muller said sweetly

Ah yes, Nurse Muller! She bent over to remove something from the metal side table replete with bouquet of pillaged Dutch tulips. Everyone should have a Nurse Muller in their lives Dagan though as both he and the Doctor admired the doubled over form of the shapely sanitary professional. She took a reef of recent newspapers and coquettishly handed them to the doctor, a curtsy was all she lacked. The doctor handed the top one to Dagan, it was dated the day after the special congress in the beer hall, page five was open and folded and a sea of gothic script was before him as Dagan looked at the page. Quite off-putting to the breakfast reader if you weren't an avid national socialist, Dagan looked up, the Doctor pointed to a small article, the newspaper, the Daily Munchener, the headline 'Foreign Dignitary taken ill during Congress. It was sandwiched in between further Congress related articles, the man who had vowed to lose 20kgs to fit into his 1923 uniform, photo of the successful slimmer included, buttons straining at the leash and the woman who for the 13th year running had bought a single lily to express her devotion to the Fuhrer and a hand-knitted jumper to keep him warm, her husband reported to exceptionally understanding also received one.

The show continued on the fourth page in the following day's papers which expanded about the previous day's case; a member of the Red Cross committee specially invited to the event, a temperature of 102°, collapsed just as the Fuhrer had passed. The doctors don't know how the man managed to stay on his feet so long; the editor suggested it was as if the Fuhrer's oratory and presence had given him superhuman strength to continue till his hero was near. The editor stated it wouldn't be the first time something similar had happened, the article went on in that vein, helped to his seat by Red Cross colleagues, received the best health care from the hands of Germany's finest doctors under explicit orders of the Fuhrer who had taken a personal interest.

- I didn't realize I had created such a fanfare – Dagan was astonished, must be the Red Cross angle.
- There is more – Nurse Muller sweetly said.

And so there was in the next paper, the evening edition on page two included news about the unfortunate Irish American taken ill at the congress. This time he was named, his age given, his ex-wife's celluloid career, his work for the Red Cross (sterling it added), his fever and high temperatures, sweating beyond normal human limits (here doctor's comment inserted about patients dehydration and recovery). Jeez he felt he was being gutted like a kipper in black and white print in front of the readers, it got worse, the visitor had been shouting Father at the Fuhrer before collapsing as he valiantly tried to raise his arm in salute. Had he been shouting? Next came his transfer to hospital, attention given, no public alarm needed, flowers sent. A photo. Dagan peered, it was like he was dreaming and looking down at himself, he could barely make out anything but he looked as peaceful as a lamb, his doctor and nurse were beside him, tubes inserted and a drip on the go 24 hours a day.

- I was quite a piece of news – Dagan saw Goebbels hand behind this.

Dagan couldn't image what the British would think when they saw the newspaper. How many papers did they get, can't exactly place an order but the Portuguese consulate, for example, could send them on and in terms of espionage costs, a few *escudos* for the Portuguese, allies of old standing, wouldn't be too taxing on the budget. The British will have to open a new file on him. The present ones will have been bursting with his cuttings. He came to the last paper edition from the evening before, he'd been out cold three days, his cuttings disappeared back in the press. The doctor said he was tired looking and Dagan took him at his word, his eyes drooping as the nurse helped him lie back, he smiled at her, she smiled back, so happy to be alive and not in a cell he thought as he drifted off.

That evening after a solid meal of rye bread, chicken broth, cheese, sausage and sour kraut he felt a whole lot better. His appetite was returning as was his will to live, his first visitors were the expected ones, his fellow committee members. In they traipsed trailed by Hoffmann, obviously, the Red Cross couldn't go out on their own. Sheepishly at first they wishing him well, soliciting after his health, inquiring about the "excellent" care and attention he was receiving. The usual platitudes, though give Hoffman his due he didn't bother too much, a nod of the head before standing there rigid as a flagpole swaying in the wind and looking around him, very taken with the flowers and the sender though. *Quelle surprise.*

- We couldn't get any grapes so we brought you some apples and some sad looking pears wrapped in old newspaper, they are just out of season – Neilson said.
- Very welcome, the pears as well thank you. Feeling good, a lot better than yesterday, tomorrow they say I'll be ready to leave and rejoin the team – Dagan answered in a chipper tone.
- Rejoin yes, but return to work no! You'll come along while continuing to recover – D'Silva had been talking to the doctors and seemed to know more than anyone, what had happened to safeguarding the clean white lines that demarcated German wellbeing. Better for me though back on the original mission after deviating to jungle fever and historical landmarks. The rest

of the group was taken on a tour of the hospital leaving Dagan alone with D'Silva.

- You've been in the papers a lot – D'Silva ventured.
-

Dagan looked him up and down without replying. He knew that D'Silva knew something, had helped or hindered him, Dagan had been thinking on it a lot and it was the only logical possibility to explain the events in the order they happened. Eventually, he said.

- Help yourself, here take a look at the press cuttings they saved for my scrapbook. You get a nice mention as the Good Samaritan catching me as I fell – D'Silva fished them out.
- I didn't catch you, you fell on me, I was just in the way – D'Silva said warily.
- The doctors changed his mind, he was all ready to quarantine me for next to a month, I wonder what made him change his initial position – Dagan challenged the South American for an answer.
- I did – came the simple reply.
- And how did you do that? – By knowing more than you were telling Dagan thought.
- I'm a doctor from Brazil, besides, when they told me of the diagnosis I was asked to give my opinion, my expert opinion, you don't incubate a fever that long, you were suffering severe stress to your system, extreme tiredness, overuse of alcohol, lack of exercise along with a severe flu. That's all, the heat and the high running emotion did the rest and the second test showed no results for the dengue fever.
- You told them I was a drunk! – Dagan was indignant; he had his drinking under control always and could stop anytime.
- What I told them was the truth, I've seen you down bottles of whiskey with alarming speed and on more than one occasion. Imagine then when you are done in physically as well, enough said end of argument – The Brazilian replied innocently.
- Why that's a God dam....- D'Silva hushed him with a finger as Dagan opened his mouth to defend himself.
- Your take offence as fast as you take a drink. You are a fiery person. Everything fast and fast and faster. Anyway, the important thing is we'll get you out of here. Let's look at the papers?

Dagan was dizzy, why did he want to look at the papers? D'Silva laid them on the bed in front of Dagan upside down to himself. Great view he was going to have.

- Look at your press photo. You are even having a drink in that – D'Silva pointed out.
- That was at an ambassador's reception; drink is the only way to get through them – Dagan retorted.

D'Silva wasn't listening but pointing at a letter K in the paper, Dagan clocking what was going on took note, then I, then L and he indicated two fingers, finally next he pointed at a photo of Hitler and shrugged looking at Dagan. KILL HITLER, he'd spelt it out, D'Silva had known all along, now it was obvious who'd taken the lighter first in the hotel, then later in the beer hall while pretending to help him after his collapse D'Silva had extricated the pen and cufflinks. The Brazilian held his gaze; Dagan glanced sideways at his side desk and then around the room. There was nothing to hand except his bare hands. He looked back at the Brazilian and racked his brains for a weapon close by apart from his pyjama cord, slowly D'Silva took his hand out of his jacket, the glint of the scalpel blade, recently sharpened Dagan didn't doubt, could be seen. No better man to find a major artery in a swift cut, Dagan swallowed involuntarily.

- You're looking much better, a clear path to a healthy future if you're smart enough to take the opportunity – D'Silva ran a thumb carefully along the sharpened double edge never taking his eyes off Dagan nor Dagan off him. With his other hand letters pointed at spelt out U ME AMIGOS.
- Never doubted it – Dagan smiled and relaxed so did D'Silva, the scalpel returned to his pocket. He looked for the German word 'und' on the paper - I feel a lot better, especially in the last minute. At the same time, Dagan pointed to M Y while he nodded and continued with the next letters P E N and he shrugged at D'Silva.
- Ah that's good to hear – D'Silva said noncommittally adding - we always leave something of us behind whenever things like this happen.
- I always thought you start over, new beginnings – Dagan pointed to P E N again and shrugged again more emphatically looking for answers.
- A common misconception I assure you – D'Silva pointed to another photo which had the river in the background – how did he manage to get a walk around in Munich near a river and stealthily divest himself of the incriminating evidence? There's more to our friendly Doctor from the Amazons than you think.
- But you mustn't worry yourself about that, from now on I will be keeping an eagle eye on developments – the tit for tat continued.

189

- You needn't worry about a thing, you are so kind though – Dagan spelt out N O and E Y E. Keep his eyes on his own road the message.
- Of course, as a medical man, I am honour-bound to do it and will not fail you – Dagan had the measure of the man and thought he could deal with the 'additional' surveillance but still had some questions.
- You mentioned my illness and that you knew more than...- a strange look from the South American
- I have a lot of experience in the tropics and symptoms that appeared to be one thing can turn out to be something else entirely - At the same time he pointed out M E - Strangely enough in the jungle you eat certain plants you die, you eat others and you look and feel like you're going to die. You eat some others and its food. You have to know and I know – D'Silva was the mixer and maker of potent potions it seemed.
- Something I caught then? Just like that, Germans are using Amazonian salad vinaigrettes - pointing out H O W.
- You drink too much, far too much, you enter into hypothetical questions, 'what happens to the world if this happens to....' – he trailed of. Dagan's big mouth obviously – I was already alarmed as you dashed to the bathroom, more so when I went later, anyway add all that to your poor physical shape and thus – D'Silva trailed off again as he filled in the gaps in code.
- We have lots to talk about – Dagan was relieved, he was off the hook at least for now.

Dagan doubted the gloss his friend was putting on the facts, thinking over it he'd gone to the bathroom, which in hindsight seems to have been a big mistake because that was when his drink had been tampered with, doctored by the doctor. Don't they take an oath? Dagan remembered he'd come down rapidly with the symptoms of a heavy flu and a fever after that. The solicitous attentions of D'Silva during and after made more sense, he'd been checking to see if he'd administered enough of the jungle juice to keep Dagan immobilized until after the Munich Beer Hall, might have even given him more. He'd also taken the lighter as a further guarantee of inaction by Dagan, but how the blue blazes did he know? Did something slip out in conversation, did he go through his pockets by chance and put two and two together when he saw the cufflinks and lighter and pen in the same pocket. Who was D'Silva working for? Not the Germans obviously so Dagan wasn't the only one with hidden agendas. In certain respects, Dagan was secretly happy his plans had been foiled but in other ways, he was raging, if he'd been his old self instead of negated by the voodoo brew D'Silva had given him he might just have managed to do away with Hitler, something millions yearned for and dozens had tried to do before him.

Prague 5th Dec 1941

Dagan sat at the window of his hotel, he liked looking out hotel windows, lots of people did, he remembered an artist who told him he liked painting people as if from through a window. Incredible genius, the number of talented people you met in Manhattan or LA never ceased to amaze him and he was once again drawn to the inverse logic that this later chapter in his life had started in a meeting room in New York. This window was in the best hotel in the city and the views were of the main thoroughfare and right beside the main square. The room and window were all belle époque effigies of brunettes with their hair in circular buns and white toga dresses and bare arms. Risqué in its day, lots of them held aloft books, torches, bridges, trains and primitive planes. Girls with an eye on the coming future. The furnishings and finishing's were of good quality and had weathered well though were tarnished by enviable passage of old man time, lack of care and not many visitors these days meant not many reasons for spit and polish. Dagan gazed at a light scattering of snow covering the roofs. Since Munich and during the journey southwards they had noticed the sudden downturn into winter. Here in Prague, an occupied capital of an occupied country, the faces were more guarded, more circumspect. No laughter in the streets, no lovers with intertwined hands, no joyous impious children kicking balls back and forth. Grim streets for grim times added to grim weather, it might not be so oppressive in July but the dark grey low cloud made the daylight permanent twilight. Dagan felt as gloomy as the scene below as a knock at the door ushered in his shadow, jailor, doppelganger D'Silva who stopped before him.

- A beautiful new day isn't it? - D'Silva announced cheerily.
- It is a new day but beauty is in the eye of the beholder in this case.
- Ah but the beauty is not in the day but what it promises, soon we will be finished our work and will go home. Me back to Rio, the beaches, beautiful ladies, carnivals, caipirinhas, sunshine and the good life. Away from this – he pointed or waved at monochrome scene below - and this – this time he waved breezily in Dagan's direction. He was smiling while Dagan just looked at him.

191

- Any dietary supplement for me this time doctor – Dagan replied in a similar cheery voice; he didn't bother sneering, what was the point.
- What foolish things you say my friend – the Brazilian pulled his ear, microphone alert, was D'Silva mocking him?

I'm the spy being doubly spied upon and heartily sick of it too. He saw his reflection in the glass, unmistakably himself indeed but thinner, whatever the Brazilian had slipped him it has killed his appetite. And if he managed some stodgy Bavarian or Tyrolean food he often saw it again later as he talked to God on the big white telephone in the corner of every bathroom. A miracle diet he could market it but with limits because apart from his lean visage he looked downbeat, sad and withdrawn. The last weeks had taken its toll but the umpire had reached nine and he had got up off the ropes to use boxing parlance. He loved the noble art, had known some distinguished purveyors of the canvas and had even done some amateur bouts in his medical pre-revolutionary student days. It turned out to be a very handy skill knocking people cold with a good right hook, he'd given some bruised jaws to members of his majesties forces in his time and had polished his pugilistic abilities on numerous henchmen, thugs, hired toughs, strikebreakers, opium runners, and Ukrainian hajduks. You name it, the last in the line being Cuban prison officials and fellow inmates.

This morning he woke dazed and overcome, had dragged his corpse down to breakfast as he had over the last weeks, more in spirit than presence. He'd gone through the motions of camp visits, sometimes not even letting on he spoke English, to avoid conversations from sun up to sundown, he'd shuffled along even his Brazilian shadow had begun to leave him alone. So it was as much a surprise to him that morning the effect the smell of coffee on his nostrils, where did they get it? That coffee aroma moment was when it all snapped back into place. The jungle was shunted out of his bloodstream for good. The eggs and sausage and cheese and toast and pickled fish disappeared down his gullet. He ate with unrestrained relish. A man renewed, he felt the nourishment soak into his wasted rundown body, by this 3rd cup of coffee he felt his old self and sod's law that's when it came crashing to halt.

- An excellent breakfast – a voice from behind right in his ear claimed his attention. Sure enough, it was Hoffman of the SS on each lapel, death skull in his peaked cap, all in black, clean-shaven, cropped hair shiny riding boots. The human form stretched to its mortal limit beyond which just lay pain and the promise of more death though Dagan never got that direct impression from the SS Captain. Another actor but on who's stage were we, his or mine. Dagan still felt the bile rising along with his fear, he swallowed another gulp of the coffee and grinned like he'd struck the Klondike mother load.

- Sets you up for the day – Dagan said as a shadow passed over his grave.
- We haven't seen you in a while? – Hoffmann said in friendly fashion – But you've been all over the papers though, the Fuhrer provoking mysticism in even the most un-German of hearts. Father. Mother – Hoffmann jested, Dagan asked himself how had he got on such jokey terms with the secret policeman.
- I had a fever of 103; even you'd look like my mother in those circumstances – leg pulled pull leg - and thanks for the visit by the way and the pears of course.

The smile on the German's face broadened, Hoffmann liked him, could it be worse.

- A pleasure, the pears were my idea. Like my mother – the joke arrived at its destination - I am German, you must excuse me as I don't really understand sometimes – the bonhomie continue – but I am "getting it" this time. 'Like my mother' Yes terribly good. I saw you on the stretcher in the beer hall you looked like a ghost. Luckily you had D'Silva to attend to you, he loosened your clothes and took your vital signs
- Ah yes, D'Silva a marvel of a man. But you must ignore my Irish scene of humour, it's not to everyone's liking, as from me I should develop my German side. I salute many German strengths and historical figures such as Goethe, Beethoven, and Luther. Great thinkers, great humanists.
- I'll give you some more great Germans, Barbarossa, Fredrick the Great, Bismarck, Hindenburg and of course new to the pantheon Adolf Hitler.

The last bit said in a raised voice, the fervent Nazi back, never mind that Hitler was Austrian, Austrian German all the same thanks to the Hitler's machinations, Dagan thought it best to keep that to himself, that and more. As a sop to his 'friend' he said that special mention could go to German science and a special mention to the German sausage. It led to a pause. Maybe too far with the sausage comment

- You jest – Hoffmann sounded amused but Dagan wasn't messing.

- Seriously I am a big fan of the German sausage in all its varieties, the dark, the light, the spiced, the frankfurter, the smokiness of those from Alsace, delicious all - The German softened at the obvious sincerity of the statement.
- My favourite is the Munich breakfast white, you should try it.
- I will if I get the chance. What about these – Dagan pointed to those on the breakfast side table.
- Bah if you have nothing else, what do the Czechs know about sausages – came the dismissive snort. Just a veneer of civilization, gossamer and the animal suddenly bares its fangs. Don't forget for a minute who you are dealing with. Go neutral, go smooth, go to the dogs morally.
- What's the weather like today?
- Cold but it is December after all, a good coat and a hearty breakfast and you will be fine - the fangs sheathed just as quickly.
- Good advice I'm certainly doing my best with breakfast - Dagan reached for a slice of toast, his third or fourth - Suddenly today absolutely famished.
- You seem more excited. Is your fever coming back?
- God I hope not, even the thought gives me shivers – Dagan reassured Hoffman.
- Ah some news, our American friends have located your predecessor at last – Dagan froze, toast in mid-air, tried to dissimulate, continue as normal. Inside his full stomach did full somersaults.
- And how is my esteemed predecessor? Tell him thanks for nothing - Have they spoken to him? That was the deal-breaker, from what they'd told him of the American he didn't come across as any bright light, could be tripped up with a couple of cheap lawyer tricks. Wasn't he supposed to be under lock and key, a gilded cage somewhere out of sight? Dagan knew he had days left at most even if he wasn't planning to skip he might have to anyway.
- Any message for him when we finally talk to him – Hoffman inquired.

Hoffman knows that I don't know him. What do you say to a complete stranger? Screw your wife and any others who'll let you! Okay seriously play with your kids and drink good bourbon but not at the same time, do more good than harm, ah come on Dagan that's the piss artist talking. How about never leave justice undone, never talk with our mouth full never talk about someone behind their back, never interrupt the speaker, never pick your teeth, never scratch your balls in public, keep your hands by your side unless it's to put them on the small of a woman's back as you usher her through a door. Dagan giddy and light-headed after that rush of ragtime epiphanies finally said.

- Tell him to always give it his best shot and hence there's no shame in coming second - The German burst out laughing – I don't know the man so I had to keep it inoffensive – Dagan said in his defence - that and tell him he owes me a case of finest bourbon for getting me into this.
- But you volunteered – Hoffmann corrected him.
- But I wouldn't have been asked if he'd gone along – Dagan corrected Hoffmann.
- Touché. That is interesting about how you did get to be asked.
- I was available, it came up in a conversation, they got in touch, Stockholm is a small place and you meet all the right people quickly – Dagan fudged vaguely.
- Who did you have the conversation with, when and where – no fudging here, give me names, dates and places, wow?
- Any witnesses needed – Dagan butted in.
- Forgive my directness, it's the policeman combined with the German in me. My government likes to know these things. For example, who contacted you, you think I'm being nosey even rude but let me put it this way we know all this information about all the other members so we just want to complete our files, very German I know but you understand – the secret policeman was nearly apologetic.
- I never knew, well I don't want you tossing and turning at night so I'll do my level best. The subject first came up at a cocktail party in Manhattan, a member of the New York Red Cross, mentioned it to me, would I like to serve humanity and so on, the committee knew of my disposition and willingness to help.
- Very selfless and noble of you, I begin to understand, in the US there are a lot of Zionist groups attempting to blacken the rebuilt and proud Germany, we are attempting something new, revolutionary ideas, national socialism is the new revolution. Are you surprised by the word socialism, it is there for a reason. Germans are nurtured and cared for by the state, their every need, spiritual and physical is thought of, we are building a new country like nothing seen before. An Aryan nation built on Aryan principles. The children learn in school and in the youth movements the new nation will be theirs, the non-Aryans are being removed, this is difficult and hard, there have been

195

mistakes like *kristallnacht*. Yes, you heard me correctly, a mistake. We have understood this and reached a temporarily compromise. Aryan and non-Aryan nations. The non-Aryans are grouped in separate locations away from the main Aryan population. In this way everyone is happy, we do our best to make these places as comfortable as possible, in exchange the guest's needs are looked after and those who want to can work.

It was a miracle Dagan's jaw didn't drop to the floor with amazement at the bare-faced pack of lies he'd been subject to, he'd kept on eating as by now he was used to the gigantic exaggeration day in day out, he swallowed and drank some coffee while Hoffman awaited a reply. It came.

- The German government has been badly misunderstood abroad I fear to tell you and that's partially why I came, I couldn't believe that the Germany of Goethe, Beethoven and modern thought could be responsible for the acts they were attributed to in the press and by word of mouth.
- Do you see! The newspapers in the US are mouthpieces of Zionist warmongering? The blame lies with us for our honestly, our bravery. Two nations two futures, the Jews were expelled from England, Spain, Russia, attacked, pogroms on countless occasions. We protect them, keep them together, save them, plan for them and for that they call us monsters! - The Nazi gleamed and shone with the party message, he really believed what he was saying. Dagan didn't know whether to laugh or cry, this was so deluded, he didn't need the secret service in American to know about the desperate plight of the Jews in Europe nor to listen to the numerous friends in the US who lamented the tribulations of relatives since 1933. The lucky rich and talented ones who managed to escape told all and sundry exactly how well the state had treated them. And even without those witnesses, all you needed was to watch the newsreels about the brutal jackboot on the neck of the common German Jew - It promises to be an interesting day for just that – Hoffman flushed.
- Will we have total access to the camp? – Dagan wanted freedom of movement and at least five minutes without a guide or guard or spy or fellow Red Cross member anywhere near. If everything was sweetness and light the Germans couldn't object.
- Unfortunately not – object they did - I would like that but even in the POW camps you couldn't go everywhere, the guard's areas, administration, storerooms are out of bounds and now you are visiting a different type of camp, these are not POWs, you have no

predetermined rights to be here but as a special favour. The German government which has nothing to hide still had to respect certain rules the camp commanders make. Our hands are tied but you will be surprised. The camp has been preparing for weeks for your arrival – What baloney! Camp commanders do what they are told not what they want Dagan knew, especially under this regime.

- The Red Cross is truly grateful for the access to Tzelsteinstat and if we could organize a regular visit, to this and other camps, it would go a long way to dissipating these unfound rumours that are blackening the honourable name of Germany in such powerful neutrals like the USA, Brazil, and Argentina. A LONG WAY, I guarantee it. German civilization and culture is admired throughout the world.
- An interesting proposal but what "other camps" are you talking about, there are no more that I know of.
- Oh, I don't understand – Surely he wasn't serious – Dachau for example.
- Understand what? Dachau is a German camp solely.
- Nothing so just please pass on the request for consideration, that's all.

Right! Just the maths made liars of them! If there are or were three hundred and fifty thousand Jews in Bohemia and Tzelsteinstat holds fifty where are the remaining three hundred? Stuffed into camps in God only knows in what conditions, unvisited, unseen but it wasn't a good idea to play the smart ass. With these thugs and with each passing day who knows the infamies being committed. This was a stain on the human soul, every person with a shred of decency had to do their utmost to stop it, Dagan had never been so focused in his life. Even his involvement in the struggle for independence in Ireland had been a jolly jape compared to this. Vindicating a free Ireland, a noble and just cause of hundreds of years was always only going to change a small corner of the world, Ireland and the Irish but this was begging your pardon to all his fellow Irishmen and women on a different scale altogether. If I can get through this in one piece I'll be back for more he thought, just like he and the other lovers of wine, women, and song, of life, culture and diversity, of brotherhood, humanity, and goodwill who had set aside all that to take up arms for a vision of Ireland, he the callow med student who'd known just enough about explosives not to blow himself up and finished the job. He and the others would see this new crusade through to the bitter end. And the ends were often more bitter than you could have imagined as you come to them, Invictus and

197

unbowed you stood maybe but changed throughout completely. Dagan dreaded it but he knew this present battle was for the soul of mankind and dominion here on earth. The deadly duel was joined. Inwardly he rejoiced to have taken up the sword, the fight was on and so he switched on the charm, told tall tales, listened to blood-curdling ones with superbly feigned interest and told the old risqué joke. Buddy level was where he wanted to be as it was easier that way, Hoffman and he even shared their admiration for one of the Czech waitresses, it felt like the thing to do. If she had a friend they could double date!

- I will introduce you if you like – his new *amigo* had offered.
- Please do – Dagan said with a wink while inwardly thought how low did he have to go.

It was as good a way of any of breaking off the conversation, he saw the flash of favour in the eyes the local waitress, party badge was evident on the lapel of her jacket, one of the converted. Hoffman left them with a jolly slap on his shoulder and a wink. He'd introduced him as a special guest of the party, a special friend of the government.

- Ach, you are so important – she had simpered.
- The Fuhrer sent me flowers – Dagan has replied.
- Ah so! – Gosia was her name, she giggled genuinely impressed and so she should be.
- I can show you a pressing I saved in a book up in my room – straight to the chase.
- I would be so honoured – hand to her heart, breathless admiration, that easy it was. In minutes it was all arranged, she'd meet him later for a drink.

He strutted out like a peacock, king of the hill until he noticed a piece of paper in this pocket, he didn't take it out, back in his room in the most furtive manner he saw written on it 'Room 64, 23:00'. Damn he'd have to have bedded the girl by then, he always hated rushing them out, such bad manners it was.

On the other side of the room Hoffman while talking to a colleague watched the Irishman leave.

- You know at first I had my suspicions but as I've come to know him I would vouch for him without a thought. Grouchy to start with but underneath he's charming company and very pro-Germany – Hoffman said to his colleague as they observed Dagan on his way.

- We still have not had an answer from the American network, it is being compromised constantly by the English who report everything to the Americans to curry favour. South Carolina, unfortunately, is too far for an embassy officer to travel without arousing suspicions, no reason to go, it was not a popular destination with German emigrant's last century.
- It should have been. It's a lot nicer than where they did go Minnesota is not that appealing even in the summer. A pity our friends in US espionage are so limited – Hoffman pointed up the limits of his overseas colleagues.
- They are trying one last time but why bother? This man and the group are leaving next week, onwards to Switzerland to present their reports – Hoffman's colleague noted.
- Which will be excellent, we have done everything to make sure of that and they know we have, they have seen nothing untoward, and our colleagues in Poland and beyond can continue their work in the shadows – Hoffman noted.
- Ack, they see what they want to see, we have painted, cleaned, given out clothes and medicines preparing for the visit, the choir will sing, the Judean committee will do what they are told or else they will be sent East and even if they don't know what East is everyone knows not to go East. And besides, the Red Cross won't be allowed there again. Why do we even have to play hide and seek – the second German failed to see what all the effort was for.
- No less than cleansing the soul of Europe – true Nazi fervour gushed out of Hoffman - Realpolitik is what Bismarck said and that's what the Fuhrer is playing at. Look how much he achieved for Germany without firing a shot, by playing the peacemaker and with realpolitik. It is the same, later the truth will be broadcast and the world will marvel but now we must work out of sight – explained Hoffman.
- Why do we care what they think?
- Were you listening *dummkopf?* – Admonished Hoffman savagely.

Dagan returned to his room taking the lift up escorted by the bellhop who's burly back was visible as the doors closed, the bellhop spoke to him 'don't look round, don't remember my face. London has told us about you, we will help you in every way possible, if you need us, go to Karol bistro in the new city, Rejok Street, tram 79, ring the operator from the public phone, ask for number 127, say it in the best Czech you can, say it twice and hang up. Clear.

- Yes thank you, do I need.....- Dagan tried to get a question in.
- Quite! No questions - the lift stopped at the 3rd floor, the man still with his back stepped out as the actual bellhop, a frightened and pasty bare teen walked in at the same time.

What if the lift was bugged was all Dagan could think, they must be sure it isn't to take such risks, if not the next time the door opens it could be jackbooted devils ready to take him away. As if to tempt fate the lift did stop at the next floor and two German officers entered. Dagan nodded politely and smiled as his heart was thumping.

Guten tag – one of the officers said and turned to talk to his colleague. Dagan sagged internally, next up his floor, he went to his room, showered again, dressed and went back down to the lobby to meet his colleagues and start the day's activities.

- You showered again – D'Silva asked – a recurrence of the fever maybe?
- You should know – Dagan barbed back.
- No chance, it's the sign of a guilty conscience – D'Silva retorted.
- That's between me and my confessor then - What was the Brazilian up to now?

Dagan peeled off and they all started the tour of Prague that was rapidly recovering its Germanic roots or to put it finely it's not inconsequential Germanic roots were being magnified, blown up, glorified, and superimposed or simply replacing the Czech Slavic ones. The Hapsburg Emperor here, the renowned German writer there, plays and battles, architects and statesmen. All helped by lashing of swastikas and German troops visible in all directions at all times, loitering, adorning or spoiling each corner. The day did its best to help the conqueror, a blue sky giving rise to a tepid sun doing its December utmost to heat man and beast. The Germans made it seem like nothing, not even noticing the icy day from a car with a retracted roof, all the better for a good look around, to be seen, the victors enjoying the spoils. Just push your collar and you'll be fine.

The people in the street went about their business, the uniformed ones saluted, police and all, Dagan jammed up against Takenaka, both uncomfortable in the extreme it was the short straw for both. Dagan had been more effusive about the current regime in front of the oriental representative and the initial open hostility was melting. This was helped by his new Gestapo chums. He wasn't a fervent open Nazi sympathizer but he was giving out all the right signals to the right people for them to believe it. He'd been too aloof and distant at the start buying into the Red Cross neutral role but with a pressed flower from the Reich's Chancellery in his wallet, he'd been making up time. Even D'Silva couldn't quite believe he was dealing with the same person who'd tried to take history in his own hands in the Munich beer hall. Takenaka wasn't uncomfortable with him in particular; he was with anyone in close contact, wife and mother included. Code of the bushido and all that. Dagan remembered how strange and compelling he'd found Japan during his visits there.

They passed a straggling line outside a bakery, weary grandmothers and grandfathers and young children in the prams. 'How did you spend the war Mummy?', 'Queuing my sweet, queuing', and there were many who'd settle for that now. The home front; less bullets just as many uniforms.

Prague was so full of troops just who was at the front? Whoever was they got first call on the food, then the German civil population obviously, so where did that leave the Czechs, Poles, Romanians in the long queues for bread that tasted of sawdust more than your Hovis loaf. They drove through the central square with the cathedral behind and right on time they stopped for the cuckoo clock spectacle. Every hour on the hour with Germanic efficiently and they had to wait no more than a minute or two. The atmosphere was jovial comradely, festive even, Christmas was approaching as was the end of this tour which meant home and family, normality after the madness.

- People are very proud of their small peculiarities – D'Silva stared at the much-heralded appearance of the cuckoo and the applause and cheers of the waiting crowds milling around the street, Germans and proud Czechs.
- In Brazil we have our Marti Gras and we think you should travel across the world to see it and have the experience of your life – D'Silva looked quizzically at the wooden bird flashing in and out of the wooden box - Have you been to Marti Gras?
- I have – said Dagan.
- This is a bit underwhelming in comparison – D'Silva said underwhelmed.
- It is – Dagan agreed – but they love this sort of thing in these parts, it's not a sad wooden bird springing out of a sad wooden box, it's planned meditated organized and ordered. It worked just now, an hour ago, this time last year, this time next year, in 10 years and 10 years ago. It stands for stability and order, as long as the birdie goes cuckoo the world is working as it should. Marti Gras is a bit more chaotic wouldn't you say?

- As you Irish say *tis* – the Brazilian agreed – I see you are getting along very well with our hosts.
- That is bad? They are our hosts after all – the fission of deep mistrust was evident in each phrase they exchanged.
- No that is good! But it's surprising, back-slapping chums checking out the girls, being very happy with the state of affairs in the world.
- Just like Marti Gras except what's going on here is even more exciting. Anyway, I'm just trying to fit in better. If the Germans are happy with me they are happy with the Red Cross and that's good? – Dagan put forward.

D'Silva glanced around to make sure no eavesdropping was possible.

- Its good but I don't understand it, especially after the beer hall, I still can't believe what you were about to do, what are you up to now, I should have turned you in.
- But you didn't and that makes you an accomplice - the Brazilian boiled at that, his face flushed with anger.
- I could do it now – the Brazilian hissed.
- And ruin the tourist spectacle. – Dagan snorted - If you do it here what will happen I'll shout *'Traitor, I trusted you'* and will bite down hard on my cyanide pill, me gone to Valhalla and you here trying to explain to the nice SS people that you are a total innocent even though you covered up an attempt on the demi-God. They'll take you apart piece by piece trying to find out more which you can't tell them because you don't know any more, but they don't know that, they'll keep on asking, talking out your fingernails, your teeth, electrocuting your *cajones*, cigs burns, glass, they can keep you alive for weeks. Finally, after an eternity they'll overdo it and you'll die, if that sounds like fun then go ahead.
- What are you up to?
- Trying to get home, I didn't do what I'd come to do and now I'm being extra pally so I can get the hell out of here – Dagan fed him a line to get the Brazilian off his back just long to vanish.
- *Eres el Diablo* –D'Silva hissed.
- I believe in what we're doing you know even if its scant consolation, if we go someday to the cafe Columbia in Rio, we'll have a plate of fiajodas and remind ourselves that the world continues, the object is to enjoy it and survive, especially that, survive – the Brazilian looked at him long and hard.
- You nearly ruined everything – he said enigmatically and before he left added – this is not over yet.

Dagan knew it was, he'd have no more trouble from that direction, but I'll still watch my drink when that fella is around, shame to lose the friendship though. Or not! What the feck, didn't the guy put some vile near-dead inducing concoction in my drink, not what you do to your friends? Back in the car, Dagan was actually glad to see the Japanese adversary so much he gave him a broad warm smile that was so open it was plainly disconcerting to Takanaka.

They then passed by the Rothaus for photos, a press call and handshakes with the great and good of Monrovian society. 1941 version, very different to 1938's, either way, Dagan was a practised hand at these sorts of events as he had been the whole trip, he found 'everything' to his liking, usually had a disarming comment to make about the gathering, charmed the ladies, flattered those who liked being buttered up, went into 'hombre' mode with the uniformed types and if all else failed, everyone loved talking about the food and drink. Basically, he left a great impression behind which is what he wanted. He even saw D'Silva look over at various times when a particularly loud laugh burst from someone in Dagan's company.

- That's a very unique dress and the colours suit you to perfection. Moyra Loy wore something very similar to a party once, one of her favourites she told me – Dagan charmed one lady.
- Oh really my goodness – the lady gushed.
- Yes, Pamplona can be dangerous but the trick is to be sober and always have someone between you and the bull. Hemingway himself told me that – he followed up on a senior government official.
- Ah Ja, how interesting, now that Spain is our ally maybe it might be possible to visit soon – came the enthused reply.
- Dearest Excellency I was wondering when we'd get a chance to meet and talk – he said to the deputy of a department of Procurement and Economic Planning.
- Really? – The delighted reply.
- Of course, my friends in the SS/army/party have spoken very highly of your bureau and the vital work it does, now tell me... - Questions that were not too easy and not too hard but allowed the other person to shine. Dagan worked the room like a real pro until he found what he was looking for.

Imperial Japanese Fleet, North Pacific, 500 miles from Hawaii

Gunnery Sergeant Nobolt and his three-man team ever so gently raised the Hero 3 torpedo from the ordnance cart to the undercarriage of the H5 Miashugshi torpedo bomber. The pulleys back and front had to be exactly in sync.

- Thabo put on the rope – to the mechanic at the back then to another - Huso continue.

The main hanger flight of the carrier Hishyu was heaving with activity and mechanical and ordinance teams prepared the sixty planes they were to launch against Pearl Harbour the next day. Nobolt secured the first clip and locked it and then the second as a broad smile broke out on his face, he ran his hand smoothly over the torpedo with its cold metal head painted black to distinguish the warhead from the rest and felt a tingle along his round calloused hands.

- Well done – as was the custom he took out a piece of chalk to write Bonsai!!

The rest of the team grinned as well, happiness all-round till Nobolt shouted - To work! Five more aircraft to prepare – and the whole team snapped back into stoic oriental visages and became worker bees again.

6th of December. Munich

Rudolf Kapler finally got the photos back from the developers, it had taken an age, he usually did it himself but you just couldn't get the materials or chemicals these days. A keen amateur photographer his opportunities had been limited by his diminishing stock of film. But those considerations had gone out the window for the beer hall meeting, he'd wrangled an invite easily enough as he was a long-standing party backer. While he'd lavished contributions from the easily days on he was not an active member, he had however spoken to Hitler on two separate occasions and was in awe of the man so jumped at the chance to take some pictures of the event.

He opened the envelope with the name of the photograph shop, this was always a special moment even after years of practice and study and dedication you never knew exactly how a photo was going to turn out. The first pictures were those you normally liked most, family, friends, parties, days out in the country. Kapler was old Munich stock of high social status, life was leisurely and comfortable but these photos he would savour another time as he was anxious to get to his big prize of the anniversary meeting. He had been so close to the Fuhrer that day, he controlled himself not to go straight to the end but forced himself to look at the snaps of the build-up, the faces in the crowd, expectant high ranking party members and friends joking and laughing, the hall, the musicians and Hitler arriving, too far to photograph so Rudolf always liked to show the faces of the audience as they listened and responded to the emotion and the clamour. Perhaps some of these could be sent to the newspaper. He saw photos of friends, their spouses and some of the group of Red Cross people who'd been just behind. They were more stoic than the rest as you would imagine but some less so. They were also the people who had caused all the raucous when one of them fainted, some exotic fever from overseas.

The temerity of it, with all the responsibility and work Hitler had, the last thing the country needed was for him to come down with yellow fever. I could have caught it too but I wouldn't be a catastrophic loss to the nation. He passed on, some pictures caused him some apprehension, a shudder along the back of his spine, especially close-ups of the man who later collapsed, he did look very ill indeed. In the graphical black and white photo you could clearly make out the fevered face, beads of sweat evident on his forehead but the most frightening thing was the eyes, they blazed as if from hell itself, the glare fixed on the Fuehrer, a portrait of glycerol empathy. Kapler moved with bated breath to the next, a wide lens photo and even though this photo showed Hitler approaching down the aisle he looked away for the strange figure of the feverish man. Rudolf remembered the excitement nearly giving him a heart attack, how he'd trembled taking the photos, one after another, trying to get the right light, focus and angle as the central figure surrounded by admirers and entourage approached. He looked at his photos, the ones with Hitler closest before he'd put the camera down to shake his idol's hand were telling, the man in front, the sick one with the glaring look was raising his hand, his mouth was open he was saying something. He looked less the ravished stricken ill figure and more the charismatic Christian in evangelical ecstasy, in the next photo the arm at the photo's edge was higher, the face of Hitler clearer, looking the other way, shaking somebody's hand, Kapler flicked to the next photo, again the damn man's arm in front, higher still, nearly blocking what could have been the definitive photo of Hitler among his people. Kapler sought no less and here was the man's other arm was coming across. God in heaven, only one more photo left, Kapler slid the present photo up and behind to the back of the pack.

The last photo, Hitler again centre, beautifully in focus, Rudolf was thrilled, and the photo was spectacular. Hitler as a man of the people

205

loved by them, a stern but loving father. This was also the moment the man in front collapsed, Rudolf had caught the moment, to the left as the strange man was caught by his colleague whose arms wrapped around him, the feverish one seemed absent, vacant, Rudolf pulled his gaze from the Fuhrer, something about the arm, the hand of the man that had been so annoyingly raised in previous photos, Rudolf swore he could see a hint of something he wasn't sure of, he looked at the negatives and decide to develop enlargements of the five final photos. Rudolf dashed home, out of breath and sweating he didn't even take off his coat before bolting down to his basement darkroom, precious chemicals came out of the cupboard and mixed, paper he'd been saving for this moment soaked. He was enlarging the perfect portrait of Hitler after all.

Rudolf set to work and in ten minutes was ready; he left the paper to develop in the bath of chemicals and wearily went upstairs for his supper. When he returned the photos were clear and he hung them up to dry. Now he could examine them closely with his magnifying glass for the crosswords, in the first the man's hand was down to his side as if shielding something. He looked at the next in the sequence, there was something small and solid, tube-like, cylindrical, barely visible, Rudolf racked his brain, what could that be? One or two centimetres were visible. In the third picture with the arm nearly fully extended he saw it more clearly, the cuffs back, it was now three centimetres long, some sort of tube, Rudolf blanched, he was looking at a barrel, the barrel of a very strange gun. He rushed upstairs and still puffing and coatless he rushed out, the cold hit him so hard he remembered his coat and ran back in to get it tripping as he did so on the doormat, fell and hit his head on the porcelain umbrella bin. The bin smashed at the impact and Rudolf's lights when out, he thought no more about what he'd been so interested in or anything else as everything went dark.

The Carolinas, USA 6th December 1941

Just as Rudolf smashed to smithereens the fake China wedding gift from his cheapskate uncle Walter, a knock on a door thousands of miles to the west awoke Bryant from his slumbers.

- Yeah who is it – he said unenthusiastically.
- Hotel personal sir, we have a certified letter.
- Can't it wait? – Bryant's weary 10 am reply.

- I'm afraid not, a messenger boy is waiting down in the lobby for you to sign it.
- Oh, all right coming – Bryant had gone to seed cut off from all contact, excluded from his careful mounted lifestyle until they gave him back all the photos as they'd promised. He hadn't been home in months holed up here like a monk, hadn't even got his oats in so long his member was getting cobwebs on it. He opened the door after checking through the peephole, an attractive looking woman; he slicked back his hair, took a swig of whiskey from the bottle and pulled his bathrobe on tight.
- Sorry about being so grumpy, I have a terrible night tossing and turning – he said opening the door.
- That's not a problem sir – he hadn't seen her before.
- You're new? –he asked.
- Started last week sir – the attractive hotel staff member replied.
- You must let me make it up to you, I'd feel awful if you didn't – Bryant hinted.
- And I can allow that sir, the happiness of our guests is paramount, meanwhile, I have the letter, can you read it please and give me any reply and sign this too.
- Okay business first, pleasure later.

He gave the young woman a leery look, she, in turn, smiled sweetly seeing a young man in his prime already going to pot, too much high living, dour bloodshot eyes, receding hair, soft hands, dirty nails and whiskey breath at 10 in the morning. Despite that, she'd give him the best screw of his life if she had to, equally she could eviscerate him straight from under the diaphragm to the heart with the long thin razor-sharp knife she had hidden up her sleeve. Anke didn't think either drastic option would be needed but an agent did what they had to do to get what they had to get. The letter was cleverly done up, forged on Red Cross stationery stolen days ago and a lot of money had gone just into that. The devils in the detail, Bryant started reading, his face changed for early mooring slackness to sharp alertness, excitement and relief.

- I'm going home; I can't believe it's finally over. Before I get dressed I'll send a reply – came the excited breathless response.

He sat down took some of the monogrammed paper hotel and wrote fiendishly signing his name with a flourish then put the letter in an envelope before handing it over to the girl before rapidly retaking it to seal it by licking the edge of the flap.

- Thank you - he said heartfully.

- The messenger is waiting so I'll be going – the "employee" Anke said sweetly.
- Like to have some fun later. In this place what's there to do anyhow?

It might have gone down well with hat check girl and the like but Anke had other things on her mind like leaving the scene right quick, going down the service stairs, removing her disguise, changing to nondescript clothes, return to anonymity, she could be very plain if she tried, then get to Washington DC and get the message back to her spymasters.

- I finish late today why don't we plan something the three of us.
- You going to bring a friend, I like that
- A friend no! My husband he'd love to go out to a show or a jazz club, he's bored in this town too.

Anke enjoyed the expression on the face of her mark before she waltzed out to the stairwell where she'd stashed her change discretely, then down to the taxi waiting out back, hang the expense she wasn't paying, to catch the first train out of town, she was amazed at the innocence of the prey, she'd spent a lot of time with grafters in the 30s and still thought of her takes like that, the game had sealed the envelope but as she was not going to deliver the letter she ripped it open without preamble and read the contents at a gallop. Bingo! It confirmed what was had been suspected, now all she'd had to do was get back to DC and arrange a meeting with her handler.

Chapter VII

Theresienstadt, 6th of December, 1941

The entrance to Theresienstadt was immaculate as they swept in under the arch of the main gate, its elegant clock marking 10:30 and they parked in front of the main administration building decked out with flags and banners as a band played a rousing welcoming tune. The musicians all had stars of David on their arms, their obvious pride along with the threadbare aspect grated when he remembered the bands in Germany, all bombastic polish and shine. This band was really good and played at a level that left earlier examples exposed as well-meaning amateurs. Dagan feeling he had been given a new lease of life and every additional minute was glorious "all my jewels for one more minute" Elizabeth Tudor had said on her deathbed and Dagan knew what it conveyed. He might have been here for one very hidden motive but meanwhile, he could contribute in his way as a Red Cross committee member. The music stopped and Dagan clapped, at first just himself then four of the five members and some of the others mostly civilians bravely joined in. The uniformed Germans to a man didn't.

- Excellent, *alles prime, toll, Wunderbar der music* – Dagan turned to Hoffman.
- There is no need to applaud they don't expect it – Hoffman raised an eyebrow.
- Reflex action, I was lifted by the subliminally of the music and the band looked happy enough to have been acknowledged. This is not what I expected – looking around – what was the music by the way, Beethoven, Straus I didn't recognize it - Hoffman would feel a bit superior as he answered, Dagan didn't mind that - I need to bone up on my classical music.
- Offenbach to be exact. This is our model, it's not so bad as you look around you, we encourage people to work, to live peacefully, to enjoy a rich varied cultural life while at the same time being apart from the rest of the population. Simple, neat and clean. No mixing among the sections that can't be mixed. Where is the harm, do you know what the British did at the start of the war, locked up all the Germans, grouped them together. Temporally until this situation is restored – Hoffman put such a glossy veneer on it but did he know how he sounded. Is it just with every conversation with a Nazi as an example in sociological backflips, these guys just had to open their mouths to get the back up in any decent-minded individual?
- 'Restored', beautiful, if I learned anything about wars it's that nothing is new and nothing is the same again but I understand what you mean about the fighting stops.
- A day the peace-loving people of Germany hope is ever closer.
- I'll second that – Dagan went po-faced all, it was all you could do, play along with the charade, thankfully that was soon to be over and what he was doing here was something that could shorten the war considerably if Donovan has been straight up with him.
- We look after provisions, security and so on while day to day issues are under the control of the council of the elders. That way the Jews themselves run the hospitals, schools, shops, cafes, we intervene minimally; they even have their own police.

The committee group was led inside and introduced to the council members who were generally white bearded wizened elders and rabbis, very Jewish with prayer hats, shawls, the typical garments of the Jewish elders but some had a more European cut to their clothes even though all of them were European. Dagan's heart started to beat faster amid all the handshakes and nodded smiles, there at the end he saw the Professor; gaunt, grey, very much thinner but still upright and with dignity, his practised German evident, much better than Dagan's, Kessler having spent years bouncing between Vienna and Prague not to mention his time in the emperor's uniform during the last great debacle.

Dagan waited till their turn came, 'Herr professor', 'Herr Malone', not the least sign of recognition, nothing to indicate a previous acquaintance, there, that's it, contact made as Dagan held the Professor's outstretched hand, soft, thinner, the bones pronounced, the grip still firm but a slight tremor, Dagan held the gaze and saw his dark blue eyes, thick dark eyebrows steeply overhanging a smooth clean-shaven face, hair grey and receded on each side leaving a triangular section still in touch with the smooth forehead. The nose was broad, more coloured than the face and the Adam's apple always to the fore was even more visible on the thin neck, it bobbed up and down as the innocuous words came out, 'good to see the committee', 'sterling work being done', 'Germans treated the Jews better than what was published abroad'.

The neck disappeared into a shirt that was now a size too big as was the baggy early 30's cut suit but there was still a dapper handkerchief, the same colour as the dark purple tie, a classy touch and no doubt the work of Maria. She'd always delighted in fashion, with her good taste and ability to combine some startling colours she'd always kept her preoccupied father dressed in rather snappy threads instead of the typical academic suits. Kessler had initially resisted dumping the tweed but later had been surprised by how well he looked in Panama hats, cream jackets with orange waistcoats and green leather shoes. It set him wildly apart from the general populace in his mist who went around in tones and shades of grey, black or dark blue, fashion in the 30s was just what Henry Ford said about his cars, if you want a suit, ok any colour so long as its black, grey or dark blue. An offer a bit more extensive than the Illinois car maker. They passed on, the Red Cross, Germans, Czechs and Jewish elders to get the tour underway, the council headquarters first, school infirmary, police cells complete with a hung-over drunk. Drunks generally have to be the most inventive of people; an alcoholic where basic necessities are scarce has to do something like distil potatoes or drinking cleaning fluids. This drunk reeked of pure spirits maybe the hospital had been obliging or some lab specimens had been abruptly reintroduced to a nitrogen-oxygen environment. The Germans were laughing.

- We have these problems too.
- Gut – he said gently, some Jewish members of the group blanched as the Germans knocked the bars with their batons.
- Ha-ha – they shouted.
- Rise and shine sleeping beauty – they laughed.

The play-acting went on a small while and then it began to seem to Dagan a bit forced or staged. Dagan began to get the impression that this wasn't the normal state of affairs rather something cooked up to make the place seem normal with normal drunks getting drunk as normal. But he didn't buy it, the shops were too full, the suits not frayed enough, the hair had brillo and mat instead of being long and dank, you'd see in the typical downbeat. The reactions of the council didn't fit either, they looked ill at ease with the situation of course but not embarrassed at a Jewish drunk and the fun-poking. When he thought about it the set up was evident and overwhelming, the camp had been thoroughly done over for the visit. The new-look feel to everything, the smell of fresh paint, the newness of the uniforms in the hospital, the bowling horseshoe hooping area looked like it had arrived yesterday and the lack of expertise in the children throwing the horseshoes begged the question whether they'd ever played before.

The group was invited to taste the food being served in the chophouse, basic soup, bread sausage and the children stared at it like Yom Kippur come early. Dagan was not naive to think that the authorities would let them visit unannounced. It's human nature to try to look your best on the best occasions and sadly to say, these days a visit from the Red Cross was likely to be way up on the list of best occasions. Still, this all rang untrue, the brush up was way out of proportion, the people were too thin, too sick looking, too scared, too silent. The ones who did talk were too forced, their eyes sad and the smiles low wattage.

Dagan remembered D'Silva stopping one woman and asking 'how is it here?' in his best German, the woman, stopped, looked at the listening visitors and their German hosts, she was dressed in a long coat with the star and a dainty hat, her shoes had been resoled and she wore woollen stockings, the face pinched the lips thin but some effort had been made, her pale cheeks were rouged and her lips redder and fuller than normal – her answer left Dagan light-headed – 'look around you' – she said slowly – 'just look around you' – and she continued.

211

Dagan had known people who'd travelled to Soviet Russia in the early 1930s; he'd even heard of people who'd immigrated to the USSR during that desperate time attracted by the rosy-tinted testimonials of the new socialist experiment as a new society of the worker. Well, those who'd visited told him things that were ringing familiar now. Potemkin villages and factories full of happy dancing peasant girls and well-built suntanned labourers and workers. It didn't ring true then or now, just look for the ubiquitous secret police, outnumbering two to one the twirling folklorists, everything was too good and hence all was a chimaera, all was false.

You had to look for other sources to verify the truth and in Russia and the Ukraine, it had been terrible famines, deportations, and forced work camps plus the Americans who emigrated and started a baseball league were never heard off again after the first Russian World series. Final proof, if needed, was the same impression that this was all too twee; all the hospital linen was brand new, same for all the starched uniforms of the nurses, the collars rashes a giveaway but their shoes were at best patched up and semi suitable for the climate. Were his opinions influenced by what he'd been told? Probably. Did it matter? Probably not. It was common knowledge how the Nazis felt about Jews and any other opponent or undesirable element. They were not nice people so they weren't going to be nice to their opponents; in fact why they bothered with the Red Cross was a mystery to him, the last shred of a thin veneer of civilization they had left. Whatever. He felt a responsibility to witness what was happening here. Unprecedented over the centuries. Witness.

Next up was a concert, the ghetto had an impressive level of cultural activity they were told, implying the rumours were wrong. How could their conditions be so bad if they had time for concerts, bands, theatre, colourful ethnic jigs and reels? The choir of young boys and girls sang a repertoire of choral arrangements backed up by a small orchestra. The singing was ethereal, ghostly, magical every member of the audience entranced and delighted. 'They're angels, pure angels' thought Dagan 'whatever happens I hope it's quick'. The tears welled up in his eyes. Time for the prison break out, time for his disappearance act, they were to spend the day giving out the parcels, the followed day seeing patients and that was it. He had to go into action but first, he had to make contact properly. Excitement grew in his gut, he was going underground.

Concert over they were taken to an open area passing another children's playground, scant it had to be said, some attempt to put a

Ferris wheel in as if it was carnival time in the ghetto. What a show we put on, no swings, a maypole, hoops for horseshoe throwing, the bored kids delighted at the free time. The parcels were handed out from trucks gathered at the side. Names called, people came forward. Close to him during all this was Kessler who approached Dagan. What could they say even out of earshot, what was the Red Cross doing, nothing if they didn't want to lose the limited access they had, would you even believe it if they told you the truth. Your eyes prefer to see what they want to see, prepared to believe the scene in front rather than imagine the nasty alternative undercurrents, just the product of an overactive mind. Dagan was beside Kessler.

- I was told to speak to you - the Czech said at last.
- Surprised to see me then – Dagan grinned helplessly.
- You never cease to surprise me, now and before, seeing you is a shock, not a pleasure.
- I understand – Dagan grin shot back into its cage.

The Kessler he'd known in the late 20s and early 30s had been a person in his prime intellectually, physically strong, secure in his profession, his country, his life, his family. His wife died in the Spanish flu epidemic so he was especially close to Maria, now his male pride reacted at being seen in this reduced state, bowed, enslaved, imprisoned, the reduction in the physical self, no dapper new clothes only old ones mended and re-mended, the crowded town camp, no privacy, baths were out of the question, eau de cologne was a luxury when compared to a loaf of bread or some potatoes for your soup. He was thinner, shabbier, duller and it did your heart in to see it but Dagan moved directly to practicalities, what he had to do to shorten the butchery was right in front of him.

- I'm not going without Maria – Kessler said directly. Without Maria, so the Czech resistance had been in touch.
- Don't worry old friend, she's coming with you and you're coming with me over the pond and far away from here.

That hadn't been part of the plan concocted by the British but he didn't care, did they really think Kessler would go without his daughter. Leave her in Prague with the resistance 'fraid not. It was going to be fun to see the faces of British secret service when he showed up with two half-starved Jews. The elder man began to sow a tear in the corner of his eye, the relief and gratitude evident, too evident, his arm began to reach over to connect with Dagan, touch his forearm or shoulder or some such but familiarities couldn't be allowed. Dagan moved rapidly and smoothly to one side.

- We've never met remember – the old man started and corrected himself - Be ready at a moment's notice – Dagan told him.
- I'm ready now, this suit is all I have, not one book left.
- Be prepared, we'll be in touch – and Dagan walked away briskly.

Let the games commence.

North West Pacific, 7th December 1941

Lt. Niaka and his navigator Sgt Kieku climbed up thc side of the Musubitsee Ankor torpedo bomber as all around them pilots and flight crews were getting into position, the noise was deafening, his chief mechanic Hiatu was ablaze, he'd even clapped him on the back and wished him a clean kill on a battleship. Normally he was a sour slave driver who never washed and sweated sake. He was from a rural background whereas Niaka was Tokyo born and bred, part of privileged elite, he'd been educated in the finest schools at home and abroad in the US.

He had mixed feeling about the attack, he knew in the war they were embarking upon they'd be up against skilled and well-trained adversaries. A strong enemy, a worthy one, unprepared yes but he knew the Americans, very pragmatic. He hoped that after Japan had gained the upper hand it needed in the Pacific the US would come to an agreement in time. He couldn't enter into the near festive spirit that was rife through the fleet – Contact!- his engine started, he could hardly see or hear, the night was calm for winter, they'd been lucky with the weather in the crossing, he had a two-hour flight with minimum headwinds, he'd come east over the island and go directly to Pearl Harbour and battleship row, even had the outline silhouette of the USS Arizona on his dashboard, he'd release his torpedo, hit ground targets then go back for more fuel and ammunition. He'd trained long and hard for this and knew exactly what to do and they would leave the US with no option but to give over control of the Pacific to Japan. His nation and his Emperor would achieve glory, his hair suddenly stood up on the back of the neck, maybe that atmosphere was infectious after all. The forward planes began their take-off while overhead the squadrons were forming up, Niaka and he waited their turn to be catapulted into the night and into a war.

Same time, Continental USA

Anke returned to Washington DC, changing her clothes and dumping each article in a separate bin. As soon as she'd arrived home she placed a plant on her window sill and half drew down her blinds. The maximum alert signal, urgent rendezvous required. Less than two hours later she arrived at the drop off point with the information in an envelope wrapped in the newspaper, she sat at the end of a bench in the very busy main Washington train station. The drops were always at busy times in busy places, a man sat down beside her, sometimes it was a man, sometimes a woman and once most curiously the contact had been a lady of colour.

They didn't look at each other, the letter was a seemingly innocent one to an Aunty in Tuscan, New Mexico, the person existed as did the address, hidden in the contents of the letter cloaked by seeming innocence was a message that could be released by an agreed code, a book or article or newspaper. Anke in swift legerdemain you'd be hard pushed to see even if you were looking closely set her newspaper down beside her quickly followed by the other person putting theirs on top of Anke's who in a flash picked up the second newspaper, got up and left without looking back. Good tradecraft. She walked into the crowd and kept going, this was the moment of truth, if American counter-espionage were to pick her up it would be now. She was sweating between her breasts and under her armpits and often had severe rashes after drops, she reached the rotating door and taking a breath pushed it out and forward she went disappearing in a rush of daylight.

Munich, 7th December, 1941

Rudolf woke up, blinked, let out a whelp of pain and looked around, a hospital bedroom? After a moment it came, he'd fallen rushing into his house but what had he been doing? He moved to one side then the other, couldn't see something to call the nurse, his head was thumping, he gingerly put his hand up to the bandages and touched the part above his forehead, he let out a shrill scream which attracted a passing nurse. Rudolf saw her and tried to talk, the nurse helped him to sup some water, his tongue felt dry, sickly and swollen as if it repelled the water.

- Take it easy – the nurse said, a pretty woman, early 20s, blonde, one nostril smaller than the other, something that in no way took

215

away from her charms, a credit to the nation, he garbled something but no coherent words formed and in frustration, he pointed at himself and the bed.

- You fell outside your house, you'll be fine, slight concussion – the angel in white replied.
- What was I doing? - he asked himself, somewhere just beyond his grasp was the answer, something vitally important, his tax bill, club subscription, flowers for his mother's birthday but that wasn't till March – Where was I going?
- We don't know. Going out! – She said cheerily, she smelt divine.
- But I must remember, it's of vital importance.
- You will, doing worry, I'll call the doctor – Who duly came.
- Good morning – he said cheerfully to the patient as the nurse explained the situation.
- Not to worry, temporary memory loss, sometimes it's better to forget in order to remember and something's are better forgotten – good-humouredly he continued - meanwhile relax and get some rest. I will pop in again later – he made to leave – move your head, ouch, follow the light with your eyes, slowly up and down with the jaw, how many fingers, two, yes, name, Rudolf, very good, no major damage, what did you eat yesterday for breakfast? Oats, how many fingers now - he raised his thumb stuck it out along with the index and big finger – Three - came the correct reply – Good, rest and everything will be fine. Rudolf slumped back unsatisfied.
- This is something very important – a thought occurred to him - What did you find in my pockets?
- The usual, keys, wallet, money and some film negatives, that stuff is priceless where did you get it?
- Pre-war, was saving it, where am I?
- You are in a fine hospital in central Munich in a private room, relax and rest, it did the previous person in here the world of good, he had flowers from the chancellery, from the Fuhrer - something vital came to the fore, it was there just beyond Rudolf's grasp.
- What person, ouch, the previous patient I mean – Rudolf's head gave a thump.
- Oh, I'm sure you read about him in the paper – The nurse said, Rudolf looked at them blankly and shrugged.
- I'm lost so please help - excitement made him move his hands making slices in the air, the Doctor ducking under one slicing arm said.

- Steady on there. The foreigner who fainted at the November rally, he was here in this very bed a whole week - The doctor let the information sink in slowly. And just then a light came on in Rudolf's throbbing swollen leaden head, he inhaled swiftly, involuntarily, his arms dropped.
- That man was here! – Big inhalations, fists clenched, rage appeared on his face as the devil took control.
- Yes – confirmed the Doctor looking at Rudolf with concern.
- That man in front of me raising his hand and the hand....WHY THE HOUND – Rudolf went off again arms akimbo, bouncing on the bed, his head from side to side.
- Pardon, the hound? That's a bit strong – the doctor said as his patient went into violent overdrive.
- THE INFAMOUS BRIGAAAAAAAND – Rudolf shouted at the top of his voice, as the big burly orderlies rushed in as the racket reached out.
- EXCUSE ME! There is a lady present – the doctor and the nurse looked at each other in shock, in panic, both feared for their safety as colleagues came rushing up to aid them.
- He was so sweet – tears were coming to her eyes remembering the previous patient.
- STOP RIGHT NOW you are making yourself ill – the doctor grappled with the trashing man in the bed and indicated to the nurse to hand him a sedative urgently.
- DOCTOR – he shouted - get me the police, I have a heinous crime to report DOCTOR – Rudolf now bit an arm that was restraining him - Nurse Nurrrr – Rudolf fell back limp on the bed.
- Phew, what a carry on, old man, what a carry on. Throwing those insults at Herr Malone, please don't be upset Fraulein Muller – the doctor said sweetly to the nurse as he took out the syringe he'd plunged into Rudolf's side.

And that was how dear sweet Herr Malone gained the precious hours he would need before Rudolf came out of sedation.

Prague, 7th / 8th December 1941

As they entered the hotel, exhausted after one of the most trying days of the whole itinerary, the various members of the Red Cross grouped in the foyer.

- You did very well today – the Swede said to Dagan.

- We all did, we deserve a drink of whatever they drink around here – Dagan suggested while D'Silva looked at him in such a way that the Irishman considered the Brazilian might have been right about his drinking after all.

But D'Silva approached and clapped a hand on his shoulder, this time Dagan could feel honest comradely sincerity in the gesture. After such shared trials they were brothers in arms again, Dagan knew he'd be taking his leave soon and ignoring the evidenced dangers of drinking with the good doctor put his arm around him and with unfeigned good nature said.

- We've done good, if only we could do more.

Mutual pats on the back with the Swede, it was only then that they noticed a murmur of voices in the lobby, reception staff hurriedly rushing between each other whispering, gesticulating, some smiling, some frowning, soon the murmur spread to the Germans closest to them.

'Damn them', 'Unstoppable', 'Like they did to the Russians', shouts of hoopla all in German, the senior officers started to remonstrate the chauffeurs, bodyguards and outriders.

- What's going on! – said one officer
- Respect for your uniform! – shouted another
- Remember who and what you represent with this schoolboy behaviour – the first one added.

A dozen uniformed figured snapped to attention, the nearest was directly addressed by that first official.

- You there. What is the meaning of this Corporal?
- Captain, the Americans have been attacked by the Japanese Sir, it's over the radio.
- *Ya ich seis nich.*

For a moment the gulf between enlisted and officer rank was bridged by sheer incredulity, they were mortals faced by monumental events that changed everything. One so big it has a before and an after. The moment quickly passed as military discipline reasserted itself.

- 'Attention!' - The assorted uniformed men, snapped out of their stupor.
- You are soldiers of the Reich, honour your fallen comrades and your fatherland and remember that. Heil Hitler!

- Heil Hitler! – came the resounding reply.

The word spread among the delegates rapidly, Takenaka was ecstatic as he realised his side was in the fray at last.

- The Yankee dogs will soon be muscled over to their side of the Pacific with the rising sun triumphant on the other – was how he diplomatically put it.

The Swede was cautious and the South Americans surprised. So many questions? What did this mean? How close was the coming conflagration? How much business would it bring to their countries? Would they be able to keep out of it? A sneak attack on the Americans. Dagan felt a charge of hope; this is the pivotal moment like the last time he just knew. It will take a while but once the US gets its act together its immense industrial potential and manpower will crush the Japanese whatever the odds, a surge of hope coursed through him, the US versus Japan was all over before it began. The Germans mingled, their faces flushed, excited, rabid dogs ready to savage North America.

- The emperor has ordered it, the Americans were asking for it - Takenaka said to Hoffman - Once they stopped the oil it was a sign they wanted war with Japan, now we will sweep them from the seas.
- You have heard? – Hoffman directed himself to the Swede.
- Yes, unfortunately, very regretful, more war, more deaths, more innocent victims - Neilson replied morosely.
- More work for you then. We will measure ourselves against the Americans and this time will triumph – the German replied cheerfully.
- It was the Japanese who attacked the US! – D'Silva pointed out.
- They are our allies and we stand by our allies – Hoffman proclaimed the generally held position, insane as it was.

'Christ' Dagan thought, they're seriously thinking of coming in on the side of the Japanese, didn't they learn from their recent history, last time America made all the difference.

- Italy didn't come in on Germany's side the first time or in 1939 – Dagan pointed out.
- A terrible oversight on their part and a slight on their honour they only removed in 1940 – Hoffman said po-faced.

Yeah right, perfect timing by Il Duce for the victory parades as France was on its knees and the Brits were swimming home Dagan thought.

219

- That would put you against the Soviets, the Americans and the British and that's a lot – he quite rightly pointed out.
- The British are finished, the Russians about to be, we are at the gates of Moscow remember, German scouts have been as far as the end of the metro line – Hoffman gave the armchair general's take.
- Scouts are one thing the main battle force is another – Dagan couldn't help pointing out.
- All their battleships sunk – Came another shout as news continued to come in over the radio.

Cripes, they're getting their first blow in goodo, how many battleships was that, six, seven, eight! They've ripped in, the Japanese will be all over South-Eastern Asia in no time. The Dutch East Indies and French Indochina are all but begging for it, like Spanish South America at the time when Napoleon came knocking on his Iberian neighbour's door. The Ultramar quickly falls apart, China will have even more Japanese hordes over it and the British won't be able to do much about Hong Kong. India's a long way away though. Dagan remembered Easter Sunday, revolutions in Russia, the day of the truce, the treaty, Collins being shot, the roaring 20s and the crash. Again today in some place called Pearl you heard the thundering gallop of history with a capital H running right over you.

- This is terrible – the Swede spoke in his ear – another outbreak of fearsomely armed nations fighting each other.
- Doesn't look good I agree, America was very isolationist but they went and attacked her without warning the idiots – Dagan whispered in case Takenaka overheard.
- From what we hear on the radio the Japanese, no friend of the Red Cross I can tell you God help any man who falls into their hands have all but wiped out the US fleet. Surely the war is over before it starts? – Neilson was terrified at the thought.
- The Japanese are finished, they're going to be plastered, steamrollered, squatted, smashed, they just don't know it yet, the might as well give up now – Dagan acquainted him with the facts as he saw it.
- Surely you're joking, they have just won a mighty battle – the Swede couldn't give credence to what he was being told.
- The worst thing they could have done, they have just seriously hacked off the Americans who will now do everything they can to utterly defeat the Japanese; it's going to be colossal and the most terrible merciless struggle imaginable without quarter on either side. Sure the Japs are going to make hay while the sun shines

and they'll set up themselves in Southeast Asia but the Americans will come at them with everything again and again and again. They will never forgive this attack until they have crushed the life out of the enemy. You cannot imagine the Americans once they are railed up, this is going to be brutal but the outcome is already decided. Hirohito is going to swing from his palace rafters, he and his whole government and the remaining lot will have to pick themselves up from the rubble and ashes and rebuild.

- You seem remarkably sure of this – the Swede was taken aback by Dagan's utter belief.
- I'm telling you now that the Japanese don't know what they have started and are as good as dead and if the Germans take sides they are finished as well. The world and especially Europe just got the big break they'd been waiting for – Dagan gave him his read on the future.
- I hope the Americans don't come in against Germany for your sake – Neilson's turn to say something surprising.
- Why should I be concerned?
- Just pointing out the obvious. You'll be arrested and retained – Dagan looked at him quizzically - you're travelling on an American passport? – such was Dagan's and everyone's surprise and commotion at the earth shattering news he'd forgot clean forgot the passport angle, he was as Irish as any Irishman on the dewy isle but he'd come here on his US passport.
- Herr Malone this had been a big shock and we are still adjusting, Japan is our ally and we could be very soon at war with the States. You are travelling on an American passport, is that not so? - Hoffman came over with the same idea in his head.
- Funny you should mention it, I just became Irish again, I would like to contact the Irish embassy in Berlin, they will furnish me with new papers – Dagan blindsides while Hoffman just looked at him.
- You can't just change your nationality like a raincoat.
- Tell that to the Sudetes, you just watch me, the US passport was just for business purposes, the Irish authorities will be delighted to help me out – Dagan doubted that but he needed to buy time - The US and Germany are friends of peace and friends of each other.
- Today for sure buddy as you say in your movies.
- Movies! What the feck! I'm Irish remember we don't make many movies in Ireland. 'Man of Aran' was the last.

- Your Irish-American movies then and as of today the US and Germany are friends, tomorrow well, if I was a betting man the odds are long ones my friend – Hoffman said to Dagan sadly.

Malone had a sinking feeling, he sensed the tide turning against him, if he was lifted now he'd spend the rest of the conflict interned, not something he relished but worse ways to spend a war, he'd be safe but as he'd seen in the POW camps he'd be cold, hungry, flea-ridden and celibate to boot. His mojo already shrieked out at the thought of that but he mentally started planning for the worst; the positives, improve his German and his French, Russian maybe, exercise, clean-up his system, a prolonged stretch off the booze, no bad thing and write, he was dying to write, he'd so much to tell, seen so many things, met so many people, those known to history and other extraordinary people who'd made such a difference to him and the events of the tumultuous century, aristocrats, diplomats, smugglers, jugglers, mathematicians revolutionaries, sportsmen and sportswomen, actors and beggars, priests and shamans. He'd write it in heavy code, a lot of people still in very powerful positions wouldn't like the portraits he'd paint, starting with the biggest of them all, the red Czar. Even the American Czar had some secrets that would take some of the tarnish of his reputation as a great leader. Sit out the war, sounds idyllic, me and my memories and my novel, in hibernation many a year from now nought but a dusty set of folios in a drawer, a testament to a languishing dream, sum up the first 25 years of Irish history of this century in a sweeping broad novel. He'd do it one day and this could be the necessary peace of mind he needed to get it done, a burst of creativity amidst the barbed wire fences. That and escape attempts and language studies. He'd be a busy man.

Sounds great except *dummkopf*, he was an espionage agent and sooner rather than later his cover was going to be blown. The Germans won't even have to go looking having him already in custody! Best plan stay free. There were too many loose ends and the laws of probabilities meant one or more of those loose ends would unravel.

Back in the hotel, the uniformed and non-uniformed were fired up by the great event and what would lead from the attack in Hawaii, unbelievable suffering and terrible warfare- The Germans and our Japanese openly elated, the neutrals appalled, they wanted to stay neutral and this latest twist made it much more dangerous. Those opposed to the triple alliance or under their boot, like the Czechs were hopeful but covertly so. This was America, great huge mighty America, for decades the destination of waves of immigrants, a new land that gave new chances, free and dynamic, above the petty squabbles of old Europe of which it had been aloof and uninterested but would be implacable and unswerving to the end once joined. Half of Europe was cheering. The end had begun. Hitler would be defeated because he faced endless Russians hordes and endless American resources.

People were drifting off to bed, the long dramatic day had left them worn out. Not before the final jaw-dropping piece of news came over the waves, the radio announced that the Fuhrer would address the nation shortly. That could only mean one thing he was told, Germany would declare war on the US soon afterwards. Germany would honour her obligations and stand by her allies.

- Enjoy tonight Herr Malone, who knows what tomorrow will bring – Hoffman called to him as Dagan said his goodnights and went up to his room, the lift door closed and Dagan signed with relief, D'Silva and he exchanged pleasantries.
- You will be detained after Hitler had done his madness and launches Germany into a struggle it can't possibly win –D'Silva's parting shot.
- Will the Red Cross do anything to help me?
- Kick up a fuss, hammer on some tables, call them names, this is serious but if you are Americans there is nothing we can do, we have to be completely neutral – he informed Dagan.
- Like the German Red Cross packed full of Nazis – Dagan said this in a low voice as the floor guard was lurking at a short distance away, 'protecting them' - Is there a lot of anti-Red Cross sentiment - Dagan had ventured to his bemused hosts. Everyone knew the reason, to stop them from wandering around and finding out the truth rather than the adulterated version of it. They were exposed to what Germany wanted them to see.
- This is not my problem, the Red Cross cannot interfere, we are dependent on the goodwill of the member nations – D'Silva was resigned to the current set up.
- So no 7th cavalry from your direction then.
- I don't understand we don't have any leverage; we are a non-violent organization dedicated to the welfare and safeguarding of POWs, nothing more.
- I'm not even American – lamented Dagan feeling sorry for himself.
- You English speakers all sound alike to me – that put Dagan in his place.
- Goodnight – Dagan said – hope to be here in the morning!

- Good night to you and I hope to see you in the morning too – D'Silva smiled.
- You're such a comedian - Dagan finished on a dry laugh, turned and went into his room. He never saw D'Silva again.

Down in the lobby, the Germans remained talking among themselves but gradually the back-slapping high spirits died down, more drinks were ordered, more female Czech waitress's were pinched. The talk turned to military analysis, strategy and the strengths and weaknesses of both the USA and Japan.

- China will be taken over completely – said one junior officer.
- Japan said China was finished years ago, they still haven't taken a third, it's so huge – Interjected one.
- So is Russia but we just keep pushing and Moscow is next – disagreed his fellow.
- The Dutch East Indies then Australia – a third pointed out.
- Why not Siberia and we finish Russia off together?
- They are running shy of the Russians after the 1939 clashes, I thought everything was going to happen that year, in the end just Poland and the Finns.

The debate ebbed and flowed, Japan south or north, India or Australia, Alaska or Hawaii, really knock the US for six, where were they going to land troops, on the Hawaiian islands maybe, the Americans were defenceless now. Amazing developments kept coming in. Guam attacked, then Hong Kong, East or South the events were confirming their hypothesizes, almost instantaneously. It was obvious the Japanese were vastly superior to the local opposition. They'd showed in spades they were not afraid to take on the biggest boys in the yard and win. Confident of a quick knockout the Germans turned their attention to the European zone as it was now a world war again! What could the US do, Europe was done in, the Brits refused to see that, refused to face the truth.

- And our Red Cross American. What do we do with him now? - an army colonel asked Hoffman, superior in rank but innately cautious of the black-clad raven like SS figures, this Colonel had fought in France in the 1914-18 engagement beside many valiant Jewish Germans, something he never forgot no matter how much venom was aimed at them by the government, he was even guarded with his wife who mindlessly aped the official party version word for word. Not safe even in your own bed so he spent as much time as he could at the front, what times to live in!

- Malone is Irish, not American besides he is an old friend of the fatherland, have you read his file or perhaps you don't have clearance – Hoffman smiled at that.

The Colonel didn't react to the verbal slap in the face from an insubordinate twenty years younger and two ranks below. He would love to stick this strutting peacock in the trenches between the mud, the shit and the corpses in every direction. The only bullets this one ever heard were those fired into the backs of people's necks.

- But he is travelling as a US citizen, it is our duty to place him in our custody – insisted Colonel Heiser without missing a beat he continued.
- Are you mad, we haven't received orders, we aren't at war with the US, not to mention the scandal it would cause, arresting a Red Cross member – Hoffman blinded by his ties to Malone resisted acting hastily?
- Have you ever been in battle under fire Captain Hoffman - the rank and name came slower and with emphasis – assuming you have clearance for that?
- We are here to serve the Fuhrer. Sometimes in different ways and I was a proud member of the storm furry, we battled communists' right up till January 1933.
- Street battles well then you know that if you have an enemy at your mercy you finish him off, you don't allow him to escape, else he might be back one day braining you or a comrade.
- Do you suggest we arrest him right now? – started Hoffman.
- Far be it for me to tell you how to do your job but we can always un-arrest tomorrow - the old army hand said fearlessly.
- You speak your mind.
- And you would do worse than to listen – the Colonel said looking implacable at the representative of the new German order.

A strange reversal of the roles, with the member of the state security pausing over an arrest.

- I will call that acting without orders which goes against the grain as much as not arresting people – admitted Hoffman. He reluctantly approached the reception desk, the SS thought of itself as first among all state organs and was not one to be told what its duty was by anyone except the leader.

Hoffman's colleague Muller shouted out that the Irish-American was putty in their hands, completely identified with the cause and that they should leave him for this night. Hoffman heard but decided anyway to

225

put through a call, the phone lines were chock-a-block but eventually he got through to Berlin.

- No order issued concerning the Americans. Proceed as you see fit – came the response.

- There we are. There is no need for haste – Hoffman declared.

- The soldier in the field would say differently - the weather hewn features of the elder officer brooked no reproach.

- The German state always acts within the limits of the legality - said Hoffman with an easy grin, the Colonel thought that if that was the case the Nazis wouldn't be where they are today.

- Come let's have one more drink to inter-service cooperation, the SS is inviting, drinks on us – Hoffman pronounced loudly and which was well received by those present.

With that the discussion was over, Hoffman knew he should be lifting the Irishman and he knew it wouldn't be nice. Gestapo detentions rarely were, he wanted to spare the man, one more night on a comfortable bed before the less salubrious confines of the holding cell. He liked the Irishman, a failing in a policeman he knew but people had the wrong impression of him. He was not the mindless Nazi he made out to be either but did what he did first as a policeman, his true vocation and second as a witness. What he did would be done by others so he did it and it was their duty to their fellow Germans, it could be unpleasant especially the interrogations but people could spare all that if they told the truth from the beginning, a simplification maybe but true all the same, they weren't savages they were just instruments of the state ensuring its security. And he gave testament to poor unfortunates in their end. They would not be forgotten. The group sat down again in the foyer, the Colonel wanted to leave being late enough but an invitation was an invitation and it would be churlish and unwise to refuse. Barely had they settled into savouring the fresh round of drinks when there was a call for Hoffman or any representative of the Red Cross security detail.

Hoffman got up and took the phone.

- Can't it wait till the morning? What! A cable from the Washington embassy! Aren't they busy burning important documents? - Hoffman said in an aside to the listening audience who dutifully laughed imagining the discomfort and anxiety of the German diplomatic staff over the pond – Go ahead. The substituted

American of the Red Cross, we have him at last! What of him? – a pause while Hoffman listened - He was what? An underage girl, well unpalatable to say the least but what does that have to do with us? The Red Cross should choose its representatives with more care, no wonder he didn't come, he was in jail and no wonder the American Red Cross didn't tell us the real reason. What degenerates, the Japanese will be in Washington in no time – Hoffman stopped talking as the voice on the other line spelt out more - ....What?...Hold on he said he was innocent, they all say that believe me.....How again? A camera, photos....he was filmed!

The details filled Hoffman's ear, men in dark suits, federal agencies, hideaways, incommunicado, charges dropped for cooperation, in exchange recommend a certain person, reference letters. The more details that came down the line the longer Hoffman's face became. This sting carried out sounded a bit like what some colleagues had done in certain cases with high ranking German army officers who were less than enamoured with the regime, who were not totally under the iron control of the party, who did not bow to its dictates. These loose dangerous canons had been subject to similar staged incidents of a honey favoured nature whose subsequent pictorial evidence had left the mortified officers no choice but to move aside and leave their posts, which were then conveniently filled by more acquiescent generals. The modus operandi of the Americans was thus all the more creditable. Hoffman's expression became clouded, his eyebrows knotted, he slapped the counter as he realized he'd been a damn fool. Malone was a witness as well but to what, what did he come for. A camp tour hardly likely, they were in the public domain.

- Enough - the Captain's composure disappeared completely - Sergeant! - He shouted at the security detail – Sergeant! - Again as the Sergeant came running.

His Sergeant had been a bookseller in the '20s, some of his best clients had been Jews, then the 1929 crash and people stopped buying books except the Jews, enough evidence for him to believe the conspiracies banded about. Then his profession became yet more endangered, being burnt not bought. He'd decided to join the SS which he saw as an expanding business with a future, he loved the uniform, the respect in people's eyes and especially in those of the women. His reservations at book burning had been assuaged by the fervour of the crowd pressing the books into his hands, young starry-eyed maidens eager to please and integrate with the new forces in accession. He enjoyed it all and the job was not difficult, people did the work for you themselves, compliance was now natural among the population and were all too busy with the cult of the body to be detained by the dangerous libidinous demands of the mind. The Captain he didn't much care for, he thought him too cerebral and eclectic but he respected him as a good policeman and an excellent national socialist.

- Sergeant, take two men and accompany me to - he turned to the receptionist – what is the room number of the Irish-American Red Cross member?
- 504 sir - said the receptionist wide-eyed, preoccupied by the ominous events unfolding in front of his tired eyes, it was now past two in the morning and he was praying not to be involved.
- To 504 now!
- Block the front and back entrances Sir?
- Of course! Do I need to spell every God damn thing out to you?

The sergeant issued orders to the units within his reach but as they were all not SS some remained rooted to the spot, a second blast from the sergeant got them moving. Arms were procured, readied, boots stamped, legs started to march.

- Area secure sir - the sergeant reported back.
- Good, let's go, you with one man up the stairs and I'll take another with me in the lift.

Officers ride soldiers march luckily it was only the 5th floor thought the sergeant, just then the phone rang, the receptionist at the desk answered it, listened, his face fell as his prayers went unanswered, he then timidly asked Hoffman to come to the phone who naturally distracted by the task at hand did a double-take and exploded.

- I have more important things to be doing than babbling – he said.
- But please – begged the receptionist after passing on the message and receiving the reply auditable at ten feet - Please sir - the pitiful request ignored by the visibly annoyed Hoffman who stepped in the lift followed by his escorts.
- Whoever it is, tell them to wait or take a message or to go to hell on a high horse as the Americans would say.
- But sir it is the office of Reich Fuhrer Himmler waiting on the line, I can't give them that message.

Hoffman's hand came shooting out of the closing lift, the doors squealed and groaned and there began a short struggle as Hoffman, the soldier and the lift fought to open and close the door. Finally, German brute strength overwhelmed Czech engineering.

- Fool! Why didn't you make that clear from the start – flustered Hoffman grabbed the handset - Captain Hoffman at your service, Heil Hitler – A short pause – Yes of course please put the Reichs Marshall on the line - Sweat broke out on his forehead, the heat of the lobby, the heavy clothes, the rich food, several drinks, the discovery of an imposter and now a call from the RM himself at 2 am. His detention of the American and possible spy could wait five minutes, sweat now broke out on his back as he suddenly realized with dead certainty that the call from Berlin and the American Irishman were linked. Policeman's intuition.
- Yes, Sir yes he is in the hotel, yes we will act on those instructions and detain him. Yes, he will not get away, as a matter of fact, we were proceeding to arrest him when I received your call, no I don't want you Sir to go to hell on any type of horse, it is a vulgar American expression, Sir.

Hoffman grimaced as Himmler's views of vulgar US expressions were made clear. After the tirade, Hoffman asked what the American was being taken into custody for. Expecting to hear something along the line of 'being an American' or 'being a possible impostor' his jaw dropped when he was told the real reason, he was ordered to secure the area while reinforcements arrived. Two brigades for one man?

- Of course, how is it possible! - He gasped and floundered not believing his ears, his career nay his very life were in jeopardy - Of course, I believe you sir - Hoffman couldn't take in what he had heard, the phone went dead but not before a final chilling warning from the RM telling him not fail in this, the Fuhrer himself was anxious to have this man questioned and to the Fuhrer, he would be answerable.

After the call Hoffman just stood a brief moment, three seconds at most, it seemed longer to him and everyone in the immediate surroundings, the sergeant coughed politely, Hoffman reacted.

- Infamy! Traitor! Scandal! - he shouted - lock down the hotel, everybody on alert, nobody in or out - The veteran colonel was visibly shocked by the outburst of emotion - He'll pay dearly he will scream for his mother, we'll be piteous - Hoffman shouted - Remember this day, a great service is being rendered to the Fuhrer and the Reich, we will arrest the imposter.
- On what charges?

- Imposter, American, spy. Yes, all of those because he is all of those, but he will also be charged with attempting to assassinate the Fuhrer.

Like Hoffman they couldn't believe it as he told them all that Himmler had seen the evidence, Malone had smuggled a specialist firearm into the beer hall meeting in Munich, had pointed it at Hitler but had been unable to fire due to a high fever incapacitating him. They had photos that proved this beyond doubt.

- This is a dangerous man. All men and officers to have weapons ready and to hand - Hoffman upholstered and unclipped his sidearm without drawing it out - No one to leave the building. Colonel may I call on your experience and beg you to take charge in the lobby while we apprehend the assassin.

The Colonel like all the Germans and Czechs present was trying to picture a Europe or a Germany without Hitler but he snapped into his training and knew exactly what to do, he insisted on accompanying the SS officer, not for the glory mind but to ensure this greenhorn didn't let the suspect escape.

- Your name Sir – Hoffman asked still not himself.
- Colonel Heiser at your service and your side, my aide is perfectly competent to take over the lobby and I will go with you upstairs – Heiser said in his field command voice and Hoffman about to protest but the Colonel drew himself up and using his moral and physical superiority exclaimed - This man is a great danger to the nation and must be tackled immediately with maximum force - and he started for the lift leaving Hoffman no other option but to follow suit with the sergeant and two troopers. As the lift rose he and Heiser worked out a plan.
- We can ask the guard on the floor if he has seen anything suspicious – Hoffman thought like a policeman on a case.
- And he will be a further help in case the suspect is armed and or resists arrest – The Colonel like a soldier attacking a fortified position.
- True! I've seen it take five or six big men just to subdue one scrawny communist; it's amazing the strength they can show – Hoffman saw Heiser wince at the comparison.

The lift arrived on the floor and they silently took in the deserted passageway as ominously the chair of the watchman was empty.

- Where is the fellow, should never leave his post, he can piss in a bottle if he has too. We'll see him severely reprimanded – Hoffman hissed.

The Colonel however tensed and so did his men; he drew out his firearm and put his finger to his lips. Hoffman took note, it seems a reprimand wasn't going to be needed; they approached the door of the room and positioned themselves, Colonel gestured to one trooper to try the door handle, it didn't give, the Colonel nodded and the burly aide burst through followed by the Colonel, Hoffman and the two soldiers.

- Get up! Get up! You are under arrest for....! – Hoffman shouted and stopped.

The light was on as the group stood agog in the middle of the room, the entire space was uprooted and thrown around, bedclothes lay strewn along with personal items, the telephone cord pulled from the wall, side table smashed, the broken back of an upturned chair, feather down littered the room like a dusting of snow, all the signs of a violent struggle evident everywhere as the Germans stared around.

- Check the bathroom - said Hoffman finally.
- God alive what's going on here? - It was D'Silva entering through the open door - What have you done? - He said in a stunned voice as he looked around at the ruined state of the room.
- Sir! - A shout from the bathroom.
- You are not permitted here D'Silva – Hoffman ordered the Brazilian to return to his room at once.

By now the doorway was blocked by the curious and the sleepy awoken by the disturbance. Hoffman made his way to the bathroom followed by D'Silva protesting extensively.

- This is a violation of the norms and protocols you cannot do this – said the indignant South American - We have diplomatic status.
- You see that - Hoffman half-listening pointed to the lifeless figure of the guard, bareheaded, eyes open, thrown in the bath and partially covered by the shower curtain - this is a violation of all the so-called norms and protocols – D'Silva's shocked expression, the slack open mouth was in curious parallel to the deceased man's- How was it nobody heard anything? – Hoffman asked.
- I heard a bump but didn't think anything of it – D'Silva said - I am a doctor let me see if I can do anything - he pleaded.
- Little in my opinion but go ahead and try – the Colonel said.

- You - Hoffman shouted at a figure behind, a member of staff with the master key cowering close to the remaining Red Cross delegates - Yes you yes - Hoffman signalled at the apprehensive Czech - who is occupying the rooms on both sides?
- Empty and being painted on one side, lift shaft on the other – the man managed to say.
- That would explain why nobody heard enough to be disturbed, secure the room. Everybody out this is a crime scene – Hoffman said looking at the corpse and thinking.

Eider was his name a big man who dwarfed the bath he had been ignominiously dumped in. Hoffman thought of the titanic struggle and the hero's death of the trooper, more people than Malone had been involved; Eider had five or six centimetres on the Irishman.

- I want the hotel searched high and low. Nobody in or out. SS reinforcements on their way. And we are going to need lots of people the whole building has to be searched from the basement to the roof - Hoffman turned to D'Silva who was coming out of the bathroom - The body is cold, estimates of time of death?
- That would be helping an official German investigation – D'Silva said without much zeal.
- Of a German killed protecting your Red Cross team and who was also almost certainly killed by one of them – the stone was chilling – you were most friendly with this Malone, we could bring you in for questioning.
- I wouldn't be overstepping my remit, in that case, were I to say, to no one in particular mind but overheard by you that my provisional estimates would indicate death occurred 2 hours ago plus or minus 15 minutes – D'Silva knew he'd better cooperate, he had been Malone's closest colleague as Hoffman had pointed out.
- Damn! That means he and his accomplices have a good head start, search the hotel anyway, question everyone, somebody helped him, I'm sure some he is linked to the resistance or British secret service. Call Prague HQ, order roadblocks on all bridges and exits from the city in case he's being spirited outside the centre.

Hoffman stood in the centre of the shambles and asked himself 'Where are you now Irishman? You fooled us all but you are now my quarry and even if you run far and fast I won't stop till I have you. I'll move mountains to do it, the hounds are after you and when we find you we'll rip you apart'. Blind rage receded and cool analytical calculation took over. 'No one had ever escaped me; to find you first I need to know what you are up to. There is more to this than meets the eye. Look at the big picture and the detail at the same time', Hoffman's mind raced over different possible motives, why would the British use an organization like the Red Cross, so highly considered by both sides, why put that in risk and all the benefits it bestows on their POWs. What if the Germany now decided to cancel all Red Cross visits, stop the work of the German Red Cross, stop the exchanges of children, of some POW's even.

Why do that? It is a big risk obviously, to kill the Fuhrer yes and Malone got away with the attempt and it was blind bad luck for him that a photograph turned up that clearly showed the gun barrel. Why didn't he run as fast as he could then? Because he's a very cool customer or because it wasn't his primary mission. The gun was not found, where did it go? Were more of the Red Cross members involved? Meeting Hitler had been a last-minute switch of schedules and it was to attend the meeting not meet him. They couldn't have known it would happen. There had been other attempts at the beer hall on previous occasions and so the whole building and everyone going in had been thoroughly searched. But not enough it seems. A severe reprimand was due the men assigned to search that night.

The policeman in him switched back to mulling over the factors and possible solutions. He loved tracking fugitives, communists, Jews, dissenters anyone tainted with the flag of anti-Nazism or non-Aryanism. Normally the chase doesn't last long but this was certain to be much more difficult more challenging and more exciting. The low buzzing noise was still there and getting louder, what was it? His mind was working on the problems at hand so he could focus on the first steps, he was certain there were people among the staff who know something. They'd start straight away by questioning the receptionist, here beside him and quaking with fear. The Red Cross grouping were another matter, he doubted they were involved but they could have helped inadvertently.

Then two simultaneous events crystallized into one and general panic broke out. Just as the thought came crashing into his head, that noise could only be one thing but this far into central Europe? Aircraft? A raid? That thought dropped into his head just as the air raid sirens went off. He couldn't believe it! People started crashing out the door.

- Stop! Two guards here. You and you stay by this man, he was a brave comrade – Hoffman stopped the panic.

233

- The dead don't complain – objected the Colonel - It is the living you have to take care of.
- It's also a crime scene, everyone else can go to the shelters – Hoffman countered, as a policeman, he was more in control of the situation, a crime scene.
- Have you heard any explosions? – Heiser pointed out.
- No, and that is odd, as odd as the raid.
- It is and that's why I'm not going, that is no more than a dozen or so aircraft at high altitude and going in the other direction, you'd be very unlucky to be hit by 12 aircraft in a city the size of Prague – Heiser was also at home in his natural habitat, the combat milieu - What the devil are the British up to because they're British aircraft, where the hell have they sprung from they're a thousand miles from any British airbase?

As if to validate Heiser's argument the flak guns which had only started now stopped firing, the droning noise of the aircraft started to recede and the sirens gave the all-clear.

- They were using Prague as a marker, the cathedral on the hill is a glaring landmark even at night and tonight there is a near full moon, they're heading west, the Skoda engineering plant.
- Away from us is our only concern now we can get back to work – Hoffman summed up.
- The raid is a footnote in this story here, a mere distraction – the Colonel said as he looked at Hoffman pacing around the room for whom the word distraction set in place the half-formed ideas in his head
- Are you sure that it isn't about our work, think about it, two such disparate events occur within the space of a few minutes, a spy assassin imposter take your pick appears just as he disappears, pretty unusual in any policeman's life even if the two pfennig pulp novels tell a different story. Then something even stranger happens, a squadron of British bombers wanders along as if they had got lost on the way to Cologne but here over the very same city Prague hundreds of miles further inland than any other raid so far.
- You think they are linked. How, please? - The Colonel didn't believe in the randomness of everyday life either.
- I don't think they are linked, I KNOW they are linked, it seems so blatantly obvious – Hoffman said it shaking his head in amazement at the clarity of it all.
- And suppose you are right, which I don't for the moment as it's a big shot in the dark, then the fundamental question now is where

the bombers are going to? – Heiser went connecting the dots; Hoffman looked at him and thought it must be like this to have a Watson.

- Eureka! Find out and you will almost certainly find where the renegades are heading now I'm sure.

- This guy strikes me as a very smart operator who managed to integrate himself in the group, travels halfway across Europe without raising suspicion from the most untrusting organization in this day and age. Your own! Put all the roadblocks you like but you won't find anything - the Colonel nodded at Hoffman who returned the nod.

- Although we still had to clear his background it was more pro forma that actively trying to catch him out. Indeed far from being suspect, we had even begun to harbour hopes of him collaborating with us when he returned to the US – Hoffman confirmed the scale of the wool pulling.

- As I say a real charmer, damn it, he even tried a pop shot at the Fuhrer, what balls, and nobody even noticed till a photo turned up a month later. This guy is clever and not above physical violence - an involuntary glance to the corpse in the bath being moved at that moment.

- Speaks the language? – Hoffman asked his Sergeant to start building a picture.

- Seems so sir, one of the staff heard him talking to a member of staff, a new guy he didn't recognize and said they were speaking in Czech – answered the Sergeant who had been busy taking statements as he knew Hoffman would ask him to do so anyway.

- When the hell was this? – Hoffman's gratitude at his Sergeants initiative conspicuously lacking

- Earlier this morning before the departure for the day's activities Sir.

- And did this person overhear any else of the conversation? – Hoffman could scarcely believe he had not been informed of this exchange.

- Wait and they will tell you themselves - the Sergeant gestured and one of his troopers brought forward a rake thin badly shaven crooked man in a loose shabby suit - This is him, the night porter, says he saw them early this morning in the stairwell. He thought it odd as staff and Red Cross members don't talk or have reason to.

- So you are the porter. What did you hear? – Hoffman said.

He spoke in his most direct manner and the porter looked around and leaned forward in a time-honoured method of integration. A born informer Hoffman thought, surely one already. The man nodded to confirm who he was and then an inconveniently long pause. Was he being played upon? It seemed the man was drawing it out like he was putting on a show. Rather than recoil with terror the night porter, as sure of himself as any Czech Hoffman had come into contact with, started to reply in a slow methodical way, an established source already for sure.

- They said tonight was the night and that they would like the cover of darkness and that was all sir, very sorry, they heard me behind them, stopped talking and moved off. I even felt a bit threatened, the Czech fellow gave me a terrible stare.
- Is that it! At least describe the Czech – Hoffman said disappointedly.
- The man was above medium height, taller than the Irishman, not young and not old, like the Irishman, he was fair-haired and not fat nor thin. He moved very quickly and his waiter's suit was too small for him.
- Like most Czechs then; we might as well look out for everybody! – Hoffman drew himself up as his voice rose but here the Colonel moved in. He placed a friendly hand on the shoulder of the night porter and said.
- Thank you, very kind of you, you have been a great help, we will not forget that let me assure you – Heiser interrupted.

The night porter looked up at the severe ascetic face of the tall officer with wonder and awe. Here was a proper example of German true blood; the porter gave a swift small crooked salute.

- Underground sewers sir is what the Czech said he had, underground sewers.
- Very good you can go now – the porters eyes glistened as he turned and left.
- What did he tell us? Nothing! Underground sewers, what rubbish, he could just have said Autocar or on bike or by foot. How they move tells us nothing – Heiser looked paternally at Hoffman while shaking his head.
- He told us there is a conspiracy, confirmed what you suspected that the resistance is involved, that the resistance can walk in here without anyone batting an eyelid, he told us that this spy of yours has been in contact with Czech resistance, he told us there are two principal routes. Information perhaps we never had and

perhaps are useful across the whole occupied Europe if the Brits have anything to do with it. He will also be able to sit with an artist to reconstruct the appearance of this contact, male, stocky and of medium age. It will flesh out the details incredibly.

- The last of the kings may be, we know this Vaclav likes to taunt us disguised like Sherlock Holmes, perhaps he came to visit again – Hoffman said referring to the legendary Czech resistance triumvirate of which two had been eliminated
- That's not bad and he'll also tell us all we need to know about the rest of the staff. As you saw with a few kinds words he'll be willing to die for us.

The body of Elber was removed and the ex-bookselling sergeant turned book burner approached again and overheard the convincing rotund declaration from Heiser. Amen he thought it made perfect sense, he wisely kept his counsel and turned to his SS superior, and 'now you're on a spot' he thought as Hoffman reacted quite badly to Heiser's critique

- Quite the detective aren't we! – He said huffily.

Grand Prague Hotel earlier that evening

Dagan Malone, spy, imposter, thwarted assassin, and ingrate guest of the nation found himself clawing in the mud accompanied by two burly members of the Czech resistance. Both taciturn and serious they spoke only when they had to and even then mostly in grunts, pushes, shoves and gestures if that could suffice. They smelled of sweat and cheap tobacco, their breath of hard liquor, signs of hard honest work, Dagan didn't mind it at all, he'd been around polished uniformed mannequins long enough, heartless and ruthless they were while professing to be civilized at the same time as espousing half-baked theories of special evolution to enact the cruellest of regimes. Give me a decent hard-working brakeman, brickie or labourer. Straight forward hard jobs done well and survived then celebrated with a shot of something strong and starting the same way the next day, another shot and all over again. And such a grinding life didn't preclude the finer points, he heard one of them humming a tune he found familiar, sounded like one of Janacek's pre-war symphonies, Czechoslovakia's glorious days of freedom and cultural vibrancy before it had been snuffed out by rabid neighbours and fair-weather friends. A bird hooted out in the night, Dagan's musical ear was in, to him it sounded like a bird but slightly off-pitch, his companion who'd been humming Janacek in the sewage tunnel tensed. Dagan smelt right royally, a fact that helped him identify even closer with his fellow working man. Footsteps edged closer in the dark. As they approached they could feel the tension in the air ratchet up, it could and should be friends coming out of the trees into the copse but they could have been betrayed, they could be surrounded trapped and doomed. Cheery thoughts.

Betrayals were plenty as ordinary Czechs collaborated to survive so the life of a resistance fighter was short and generally ended in torture and death. Dagan had spent enough time in similar situations and had been lucky but he'd had some close shaves, and more than once had been saved by seeming miraculous intervention, he still could see the vivid disappointment of the British officer who after surrounding them in the hideout in the Tipperary hills had been obliged to let the flying column march right past them because the truce went into force the night before. That sort of pure chance was close to divine intervention.

From somewhere in front in the forest a figure in a flat cap poked through the branches sporting a short carbine last seen repelling the Tsar's troops in Galicia poked through the branches. The tension relaxed palpably. Friends and comrades saluted quietly. Dagan had escaped and was in safe hands after the long dark hours. He quietly exhaled with disbelief as he thought of the night's events and the things he had done but with what choice? In the end, circumstances had decried the outcome such as the unpleasant proceedings in the hotel hours earlier but which now seemed days ago so much had happened since. It has all started as the doors had shut on the lift, in his jacket another message he knew because the waiter had the button of the jacket open and no gloves, left-handed quite a trick to pass off. Dagan stopped the lift two floors below and walked to the stairwell, his contact was there coming from the other direction, his tray in one hand.

- London says everything is in place for tonight so we must move - he said in shaky but correct English without preamble, hesitation or pause. Confident chap.
- Perfect timing because my passport is now a major liability. What about the guard on the floor? – Dagan asked.
- Do you have to go to your room? Just come now – Some urgency audible in the man's voice, no wonder with a lobby full of Nazis.
- They are expecting me to arrive at the room and I haven't got my toothbrush – Dagan said giddily.

- Where you are going no toothpaste so no toothbrush needed - For something so deadly serious they both cracked grins and each knew they would get along.
- If I don't show the guard will alert reception, we'll lose any time advantage and the place is crawling with Germans, we'll never shoot our way out – Dagan turned serious.
- So?
- So I have to go up first and the guard has to be neutralized – Dagan explained.
- Okay, you go in the lift, in 5 minutes I'll knock on your door. Change into boots, waterproof ones if you have them, where we are going is very damp – the man told Dagan who groaned inwardly. Couldn't they just hail a taxi but no it's never that easy.

Just then the night porter came shambling through the hall.

- Ah, good night to you both – said the new arrival.
- This guest is lost, good night brother, you can go on your way.
- Yes yes - said the older man showing no great signs of moving on - Have you worked here long, I thought I knew everyone.
- And so did I and I think it is the first time to see you as well. Now vyčistit – the "waiter" added in coarse Czech. Piss off.
- God be with you – the face of porter paled at the verbal blow.

Dagan went off to the stairs as the night porter ventured – Lift is there all the Red Cross people are two floors up?

- I like the stairs its good exercise – Dagan told him.
- Exercise? - came the incredulous reply.
- Yes to help digest these big heavy meals they give us, Czech food is very wholesome and filling.
- Ah, that is true – the night porter said finally moving off. To him, that made more sense than the fanciful notion of exercising, for a person who worked long and hard physically all his life the thought of doing more in your free time was a perverse occidental notion or even worse. Stretching the legs after dumplings and rich pork stews was altogether more reasonable in the mind's eye.

Dagan left them behind and climbed to the next floor, called the lift and rode it up, as he approached his room he nodded to Kerber from Baden Baden. Bath bath, they had joked about it. Kerber had a clean childhood his mother says, better not to have so many personal details but Dagan spoke to all and sundry in his immediate environs, always had, verbal diarrhoea.

Dagan told Kerber that he'd called up for some painkillers as he had a stunning headache.

- Not as much as the Americans - Kerber joked, he had heard the news - Does this mean war with the Americans?
- I hope not.
- Yes, it would be a shame. I like American movies, the gangsters just not the filthy black jazz musicians and that boxer with the white women, it's sick and poisonous - Kerber shook his head sadly.

Dagan just said good night, inwardly aghast once again by the hate lavished on fellow human beings for nothing more than the colour of their skin or their religion or gender or whatever. One last look around the middle European room, then to the bathroom with its big cast iron bath, he looked in the mirror and saw a face he hardly recognized, hair slicked back, small pencil moustache, short dark tie. He looked a proto blue black brown pick your shirt colour fascist. He gathered the papers he would need, put on double socks, boots, two vests, filled his coat pockets full of hard cheese and ham pilfered over the last few moorings and squirrelled away till he was out there in the middle of winter and on the run from some very bad people. The thought of persistent vengeful, despotic pursuers awoke the need for a shot of whiskey and he swallowed instinctively. Everything was ready but he decided to do one last thing while civilization was available to him. He took off his shirt, the vests and started to shave his moustache, once done he rinsed out the gel and his hair fell naturally in position. Rich sandy dark luscious Celtic curly hair his mother Grainne used to run her hand through as she baked apple and rhubarb tarts and make her stews on the huge iron stove.

- Great hair you have strong Malone hair just like your father and uncles. Doctors and engineers all, that's why you are named after the great William Dargan except the registrar couldn't read your fathers writing and you ended up as Dagan but that's a beautiful name as well.
- Stop that - he'd say as she ruffled his locks - You're messing it up - but he secretly loved the attention, the words, the maternal love.
-

Well, Mam, your boy is back - he said looking in the mirror and he's going to make you proud. A knock at the door – look away now Mam, this is going to be ugly and I don't want you seeing this.

- Who is it? – He asked continuing the charade.

- Hotel service. I have the Alka seltzer and soda water sir.
- Okay come in please – behind the Czech he could see Kerber was tense and watchful – Yes yes I rang, put it over there, I'll get you something from my jacket.

A mistake, Dagan didn't have any of the local currency, the Germans had replaced the pre-war Czech one and the dollars he'd been giving out up till now hadn't met with the same expectation as in German hotels. Kerber prevented the door from closing.

- *Was ist los* – he said and put his large frame in halfway – leave it there he barked – the waiter deliberately let the tray give way a bit which rocked and nearly fell.
- IDIOT – hissed Kerber.
- Excuse me – said the man in white-jacketed livery bent over as if lashed by the words, a typical submissive stance shown to any German. Dagan felt a melancholic wave roll over him; he knew what was coming next. His contact was as big as the German well-fed, unbroken, lithe. Kerber was beginning to sense something was awry.
- Excuse Sir I will get a cloth in the bathroom – the waiter moved.
- *Nein! Komen sie hier.*

Kerber followed the waiter to the bathroom as Dagan silently placed himself behind to close the front door lest the noise awake anyone but Kerber turned around and reacted. Cue two minutes of mayhem and bloody violence as his contact reacted too, clipping the guard with a knuckle duster as he went for Dagan. The Czech jumped on the stunned German and both staggered around the room knocking over furniture as Kerber tried to shake his assailant loose who was desperately trying to garrotte him with a thin wire-line. Dagan immediately sensed the mortal danger if Kerber got free and dived underneath the lumbering German who toppled over and crashed into the wall. All three fell in a heap but still the Czech even as the German thrashed, thumped, swayed and jerked violently as now Dagan drove his elbow into the solar plexus and the windpipe. That was enough as with a violent sag the struggle ended, Dagan turned away as his contact kept up the pressure till the twitching stopped, Dagan heard the release of breath from the resistance fighter as he now slumped down beside the dead body of the man he'd just killed.

- What's your name? – Dagan whispered as he could barely talk.
- Václav is all you need to know, the last of the three kings – Václav said proudly but wistfully as he lingered on the last words.

241

- His name was Kerber – Dagan said sadly pointing to the inert dead German who's necks deep bloody gash was horridly visible.
- He got what all Germens in my country deserve, don't be so sentimental, did you Irish give the British kisses so they'd leave? – the words fairly spat at Dagan.
- Kick and more kicks even as they kicked back – Dagan didn't need to be told how tragic war was.
- Quite! That about sums it up.
- Still, I don't like to do it or see it done. I take no pleasure in it.
- Who does? – Vaclav shrugged.

Dagan knew he was right, certain people could be very nice to him personally and viciously awful to others not to their favour. In the calm they both listened intently to see if anyone gave the alarm, the moment passed and their breathing returned to normal, no one came, no one called, not a sound could be heard, people in these difficult days knew bad things happened at night, others just 'disappeared' and keeping out of the way of such 'extrajudicial processes' was the best policy, this time the docile behaviour inducted in the population worked against the Germans. A relief at least but it didn't mean someone hadn't rung and the German cavalry was charging up the stairs.

- Put these on, goloshes to fit over your shoes – Vaclav whispered.
- Let's go - he said to Václav picking up this coat and pocketing Kerber's SACM M1935A French sidearm, booty he had helped himself to in 1940 and had proudly shown Dagan only the day before. Dagan felt better now that he was armed, he'd kill a few before he was finished. Václav took the MP semi-automatic removed the magazine and put it under his valets jacket.
- Follow me, put your collar up and your hat on, don't stop for anything, if we get separated go to the corner of Eccles church and wait in the shadows till somebody comes.

They opened the door a crack, nobody on the corridor. Václav ushered Dagan along with him to the service elevator, down the flights of stairs, through the laundry, past the rubbish bins and empty bottle crates and out into the night. They sprinted around two back streets always keeping to the shadows and with the goloshes on the shoe soles dampening any sound they glided silently and stealthy through the neighbours because if they were stopped by a patrol they'd have to shoot their way out. From shadows to doorways they rapidly progressed, the quiet night was unbroken by any sound, once a German lorry passed through and Dagan and Václav hid in a portico of a church holding their breaths, guns to hand faces towards the wall, the blinding glare of the lights like a blazing summer's day, shadows flashing across the walls as dawn led to dusk in a matter of moments, the Germans were singing as they passed and in a flash were gone leaving Lily Marlene wafting in the air. Both men signed with relief but Dagan's heart was pounding at each corner. One street had no cover and they were completely exposed as halfway along they heard running wheels on the pavement cobbles coming towards them, they tensed reaching for their firearms as around the corner came a pushcart laden with potatoes and root vegetables. An old man and young girl dressed as rural Moravians passed and didn't even pay them a blind bit of attention.

- Market time soon, they have dispensations for the curfew and a few potatoes helps too, everybody is hungry including the Germans - his guide explained once out of sight.

Finally, they stopped at a dark looming house and knocked softly, a scratch was heard and they as scratched in return the door was opened by an old man, no light escaped to the street as his guide entered and taking his arm they stepped slowly along a passageway as the door shut behind. Along they crept through another door covered by an ancient horsehair blanket as were the windows, the room hermetically sealed smelt strongly of everything, sweat, urine, boiled vegetables, rancid kerosene, furnished with a bed, fireplace, table, chairs and a partitioned off area with a sink and stove. Clothes hung everywhere, a small child's face peeped out and was shooed back by an ancient man in the corner, two indiscriminate figures curled up together in the other bed keeping each other warm in the bitterly cold. Another blanket-covered door was unlocked by the man who'd let them in and down some steep steps they went to the basement. There in the musky cold damp, mercifully free of slumbering bodies, he removed a grill from a small gap while Václav took off his coat and jacket and put his bag and gun down, the grill had an abandoned aspect, rusty and filthy, covered in the dexterous of time, insect droppings, webs and baked soot but as he pulled it back it was surprisingly well cared for, fitted to perfection and moved soundlessly.

Václav started to back himself in feet first, wiggling his way down as his legs and lower body entered easily enough, then one arm and the head disappeared. The old man gestured to Dagan and said 'Your turn' or some such phrase in Czech. Dagan still couldn't get his head around it, he'd not had many opportunities, the lingua franca now in Europe was German, Dagan lowered himself on the cold stone and reversed through the gap, within seconds his legs were being supported, down he went and their belongings quickly followed, within seconds they set off as the grate above slotted back into place. The air in the brick passage was rancid, fetid, slightly sulphurous and bone dry. Dagan dry retched, the fine foods and wine consumed that night disappeared into the culvert beside them. Once he recovered they continued, a rat ran over his shoe, then another one. He stumbled on an uneven slab, they were all uneven. He fell a couple of times, banged his knee, an elbow, both shoulders, he nearly fainted and retched again. All the while Vaclav piteously hushed and shushed him, prodded and dragged him and even carried him up partitions as Dagan was frog marched through the sewers and out of the city.

Several times they changed tunnel and all the time the rats, the stench, damp walls wet and encrusted with cooking and lighting oil, yellow and ubiquitous it would have required a crowbar to move it. The smell kind of went away or your nose got so overwhelmed that it didn't register so much but the danger was ever-present, drowning, getting lost, diseases, falling, slipping, poisoning. Germans were the least of your problems down here and it was also very claustrophobic, if Dagan had any real fear it was confined places, they often had to crawl through small subsidiary tunnels, seven Dantean circles doesn't do it justice Dagan thought as he contemplated the contrast of piping hot steamy sections with freezing cold segments.

- Sweat suffering saints why not go back fruit seller?   - Dagan economized to save energy.
- And be in a German prison come day time, be quiet. Me before in sewers never, now every day, after the war never again – and Vaclav blessed himself.

The pace was relentless. Dagan had voided his gut and felt better, to begin with but the lack of solids and nourishment began to tell and left him light-headed until the blessed marching rhythm took over, he just cornered away the unpleasant aspects and focused on keeping up, his guide knew way well and went at a clipped pace so Dagan concentrated on matching him and not being a burden. He even came to notice his surroundings a bit more, the different building periods, styles and eras. The cantilevered imperial elegance of some of the large culverts they passed through against the poor state of older black sooty sections. Time and distance passed eventually they began to climb towards a higher section and street level and came to a narrow storm drain runoff where fresh cold air made their faces tingle. The approached the grill very carefully, nothing could be heard. The grill again in apparent ruin and rusted shut but it too came away cleanly.

They were in a small clearing on the edge of the city near some wooded uplands, the bright nighttime stars and clean crisp air a tonic. Dagan stood upright with glee, took deep breaths that filled his lungs and once he had his oxygen fillip brushed himself down as best he could and looked around, Václav with a movement of his head and his finger on his lips urged him to quiet, Dagan noticed he has cocked his gun. They moved quickly and entered the wood along a trail of two hundred meters which they traversed half crouched and on alert. They came to an old battered enormously high truck guarded by a young woman, dressed in the tradition heavy floral skirt, white blouse, tight black waistcoat, head covered with a scarf but strands of exuberant deep thick auburn hair still escaped. The guide kissed this strong limbed slightly plump girl on the cheek with affection. Dagan was ushered into the open back which had its tarpaulin pulled back over the rails and it was here out in the open the Vaclav rode up behind while the girl climbed up to the towering cabin and started the engine which trundling into life in a powerful restrained manner given the state of the rest of the vehicle. Then without lights, the truck set off through the clearing in the forest, how the hell did they know which way to go, Dagan could hardly see a thing. They motored along at a lively pace and each change of direction in the forest path was indicated by Vaclav with a tap on the side of the cabin roof the truck was to turn if the curve was severe two or three taps was enough and thus they advanced along the route in total silence.

At times they had to stop suddenly, a palm fist slapped hard on the centre of the cabin roof and Dagan and Václav would jump down and remove the logs or branches that blocked the path, occasionally they jolted violently over objects they hadn't managed to make out but the pace was maintained. Václav explained that it was much safer to avoid roads if possible, where they were surrounded by the dense forest, protected, insulated. Where did they get the petrol, liquid gold in fortress Europe Dagan asked? If the Germans cared about popularity, which they didn't, then they'd go straight for the Caucasian oil fields. A round of the black stuff for every man, woman and child in Europe. Hurrah. As the signs of daybreak began a cacophony of bird song accompanied the last nocturnal pathways and forestalls clearings. Finally, they stopped in a forest glade; his guide again kissed the female driver who'd navigated them through twenty-odd kilometres of pathway in the dark aided only by vapid half-moon light and incredible night vision. Though that hardly explained it, Dagan in comparison couldn't make out where his trousers ended and his shoes began.

Silently Václav set off again as the truck took another barely perceptible path and disappeared from view. Not much of a talker. Dagan and Václav quickly moved along to the copse where they had been told to go to and find their contacts. This time they were met by a group of five men ranging in ages and social backgrounds and the tense assembly over day began to break and the sound of approaching aircraft could be heard. The partisans moved into position and Dagan in the dim pre-dawn recognised where he was, on a verge close to the remotest wall of the Ghetto town. The shelter afforded was minimal, a small break in the ground with dirt, scrub and low bushes scant protection against the 10,000lbs bombs that were about to fall nearby from 8,000 feet as the aircraft were screaming in.

Madness Dagan thought as the noise of the Rolls Royce engines got louder and louder, he'd suggested several different ways to create a diversion, all less foolhardy and dangerous to innocents asleep in their beds and themselves out in the open, who knows where those bombs will fall. The RAF and the Luftwaffe had both demonstrated that the art of precision bombing was just another example of their respective high command's mixture of canards, falsehoods, hopelessly overestimated target hits and unhealthy amounts of propaganda. It was more the inventive use of words rather than a sound military achievement. To prove Dagan's point the first of the nights 144 bombs, around baker's dozen, fell a mere 50 yards away. The noise was deafening as a blinding flash of light left them all starry-eyed, the lookout was thrown off his feet and backwards and a shower of earth rained down on them all, the man beside him swore while on the other side a third tried to cover the embarrassing stain that could be seen on the breeches of his pants. Dagan looked away, he understood but didn't sympathize, it was always a shock the first time, no one could prepare you for it and you either got to grips quickly or you fell apart. You needed to be with the first to survive and avoid the second group of unfortunates. Damn Dagan thought, if that was an indication of their shooting prowess there was going to be a lot of dead Jews.

The RAF had been given detailed plans of the whole setup of the Ghetto camp and surroundings, pinpointing the barracks, work compounds, storage, living areas and open ground, everything that could be hit with minimal danger to civilians and maximum collateral damage. By now sirens were blaring out the air raid warning, all the lights had gone out which was expected and which was the signal Kessler would have been waiting for and should now be making his way to the part of the wall furthest away from the guard posts, official buildings and the Kapos barracks, lodging of the despised Jewish collaborators and Ghetto police who did the job the Germans didn't have the manpower to do, in return Kapos enjoyed special privileges that made life in the Ghetto easier, better food, drink, women and rest time. Beggar thy neighbour at its best.

The bombs continued to fall at random over the fields, a few searchlights lit up the sky as Theresienstadt was hardly tooled up in an anti-aircraft line and one direct hit in the administration and the German garrison area in the new part of Theresienstadt to cause some fires and create distractions. Maybe Princip's cell just went up in smoke, he'd been imprisoned here after the murders of the Grand duke and his wife in Sarajevo. I just missed joining your club Dagan thought.

The whole raid had to look like a random dumping of bombs over open land but unfortunately, they needed some causalities so the Kessler's could disappear. The plan was a German or two or some Kapos. The first bomb had been a shock but also was the sign for the man beside Dagan to push the plunger down and immediately the yellow painted wall 100 yards in front exploded at one section, leaving a gaping hole in view after the debris had settled, clean with just a couple of rubble mounds of debris to clamber over.

The man began to disconnect the plunger, wires and detonator into a bag over his shoulder. Václav motioned to him and they rapidly covered the open ground, retrieving the cable from the dirt, they couldn't afford to leave and evidence and would need the cable for another day, why waste valuable sabotage equipment. Dagan and Václav guns to hand arrived at the sundered gap as surreptitiously as possible, from the other side came screams of women and children, dogs barking, guards shouting and all the time the wail of the air raid sirens. The blind terror of the innocent was heart-rendering but it was the only way. One more nasty experience to add to their collection, these days childhoods were being truncated with bewildering rapidity. Dagan and the Czechs crouched low beside the strewn rubble and waited, time passed, seconds but it felt an age, Dagan counted seventy-three heartbeats of his own. Then some scraping sounds against the other side of the wall indicated the presence of people, rocks were moved and a faint whisper was heard above the din.

- You Irish son of a bitch, where are you? – Kessler's head appeared above the remains of the wall.
- Here ready to blow your sorry Yiddish head off – Dagan replied softly as the physicist looked down.
- Still under my feet, always under my feet! - Kessler scrambled out

247

- Is Maria with you? – Dagan said worriedly, a chill came over him perhaps something had happened but Kessler ignored him as he got over and was led away crouching, in slow deliberate steps, muttering as he went while the Czech with him was hushing him along the way.
- Here I am, I'm missing my bridge club tonight – Maria's voice came quiet and businesslike from nearby.

Dagan watched as a trousered leg, long and firm if he remembered correctly came over the wall, her delicate foot shod with big boots for the tough road ahead. Next came the glimpse of a wonderful sheepskin coat swaddling the slight figure, Dagan took the outstretched hand and from the deep shadow came a fox fur collar then a stalkers hat and finally the lovely oval face of Maria under it. Gaunt and thinner yes but essentially she had hardly changed with her porcelain skin, high Slavic cheekbones, and full red lips under and lower, unusually large eyes of a penetrating deep cobalt colour. What children they would have had and could still, Dagan felt a jolt in the groin.

- Hello Maria, you look as beautiful as when I last saw you – Dagan squeezed her hand.

The steely gaze of the blazing blue eyes beheld him as he held his breath awaiting an answer which came in the form of a resounding slap to his face from the flat palm of Maria's other hand, like the sound of a low calibre gunshot, she might have been suffering from poor diet unhygienic living conditions and overwork but could still pack a punch. Dagan's face spun 90 degrees so fast his neck hurt almost as much as his face and his pride let it not be said, a deeper wound. Okay, their relationship had ended rather abruptly, had ended with Dagan upping sticks and moving on, had ended with Maria in the dark about where he'd gone, had ended with the wedding invitations printed and ready to send, had ended really badly. But he had sent his apologies, eventually, had phoned, eventually, had send flowers within days, paid for the church and the dress, he had even considered not asking for the ring back but it was a family heirloom in his mother's family over 200 years. Surely her knight to the shiny rescue deserved a better reception than this, time was a healer, after all everyone said so and years had passed.

- Maria, how are you keeping? - Dagan said to no one in particular as Maria marched off to join up with her father and the rest of the partisans - I'm here all on my own and that's hardly a good idea - Dagan said glancing over the wall to the gloom and quickly followed on. By the time he reached the group, he found a mild discussion nay argument going on in hurried whispered voices between the scientific father and daughter and the rest.

- What the blue blazes is going on? - Dagan asked.
- They don't want to go with us, they don't trust us, they say their friends are better and we are too infiltrated by collaborators - Vaclav answered.
- No Czech stopped the ghetto happening, no Czech spoke for us, they abandoned us, left us to the dogs – Maria spat out this last phrase. Dagan turned to her.
- Which friend? Please tell which friend you think you're going to? I am here to get you out of occupied Europe not into hiding if that is what you thought. It is far too dangerous for you and the people sheltering you and I so again ask 'What friends?'
- We are prepared to take our chances – Maria said defiantly.
- I don't think you are, again what friends? – Dagan insisted.
- Rosický or Procházka or Železný, all good men all good colleagues.
- All Czechs, the self-same group who are collaborators and left you to the wolves as you just said to my friends here, those risking their lives for you now. Rosický is dead, sorry that you didn't know. Železný was arrested because he was a Socialist and we don't know where he is. Procházka is an active member of the Moravian Nazi party. He now occupies your father's position and denounced you to the University rector the day after the takeover.
- Oh no! Poor Tomáš. No! Lies – shouted Maria to his face – You are a liar, now and before, you haven't changed.
- We should go – Václav took Dagan's elbow forcefully, the last of the Aircraft had passed over, the sound levels would be dropping, the sirens were still sounding but soon they would stop and that would leave burning buildings, ringing bells with the shouts and screams of the frightened and injured. Dagan could already hear guard dogs barking rapaciously. Guard dogs or strays, either way, it wasn't a good idea to stay close to a TNT'd wall.
- We're moving out – Dagan said - you are putting these people's lives at risk. Jan here has several young children and they will be forced to watch him hang if he is caught, I wouldn't want that on my conscience.
- We'll take the risk of going alone – Maria said less stridently – Lukomski - she quietly named another former colleague as the group started to move off quickly.
- Single, lives in the centre of the city, an irredeemable bachelor, you wouldn't last a week in his apartment and if you were mad enough to try if his landlady didn't shop you one of the

neighbours would – Dagan said refuting Maria and in a sangfroid voice – See those people there - he pointed at the rapidly retreating group - That is salvation, you can come with us with me to where there are no Nazis, no camps, no shootings, no random brutality, beatings, savage dogs and vicious guards or you can go back the way you just came where dying of starvation or consumption is the best option you can hope for – Dagan started after the nearly out of sight grouping he didn't look back and within seconds the two escapees followed, Kessler with an insistent 'Come on Maria' who could be heard swearing angrily in the crudest possible Czech. 'Blimey' thought Dagan 'she'd never even uttered the word damn before, seems the sweet girl has had the sweetness knocked out in lumps by the war'. The camps have hardened her, made her tougher, dehumanized her by the forced labour, hunger, cold, misery and bleak hopelessness but they were free now and the healing could begin. Without any sense of triumphalism, Dagan turned and whispered 'Thank you' in Czech, which gave Maria pause that she stopped cursing him and the world.

- I'm sorry I called you a c**t, I never used to use such language, you will think I am such a guttersnipe – she said by some sort of way of apology.
- I never knew that word in Czech, could come in useful. Come on we have to catch up – Dagan ever the pragmatist said smiling.

They set off at a good pace and they reached the wild paths of the forest as the light strengthened, the sexagenarian physicist soon started to lag but it was imperative to keep up the pace and put as distance as they could between themselves and any likely pursuers. It was unlikely as they had been careful to cover the 'prison break' with an air raid but the Germans weren't idiots and would eventually figure out someone was missing, hopefully too late as the escapees only needed a half-day to disappear.

- Kessler let me help you - Dagan took one side as Maria slipped her arm behind from the other and together they both helped the aged scholar keep up.
- I feel like I'm floating, a moon dweller, gravity, ordinary not applied to me. Exception to rule. Kessler co-efficient to be calculated. Malone offset - Maria and Dagan were practically carrying him; no wonder his feet barely touched the ground.
- Ever the theoretical physicist - Dagan grunted.
- It is my life, my vocation, ever since I was young I have wanted to know why? So many questions in life and physics gives you so

many of the answers. Why does the sunshine, why is the sky blue, the night black, where do the stars go during the day. I was a good boy but a curse to my parents, not a minute's peace from the ages of three to six then I discovered books, THEY had all the answers my parents didn't have, it was all in books, I read everything in the library. Then I wanted to write books, I saw things I knew were right and some that were wrong, I wanted to understand, to correct. I remember my poor Ompha when I repeated Galileo's falling bodies experiment, so simple, she got such a fright when the lemon and melon landed beside her from the upstairs window. Wheeeeez over we go floating floating faster faster – Kessler came back from the past to comment on the present and to cajole his porters to up their rhythm – I explained what I was doing and said sorry of course, I was a good boy but she still clipped me around the ear. Science is suffering, she didn't tell my father thankfully and later she gave me a half-crown, I think she was secretly pleased.

Such euphoria, such jubilation, Dagan got a hand free and put it to Kessler's forehead.

- Slight fever, dizzy spells, tiredness, weeping eyes, he needs rest and comfort – was Dagan's evaluation, didn't they all.
- Mere conjecture, I've never been better - Kessler was babbling, well he'd been doing that ever since they'd left the camp despite the persistent hushing and shushing from the Czech party he'd kept up a stream of gad flying pedantry totally out of keeping with the predicament they found themselves in. The rested in a glade at around 8 am. The partisans on one side, Dagan, Kessler and Maria on the other.
- Most of the time he coped very well, he was a respected leader of the community in difficult moments but sometimes it became too much and he retreated inside, babbles about events decades ago, I now know more about my grandparents, my Omphas and his childhood than I ever did before. He seeks refuge there, sometimes he talks about the imagined future, life from the perspective of a comet, a time traveller, an electron, a magnet. As if it were the laws of physics against the laws of man, rational versus the irrational – Maria spoke softly while they divided the husk of hard bread and sausage given to them by the Czech freedom fighters.
- Aren't you going to eat some? – He asked.

251

- No, I'm on a diet, all these diplomatic receptions I've been to lately, I'll give it to him, he needs it more than I do – Maria answered.
- We all need it, you are no good to us if you can't walk or help, you think your father, with the best will in the world and the best food from the Ritz will make it without your help – Maria looked at Dagan and then Kessler and took a small bite out of it.
- Seriously that's enough. You always thought I was carrying a few kilos anyway – she said slowly clewing and savouring the best taste in a long time.
- Nonsense, you need a bit to lose a bit my old Mum used to say - Dagan came chivalrously to the rescue.
- Your gallantry is noted, I might even stop having the overwhelming desire to slap your face which arises now and then. What have I been doing, waiting perhaps for my knight in shining armour? Amor, armour so close those words in Spanish and English but your gallantry is misguided although it saves the face I so badly want to see red rare with my slaps. They did not ban mirrors, everything else yes but not looking glasses. I know exactly how I look so please spare me the platitudes, it hurts more than helps – Maria said
- I heard. I was trying to make a difficult situation a bit more bearable but relay on me to be your lighting rod. Soon we'll be able to talk honestly and openly but now the important thing is to get to safety far away from here. You mentioned Spanish, a curious thing is the way in Spain they use 'guapa' or pretty all the time, to pretty girls obviously but as well to eighty year old grannies and everyone is happy, it's the well-intentioned good feeling behind it even if the 'guapa' is wrinkled, white-haired and toothless. No bad thing methinks.
- It was horrible the camp but it didn't affect me, it was just my body they had control over not my mind my spirit.

Dagan knew a cry from the pits of despair when he saw one. The mind and the body are one and whole and indivisible, both suffering or both healthy and both heal together. The body will be quick, a month's rest, some good food, some new clothes and a hairdo but the mind, the mind can't be disinfected so easily of what it's seen and heard. Still, there was hope, Kessler had gone around as an electron, very distant from the centre the theory went and Maria was young and resilient, things will become easier, more normal like but the horrors and the nightmares were your everlasting friend. Dagan still have the vision of the face of his friend shot beside him, still had the vision of mass graves, mass slaughter, fallen foes and their surprised looks as they slipped beyond. Dagan stopped himself thinking anymore and switched instead to sunny meadows and forest walks, summer regattas and lawn tennis, picnics, operas, cheili's and fine wines. He felt the cloud lifting, he thought of Maria's face after they made love, he had liked that face a lot.

- What are you smiling at? - She asked - what can you remotely find to smile about, you amaze me! – The question brought him back from that nice place to reality. He saw Maria's face as it is now and focused.
- You would be happy if you knew believe me - his soft tone mollified her.
- I want to be happy again – she added equally softly.

The five minutes rest felt like five seconds before the Czechs who hadn't even sat down began to make noises that it was time to move on. Dagan stopped massaging his calves, got up in three bone-cracking movements each accompanied a small whooh, or 'life on the open range' and he then helped Maria up. Her father presented a curious spectacle and was refusing to budge.

- Five minutes is the wrong amount of time, the body is better continuing straight on or a quarter of an hour repose, feet in the air, higher above the heart. Diminish blood supplies to overburdened areas by simultaneous application of cold presses - he had been eating with his back on the ground, his feet on a rock above him, cold hand in and out of the river applied to surface of his forehead.
- Right ready to go? – Maria asked, Kessler jumped up spritely and flexed.
- Ready when you are! – He said energetically.

He'd held them back before but not anymore, he was positively skipping along, looked younger, more dynamic, a rejuvenated Kessler chomping at the bit as the guides checked the ground to conceal signs of their passage. They kept up a clipping pace and the mood was buoyant, 'Can't last' Dagan thought after as if the Devil heard him just minutes later someone said 'Hear that'! They all stopped to listen. 'What' said Kessler, 'Schhh' said Maria with a worried look, because she along with all could faintly distinguish a distant howling. Dogs. The Czechs looked at each other alarmed, word rapidly passed between them, dogs were a shock, dogs were really bad news. Dogs were an indication of organization and chillingly the howling was coming from whence they had come. 'Move it!' Vaclav said and they picked up the pace, thirty fanatic minutes half-hoping but exhausted one and all after the effort it was obvious it had been in vain. In that time the sound had gone from being barely perceptible to fairly apparent, the far off pursuers weren't just searching blinding they were tracking the runaways.

Chapter VIII

Prague, 8th December

Hoffman stood beside Heiser now ordered everyone else out of the room except one soldier and his Sergeant.

- Stand over your fallen comrade who will be avenged – he said sternly to the trooper and then to the Sergeant - Get the cars ready, we're going follow the sound of the aircraft.

The sirens still sounded as the last of the aircraft passed out of range of the anti-aircraft batteries still firing into the skies above. 'How can they even reach Prague and where will they go now?' – Hoffman wondered to himself. The searchlights still sweeping the sky at high attitude caught barely perceived bomber undercarriages in their crisscrossing beams, soon even that fleeting sight of the enemy gave way, still, some anti-aircraft banging continued sporadically.

- What are the idiots firing at? – Hoffman was annoyed at the interruption to his thought processes.
- Combat tension it will die away presently – the Colonel added sagely – or practice, can't get many air raids on Prague.

Down in the foyer of the hotel orders were being issued rapidly. Motorized vehicles couldn't come because of the air raid Hoffman was told.

- What air raid? – Hoffman snorted ironically.
- Circulation of motorized vehicles prohibited for 20 minutes after air raid sirens have stopped. To avoid collapsing buildings, orders of the city *Gauleiter*.
- Tell the dispatcher there weren't any bombs so no fires, no damage, no falling buildings and if the vehicles aren't here in ten minutes a ton of bricks will be falling on him I promise - Hoffman spoke as he collected his thoughts - You have transport we can use – he asked the Colonel.
- What do you need cars for if you're looking for a sewer rat – Heiser was thinking of Malone's chosen escape route.
- He's long gone from the sewers, it is useful though and we will set guards on all exits from now on, pump gas in and see what vermin we catch. But for Malone it's already too late so we need

the cars to go where he's gone, dogs to follow and catch him and rope to hang him from the nearest tree.

- Dogs? – Heiser ignored the bit about rope, the SS loved a bit of rope.
- Yes, dogs – then to the Sergeant - Get me the city *Gauleiter* on the line again and tell him I want the best pack of hunting dogs he can muster and I want it quickly and that building is still hanging over his head. We're going hunting oh yes and this will lead us right to the prize fox - he flourished a garment of Dagan's from the hotel room in the air.

The phone rang. Hoffman grabbed the phone in an exultant gesture.

- That will be the *Gauleiter*. You have my dogs I hope – were his first words before he listened and his heels clicked to attention - Yes Reichsfuhrer Himmler! Please let me explain, we need the dogs to track the escape. No, he was not in the room, we found the guard dead in the bath, yes Sir dead Sir. Yes, a great pity and a true German who will be avenged. No Sir, not alone, it is conclusive Sir. A British agent – pause as Himmler spoke - Good question Sir as far as we know he was aided by Czech resistance. Yes, we are now proceeding. Dogs in the city no, it's because he is not in the city anymore. How do I know? The air raid Sir. Yes, a British air raid. In Prague yes just now. The coincidence is too great. No, we won't let the dogs get at any chickens. No Sir, I've never seen what dogs can do in a chicken coop. Prague Command and Colonel Heiser of the 9th are providing transport, the raid went north dropping bombs, yes Sir, the army is closely working with us yes, we are aware of the importance. By noon we will have further news. Heil Hitler.
- Thought it was foxes and hen coops – Heiser said to no one in particular.

Hoffman hung up, sweat could be seen on his upper eyebrows. The big cases made or break you and meant you rubbed shoulders with the heads of the SS. You became a leading figure in it with perhaps a subdivision of your own, you even came into the orbit of the Fuhrer himself. Everybody knew Hitler had a particular soft spot for the service especially after 1934 and the night of the long knives. Indeed the SS had started as the personal bodyguard of the founder of the Third Reich. Those were the rewards for success, the price of failure didn't bear dwelling on for failing to catch the individual who tried to kill Hitler and hence was the most wanted person in continental Europe. Whoever caught him however would be the most lauded man in the country. Himmler told him to work closely with the army, he could mobilize it and the entire structure of occupation to do his bidding. Hoffman looked over a Heiser, a man used to commanding large groups in battle, and thought it wouldn't be bad to have another person involved, this was that big.

- Where are your vehicles? Let's get going – he said impatiently.
- We? Where are WE going? – Heiser didn't sound too keen on the mooted plans.
- Wherever the bombers went. RF Himmler just assigned you to help me till the task is done, you were the one who insisted in taking in the Irishman so now's your chance to finish the job - Hoffman broke the news to Heiser and then turned to his Sergeant – Update on the air raid – he shouted over.
- Just coming in Sir, reports of bombs dropping twenty 20 miles north, in and around the river Elbe Sir.
- Near the Skoda works? - Heiser suggested, Hoffman didn't know or care where the River Elbe or Skoda works were but it was the obvious target he had to admit. What it all had to do with Malone was another story but Hoffman knew the dots would start to connect once he put them on the page.
- No Colonel near Theresienstadt the report states.
- Theresienstadt? - Two dots connected right there - But what would they want with Theresienstadt
- It's just a work camp with thousands of miserable dammed Jews. Who wants anything with them? They are just bakers and labourers and ex-teachers, ex-doctors, ex-councillors – Heiser said
- Yes we cleaned them out of the system years ago, the first thing we always do, purify the public services which then flowers under enlightened Aryan leadership, gone from the ministries, schools, hospitals, universities..... – Hoffman didn't care what he was saying, he was just putting dots on the page, thinking aloud, waiting for patterns to appear.
- Einstein was the first to go back in 1933 – Heiser pointed out. They had been walking to the motor cars and mounted the Army staff car - We won't stop even for roadblocks, they'd just better get out of the way damn quick because we are not stopping – Heiser informed as they mounted – Driver! Theresienstadt right now. Let's show our state security colleagues how the army does things.

'Right' Hoffman said absentmindedly as he mounted up behind Colonel Heiser. He kept thinking on about universities, institutions, research centres, Hoffman knew that even some of those despicable Jews, a cancer to be cut from the Aryan flesh, were extremely beneficial to the Reich in the short term and others had just assimilated. Hitler's chef was Jewish. Hoffman remembered a story that went around the academy, of Himmler trying to point out to him the incongruity of the situation and to let him get rid of his cook. A Jew making the meals for the head of the Reich! But Hitler just turned and said 'Aryanise him!'.

It was very much the exception though, another rare exception was Hitler's officer from his time in the trenches on the Western front, this Jewish former officer had made it known to the Fuhrer that he was being targeted and Hitter straight away left strict instructions that neither the man nor his family were to be molested by anyone at any stage or ELSE.

But most Jews suffered a different fate and were separated, even so, the firm National Socialist control exercised over Germany couldn't reproduce some of the singular skills certain Jews had. In one camp Hoffman knew a group of expert forgeries were counter-fitting Sterling banknotes; the plan was to flood England with false ones dropped by air and with any luck to destabilize the enemy's economy. Those sorts of arrangements were due to expediency and not likely to last longer than the war itself. So Hoffman thought maybe there were other overlooked talents mistakenly considered expendable that the British wanted however and would stop at no lengths to obtain. The camps were arbitrary, in them shuffled one great mass together, controlled chaos they liked to say, street cleaners and beggars (whoever saw a Jewish beggar but he was assured they did exist) were mixed in with doctors, lawyers, scientists, bankers and all those professions of influence who if left to their own devices would once more confabulate and bring under control the great nations of Europe. Only thanks to the enlightened actions, so criticized and at the same time so envied in Britain and France that the Fuhrer had taken of sweeping this miasma from their invidious position of mellifluence, had saved Germany if not Europe. Still among those legions might there be talents that the Reich could use to its benefit, talents disregarded because the rule of no exceptions except those of personal interest to the Fuhrer. Was it wise to be so broadly exclusive and take the loss of some good along with all the bad rather than let parts of the cancer remain however tiny however useful? Perhaps those abilities were sought after by sworn enemies who would stop as nothing in their aim to defeat the Reich and bring her down, she the shining light of a revived reborn western civilization.

- It's a prison break I know it! - Hoffman shouted out.

- What do you mean? He tried to shoot the Fuhrer and is now fleeing for his life because of the attack in the Pacific – this was how Heiser saw it.
- You said it yourself, eminent scholars, draftsmen, scientists, the Allies want somebody, one of those gifted individuals. Who I don't know yet but it will be easy to find out, just do a headcount to see who's missing and once you know who they want, you know what they are working on. Driver faster have the outriders clear the roads. Keller, get on the radio to HQ, have them contact Theresienstadt to close the exits and put guards on alert, any suspicious behaviour to be reported then start checking all the houses and buildings, confirm missing or dead, most of all missing. Have reports ready in 30 minutes. Thank you. Go!
- Scientists. I've always have been one more for action than books or study or academic pursuits – Heiser mused.
- Germany needs men of action now more than ever – Hoffman said placatingly.

They fell into a silence broken only by the klaxons of the outriders and cars giving warning to the traffic coming into the capital early that working morning. Hawkers, vendors, peasants, cleaners, factory workers all had to move over rapidly as they were shunted aside by impatient Germans. 'Ever thus' more than one though inwardly as they impassively did as they were told. The road was the same the Germans had used two years earlier to enter Prague without a shot being fired. Such a victory, such a triumph for National Socialism, it was a good road Heiser thought, a few more like these and we'd have been in Moscow months ago. Progress increased as the incoming traffic thinned out, half an hour later they were slamming on the brakes outside the arched entrance to the ghetto town, the portly camp commandant out of breath came running over and welcomed Hoffman and Heiser, initially addressing Heiser as the more senior and thus mistaking him for Hoffman to which the army man took offence.

- Do I look like an SS officer! – Heiser retorted.
- Well now that you mention it the jacket doesn't quite fit in with regulations – the commandant was taken aback; him being the supreme authority for 55,000 Jews and 3000 camp staff he was not used to contrary voices.
- Hoffman here but I am only a Captain – Hoffman tried to placate the situation.
- That was before. The office of Reich's Fuhrer Himmler has informed me that you have been ascended two ranks which we now both share. Let me be the first to congratulate you, the same

call also told us that all assistance needed should be proffered; we are at your disposal Colonel, completely and utterly and let the Reich's Fuhrer be in no doubt of that – the commandant was indeed the bearer of good news.

Hoffman was now a full Colonel and the entire weight and machinery of the German occupation had been placed at his disposal, it was exhilarating. Right then two more trucks came roaring up to the gate.

- Colonel Hoffman – a junior officer alighted, came bounding over and took his turn directing himself to the wrong Colonel.
- News of my good fortune has spread quickly I see – Hoffman to one side said straight off before Heiser had time to react.
- Ah! - the young man said turning around - The *Gauleiter's* compliments, his men were now unloading all eighteen German Alsatians of the Prague canine unit along with six beagles requisitioned from a volunteer, who we brought him along just in case - Here he pointed over to a scared stiff man wearing a winter coat and boots over pyjama bottoms being prodded from the back seat of the car.
- He doesn't look like he volunteered - Hoffman noted as the man pleaded in desperation at the smirking Germans.
- His attitude changed remarkably once we pointed a gun at one of the dogs, more so than at his wife – The Lieutenant remarked shaking his head.
- Tell your men to treat him with a bit more respect, he is a citizen of the new Reich after all – Hoffman corrected him to the subtleties of the present order.
- Yes Sir, I will make sure of that. May I continue Sir – the Lieutenant glossed over the new order in short order.
- Yes of course – Hoffman said impatiently.
- We also have a golden retriever, a St. Bernard who has colic, the gas smell is horrendous, I think we should leave him behind, an Irish red settler and three huskies. The huskies are a bit thin but the cold is not a problem eh - the Lieutenant chuckled at that as he finished his recount of the crack canine force assembled.
- Enough levity, we are dealing with a serious attack on the core of the Nazi vision of the future – the new Colonel decided levity was not in keeping with the turn of events and the Lieutenant bolted upright, the smile became pinched lips, the boots clacked together resoundingly.
- Of course Heil Hitler – he said, what else could he say, it was the best answer in any case at any time.

- Good work with the canine marshalling, I doubt a better more varied pack could have been put together in such a short time in the whole of Europe. Please get your men and dogs ready, we have important work for them – Heiser interrupted and the Lieutenant glowed at his well-phrased complement. Hoffman once again marvelled at his innate ability to command and vowed to learn from the more experienced leader.
- Thank you, you have a way with help - he said while the Lieutenant went about his task with the camp commandant.
- Don't mention it, I don't consider them that and that would be a good place for you to start from - Heiser replied good-humouredly as they stood to one side around a blazing brazier, their breaths in vaporous clouds giving evidence to the season of the year. As Hoffman stamped his feet he asked the camp commandant about the raid.
- They must have mistaken us for the Skoda works but even so most of the bombs went wide and in the river, perhaps they were dumping bombs because they couldn't find the factory. Only three hit the camp, one on the gym building, one more on the east part of the wall and one blew a warehouse up sky high. Very poor shooting on the whole - he said sheepishly
- Sounds like excellent shooting to me, they hit a wall, a warehouse and an empty gym so no civilian areas. How many casualties? – Heiser asked
- Why would they want to hit us? Well, the losses are amazingly light, two dogs and a Jewish night watchman that's all. The dogs will be a sad loss of course – the commandant said straight-faced.
- And who is missing then? Did anyone use the opportunity to bolt? – Hoffman pressed the commandant while ignoring the comment about the night-watchman. If that's what camp command did to a soul he'd strain to avoid any involvement with them.
- They can bolt any day they like, the gate is open for those that work outside, they just need to invent an excuse to the guard but where would they go? Most likely they would be back in here in two hours and things would be a lot worse for them, punishment is something we are serious about. No one who is punished wants to go through it again – the Commandant explained self satisfactorily.
- I'm sure you are doing an exemplary job but that hasn't answered my question. Give the zookeeper this - Hoffman passed the jacket to an NCO - Have you done a headcount or not? – He asked the Commandant turning back.

- It's a bit more complicated than that, we have a very transitory population, children and elderly people, this is a work camp, not a prison - the Commandant vacillated.
- All the more reason to keep track – Heiser countered as a camp adjutant ran over to the Commandant to report.
- Sir all present and correct – the man said eagerly.
- There as you can see we have the situation is under control - the Commandant turned to Hoffman.
- And if I may continue Sir, we expect to find the missing Jews under the rubble of the gym, the Kesslers, father and daughter, he an elder of the council which was why he was missed so quickly. Kessler held an important university post before. The council place great value on learning and not all are rabbis who know nothing beyond the Talmud – the camp adjutant finished.
- What did this great man study, history, philosophy, languages, the violin, so many 'play' the violin? – The Commandant who hadn't finished high school scoffed.
- No sir, nothing so prosaic, he was in the Physics Institute – answered the subordinate.
- Did they tell you any more about this man? – Hoffman asked sensing was on to something, a scientist could be invaluable given the right discovery.
- To me sir no but Guzman the council of elders liaison officer talked to him much more frequently.
- Bring Guzman here at once – the SS man ordered.

Hoffman still only had a half-formed idea in the head, he couldn't quite put in together in a way that made sense. He knew he was close though, physicists were in great demand by the Reich so why hadn't this one been put to use on some project. Hitler's wonder weapons were in the nascent phase of design and Hoffman instinctively scented an opportunity. The Nazi's had been great opportunists to date and had expertly ridden their luck through a baker's dozen of conquered countries but now the luck was starting to thin out and it seems their opponents were the ones getting better at searching out opportunities. Physics. He hated it at school, all weights and pendulums, actions and reactions, planetary motion, Hoffman preferred chemistry, smellier and thus earthier, liable to go boom which is what every boy really liked. Physics was off worldly cold dark bodies, infinitely distant stars, immense unimaginable planetary forces or infinitely small 'ons', protons, electrons and all made up of space! But now physics was in fashion and being harnessed by his party's scientific colleagues. Did this Czech Jew have something to do with radar or rockets or jet engine program?

- Bring me an item of clothing each of this man and his daughter – Hoffman told the adjutant.

The barking yapping snarling growling collage of sounds of the assembled pack was now incessant. The dogs of diverse pedigree and breed were forging into a manageable pack as they sniffed and licked and circled each other, an edifying sight as Heiser's handlers struggled to keep them under control, visibly straining with the three dogs each had been assigned. Coffee was brought over to all and was very welcome after the cognac and alcohol of the night. The commandant cheerfully explained how they were getting ready to send trains loads of people east where they had new camps starting that was looking very promising, bound to ease the problem of overcrowding and so would give him less work to do.

- Camps in the East? - asked Heiser.
- More room to work, here we are very cramped – the commandant explained. The Colonel looked around at the rolling Bohemian countryside heavily forested with barely a hamlet or farmstead insight.
- Yes, I see - he said, although he didn't but as a veteran of France, Poland and Russia he knew the further away you got from the Fatherland the easier it was to apply looser moral guidelines. Just then the sound of pitched canine excitement could be heard, the barking of the pack until that movement had been the normal sound of a disparate collection of hounds thrown together and dragged around by handlers trained to mould them into a coherent hunting pack but they'd found something, one of the hands came running up.
- The scent was found – he said doubling over, he smoked too much.
- Which of the scents was found - asked Hoffman but in a flash he knew the answer.
- Both Sir! Over by the gaping hole in the wall – on hearing this Hoffman turned triumphantly to his astounded fellow officers.
- Gentlemen what we have is a conspiracy of the highest order, which they have attempted to pass off as a mere shabby incompetence air raid. Nothing incompetent about it at all, it was meant to cause the maximum noise for the minimum damage and all designed to cover the base criminal act behind it.

263

The Greek chorus behaved in exactly the way he thought they would.

- What criminal act? - said the commander, the Colonel and the Lieutenant in unison and then they all looked at each other in sheepish surprise.
- It's obvious once you look at the situation in a certain way - Hoffman told them.
- A prison break? – Heiser said.
- Exactly - said Hoffman – exactly.
- Your boys organized some prison breaks in your time so you should recognize one when you see it – chuckled Heiser at the SS men.
- Whatever do you mean? What you may have heard is pure conjecture, our party has always acted within the limits of the law - a faint hint of a smirk appeared on Hoffman's face before the continued – even our leader was imprisoned for nearly a year and he did not move from that prison the whole time.

Heiser thought it was a bit rich, that high treason could work out so light-handed, five years reduced to eleven, repeat eleven months. The opponents of the current regime whom he knew existed, they had to exist even though as a career soldier he steered clear of politics, he counted himself as a German first, a soldier second and a Nazi never! But those opponents would be delighted with such a sentence. Heiser knew that Hitler had even made good use of his free time to write that drivel every German had to read or at least possess a copy of, 'Mein Kampf', his struggle was not half as much a struggle as to read it. Heiser's cousin had been in charge of the detachment of Munich police send that day in 1923 to stop the Putsch, he'd sworn never to have seen the supposed famous image of Hitler in a white trench coat at the head of the marching column. If Hitler had been that conspicuous he wouldn't have lasted the first fuselage. Heiser didn't say that to anyone present of course, his cousin had to leave Germany in 1933 due to promised reprisals and was rumoured in the family to have joined the Allies. A soldier picks his side then fights and dies; he didn't hate his cousin, he'd have done the same, none of this he shared either but just went about his duty.

- Let's go then, what is happening, what can my boys do? – Heiser asked.
- The dogs have found the scents are waiting to follow the trail – The Lieutenant reported.
- Good God, then what are you waiting for? – Heiser looked at him fiercely.

- Orders Sir – The Lieutenant stared back stuck for words.
- Even the dogs would know what to do, get after them this minute!
  – Heiser shouted.

At the broken part of the wall the dogs were given free rein to their hunting instincts and charged across the open ground to the trees that marked the start of thick forest, the handlers controlled them as best they could, the dogs were rested and ready to go and were in the throes of feverish excitement, if they'd been horses one could say they were champing at the bit, behind them the platoon of infantry followed up.

- Commander, we need to send more men with this platoon? Whoever you have available – Hoffman asked.
- But how old is the Jew? – The Commandant replied reluctantly.
- We have been told sixty-three Sir - answered the adjutant.
- Good God sixty-three and he is still here in the camp, you won't need more than you have, he'll be as weak as a baby - said the Commander.
- It's been two hours since the raid so at a moderate pace at night in winter with one elderly badly fed Jew, one badly hung-over Irishman who I personally saw hopelessly drunk at the reception and add in a woman to slow them down, I'd say we'll have them in our hands by noon. Any takers? - Hoffman was exuberant as the commander took up the challenge.
- A case of the finest champagne will be yours with my well wishes – he answered the call.
- A case of champagne throws down the gauntlet, we soldiers prefer Scotch, hard spirits for hard battles but I'll take the champagne mind, any day, whatever is to hand – Colonel Heiser said less enthusiastically.
- You don't seem optimistic! Surely you can take such odds - Hoffman exclaimed to Heiser.
- Oh, I might have to find a case of champagne but I don't believe so, not by noon anyway. This Irishman seems very lucky or very astute or both, he's handled his hangover very well so far, maybe it was a put on for the audience knowing he'd be going clandestine after the party, he'd have been warmed beforehand so for my part sounds like a good bet – The just as astute and somewhat lucky German mirrored his prey.
- In three hours we'll see. The old man and the girl for sure. The rest are slipperier - Hoffman settled the discussion.

The dogs had disappeared into the forest followed by handlers and infantry. Some four platoons of ninety men. All the ones behind could do was wait.

- Send reinforcements to catch up, who knows what's waiting for them meanwhile pass me this 'best coffee', strong and hot I hope to disguise the rich roast taste of rats droppings – Hoffman grimaced.
- That is just a rumour spread by the Jews – The commandant stood by his convictions and his prejudices.

Deeper in the forest

Kessler was looking and acting like anything but his sixty-odd years. He said so himself.

- Such a sense of freedom, I feel twenty years younger. And sorry for the lamentable scene at the wall, first draft nerves, for actors its first night, for scientists the publication drafts. Maria, apologies to dear Dagan our Sir Galahad please for the less than fulsome welcome you gave him. That was no way to treat old friends - Kessler bounded along revived by the nurturing air of liberty freedom and the pursuit of further freedom.

At this he turned to the nearest resistance fighter and said something in Czech holding his hand to this chest in a clear act of contrition. Dagan didn't need Czech to understand that the elderly scientist was asking pardon for having doubted them. The dignity and obvious sincerity of the distinguished figure had a thawing effect as the flight went on. Dagan noticed that certain people like Kessler had a natural gentleness, a mantle of secular saintliness that even the hardiest street toughs were drawn to and returned the good naturalness. It was quite a trick. The battle-tested condemned men of the resistance started offering help to Maria, passing small chunks of ham and cheese and slips of water. No wonder the Professor fairly bounded along while his daughter, thirty years younger looked like a busted flush and the man who could have been his son in law keenly feeling the effects of the previous evening's heavy meal and alcohol. He'd overegged the drunkenness bit but even so, add in the homicidal bedtime, plus the nocturnal cloacae replete subterranean flight, not to mention the dawn bomb blasts, hurried jailbreak, strenuous mid-morning Silvestre stroll, active pursuit by ravenous hounds and you could forgive the Irishman his jaded aspect.

The chasing pack could now be clearly heard, a large pack by the sound of it, still too far off to hear distinct voices. The time since they'd left the camp had been a trek thought rivulets and forest marshy ground, brushing trails with branches to remove evidence of their passing, they'd stayed close to the rivers crossing and reclosing. Sticky going but the professor was saying he hadn't had so much fun in years and how he'd been stuck too long in labs and ought to have got out and about more in the countryside.

The Czechs glanced behind and talked heatedly among themselves. Dagan wondered how the Germans had figured out the ruse so quickly, maybe Kessler was right about a breach in security. Not from London's end or he'd be dead long ago but from Prague's, a more hit and miss prospect, somebody knows something about somebody, whispers, suppositions, rumours but added together could blow apart the carefully constructed chimaera of his disappearance. The Germans had that piece of the jigsaw but did they have the rest? The false air raid had been decried far too quickly. How in the world had they cottoned on so quickly to the ruse and the missing people? Straight away near as. The dogs were following an obvious scent. They knew who they were after, who would have thought, two Jews among tens of thousands of dirty, dishevelled, unshaven shabby ones, it was as if they actually cared. The great unwashed mass all looked the same, a mega Hebrew Babel piled on top of each other and still they notice when two leaves got blown off autumn's swept up pile. What had he done wrong? Dagan sensed that luck wasn't playing so much a role as an extremely smart adversary who had seen through the smoke and mirrors straightway or who had taken seemingly random diverse events and had connected them in record time. What had gone wrong? At least it's keeping me indignant and moving he thought. Five lightly armed men, one old man, a thin weakened female and himself, getting on in life but still up the fight, against heavily armed battle-hardened crack German infantry being led on by a pack of rabid dogs with the scent of a kill in their nostrils.

It's a wonder we've got this far - Dagan thought - Was the sound of the pursuing pack changing? A flurry of anguished howls went up, the howls continued at the same spot. The chased kept moving.

'Pepper' the man next to Kessler said but in such a thick accent that Kessler had to repeat the word to Dagan. For a couple of minutes, they advanced steadily without being gained on, the tension replaced by smiles and shared glances of complicity. They'd make their escape. The howling of the dogs, maddened with the burning in their nostrils and throats, grew slightly fainter as the distance between them and the pack widened. Suddenly shots rang out in quick succession followed by more howls of anguish, the shock wave caught the group on higher ground. They could see that the shots came from two valleys over, too close, two more shots. The Czechs began to hurry while after some heated exchanging of words the youngest, Pavel, twenty-five if a day, took a rifle, turned and without a seconds hesitation began running on down the slope towards the oncoming Germans.

- They shot the dogs crazed with the pepper and have continued after us. Pavel has gone back to delay them – Vaclav explained.

The scramble to escape their clutches intensified, everybody in the group except Kessler seemed to notice the palpable fear and nervousness. They were losing ground and they knew it as the pursuers moved perceptively closer. Half an hour later they heard an explosion, a grenade, more confusion sown among the Germans, some time gained by Pavel at what cost given the relentless chasers would get going again, another two minutes another blast sound.

- How many grenades does Pavel have? - Dagan asked.
- That was the last - Václav told him.
- What now, sets traps, tripwires, moons them? - Václav looked at him sadly.
- He's a French literature student, he gets close and shoots, he gets closer and throws the fucking grenade. Just like Balzac – Vaclav crudely put it.

Solitary shots came and were drowned out by multiple rifle and machine gunfire. A one-sided firefight, another isolated shot followed by the crackle of returning fire. It was strange to so intensely follow the unequal combat so closely but at a safe distance. Pavel's life and death struggle so real to him so at arm's length to them. That would change.

The Germans knew they were up against one or two and just kept following the trial. He could still hear the dogs, so the grenades hadn't finished them off. Shame. Another shot and another again rejoined by a return cavalcade. The firefight died down and died out, silence reined apart from the dogs and now ominously the sound of deep bass shouting voices. Sharp and clear vocal sound, words just out of reach.

- What's the plan? Are we just running or are we running to something? - Dagan challenged Václav.
- No one can be taken – Václav changed the subject.
- Sorry about the boy, he died bravely and his family can be proud

- How do you know he died? Pavel is today's Monty Cristo and will fight another day, we don't give up fighters easily, he had strict instructions to hold them up then try and lead them away. End of story, he is now running like a mad man in the other direction.
- I read you now and if I'm right then the people who you work with the same, never get caught and take as many Germans as you can to the hell when you go.
- That is my plan but not today. Give your coat and Kessler's to Sasha – Václav ordered.

Sasha, another of the partisans took both and gave his coat in return to the elderly scientist while giving Dagan a rather musky scarf and then disappeared at a run along an adjacent path into the next forest valley. The last sight they had of Sasha was him dragging Dagan and Kessler's coats along the ground and rubbing them against the trees to try and decoy the dogs.

- That's a Cromby original given to me by the designer himself, if he could see it now he'd be mortified – Dagan said half-seriously - or damn proud – deadly seriously.

The tense deadly cat and mouse morning continued, a bright day whose small amount of heat from the equinoctial sun was greedily absorbed by the upper branches, either way, the forest floor was not the place for the ill-shod or ill-clothed or plain ill at ease, all of which applied to Dagan. The ever-present cacophony of the canine pack had diminished slightly and the distance between the rabbits and the foxes seemed to be lengthening but it was a mirage, a false dawn.

What they heard was two packs, the Germans had split them after encountering two trails. The decoy got attention but not fully, the main party of pursuers continued, the rest followed Sasha. Kessler was now beginning to flag, all of them were, it was relentless, Václav however seemed to be keeping cool.

- We should start looking for a spot for a last stand - Dagan urged.
- Not necessary – he said and to the rest in a louder voice - not far now.
- Not far from what? - Dagan said exasperatedly and couldn't help asking.
- The end! Something I hope is going to work out the way I planned it. A minute late and we are lost.
- I'm sorry Maria - Kessler said to his daughter meanwhile.
- Sorry! Poppycock - she replied tenderly - If you are sorry for taking me away from that living hell don't be, we'd only have

lingered on another few months anyway. Here we'll die spitting in the face of the enemy – Maria turned to Václav – Give me a gun, any gun, I am not going quietly this time - She turned back to her father and they embraced gently - I'm even glad it was him - Maria said pointing to Dagan and addressing the Irishman - Come on, a glib answer please, just your style.

- Normally the case without a doubt – Dagan laboured in his response – and usually I have a flute of champagne to hand and a good cigar along with the glib answer but now I'm too tired for glib my sweet. Just happy you're happy.
- Well then say something to cheer me up. You were always good at that too - Maria smiled at Dagan and pictured themselves ten odd years ago.
- I tried to shoot Hitler but missed – he said and Maria genuinely surprised burst out laughing.
- You missed obviously as I wouldn't have missed that news – she laughed fully.
- Maria this isn't over yet you know – Dagan said determinedly.

The group had rested a couple of precious minutes in a grove while they'd thought they had outfoxed the fox. The effort to get going provoked audible groans and curses.

- Why not just wait here from them - Kessler said - they can't be more than five hundred meters or so behind.

But Václav ignored that suggestion and urge them on at a clipped pace moving them down the valley and over a small hillock. As they made their way the pursuers could be seen on the adjoining rise, shouts rang up and a volley of shots whistled over their heads.

- I will go back and hold them off – Václav said passing the cowering group – you move move move.
- Brave and stupid – Dagan countered - you are the Czech resistance here, where the blue blazes are these two and me going to go without you *dummkopf*. Give me the rifle. I'll delay them, will give them something to think about – Dagan grabbed the rifle as Václav looked at him disbelievingly.
- We are to rendezvous with the truck from this morning - Václav came clean - just over the ridge here; the meeting time is in half an hour's so I hope Magda is early but all the more reason to hold them up a bit and for that two are better than one. Fire this gun in the air went the truck arrives – Václav said to Pieter exchanging Pieter's rifle for the pistol Václav carried – you know

where, wait five minutes and go. Come on Irishman, let's go German hunting, open season - Václav handed more rounds to Dagan - Five loaded and here are five more, they should fit in the barrel more or less.

- What do you mean "should fit", didn't they fit before? – Dagan gasped as it was his turn to look incredulous as he stared at the collection of oddly shaped battered cartridges.
- They have been recovered so to speak, made whole again, use your judgement if they don't quite fit it is best not to try if you are not sure or brave enough or too needy.
- Stupid enough maybe, I'm going to be under fire and would quite like something to shoot back with - Dagan ruefully put the odds and sods of the Czech resistance's ammo supply in a jacket pocket - Go as fast as you can - he said to Kessler and Maria.
- You're both going to come back - Maria asked tentatively.
- Of course - Václav said with feigned bravura.
- And I go where ever he goes - said Dagan - and anyway we have a lot of catching up to do you and me.
- The others didn't come back – Maria pointed out.
- Ever the realist, you need more romance in your soul, now go quickly before my German friends arrive, there's a lorry waiting in the ravine down there.
- Quite close now and usually on time – Václav added while Maria looked at the dense surrounding forest and wondering how a truck could make it to this spot.
- Yes like the Prague trams – she said vaguely.
- Even better, come on let's go – Václav and Dagan hurried off and as they left the group in a low voice added his sign off to the Irishman – If the truck isn't there we're to go our separate ways, the old man and the girl will have to fend for themselves.
- You can't be taken - Dagan asked – neither can they.
- I already have and don't care to repeat, I have lost two good colleagues already, two lions, it will be terrible. I've raised hell and the Germans know it, they'll do anything to get me alive and make me suffer.
- Nice to meet you, Václav R. I will put in a spurt at the right time and get away, I used to spend half my days at Clongowes days doing cross country, this lot I'll leave standing, which way is west?
- That way - Václav pointed north grinning.
- Ah, the other west – Dagan pointing south.
- Do you have a contact in Prague? – The Czech man asked.

- One for emergencies but you could hardly call this an emergency, an awkward situation at most.
- You, my Irish, will be very sought after they will do anything to get to you after the hotel and this stunt – Václav advised.
- You don't know the half of it, I wasn't kidding when I said I took a pop at Hitler, aimed directly at the moustache.
- A really bad man and to add to it such awful taste as well, even the slavish doltish Germans haven't copied that fashion. You could have saved us a lot of trouble. We will have to take care of "them", we can't leave "them" for the Germans – Dagan knew who "them" referred to.
- Bit harsh, what exactly do you mean "take care of them" – he demanded.
- It's a euphemism – Václav said enigmatically.
- Your English is getting better by the mile, are you sure you are just an engineer. Quite a phrase "take care of" sounds warm and caring, solicitous, mollycoddling, spoiling even. Ok, I will take care of him and then run like hell with her, she might make it.
- Those aren't your orders, she's not even included in the rescue I know how the British work, better to be their enemy that their friend like my poor country, sold out for twelve months more of peace and we turned into Pharaoh's slaves.
- Don't get me started on the Brits. The Irish have had enough shit from them to last an eternity. Anyway who says I going back to the British. Might go east – and at that, they left it and separated.
- Fire at the targets nearest to your position – Václav urged
- Right, body shots to men and beast, maximum damage and howling, fatalities were not the priority – Dagan knew what was a stake
- No, not this time but it will be difficult not to go for the kill. Against my nature – Václav could only respond.

Dagan scuttled back up the hill, the sound of the dogs so loud he imagined them right over the crest. Václav and he approached from different sides, crouching and then crawling the last few yards. Dagan spotted a natural bit of broken ground between two rocks shielded from the front by a small bush. Václav did much the same and was barely visible fifty yards away. Three hundred yards in front they saw the Germans cross the bottom of the ground below them, perfect, the pack was a crazy mix, you'd laugh if they weren't working their damn little paws off so well together, huskies and German shepherds were leading, a civilian tagging along behind and spread out over a hundred yards three well-marshalled platoons of infantry advanced in staggered lines experts at what they were doing. If the first line passed over you the second might but the third wouldn't. The command section to the rear was made up of radioman, heavy machine gun team, sergeant and lieutenant. I'll start with them. Dagan looked for his next position first as Václav was indicating to open fire. All hell was going to break loose and these Germans were going to give as good as they got Dagan could see that the whole platoon was eying the ground ahead, they'd been attacked twice before so were very combat-ready.

Dagan chose his next spot away on the flank, let Václav take the middle, sniping was all about shooting and moving to hyper range. Dagan would try three positions before he'd attack with his pistol, okay no futile charge of the light brigade, the pistol he'd keep for close quarters and 'euphemisms', Kessler was vital for the atomic program, they'd been adamant about that. His knowledge and skills in isotope enrichment were unique and crucial to a working weapon, Dagan tried to imagine what that meant but parts of physics were the realm of the few and they were worth armies. It was still a mystery to the Allies why the Germans didn't see that but once attention had been drawn to it they might, some clever clogs might stitch it all together and that couldn't be allowed. The Allies were giving too much away if found out.

The Germans kept coming, ordered and efficient, Dagan lined up the officer, just on his side of the imaginary divide he had with Václav, two hundred and fifty yards, its wasn't a difficult shot, aim for the big tummy bursting out of the uniform of the panting red-faced junior. He'll scream blue murder and his rank will draw in three comrades to give him auxiliary.

Dagan aimed dead centre and hoped the barrel was clean and not warped. The officer stopped to mop his forehead and shouted at the platoon leader to close up. They knew they were close. Dagan looked over at Václav; he gave the fire signal and went back to lining up a shot. Dagan fired, a sharp crack resounded through the trees, not quite the normal sound of a shot but the birds and dogs reacted first with furious barking and the beating of hundreds of wings as the avian hordes launched themselves simultaneously into the sky. For some reason amid all the hell breaking loose he was reminded of the old school joke 'Johnny, 10 crows sitting on a fence, one gets shot, how many does that leave?', 'None Sir', 'Now Johnny, it's simple, one from ten is...', 'Nine Sir but that nine are going to fly off like bats out of hell at the sound of the gun Sir', 'You cheeky git you, come here while I cuff your ears'. Even though Dagan was expecting the sound he was still momentarily stunned. The officer disappeared in the low foliage with a scream. Václav's first shot was at the howling dogs high and right and one of the German shepherds went down and started rolling over again and again in agony. Dagan put a new round in the chamber using the stiff bolt. The Germans were already reacting and bullets where pinging close to but not quite at his spot, they just knew the general directions of their positions, that would change. Dagan moved a fraction to the left, lined up the frozen half crouched radioman, adjusted for the derivation in his first shot and let off another round and he moved straight after without looking to see what he hit. The second shot was enough for the on edge Germans, a hail of bullets came flying at where he'd been just moments ago, chipping rock and making gaping holes in the leaves. Václav too was moving, Dagan didn't know if he'd fired as the sound of gunfire was deafening. From his new position Dagan saw he had missed the radioman, he'd hit the radio though which was good enough, the force of the impact had hurled the operator to the ground. Dagan could see wires hanging from a hole in the equipment and hopefully, he'd put it out of order.

The Germans now stopped firing and organised, the NCOs ordered some units to advance while covering them, the officer was out of the game and was screaming for a paramedic above the background of canine bedlam and gunfire. Dagan's new position behind a pine tree was more exposed, he didn't waste time but lined up the morass of the dog pack and fired, no great marksmanship required, more anguish and the handlers lost control of the pack, dogs yanked away and bolted left and right from the two wounded ones. Dagan felt more of a twinge of conscience shooting at dogs than at humans, within seconds fire was coming in on him but Dagan had again moved back to his original position. This trick was one of desperation and would work once if lucky, Dagan reloaded and looked for more targets, he didn't have to look far as a German grenadier was straight in front, he took him down and a second later tried at the figure following him who dived right. Now the heavy machine gun blasted around him, chips of rock, leaves and dirt coated his hair. He had stalled the momentum as the dogs fell at each other but they didn't need the dogs now. Dagan from his third position saw the sergeants order the handlers to shoot the wounded dogs. Dagan aimed but the sergeant was a wily old hand and barely visible so he switched to fire at one of the dozens of steel helmeted infantry rapidly approaching, cover move cover move as precious dividing meters were eaten up. Dagan could see scars, facial hair, the size of the noses and chins. Too close. He fired but the target seemed to sense it and moved to the side, he then reloaded and aimed at a further figure. It was the trooper poking a gun at the reluctant civilian, must be the owner of some of the dogs, but before he could squeeze the trigger a storm of bullets came crashing back. He shot wildly while looking out for Václav, he couldn't see him and hadn't since near the start of the shootout. He must be up to one side undercover; Dagan didn't have time to scan around but just got to another location.

Now he had to fish out the 'reserve ammo', Dagan judged the most likely one to fit and put it by hand in the barrel, a strong push was needed at the last. The last round had slightly misfired causing Dagan to jerk ever so slightly, Dagan was glad he missed the civilian though, war is war but providence is Devine, the bullet hit the tree spraying splinters over the civilian but if a few splinters was the worst to happens to him this war he wouldn't be able to complain. Dagan fired again and a trooper screamed. Move and re-position. Pity he only had an ancient rife, just like being out in 1916 again with his Mauser, what a brute that was, he'd only been a boy but mature for his age, able to march, knew his left from his right and how to obey orders just like the cannon fodder needed then and now. Dagan scattered back along, hoping to see Václav or hear the signal to get blazing out of there, but so far neither of those lifesavers. If the truck hasn't arrived at the rendezvous the Germans would be on them in less than ten minutes, he could already see and hear them advancing relentlessly. Dagan took another cartridge and inserted it, halfway and no more, shit, he yanked it out and the next one was a bit better. He sighted the rifle on a rock he heaved over behind it and used a vine on the ground to tie it to another rock all the while trying to be coordinated and quick despite his sweating hands.

As soon as saw a figure cross the line of fire he threw the rock away, the vine tightened and the trigger pulled. Remote fire, just like they did at Gallipoli to cover their retreat. The shot missed but the Germans stopped, he'd settle for that as rifle bullets danced all around, Dagan pulled the rifle over with a stick, he wasn't remote more at a remove, another bullet shoved in, hands shaking didn't help but his sweaty palms did, finally greasing the bullet into firing position. He could understand perfectly the shouted commands of the Germans just below as he quickly as he could set up his remote firing mechanism again. He had to look over the top for a fraction and there a stone's throw away a German who saw him and fired back but not in time. Dagan threw the rock as hard as he could and ducked, as a sudden loud explosion sent sparks and hot metal flying including one shard into his left trouser leg. The barrel of the gun had burst, the last cartridge has been just too makeshift, it would have blown his head off if he'd been pulling the trigger himself starting with the rifle bolt going right through his eye, it now embedded in a tree directly behind. The explosion had deafened him momentarily but once the buzzing stopped he could hear Germans shouting in glee. They had him and knew it, Dagan saw the game was up, never mind the signal all hands to the boats, he hit the path down the rise as fast as only a Clongowes hare could. The minor pain in his leg meant he'd only been scratched by the hot metal. His coordination and speed got better as he realized he was removing himself from immediate danger and he covered the greater part of the distance to the next rise before the Germans crested the hill. He was partially visible through the foliage and zig-zagged. 'SEHEN SIE DA DRUBEN', shouts quickly followed by gunfire. Bullets hit trees and branches and the ground around him but he still just in effective range, his lungs felt like exploding from the effort but he was a dead duck while bullets could reach him so every metre gained meant a harder target to hit. He threw his body around, another jolt to the right then right left right left right till he was over the next rise, adrenaline surging trying to lead them away from the path the rest had followed. Just as he cleared the ridge a close whizzing sound caused a sting on his arm as a tuft of jacket padding came flying through the air, he'd been clipped earlier and now he'd been winged, nothing serious he thought as the blood-soaked through, have to get that cleaned. Cloth fibres in the wound get infected and that's goodnight Irene. The last volleys fell away, Dagan scarpered right and kept going out of the way into an overhanging tunnel of leaves, briars nettles and thorns. Out of sight he turned back and in five minutes arrived at the rendezvous and smack bang into Václav who strangely pointed a rifle at him, behind him in the back of the parked truck, the same one as the night before, Maria and Kessler were already mounted and it looked like they were all just getting underway.

- You didn't fire a round in the air, no one did - Dagan quizzed, panting and out of breath.
- We didn't need to, you are here now and it would have given our position away – Václav pointed out.
- When did you get here? - Dagan noticed Václav wasn't panting or out of breath – and you can put the rifle down now and I'll put my pistol away.

Dagan could see past Václav's impassive face and Maria and Kessler's perturbed aspect as if an argument had just happened.

- The Germans are right behind me – Dagan urged and that seemed to break the spell.

Václav paused once time more, looked over Dagan's shoulder as the sound of approaching Germans grew and finally lowered the rifle pointed at Dagan, who notices Václav had looked at the pistol in this hand first. Did a rough calculation go through the Czechs head of whether a shot would be enough or world Dagan get one back?

- What are you waiting for you dumb bog hopper! - Kessler said over his shoulder, his notions of Ireland were fanciful at best.
- Who need Germans with friends like this – he quipped.

With that Dagan climbed up as the truck started straight away, the sound of motor coughing into life bought a flurry of voices from the pursuers close by. The truck took off along a barely perceptible forest path, a small step up from a track to be sure and thankfully the winter cold made it hard and runnable. The truck accelerated slowly like the last time with numerous grinding changes of gear, they got to thirty mph and just as they left the first straight some Germans and dogs burst out of the copse behind them but it was too late. They tried to sight their rifles and some left off instinctive shots from the hip but the truck disappeared around a low rolling hill and into another small mountain valley. Dagan heard some more desultory shots and curses which soon subsided as they were out of sight and harm's way. Two Alsatians ran along for a while snapping and yapping till Dagan hit one with a spade and then even those loyal servants gave up the chase.

The Czechs with Magda once again driving with practised ease were upfront. They quickly put a kilometre then two behind them along the narrow paths, progress all the time accompanied by the brush and scrape of branches not accustomed to meeting solid objects at that height, this was the less travelled road for motorized vehicle or anything with wheels. The sound of the dogs and Germans faded away as they made good their escape. The three in the back looked at each other with shattered faces. Kessler beamed but his eyes told a story of the suffering he'd gone through.

- So good to be free, where to next? – Kessler asked.
- Who knows, we're in the resistance now – Dagan was still getting a hold of himself after the bullet-ridden chase.
- They assured me there was a plan; you were going to get us out of here?
- Yes there's a plan and yes I'm going to get you out of here but no I don't know what the plan is and no I don't know where they're taking us. We'll have to pass down the underground to a neutral country and cross a heavily guarded border. Piece of cake. What

worries me is my new bosom buddy Václav was about to leave me behind. A guy could take it badly, being left with the rabid dogs and not so nice Germans. Kind of like his friends didn't like him. Comes across a bit hard.

- We had a huge argument with them, they were rushing us onto the truck and about to leave, we said to wait but Václav was adamant you had been killed by the backfiring rifle which even we heard when it blew – Maria described the scene.

- It backfired alright but I fired it by pulling a string from beside, it was the poor rock behind that got the lashing on its way to me, frightened the bejesus out of me it did – Dagan thought he knew what was going on. Leave Dagan behind for the Germans to capture, nasty Germans happy enough, half-hearted search for the rest. But Dagan gets away, nasty spiteful Germans hell bend on finding him and as such whoever, he was with was in mortal danger. Dagan would bring too much heat for the resistance.

- Bejassus I haven't heard that word in years, so Irish it makes me laugh. You are a bad influence on my English, I used to go around saying things like "that's gas" and "that's grand" and people would look at me. Hey! You are wounded here and here and HERE - Maria pointed out the nicks on Dagan's face, trousers and arms. His 'trophies' from the skirmish Dagan hadn't thought about them with the adrenalin of the escape.

- That's nothing – he said touching his face - it all adds character, my arm would appreciate some care and attention though - while he moved around he spotted a gaping circular hole in the tail of his coat - Ah – he said putting his index finger through the clean round hole left by the passing hot lead.

- Oh that's terrible so it is – Maria gasped when she saw the filth caked hands, blood-stained sleeve and legs and the general shot up look - Take the jacket off gently.

She took some of her undershirt, tore it into a bandage then some water from her rucksack and went to work washing Dagan's collection of minor wounds as he stoically looked on. She then took another small brown crystal phial and poured some clear liquid on the cloth and rubbed the arm wound, by now naturally cauterized, the liquid stung as badly as the moment the bullet had traversed it the first time.

- Very professional – Dagan told her through gritted teeth as she ripped another strip and wrapped it around the cleaned wound.

- We learn no end of practical skills in the ghetto, bored we never were, frightened, hungry, cold, tired yes but we never lacked things to do. Neither gas nor grand nor great was it to be sure.

- Is it as bad as they painted it? - Dagan said quietly, Kessler looking out the back of the truck as they rattled past the enclosing trees turning and turning again onto wider paths and forest roads.

At this pace they had left the Germans well behind but needed to get much further if they were to have a chance of staying at liberty. Dagan surmised that the Germans would stop at nothing to recapture them for their importance of the escapees but also because they ruled by fear and terror. Absolute obedience was paramount to their rule of iron and who stepped out of line was smashed for all to see, who tried to escape or resist was similarly destroyed to better serve as an example. Dagan and the Czech resistance had made fools of them and that would infuriate them even more. Maria glanced over at her father and began to talk quietly.

- He didn't suffer too much due to his high standing as an elder but even they were subject to the whim of the Germans and could be slapped or beaten on the slightest pretext. I myself well – tears welled up in the big doe-like eyes – one of their savage dogs bit my leg once while the kapos just laughed. It wasn't until some brave idiot whistled at the dog that it let go. I have the marks still. Worst of all was well were to start, after a lifetime of bourgeois comforts we were so reduced, I'd never seen a potato in its skin, now it is a delicacy you pay dearly for. Before I had baths three times a week, big warm soapy ones, now a furtive wash of the armpits and other sensitive parts is all we manage, I reek like a fisherwoman I know.
- Oh, I'm worse. Seriously I spent the night in a sewer up to my neck in brown trout.
- Brown what? – Maria was momentarily flummoxed.
- Never mind but it was malodorous – Dagan corrected himself.
- I used to be one of the first to view the latest Paris fashions even if I didn't buy much now I smell like a cheese in my one good winter coat I kept a hold off, you wouldn't believe the thieving you'd think we'd be united by our common suffering but it's Darwin's theories come to life. The worst beatings aren't the Germans but the kapos, young strong Jews lending their arms to the Nazis for privileges and better bread PHAW - Maria spat out an expletive, Maria was an evolutionist as well as an accomplished physicist - bubble bath and Haute cuisine, I sound so shallow but the truth is I worked so hard back then and here I was working much harder but without any of the creature comforts. When I think of the food I use to leave on the plate because I was too bloated

279

before a dance I could nearly cry. I dream of cream cakes and hams and blue cheeses, white bread and everything else we used to have in our kitchen – Maria waxed lyrically on culinary delights of yesteryear.

- I've been in a few prisons and know what eating insects is like to supplement the lack of protein but it was never for too long,
- Why do I look at you and think of a playboy when it's far from the truth, my funny light superficial Irishman, a gadabout. When you have been through a lot of very unpleasant experiences - Maria held his face touchingly - Maybe because I loved you so much and you made me suffer so - she sighed, Maria Kessler, physicist and leading light of the feminist movement of 1930s Prague still shone from somewhere in the ravished creature before him who despite the reversals and calamities still retained and radiated an inner beauty out to the exterior, still sported a sweet good nature like her father. Dagan smiled – Champagne my dear? - she joked.
- That will be a treat, we'll head to the Cody's Bar, I always like to celebrate surviving a brush with death by toasting the health of la mort with champagne and beautiful women – Maria laughed at that.
- You say such silly things, we'd have less trouble finding a bottle of champagne than a beautiful woman – Maria kept laughing and it did both her and Dagan the world of good.

Chapter IX

Theresienstadt

Hoffman, Colonel and the commandant had remained in the field rather than retire as the commandant had suggested to his comfortable office with its fire blazing and brandy and whiskey to hand. But NO, Heiser had made a sideways comment about Chateaux Generals and Hoffman himself disliked the idea to boot, he didn't want to endure the sight of half-starved walking cadavers shuffling around. Aryan purification theory was sound but visiting or witnessing it in practice was another. So they stayed out in the open beside the Heiser's command and communication vehicle as throughout the morning regular radio contact kept them updated on the hare and tortoise pursuit that had started with the chasing pack getting off at a grand gallop. Progress had been thick and fast then slow and hard, the renegades wouldn't be far ahead according to the expert trackers if the footprints, broken twigs and branches were telling the truth. The first reverse was an hour later, the trail was lost in a rivulet as the pursued 'had taken an early bath', the commandant chuckled but the Germans had a lot of experience in these matters, half of Europe was running towards then while the other half was running away. Sufficient to split the dogs and follow the river on both sides, then news came of a still-warm campfire, a good sign then quickly another reverse, black pepper on the trail. Dogs driven crazy, bathed, dozed and one beyond help shot, the relentless chase continued.

- Most exciting, gentlemen we will be the toast of Berlin this day – Hoffman said - I venture - he added a note of caution stamping his feet and calling for more coffee. Colonel Heiser who'd been in touch closely with the men was more cautious.
- They are doing exactly what I'd do in their position and there are a few tricks still to play. Radio! - He shouted - send a message 'be on the lookout for traps and lone gunmen, locate firing positions and envelope as trained'. Those are their next obvious moves. Save your laurels for later, still have to catch the hare before we can prepare the stew – Heiser sagely said.
- Noted. Speaking of stews you don't have some sort of field kitchen? We could do with some sustenance after our night chasing criminals from one end of this country to the other – Hoffman addressed the commandant.
- We can go to our canteen? – The commandant suggested.
- No thanks - both Heiser and Hoffman said in unison looking at each other – We can't leave while the units are out there - Heiser said – on a campaign, one must stay in touch with events - Heiser pointed to the command wagon.
- Suit yourselves – the commandant said huffily.

That both officers for different units were showing the same disdain to those whom they considered were nothing more than prison guards, he the commandant/warden was offended and it put him in a bad mood. Little did they know how vital his role was as if they did they'd be a bit more respectful. He had tens of thousands of people under his care, more than most generals and certainly more than a mere colonel and over-promoted captain. He was the mayor, judge, policeman, chandler, victualer and warden of a small city, all-powerful and omnipotent. They should try it for a week then they'd be a bit more understanding and less stuck up.

Just then to the relief of all the tension was broken by a radio call, two trails found, the pursued had split up it seemed.

- Standard tactic, how many dogs are following the new scent? - barked Heiser into the microphone.
- Three of the pack just - came the reply.
- Send a troop, no more than eight and the three dogs. Kept the main force on the initial trial.
- Of course Sir.
- You might win that bet Heiser after all but I will have my recreants all the same – Hoffman said quietly confident.

Hoffman knew he had stymied the plans of Mister Mystery Malone by the speed of the follow-up and Malone and cohorts were on the ropes. The exact time they are captured was of little concern. Fifteen minutes later the next report was called in and it was dramatic. The Germans were under attack, gunfire was audible in the background.

- What the hell is the matter? Concise report now! – Heiser demanded.
- Grenades Sir, two at least, then gunfire; they hit a dog and wounded a trooper.
- How many opponents, one or two?
- One Sir, we're closing in, we've circled around the position over.

Over the radio the progress of the firefight was evident, first sustained gunfire bursts rattled nearby met by less audible solitary shots now and then, all this against constant orders and shouts to encourage the Germans tightening in. Finally, a long burst and the guns fell silent only for the jubilant cries from the satisfied Germans heard before the confirmation message.

- Target vanquished Sir. Fleeing to the west.
- Don't concern yourself with this one, he is small fry, follow on the trail at double pace, they're close and desperate.

Orders were relayed and constant reports of rapid progress received.

- We have a sighting Sir, point man saw figures ahead and the trail is fresh – came the report.
- After them then and careful – The Colonel said.
- Sir we've seen the main group up ahead – they heard two minutes later followed by a sharp bang - Sir a dog has been shot – another shot and a cavalcade of gunfire in return - The lieutenant has

been hit, more than one attacker, changing positions – Screams, shouts, howls, gunfire.

- All this caused by a couple of men? – The commandant asked from behind.
- This will be the Irishman and the main resistance leader, a final throw of the dice; it will be all over in minutes. Hoffman, we will be lucky to take your Irishman alive, he knows the stakes but your Jews you will have back that I'm sure of – was Heiser's analysis of the situation.
- Not my Jews. His – Hoffman pointed stiffly to the commandant.
- There'd be causalities but the result is inevitable – Heiser added.
- The commander is down - screamed the radio operator – A medic! A medic! - could be heard from the lieutenant close by.

Suddenly a massive spike, a thundering cacophony of metal again metal and the radio went silent.

- What the hell happened? – Hoffman's ears clanged and hurt.
- Take out command structure, then communications, these people are well trained but we'll get them their luck won't hold against our troops, they're trained to lead themselves if needs be - The Colonel proudly announced the qualities of the common German soldier which had so far lead to triumph after triumph across Europe - German soldiers never give up, falter, flag, lose formation or their heads. At every level, there is a sense of belonging and common objectives.
- Admirable very admirable, only when deserted and betrayed on the home front as in 1918 is the German soldier undone. And that will not happen because the SS is there to make sure home discipline is maintained. Let us see your troops show off their superlative qualities – Hoffman got in his spoke, the minutes passed, five, ten then twenty.
- The radio is gone so we're in for a long wait – Colonel said resigned.
- You give orders then you wait and hope for the best – the commandant this said to no one in particular.

A field dinner was severed in small metal trays. A meaty stew that was one of the best Hoffman or Heiser had ever tasted.

- Complements to the field kitchen – Heiser saluted the commandant.
- What is this meat, so damn tender? – Hoffman asked.

- Don't ask, it tastes good so who cares, 14-18 was a lot worse, we rarely saw rats in the trenches that can't be normal – Heiser interjected.
- I think I'm going to be sick – the commandant said half in jest.
- You can get too used to the easy life! When you are hungry you'd eat anything. Ask those people in your delicate charge. Sometimes back in the trenches we looked forward to attacking the British as once we got to their trenches we could stock up on all their rations - before continuing - I was joking about the rats, they were crawling over us day and night, we shot them but didn't eat them, our front line boys were well looked after with horse meat, millions of horses, they worked to death the poor nags and when they were finished they ended up in the stews before the flies knew what happened. As for the meat, delicious, never any fat on it, lean and healthy.

Hoffman looked around him, the comradery, the pleasant conditions on a mild winters day, fires burning to keep them warm, the soothing sensation of the hot food starting its digestion, the imminent news he was about to receive, great news, news that would bring him to the attention of the highest in the land, the factual lords of all Europe. The possibilities afterwards were manifold, he was even decided to be gracious to the Irishman. True he'd read him wrong, had been taken in by the false honestly, a lesson there and an important one for a servant of the state engaged in its security. But he would let that pass, he'd receive the recaptured Jews with consideration, the Irishman with good grace, the resistance members with care. Later they'd be all dealt with severely but someone else could do the dirty unpleasant work. The old man would be looked after, Hoffman had plans for him, he'd consult with the scientific elements of the SS and look at the secret research programs. If the Brits wanted him so badly then there must be some advantage some edge that could come from the man. Like bronze swords, canons, gun powder, flintlocks, it could be some huge leap that rendered redundant or put at a grave disadvantage the weapons of the enemy. Our tanks tactics were the edge now but was there more in 'the power of the atom', Hoffman remembered that as the title of a talk way back in the 30s. Hoffman was about to call over Heiser and ask to talk to his engineers when the radio sparked into life. The radio team had calmly kept calling without pause since the last contact.

- Control to sector one overdo you receive over - Again and again, it got very monotonous and almost reassuring, part of the background like working with the radio on. Then suddenly an answer came.

- Cooontrol control – it was the voice of the radio operator.
- Receiving over.
- Con-control, target lo-lo-lost over - The voice came halting and stuttering, you could nearly imagine the operator trembling and in shock.
- Control here - the Sergeant grabbed the micro - you are not speaking clearly, remember your training, drink some water, take some deep breaths.
- Is he on the Rostov front or chasing an old man and woman, a hung-over Celt and a few Czechs? - Hoffman said listening in
- Shock definitely, the bullet ricocheting and wounded him - Heiser took the microphone himself - Well done man, you did very well to fix the radio, will soon be back in a warm barracks with a hot meal and a shower now tell me slowly what happened, take your time, what happened?
- Goooone Sir – finally the voice was coming under control - Sir we were about to catch up with them when they were met by a truck and were taken away, we couldn't stop them over – Hoffman, Heiser and the commandant stood listening slowly taking in the news.
- A truck, a fucking truck! Where did they get a truck from? - A terrible sinking feeling caused a heave in Hoffman's entrails, the stew made heavy work of riding the storm and was threatening to make a reappearance.
- Casualty report, who is in charge? - Heiser asked - Do you need assistance over? - The crackle continued before another voice replied.
- Sgt. Heike Sir, the lieutenant is on a stretcher but stable we are bringing him back, the patrol is now reunited and only some lightly wounded. The radio operator had a bad cut to the neck and lost a lot of blood but is okay. Estimate another four hours before return.
- Thanks Heike, good report, you will be here before nightfall, we'll send a party to meet you and speed up your return. You will find everything ready for you, medical assistance, hot food and drinks.
- Appreciated Sir and awaiting welcome sight of our comrades over - the obvious relief and gratitude in Heike's voice showed Hoffman why Colonel Heiser was so esteemed by his men.
- You mollycoddle them - he said half-joking.
- On the contrary, I ask them to fight and to die, a hot dinner is the least I can do if it's in my power, they will fight all the harder and all the more willingly the next time - Heiser spoke with passion and radiance, his men were his charges, every last one of them

285

had loved ones, sweethearts, wives, mothers, fathers - One of the worst things about my job is the letters to the families of the fallen. I don't know if you've written any but when faced with the blank page and the name of the solders whose face you can hardly remember trying to write the most important letter about them to break the terrible news that no one wants, it makes you focus on the little details. We're at war, people die but if we can avoid many unnecessary deaths by small actions then it is our duty but what do you know about this? Your helpless opponents were in no position to present problems.

-   We're all on the same side fighting for the same goal let's remember that, divisions between us is a boon to the enemy - The camp commandant retorted.

He felt a lot better, the fighting colonel's contempt was spread evenly and applied just as much to the SS as to him that quizzically made the commandant quite happy with his lot, and he enjoyed immensely the discomfort experienced by his state security colleague. Hoffman himself was not paying attention to the little details speech, results were what Germany needed and there was more than one way to achieve that. Hoffman was more focused on the escape, his quarry had got away and while they were free his own life was in peril, it was that simple.

-   Show me the maps - he ordered his Sergeant - They've got away but haven't escaped from our grasp.

The huge operations maps were spread out on top of the bonnet. The radio operator in the background still talking to his companion, the howl of dogs every time the micro switched over was annoying. Hoffman studied the maps especially the immediate area for a radius of 30km and then a larger general map taking in Bohemia, Monrovia, parts of Austria, Poland, Germany and Switzerland.

-   We will catch them yet before they go to ground - Hoffman stated.
-   I'd go east towards the Swiss border so roadblocks here, here and here plus controls at all bus stations, trains and transit points for a start - Heiser considered the absconders best options.
-   Roadblocks on every major and minor road, every shepherd track if needs be, these people stay off-road as we've just seen and we'll put the roadblocks in all directions, they also love to do the unexpected.
-   It's good for the troops, too much barrack duty, the easy life is not good at this time of year – the commandant added wanting to

take part. Hoffman and Heiser just nodded at the rather inane comment.

- This will be a show of who's in control – Hoffman said - We'll catch any number of smugglers, activist's, criminals, and deserters and so on and I've no doubt Malone. We're going to put middle Europe under lock and key as long as we have too – he proclaimed to his colleagues.

Chapter X

Transcript W4453 Telephone conversation

Gestapo HQ Prague to SS HQ Berlin
RM. H. Himmler to (HH) & Strumpfuhrer C. Hoffman (CH)
11/12/1941 11:52 am – 11:56 am

- HH: The British organized a raid over Bohemia just to save some Jews?
- CH: And sent an agent to Prague under cover of a neutral organization via the whole of Germany to lead the mission on the ground.
- HH: But wasn't the agent sent to attempt on the life of our leader.
- CH: That might have been an opportunity that fell into his lap so to speak, too tempting to ignore, he has no history of that kind of activity.
- HH: He has plenty of other histories, I've read his file or files, so big it came in three folders. Very gung-ho, I found it distasteful. Now he is starting the fourth and final folder. Continue with your conjectures.
- CH: In 1932 he studied or dallied a time with Kessler the Jewish physicist. There may have been some sort of relationship with the daughter. It doesn't seem to have led anywhere.
- HH: That sort of behaviour is also typical according to the file.
- CH: The imposter disappears the same night as the suspicious air-raid on the ghetto transition camp where it just so happens he just visited and has dear friends there all the while we were about to arrest him on multiple charges.

- HH: Transition is a polite way of putting it, we will be applauded once we have finished our work but for now we have to operate away for prying eyes. Continue.
- CH: Following a hunch, I could see that the disappearance of Malone and the raid were connected and later at the camp we linked him with the Jews and we nearly had it all tided up in twelve hours.
- HH: Nearly is not good enough. What happened then?
- CH: They were helped to escape by Czech resistance, they were fleeing through the forest and just as our men were about to catch them they were driven away in a truck that had come eight kilometres up impassable forest paths.
- HH: Nearly! Just! And then what?
- CH: And now are hiding out, request permission to make free use of the troops in this area to mount roadblocks and start searching.
- HH: Over what area?
- CH: Monrovia, the protectorate of Bohemia, bits of Austria, Hungry and northern Yugoslavia.
- HH: My goodness, lord of all you survey, ancient kingdoms were made of less, not bad for a mere Colonel still wet behind the ears. I was advised to place an officer of longer experience in charge after this failure to recapture but it is true and can't be denied that if you hadn't done such good police work in the first place the spy and the Jews would have made a clean away.
- CH: Thank you.
- HH: Don't thank me, get the spy and the rest of this rabble and that is all, doing your duty does not need to be eulogized.
- CH: Of course.
- HH: You have *carte blanche* to use all the Reich's resources as you see fit as if it was my own person requesting them, an order will go out to that effect, don't defraud me any further.
- CH: Permission to detain and question the rest of the Red Cross delegates.
- HH: Denied
- CH: May I inquire as to why?
- HH: You may not. You have enough work to do, leave the Red Cross to me.

The line cut off: Hoffman lowered the apparatus from his ear, looked at it briefly in amazement and put it back on the phone set. The tone had been amicable businesslike but, the words encouraging, the subtext mortal.

- That was the closest I've come to death - he said to Heiser beside him.

Heiser contemplated the young official, his pallid tense face and he felt something he didn't think he'd ever feel towards one of the black crows, he actually felt sorry for him.

Farmyard Barn, 50km to Prague, 4km to the nearest village

The straw was flattened underneath by the cows that spent the dark hours chewing the cud or lowing, the warmth they generated a blessing that kept the night from being unconformable instead of scarcely bearable. To one side sat the truck looming over them, sainted salvation on eight wheels Dagan called it having saved them from certain capture. Václav had told them it had been a huge sacrifice because now it couldn't be used, fortunately, it couldn't be traced having never been registered, it had arrived in one of the sweeping convolutions that had moved people booty possessions and material from one end of Europe to another and here it would stay till the end of German rule whenever that was going to happen. You could never think never but it did seem a remote outcome judging on the state of the present world. Dagan knew what he was doing could shorten the conflict but would it and by how much was pure conjecture. At the start, Kessler had been euphoric about their escape and had put a brave face on the surroundings, better than any German cell. Dagan had time to start rethinking what he knew of atomic theory, what he had learned in the early 1930s and what had happened since. He'd been in Dublin for other reasons altogether that time but had always been interested in Science and Medicine and had joined Kessler on several projects during a period when he'd had the time and having met Maria early on had stayed longer than originally intended. Splitting the atom had been all the talk at the time and finally, Kessler's friend Ernest Waston had been succeeded with his team in Cambridge and that had given an impetus to the whole field. Now it was all about maximizing energy release, radioactive isotopes, uranium, plutonium, heavy water, enrichment, all big discussions about tiny things as Kessler was fond of saying. You're not keeping up he scolded Dagan on more than one occasion.

289

- I'm a mere passenger, a pedestrian in the quantum paths, in the foothills of the issue – Dagan aggrieved had countered, he had a headache with the soup of calculations.
- Lazy boy, always a drink and a cigarette to hand, my parrot has a greater understanding of the problems – Kessler said.
- Badger the budgie then – Dagan then had laughed uncontrollably, for the alliteration maybe, he felt dizzy again.
- I thought we had got rid of you in Dublin. A serious business should be left to serious people - Dagan had forgotten how exacting Kessler could be. He'd be revitalized by his escape, the physical exertion, the emotional uplift of a last-minute saving from the wolf's jaws, he was rejuvenated by that sense of a second chance and a pain in the butt as a result - If you used half of half of half of the brains you have you could achieve so much, instead, it has to be the good life   Kessler the reborn said.
- Thanks, I think – it was Dagan faced with the phoenix-like Kessler who was beginning to feel under the weather – Forty-odd years of iron constitution and here I am suffering from jungle fever.
- What? Jungle fever, where have you been? - Maria asked.
- A long story, moral of it is, watch what they put in your glass, make sure it's just alcohol and lo and behold a week in a hospital, three weeks without missing a camp on the way I was and a lovely brisk walk in a wood and I find myself a tad feverish - with that he sank on the straw, alarmed when she saw his face Maria put her hand to his brow.
- A temperature of at least 39°C or 40°C, no wonder you physics is so at odds – Maria said shocked by the strength of the fever.
- I'll prove it's a flat earth yet – Dagan rallied from his prone position.
- Drink this water now – Maria brooked no opposition.
- Phah water, are trying to poison me, I must be really sick if you expect me to drink mere water. In fact water will make me sicker, it's for the animals. Irish people drink two things, tea and alcoholic beverages – pronounced the deluded Celt.
- Water never hurt man or beast, worse of all that Scotch you put away, I can't imagine your kidneys – Maria wrinkled her nose.
- Scotch! - Dagan said taking a sip then a great gulp as thirst came over him – Scotch! How little you know about me, Scotch! she says to be sure, drinking water from pigs troughs is better don't you know.

With that damning Irishman's verdict on the uisce beatha albain or Scotch whiskey in the vernacular Dagan slumped down. Over the next day or so he was nursed by Maria as his strength ebbed and waned, it was a combination of the fever he'd been injected with, the endless round of visits and the tension involved in watching his every move as any slip up by him or any by many others in London Prague or the US might give him away. You heat a kettle and sure as night follows day you get steam bursting through the spout and from under the lid. Maria covered Dagan with straw to keep him warm and fed him fresh cow's milk she extracted from the udders of a cow that was their housemate, she helped him do his needs asking her father to go for a slow walk to the other end of the barn to save Dagan's blushes, she kept him warm at night as she slept beside him, her firm curved back and behind pushing into Dagan. On the third morning, she woke up to notice a new addition to Dagan's posture, his revived libido nudging into her showed he was firmly on the road to recovery. Maria turned her head to Dagan who was wide awake and looking at her with a small guilty smile on his face.

- Firmly on the road to recovery aren't we, forgive the pun – Maria tut-tutted.
- I feel a lot better, the fever has broken though and I could kill for a bath – Dagan voice was clear and steady.
- You could have told me earlier.
- I didn't want to rest you from your slumbers as you looked so peaceful, better than when you wake up it's a different reality awaiting you – Dagan said well intentionally.
- I'm used to this new reality as all Czechs are and even more us Jews. How can people hate us so much – Maria's sheer disbelief at ephemeral civilisation's rapid disappearance showed?
- That's history. Now in your case whatever happens you're not going back - Dagan put in the positives.
- How can you guarantee that? – Maria was openly sceptic.
- I can and I do now tell me what the hell has happened while I was away in dadalala land, how long was I *non compes mentus* by the way? – Dagan needed to get a grip on the situation.
- Your Latin is a bad your physics. You were out days, Václav was here meanwhile. He told my father off because he had wandered into the farmyard, he says that the Germans are up in arms and are putting controls and checkpoints all over, the whole country and resistance activity is on hold, nobody can move anywhere clandestinely. It beggars belief he said that they would be so

291

interested in you and me! Václav said that the Germans are very unpredictable and it's likely they are planning something.

- The Germans are planning to find us period, they won't stop shaking the tree till something falls. What did Václav say about us moving, when do we start?
- Stay put and wait is what he said – Maria related.
- Christ! – Dagan swore in frustration.
- He will try and come soon; the farmer told us not to go outside, not to show lights at night or even pop our heads up at the windows and of course, hide from anyone in the barn. We have all the water we need, paper to write on, animals to keep us warm and no one is beating, whipping or working us till we are exhausted. This is a holiday! My father looks ten years younger.

They both glanced over at the physicist sitting by the window, making the most of the daylight and scribbling furiously in a child's school notebook while muttering to himself, he certainly had a burning energy not visible the first time Dagan saw him in the camp less than a week ago.

- Great! Happy for the man! He got those ten years from me, read the 'Third Policeman' it explains how; I in return must look ten years older. I'm glad I don't have a mirror to look into.
- I was about to say... - Maria said playfully.
- How's your father's work going? Not a lot you can do with pen and paper – Dagan interrupted quickly.
- You'd be surprised, you can theorise and calculate what the results should be and just wait till you can get to a laboratory to prove it by experiments. They identified an element like that once, theoretically and there it was when they went looking for it in the laboratory. He has already filled twenty pages just this morning, he's gained weight, he sleeps like a rock, and he even does some light callisthenics, I really can't get over the change; he looks like lasting longer than me!
- You don't look so bad, the flush is coming back to your cheeks in fact - Maria obligingly blushed – I stand vindicated, except I can't stand. Temporally. Anything to eat? I am famished – Dagan looked around hopefully.
- I'll get some stew and bread we were left and some milk from our friend over there – Maria went and brought over the food - The stews a bit cold but it tastes like caviar to me all that gristle and hard to identify meat cuts - she started to bring a spoonful to Dagan's mouth - Open up – she ordered.
- Oh, come on I'm not a baby, I'm perfectly able to feed myself.

- I'm sure you are - Maria said looking at his raised handshaking in the air, she didn't put the spoon in it but continued – this is too valuable to waste being spilt on your jacket so cooperate, it's feeding time at the zoo.

Dagan took it like a man and baby, the nourishment flowed into his system and he slept for most of the rest of the day. Sleep glorious sleep, he might be in a barn on the run but he felt he hadn't slept like that since his teens. The next day they repeated the pattern and by the following morning, Dagan exhibited signs of full recovery, relishing his breakfast of oats and barley boiled with fresh milk and salt. The day had turned mellow and bright, they'd been there a week which was okay by Dagan as they needed to regain strength for the coming ordeals. The downside was the longer they were in hiding the more chance they had of being uncovered or betrayed. Václav came late that day bringing food, clothes and news that was not in the newspapers, everything the ardent Nazi didn't want to know.

- Shut down! The country is starting to feel like it is in a straitjacket, we can't leave here for the moment – Václav was exasperated
- How did you arrive here so? – challenged Dagan.
- With great difficultly but I found a way. Now the sewers are off-limits too, they have been fumigating nonstop since last week, rats! They say we have a plague, rats! As if the Germans care about Czechs being overrun with rats, now rats are in danger of disappearing like from a ship on a long voyage.
- They knew about the escape routes before it's only now they care – Dagan couldn't get the faces of the families out of his head, sleepy and resigned, I hope they blocked up the grill we passed through if they were going around fumigating - They always knew, people knew and people for a loaf of bread tell everything, a reassuring thought, how many loaves of bread would somebody get for me. Which is why after a week here I think it's time to move on and out of this area and country, go anywhere else, by walking or cycling or train or in another super-truck but we're got to go. What does London said this week, what code did they use?
- The code was blue – Václav told him.
- South towards Ljubljana – Dagan told him.
- Not west to Switzerland? That is where we figured you'd want to go especially as you didn't tell us from the beginning.
- Everything boxed off, safer for all concerned even I wasn't sure till you told me that. London didn't know themselves till now, these

things take a lot of organization and we're far from Allied held
territory

Dagan told a few pork pies and some outright lies, his nose Pinocchio'd
to the door unaided. The various escape routes had been long and
thoroughly explored by British SOE agents using them and the
Germans chasing after them. The routes varied but all were far from
friendly ground to start with. Switzerland the nearest but Austria is in
the way and even if you made it through the Tyrol's and over the
mountains at the same time as avoiding the Germans unless you
avoided the Swiss as well you might end up interned and spend the rest
of the war there. No offence Geneva but no thanks, Kessler would find
the mountains tough going though heck Dagan was dreading it too.
East playing catch up with the German advance (stalled temporally by
General winter which was as hard on civilians as it was on the military)
in the middle of December crossing two front lines and the best
outcome of all that is that you are in Russia. Geneva begins to look not
half bad by comparison. Next roll of the compass, north, back through
the dark heart of the dark empire. Dagan had seen enough by now to
know it was a suicide mission not even worth contemplating.

And that left one point on the compass. The Brits could move around
the Mediterranean more or less and the Adriatic was long and rugged
and full of islands and inlets. It was so close to Italy the thinking went
that the Italians could safely ignore it and so was less protected. Blue
for the blue sea, that's British thinking, white was Switzerland, black
Germany and red the Soviet Union. The sky is also blue thought Dagan
but he hadn't told the Brits that. They expected Dagan and his charges
to make their way down into recently occupied Yugoslavia (and hence
lots of remnants of the previous regime, hiding out in mountains and
forest that the Nazis hadn't had time to clean up), first the top bit,
Slovenia, then cross into Croatia staying away from Serbia. The ancient
settlements of the Pula peninsula dotted with Roman ruins, there in a
small bay they'd be met and transported in a midget submarine, the
one size that could travel the length of the Adriatic unobserved abet
very very slowly, maybe the war would be over by the time they get to
Malta. The plan was crazy maybe but claustrophobic definitely. Dagan
hoped they had brought plenty of blank paper for the good doctor; he'll
cook up a storm under those conditions. There were faster ways he had
told the British but they'd ignored him so he had made his own
arrangements.

- Václav we're been here a week, enough time to regain our
  strength, now it's time to move, staying here is inviting trouble,

someone might say something to someone and the bad guys will be in here a New York minute.
- A what? You're not in some gangster movie, talk to me in English proper – Václav smiled.

Dagan couldn't help a small smile to himself at that, suddenly he cheered up immensely. A small crack of humour in the bleak scenario meant a lot, the augers were pronouncing in their favour he thought, the tides were changing. It didn't mean much but he'd always been a bit superstitious. Might get out of this after all.

- I want to move on, start travelling again, the four of us - he said deliberately and clearly. I feel it in my bones, south, Slovenia and to the coast.
- South! That is full of partisans, lots of defeated Yugoslav troops mad as hell and armed to the teeth.
- And so no friend of the Germans, just the sort of people we'd like to meet.
- Don't be too sure, they've gone cold on the British like half of defeated Europe, must have been for all the help you didn't give them. That's if they wait to hear what you say and don't slit your throat for the gold they know you are carrying. British agents are famous for the gold they carry for the food, drink or for a girl. They are brigands outside the law.
- The Brits or the partisans? Anway that's where you come in. You know the good guys from the bad guys, who's going for gold, who's going for revenge, who's pro-Peter and who's pro Joe, pro Adolf, pro yo. You know your way around, you have family there, your wife was Slovakian, you traded there, lived there, played there – Václav looked astounded, so did Maria. Kessler, on the other hand, was like a child in the corner, just interested in one thing, being led to a physics lab to get working and everything else was just static in the background.
- You know a lot about me – Václav stated bluntly.
- Our lives are in your hands. We know when and why you joined the resistance and we know you are in this till the end - Maria caught the last bit of this conversation and looked appalled and intrigued.
- So many bad things happen these days my circumstances are not worthy of broadcast – Václav turned away.

Dagan put his hand on Václav's shoulder who had the look of a man lost in his thoughts, lost in happier times.

- What you're doing now will help turn everything around, more than you can know you can trust me. This man could be the difference between which side has a superweapon and when and again it's more than I can tell you. To be honest, the less you know the better.

Dagan pitched his words and his tone along with an open stance, the tantalizing snippets hoping to create a level of trust and confidence in the Czech, the what and why of this whole operation but still Václav took it badly.

- I don't need cheering up pepping encouragement backslapping sweet words hard words or words of any sort. I know what I have to do, kill Germans until they are all gone from my country, packed off to hell for all I care – he said.
- Or Connacht – Dagan said under his breath.
- All I care is a free Czechoslovakia or die trying. Right now I like you, we killed that German in the hotel, you shot another and then some more and their dogs in the forest. That makes you a friend for life.

A horror movie of images unconsciously flickered across his mind's eye, the dance macabre of grotesque dead and dying the past week by his hand. On the whole, he'd rather forget the way he'd gained Václav's friendship but all the same, he nodded at the comradery of those who fought and killed and lived to talk about it, made you closer than brothers united by links difficult to explain.

- South it is my friend and as soon as possible – they shook hands as their eyes meet. Dagan again felt a looming sensation of foreboding, he itched to get moving, he didn't what to be on the farm and in the barn any longer.
- South – repeated Václav – towards all the roadblocks, patrols, spies, informers, partisans, ultras, SS, Gestapo, idiots, police and sympathizes. South when you could stay here in this nice warm comfortable home from home, here away from the badness, here till the war is over, here with your cow - he swept his arm around the barn.
- Putting it that way I'll stay – Dagan said.
- Of course, you won't, south it is, the cow insists, sick of you she is, we leave tomorrow at first light – Václav added.

Prague, 15th of December

Hoffman was beginning to feel the build-up of tension, one week had gone by and not a sniff of his flown quarry. This was the sum of it and it wasn't enough, one week of activity directed by Heiser that had been frenetic, close on one hundred thousand men of the occupying forces, police, auxiliaries, soldiers on leave, the resting, the walking wounded, Frei Corps veterans, 1914-18 Austria Hungarian loyalists had all been drafted in to help, 'it was all bigger than most army groups' Heiser had told him and was twenty times what he'd commanded before.

Hoffman also knew about what it was like to be the centre of the opprobrium of thousands of military and millions of civilians of middle Europe. The constant roadblocks, checkpoints and lightening inspections may have yielded a bonanza of smugglers, petty infractions, ration hoarders, black market operators, deserters, political opponents and some Jews but that was just not what he was looking desperately for. The jewel in the crown had been some well-known resistance members caught with incriminating papers or small arms. Two had been killed trying to escape measured against one German wounded in the leg, curiously such lawfulness was having strange advise effects, with smuggling all but wiped out the daily situation began to be critical.

- If this goes on I'll run out of whiskey in a week – had been one comment. Hoffman suggested comprehension and recommended the local wine.
- But the whisky was the only way to make the local wine palpable – came the half-serious reply.

The whole of the protectorate was at breaking point. The whisky complaint had been jocular but the grumbles and genuine hardship were beginning to manifest itself in the civilian population, it couldn't be called opposition but it was becoming more vocal as the yoke was tightened. Not that Hoffman cared about the privations of the locals, he had but one concern, he knew that if his quarry moved he'd get them and if they stayed put he'd get them too, time was all he needed so stuff the rest, Himmler was behind the actions he was taking and that was all that mattered, 'Acceptable decrease in iniquitous activity' he said to Hoffman during one of the many phone calls.

- HH: As a policeman first and foremost it makes me very happy but I am a secret policeman with all the excitement of our new adventure against the Americans. We must move against the Russians hard and turn to what's left of the British and their new ally. Busy times so I have not been as attentive as I hoped in this matter, perhaps you should be grateful for that.

- CH: It's only a matter of time if they move it greatly increases our chances of finding them. If they stay put we'll find them so they have to move. We have gone through the towns and villages and are now starting on the farms, outbuildings, summer homes and anywhere else that would be easy enough on the old man.

- HH: We have been rounding up all the Americans we can find, even a famous poet who is quite happy with us and who will cooperate on various activities with Goebbels, we are delighted.

- CH: Quite a coup.

- HH: But getting back to this matter - the voice went cold – your reasoning seems sound, this was not Churchill attacking Hitler but an agent on another mission who decided to take advantage of an opportunity that presented itself. An opportunity thankfully the Gods were not in favour of – Hoffman thought 'what Gods did he have in mind?' Hoffman was a Catholic who'd spent time in a seminary but had realised his mission was else were, beside Himmler and the rest, Himmler didn't know that no one knew it. Hoffman has his reasons for leaving, he was more concerned with this world and those who lived in than in God's. Himmler then mentioned some scientific missions he'd sent to examine powerful legends with the idea of bringing back for the benefit of the SS and the German people – The Ark of the Covenant was probably destroyed at the same time as the Temple but no matter, we are modern knights templar in service of the Aryan nation - he concluded - and you Karl Hoffman have devastated Czech resistance in ten days, which is to your credit but have not found the renegades. That is not so creditable; having these people in liberty is a direct personal affront to me, Germany and the Fuhrer.

Hoffman knew he'd built up some goodwill but it was unlikely to last unless he caught the big prize, a British agent, how Himmler would love that. Behind this was a lot of politics and jostling for position as always with the high couturiers around the supreme power. Himmler would love to trump Admiral Canizares, the actual head of German intelligence. Canizares and his huge powerful organization was, strangely in Himmler's eyes, separate from the SS and Gestapo, it irked him as he wanted all the state security bodies under his control. The fact that Canizares had been less than successful with British espionage was a key factor now. If Himmler could get his hands on this agent, uncover the plot and present the spy who had tried to take a pot shot at Hitler what a coup that would be. As if the stakes weren't high enough for Hoffman that made them higher. Crippling Czech resistance, rounding up dozens of criminals, Jews, deserters and whatnot, wasn't enough.

- HH: We'll give it 48 hours. Good night - Himmler hung up.
- Brotov! - Hoffman called his adjutant who came running up smartly. Hoffman's adjutant was not an officer, not a mere sergeant.
- Sir! – Hoffman could see the relief in the man's face, rather not have to speak to Himmler himself – Did everything go well with the status call?
- For the moment but not if I don't find Malone – Hoffman shouted, he crumpled a piece of paper and threw it on the huge table laid out with an equally huge map of middle Europe. It was chockablock with pins marking roadblocks and troop dispositions, others pins were colour-coded, green for acts of common dissent and agitation, red was physical resistance, blue meant vulgar criminals and black showed were deserters had been found. The areas around Prague and major urban centres were replete and the centre of Prague a bouquet of pin flags, green ones in the more affluent zones of Prague as you'd expect, blue in working-class neighbourhoods and red evenly spread. In the countryside, the pins were more sporadic. Heiser came in the door - You still here? – Hoffman asked.
- Let me guess, Himmler was very supportive of our efforts and is urging us to even greater heights – Heiser also asked for an update of the latest Prinzestrass prep talk.
- Exactly, his words were very similar – Hoffman bluffed.

The pair so different in many ways had formed a close working relationship based on duty and being squarely in the eye of the RF. Their lives hanging by a thread they knew the cost of failure, Himmler hadn't got where he had by being nice to people especially those who weren't giving him what he wanted.

- We have forty-eight hours – Hoffman admitted.
- That much! I thought he'd yank us back to HQ now or give us a day at the most - Heiser looked at the map.
- We have done everything in our power, the entire resources of the protectorate have spent this past cold week ransacking rummaging and shaking Bohemia from top to bottom. Informants have been squeezed, rewards offered, criminals locked

up, deserters shot. Now it all depends on luck and that she smiles down on us in the next two days.

- Luck doesn't enter into it just hard work and statistics. The more we do the more chances we'll have, some unknown factor, seemingly unconnected will lead them to us. They have to be lucky all the time, we have to be lucky just once – Heiser tried to encourage his young cohort - So what's next?

- I dare … – Hoffman started to say before a knock on the door was followed by Bortov entering in eager haste.

- Sir, I think you should listen to this. There is a farmer outside who is very annoyed with his neighbour, he says they have filled his barn with strange people, his favourite cow is off-limits and has possibly run dry and not only that they have parked a huge truck inside and won't remove it.

- A flaming great big truck you say –Hoffman and Heiser looked at each other in amazement.

- Tell him to come straight in – the army man ordered Bortov.

Chapter XI

Czech countryside, 16th December

The group were now two miles away from the farm resting in a culvert at the side of the road which they had just crossed one by one crouched down. Václav was adjusting his backpack when his ears picked up, 'Sssshhhh' he said quickly and gestured to his straggly group to follow him immediately into the undergrowth a bit further away as the sound of motors approached. The woody copse offered the perfect protection from the road as the cavalcade of vehicles approached with a roar of the engines around the corner. The column consisted of several trucks full of troops, armoured cars front and back, two motorcycle and pillion outriders and taking up the rear the command unit of the officer's car plus communications/radio van. The convoy of vehicles stopped at the turnoff that led to the farm, the same road they had walked down ten minutes earlier.

The commander consulted with the first of the outriders and both looked at a map, they pulled a Czech civilian male from the lorry in front, the man was elderly and walked with difficulty as he was prodded forward. Václav cursed silently, he recognized the figure even at this distance as Kveton, the neighbouring farmer, Kveton did what was expected, he pointed down the lane jabbing his finger in the farms' direction. Reading the scene from afar was easy enough being one oft-repeated throughout history. Dagan knew all about sell-outs and they were nothing the Irish had invented, the commandant in charge ordered the column up the side road. Dagan and Václav now focused their attention on this figure as it was Dagan's turn to curse inwardly. 'That's the SS Captain who shadowed me throughout Germany' he whispered as there in front of them was indeed Karl Hoffman, the tall pale bearing, sharp features and slicked back jet black hair evident even at this remove. 'Very strange' commented Václav who took out a small pair of binoculars and looked over.

- Yes, it's Kveton all right, I'd know that sour son of a bitch anywhere. Don't know the German, SS alright but he's a Colonel now - he gave Dagan the looking-glasses - They're going up to the farm. We're fucked.
- Looks like we outstayed our welcome alright and I'm beginning to get the reasoning for the shutdown – Dagan added.

- What now? - Maria asked as the most of the convoy took off around the turn and was rapidly swallowed by the dense forest foliage.

The outrider and pillion stayed behind with the sullen Czech farmer who would not want to be seen pointing the finger at a fellow countryman for the hated occupying forces. What he didn't know was that he had been seen and was a condemned man. Václav answered Maria by drawing a hand across his throat.

- We're on foot and are thirty or forty minutes ahead of the Germans – Dagan summed up the critical situation they found themselves in.
- We need motorized transport to get away, without it we might as well put our hands up now – Václav looked around.
- We shouldn't have left the truck in the barn – Dagan argued.
- We had no choice, it was too well known – Václav muttered.
- Well as for motorized transport I think we have some to hand – Dagan gestured below, Václav thought it over a second and didn't hesitate.
- Kveton your time is up, listen we'll go down to the end of the road, they aren't expecting trouble. We'll be so close we can't miss and we'd better not. I'll take the officer you take the pillion. Kveton we'll deal with later. Clean shots and don't mess up the uniforms. You two stay here and don't make a sound – he said to Maria and her father who both nodded vigorously dump struck by the turn of events.
- And best not to look either, turn your backs it won't be pretty – Dagan added - Václav these are hand signals we used back in my rebel days, this means stop, this means go, this left this right - Dagan quickly demonstrating with his fist the signalling system they used crawling around Irish bogs on their way to ambush Black and Tans. – An old pal of mine Dan taught me it and boy did he know how to sneak up on people.
- This means take cover, this is retreat, this is to give cover fire and this is thank you for the advice – Václav held up Churchill's two fingers victory salute the other way round that meant something completely different as they both knew, then he reversed the signal and smiled - You friend Mister Breen and his book are very popular these days in lower Bohemia the same goes for Mister Collins. We are learning a lot from them and it is pleasing that you were a colleague of theirs, now come on we have little time to waste.

With that he and Dagan stealthily approached the edge of the road to within twenty meters across and to the left of the three figures, the two Germans were talking together, the soldier was smoking while the officer had just put his out by throwing it into the undergrowth. The elderly Czech turncoat grumpily remonstrated about it in his language which was lost on the Germans who ignored him either way, they just continued their conversation, words floated over about the usual soldierly concerns, not enough food, food not hot enough, not enough women, not hot enough...roars of laughter....Bohemia woman came in for rough appraisal.

Kveton approached them and asked for a cigarette, they laughed and pushed him away adding a coarse Czech expression that even Dagan knew. Dagan lined up his sights, it was easy, the distance was point-blank, he decided against aiming for the heart as it would ruin the uniform but it did run the risk of missing if the rifle wasn't in good condition. The head isn't that big even at twenty paces but any hit was normally enough. Václav made the signal, Dagan was to be the first to fire as the convoy was well out of earshot, it was now or never, he tensed the trigger, kept his sights level and fired. The retort and deafening sound didn't impede him see his shot slam home into the unaware German who dropped instantly blood-splattered cigarette still stuck to the lips. The shot from Václav just after hit the other German who had a fraction of a second to be shocked but not long enough to react or suffer unduly before he was bundled over the bike by the force of the blow. Václav and Dagan both broke cover before the second corpse stopped falling, they sprinted over as Kveton looked on in wonder and bewilderment at the crumpled figures in front and the rapidly approaching armed men. Kveton's eyes budged wide as he recognized the onrushing figure and he tentatively reached for the dead Germans pistol rifle but Václav was up to him before he could put thought to action.

- Gregor, surprised to see me, we had arranged to meet in your barn later today but I see you made new friends.
- I-i-i-Ivan –the old man spluttered still unable to register the dramatic change in events – it's not like that, I was informed on, I am innocent, I would never betray you.
- Sounds familiar, they all say that. I have no doubt somebody informed all right and all the evidence is pointing to you.

The scenario was a bleak much played out theme in Dagan's life and he supposed in Václav's as well and here it was his problem to deal with so Dagan wasted no time stripping the dead Germans of their helmets, blood-splattered overcoats, boots, belts and guns. Dagan didn't pay much attention to what Václav was saying to Gregor as the pleas and accusations flew between them finishing in some sort of 'Proper tribunal in front of the people' from Vaclav. The old man must have gladly taken the bait and relaxed before a gunshot rang out and Václav now heaved the body of Gregor on top of the bike. Meanwhile, one of the inert Germans coughed somehow and moved, Dagan knelt and held his hand, the barely conscious man managed to whisper something like 'Gretchen Greyhen' in a sputter of blood and spittle before starting to shaking all over, Dagan held on tight as he finally slipped away, it was heart-rendering as the grip went limp and the eyes rolled upwards, he hadn't felt pain. Dagan got up and finishing stripped and heaved them both on top of the Czech.

- According to the uniform tags you have just become Lt. Ernst Kaufman and I will be the good soldier R. Werner – Dagan said mournfully as Václav just grunted - Take the bike up to where the Kessler's are waiting, dump the bodies as far as possible. I will clean up here and leave it like my grannies front parlour – Dagan proposed.

Both knew they had to buy time, had to make the Germans think that the guardians and the Czech had got bored or fell out and left so they would be able to put as much distance between themselves and this spot before the Germans figured out what had actually happened. Václav started the bike, he looked well used to two-wheel vehicles.

- Mechanic? – ventured Dagan.
- We don't have time for swapping work histories. Here we do a bit of everything and long before today, I was a dispatch rider.
- Well don't over gun the engine and sorry for taking an interest – said Dagan gruffly.

Václav grunted and took off down the road where after thirty metres he turned off then disappeared as he pushed the overladen bike past the overhanging branches taking care to leave as little sign of passage at that point as possible. Dagan cleaned up the action, removing any evidence he could see, he picked up cigarettes butts, tufted up trampled grass with branches of leaves, smoothed over footprints and wiped blood and other organic matter he didn't care to identify with handfuls of grass. Five frantic minutes passed, too long, he ought to be going. Normally at an ambush scene, you want to leave as much mayhem as you can lying around so he wasn't used to all this whitewashing. Once he was satisfied the stretch of road superficially looked like the rest he ran down to the point where Václav had gone off, Dagan gently parted the canopy as Václav had and was off the road. He hadn't realised he had been pumped up by being exposed out in the open and now that he was out of sight again he felt a charge of tension drop from his shoulders. He tufted up grass, removed tire marks with this boots, picked up broken twigs and brushed leaves, trying to make it hard to follow the trail, hard work as the bike had been heavily laden but anything to gain time. After about twenty meters he got faster as he only did the bare minimum, the bike tracks only and he quickly came across the group, ten minutes had passed since the ambush. Václav meanwhile had cleaned the bike and the rescued Jews were mounting up on the sidecar, Maria had armed herself with a machine gun pistol and looked well for it.

- I want to find some Germans to use this on - she said coldly – if it were the last thing I do it will be a good end.
- Just so you know not a drop of German blood in me – Dagan said looking around – Where are our the...those...heck you know what I mean.
- Two dead Germans and a dead traitor. We are making up for the havoc you have caused in the resistance. Dozens had been caught because of your pop trick at the moustache - Václav was contemptuous and jocular at the same time – They are in a ravine just over there and won't be found easily, with any luck the animals will take care of them.
- There poor mothers – Maria intoned.
- My poor mother! - Václav responded exasperated – There's no room for sentiment, they should have stayed with their mothers in Germany and then nothing would have happened to them.
- Mine only drinks gallons of tea during the day and wine at dinner, is a demon hand at Bridge and is fine TG – Dagan added to break the tension putting a hand on Maria's shoulder.

Maria and Kessler were making themselves as comfortable as possible in the sidecar while Dagan mounted as pillion passenger behind Václav as this revved the engine.

- Let's waste more time, we need to go fast and far before they start after us. Don't worry about Maria, it was she who helped me drag the bodies over to the ravine and push them in - Václav said - and she did it dry-eyed - he grinned – babushka – he added sweetly – now we go or else we are next into the ravine.

Down the forest path, he moved on the motorcycle, similar to the type of lane they'd traversed in the lorry a week earlier but even narrower. Dagan had to turn his head and hang on tight to Václav who kept gunning the engine to get over bumps, outstretched roots, ditches and dykes. All the usual terrain you would expect of a country lane. Maria and Kessler beside them managed as best they could and blessed by all were the clear straight flat parts, regrettably few as once encountered they disappeared to be replaced by rough tough bone jarringly terrain, more than once they had to dismount as Václav took the bike down a stream bank over and out the other slope. The physical effort of dismounting, walking and remounting felt like you'd been in a car crash, a reasonable approximation, the cold didn't help but at least it was not snowing, the unusually mild weather had played in their favour even the sun made brief appearances between the overhead leaves. Dagan and Václav gave their heavy German overcoats to the sidecar passengers who not a bit squeamish about blood stains and brain matter took them gladly.

Back at the Farmyard

The farmhouse and yard seemed empty. Of the three dwellers, they knew where the Gregor the farmer was but the old drone and young serving girl? Warned no doubt to go visit some family somewhere which also neatly explained the absence of the pony and trap. The Germans crashed into the yard as chickens and dogs fled gawking and howling in the other directions. The barn was closed with a wooden plank across it to stop the large dilapidated barn doors from swinging opening. Solid oak the plank and the barn a mix of pine, cedar and hazelnut. Hoffman waited impatiently as the doors were opened and the platoon ran in shouting 'Hands in the air. Surrender Surrender Surrender' each soldier knew the value of the intended targets, shooting was strictly forbidden in the case of Malone and only when lives were threatened for the rest. 'Alive' was the word Himmler has used most. 'I want that ingrate Irishman alive'.

Still with arms to the ready to fire, combat fever pumping and stories of the previous week's pursuit through the forest well known in the ranks anything could have happened if they had encountered more than just the cow. The sharpshooting Irishman had gained a fearsome reputation but as the barn was empty except for the lowing of the 'dry' Swiss brown cow the tension of impending action rapidly faded away. Some of the soldiers accustomed to life on farms calmed down the startled animals as Hoffman and Heiser marched in, the Sergeant came rushing up and spluttered the 'All clear Sir' to which Heiser ordered them to take parties and search the rest of the buildings and the surrounding area, the Sergeant took off.

- Sir this is where they were – a grey-haired corporal beckoned them over with a polite cough.

They followed him around the back of the truck, clear of booby traps they'd been informed. A single bullet hole in the canvas on the ground evidence of the previous week's close encounter with the Germans in the forest, everything stank to high heavens.

- Although you wouldn't think this area has been cleaned – the Corporal said before flourishing a chamber pot in the area – recently used by a female.
- Male, female, there's a difference? – Hoffman the policeman's interest in forensics came to the fore.
- Oh yes, I use to be a sewer man and the sewers below the abbey always smelt different to those below the monastery – the NCO replied.
- Let us find these people and put an end to this war early so you can go back as soon as possible to your previous...er...profession – Hoffman suggested.
- Girls' schools and boys schools the same, sweeter and less sharp the girls, funny that – added the grizzled old-timer.
- Such domination of your chosen field my good man, why did you volunteer, you are needed on the home front? – Heiser joined in.
- A bit of air, the gases down the sewers are very dangerous and it ages you. I'm ten years younger than I look you know, forty just gone so the Army seemed like a good idea and of course to do my duty is an honour as well – he added.
- Plenty of fresh air it's true – Heiser couldn't help agree.
- Without a doubt true – Hoffman added - what else does your keen olfactory senses tell you?
- Begging your pardon Sir my 'oly' what?
- Your nose man, your sense of smell.
- Well Sir, I never heard it called that, left school at twelve but smells I know, they was four, the cow kept them warm, they cooked on a Kerosene stove very dangerous too which is why they cleared away the straw - he uncovered a section beside the wall in the corner - the food - he sniffed - cabbage soup, tea and milk of course. She used some eau de cologne, one of the men wore

François Coty of Paris, another stinks of prison and one of the
countryside – the corporal pronounced very sure of himself.
- Very informative so you say, the cow is not dry after all, even I
  can smell the cabbage among the stink and a good scent is
  always Parisian but can you give us anything else? – Hoffman
  asked.
- They were here about an hour ago – the man said confirming
  Hoffman's suspicions.
- We are right behind them – Hoffman's voice rose, he felt the chase
  - Heiser let's the get the dogs out!

The canine survivors from the forest were given some of the straw to
sniff and went barking mad at the familiar smell and were soon pulling
on their leads.

- Set them loose for Christ's sake – Heiser ordered the handlers and
  Hoffman couldn't but agree. The dogs took off down the way
  they'd all come a short while before.
- As we supposed. Malone was just here, but surely we are close
  enough behind them now and this time they have no ace up the
  sleeve – Hoffman said looking at the giant truck beside him.
- How did that get through the forest? – Heiser wondered and then
  to the prematurely aged sewer man - that's quite a gift you have
  my man, we need you front with the dogs. You'll put them right
  should they go astray. Mount up! – he shouted at his cohort.

Forty minutes later they were at the main road if you could call it that
more a step up from a rutted dirt track but it could support tanks if it
had to, was open and broad enough for traffic to pass in two directions
however the dog teams paid no attention and kept on going straight
across it and into the bushes on the other side.

- Where are the motorcycle outriders and the farmer? You order
them to stay put – Hoffman observed looking around.

- I did and junior officials rarely disobey senior officers and in my
case never. If Kaufman and Werner value their lives they'd better
turn up right now – Heiser said puzzled.

- Maybe they took the Czech off for 'disposal' – the Sergeant
suggested.

- No one told them to do that either – Heiser pointed out

- Tell the dog teams to halt - Hoffman shouted at the team leader as
he dismounted.

- What are you imagining now? - Heiser asked he knew that look on Hoffman's face who lost in thought didn't reply straight away.

- You might know better than I Colonel, it's ninety minutes since we arrived here, how far could you go on a motorbike cross country in that time, say four people on rough country lanes? – He said eventually.

- They have the bike is that what you think? – Heiser conjectured.

- The only sensible answer, German troops don't disappear without orders, they just don't. The fugitives came down this road the dogs tell us that and just after crossing we came along. Knowing we'd be right behind then and having left the best-known truck across Bohemia behind they overcame the motorbike team and the informer. The corpses are somewhere over there - he traced an imaginary arc with his finger a hundred yards in front - they couldn't lose time, they cleared up the crime scene, dumped the bodies and took off after, so again after ninety minutes how far?

- The weather hardened the ground and that helps, to the rough paths you have to add in streams, culverts, hedges. I'd say they could quite easily manage thirty kilometres per hour, the bike is way overladen and that will slow them down but the bad news is that the BMX RM 75 was designed for just this type of activity, they've built a fucking beautiful bike is what the men are saying in the East, has gears for on-road and off-road and even can connect and disconnect a special axial to the sidecar to make it more agile. It weighs a ton but goes a bomb, yes 30 mph even over laden because the old man and the girl don't weigh so much, 35 mph maximum.

- We're here - Hoffman was pulling out the map and pointing to it and with his finger traced a circle with a radius of fifty kilometres - Radio HQ the Irishman Malone, the two renegade Jews and an unknown Czech resistance member believed to be Vaclav, the last of the three kings are heading south away from our coordinates, subjects are armed with MP machine pistols and are driving a stolen BMX R75 motorbike and sidecar. Block all roads in a fifty kilometres radius and jump to it. I want them in place in thirty minutes – Hoffman turned to Heiser.

- So what are the odds this time – Heiser said looking at Hoffman.
- This time I cannot be so blasé, 50:50, we are ready and relentless, they are resourceful and desperate, and the outcome is finely balanced. We can block the roads and wait. If they stay off the

roads I want the Luftwaffe involved, spotter planes flying search grids here, here and here.

- The Luftwaffe the saviours of Dunkirk, *Gott im himmel,* all we had to do was roll into the town with our tanks and the war's over but Goering said no, said he'd take care of it and lo and below most the British army and a good section of the French escaped without even wetting their boots. This time no one will be firing at them so they should manage to help - snorted Heiser. The reputation of the German air force and its charismatic leader was in freefall since the debacle on the French coast and the inconclusive battle for Britain.

- Sir Luftwaffe say weather will keep aircraft grounded in this sector until further notice – came the message from the radio van.

- What! Put them on the line this instant – Hoffman was incensed - YES pass me over YES the commanding officer. Who am I speaking too? Adjutant pass me to your superior this minute do your hear this minute. He is indisposed! I've heard it all now, put him on the line if he cares for his hide, good soldier excellent – Hoffman waited till a voice answered - Get your planes in the air searching grid pattern over the coordinates we will radio and do it now. Who gave you the authority? – the Luftwaffe area head now on the line questioning Hoffman's authority was just the sort of thing to ignite his indignation even more - You know who and you'd better take heed, the head of Luftwaffe is senior to the head of the SS but state security is ahead of all, anyone who hinders that is guilty of anti-German behaviour, they and will be suspect and will face the full pitiless response of the state. So think it over and quickly – Hoffman hung up - I have to threaten people to get some help looking for the most wanted man in Europe – Hoffman said astonished – truth be known I've never harmed a hair of anyone or their families but it gets results.

- What is the world coming to, you SS don't have to threaten anyone just the sight of the black uniform is enough to make grown men shit themselves, I love being in the army because of this – Heiser held up his sidearm - kill before being killed, Russians, Brits now Americans anyone as long as I have a bullet in the barrel I'm in control of my fate.
- I'll mind what you said – Hoffman took out the standard-issue Walther P38 pistol looked it over and checked the ammo clip - I might just be needing this too.

Deep in the Czech countryside

Dagan and the rest were making good progress along the long paths between endless forest and fields avoiding a couple of villages along the way they just kicked the barking dogs as they went past, the few country people they saw muttered oaths as they blared the horn at them. Dagan took to saying *'raus raus dummkopf'* before Václav elbowed him in the ribs – 'They are Czechs remember! We don't have to be too German'.

Towards mid-morning Václav screeched to a halt and Dagan and the two sidecar passengers were flung to one side as the bike stopped dead, the Czech had heard something out of place above the sound of the engine, somehow noticing the slightest of alterations in the background of rustic country noises, pure instinct was what you would call it because even with the engine idling it took precious time to identify the approaching sound. As soon as Dagan could distinguish it he knew it was a plane. 'Quick into cover' - he urged.

Maria and Kessler jumped off the bike, Václav rapidly cut the revs of the engine and pushed it towards the canopy beside the path while Dagan pushed from behind, the 760cc engine even in idle was more than enough to gain headway and just as well as pushing the half-ton bike alone would have been brutal, Maria helped by pushing from the spare tire on the back of the sidecar while her father on the other hand jaunted around as if on a Sunday stroll. Once the bike was under the cover of the bushes the four of them flattened themselves against the cold hard ground, Dagan was right behind Maria and noticed scratches and blood coagulated on her hand and face. She'd had a rough time with the brambles, branches and thorny hedgerows they'd brushed past, not a word out of her about it though.

- We'll look at those cuts later – he said.
- What cuts? Ah, those, nothing, my legs were so toasty warm I couldn't care, it was worth some scratches. You, on the other hand, must have been freezing – Maria played it down.
- Oh, I don't know the engine exhaust kept me toasty warm.

'Scccch' Václav hissed as a spotter plane flew overhead at about 150 meters. The plane was going so slowly, thirty of forty kilometres per hour overflying the meadow that bisected two sets of forested areas. It was a spectacle, the plane seemed as if it was going to plonk down on the grassy carpet of a meadow. They could easily make out the faces of the pilot and spotter, nearly reach out and touch them.

- So slow – Maria marvelled.
- They need to go that slow, so they can see everything clearly and avoid the trees, it's very tight for them in here.
- They won't hear us if we talk will they? – Maria said whispering and looking at the observer scanning the terrain below and on the other side of the meadow – He looks so bored and the pilot so scared.
- Best not to talk, be still and quiet till they go, you might move while talking, hand gestures you use instinctively that might catch the eye, if your watch moves for example even though there is no sun anything bright gives the same result, they're trained to spot needles in a haystack.
- Okay - just as she said that the observer switched sides and was now looking their way – Oh – she involuntarily shuddered and flinched backwards trying to shrink in size.

Both Kessler and Maria refrained from talking till the plane made another pass in the other direction and eventually flew on further ahead.

- That's very strange, the Germans never fly in low cloud weather, we know that and behave accordingly but now these planes are buzzing everywhere.

The aircraft was out of sight but could still be heard in the distance, crisscrossing the countryside in a grid pattern.

- They are out flying in dangerous conditions because someone really powerful made them do it, they are really after us. I can't understand this level of intensity for two missing Jews and a missing friend of the nation. – Dagan all but stretched his head.
- You stopped being a friend when you helped strangle the guard in the hotel.
- Self-defence – claimed Dagan.
- What guard did you kill? – Maria asked initially surprised before continuing in a more sanguine manner - Well killing Germans isn't a crime for me anymore not even a misdemeanour - Maria took her trousers out of the sidecar and put them on behind a

tree why the modesty thought Dagan not for me surely or her father or Václav, a bit of leg never did anyone any harm.

- Can we continue now? - asked Maria.
- In the direction of the plane is best. They're hardly likely to backtrack - Dagan added.
- Best wait - Václav said - rest a while and eat some. How far have we come Professor? - He asked Kessler.
- 80.5 km judging by the time elapsed, the approximate position of the sun behind the clouds, its shadow length and angle, the average calculated speed of course. I might be out by a kilometre or two but I stand by it as a trustworthy approximation - Kessler waved an arm about as Václav and Maria looked on.
- He's more than likely right - Maria added - when I was young he'd tell me exactly how far the train had gone and what time it had taken without looking at his watch and he was always right. My friends loved it when he told them how many leaves had fallen in the last hour in the park or Prague or the last year.
- All the world and nature is governed by physics and if it can be measured it should be measured - Kessler listening in added. Václav just looked at them.
- I measure too, on my Grandpa's farm, sunny days, rainy days sowing, weeding, reaping, the weight of grain, number of lambs, piglets, chickens, cattle sold at market. Counting is what I do and now I am counting the number of Germans who are looking for me, the number of kilometres to the coast, the number of days it will take to get there. We've run out of petrol and we have to go down to that local village nearby and get some.
- Bit of a scarce commodity gasoline, I'm not sure if in the village they'd be willing to give is any, we don't have anything to trade. Do you speak German? – Dagan knew well he did but didn't want to let on?
- Mother tongue, she was from the Sudetenland. I never felt German but yes we spoke it all the time at home.
- Are we near Jedovnice yet?
- It is close but how do you know of it, it is just a tiny village – Václav looked at Dagan strangely.
- I heard there is a Luftwaffe aerodrome about three kilometres from there.
- A long walk with a bike and their spotter planes after you.
- I doubt it, it's a trainer field, wet behind the ears flyboys, they wouldn't be able to do what that pilot did just now.

- Cadet flyers still have instructors but are you thinking of walking in there and asking for petrol? - Václav and the rest looked at him before the replied.
- I'm most certainly not, whoever heard of such a thing! How can I ask? I don't speak German remotely well enough and anyway you have the officer's uniform on so it would be best if you do the asking.
- What! Are you crazy – Václav's voice rose?
- And you Václav as the near-perfect German speaker are not going to ask for petrol but for a plane – Dagan said to Václav in a flourish.
- You what? And just who's going to fly this magical gift - Václav aghast spluttered in confused defence.
- Great, there you see, you didn't dismiss the idea directly and that to me means you're half sold on it.
- So this is where in the story, the other guy says 'hey buddy let's do it' you know what I mean, well this is not a dumb story this is very real life. Why would a Luftwaffe base commander give a plane to some SS officer, fake mind, who just turns up at the door and asks? - Maria and Kessler just looked on at them arguing.
- We don't want to see Germans again up close – Maria said timidly.

This was when Dagan flashed his trump card, the letter from Herman Goering's brother.

- What is this? Unless it's signed by Hitler I doubt it will help us and that's not likely as you tried to shoot him, something you keep bragging on about - said Václav.
- I wasn't bragging and indeed my relationship with him is now beyond repair; he currently wants me dead but before we were close, even sent me flowers.
- You also brag endlessly about that too – added Maria echoing Vaclav.

Václav took the letter, opened it, took the sheet of paper out and ceremoniously started to read, - I Herman Gor....ring as head of the Ger.... - he looked up, 'What the fuck is this?' And then the continued but to himself, his head popped up now and then looking at Dagan quizzically. He let out a grunt when he finally finished.

- Well this changes things – he said ruefully - Are you sure they will accept it? – Václav looked at it front and back.

- Read it again, wouldn't you and look at the watermark, the headed notepaper the signature....this is poker and that is a full house. It's a Stamfumpletreichmarshal, I am directly under his orders on a special mission, no questions asked, none taken, the SS tend to use them more but why not Goering – Dagan voila'd.

The letter had been passed to the Kesslers who read it heads bobbing together saying things like - *I don't believe it, is it possible* when finished their puzzled faces matched as Maria carefully passed it back.

- Germans in a Nazi state being ordered to do something by the second in command, the archangel Michael next to God himself yeah sure they would but without a German speaker passing for a native, take a bow Václav, the plan doesn't stand a chance.
- Okay, I speak German so I presume you can fly? - Václav asked and Dagan knew he had him. Václav looked at Dagan amazed, this much planning and not by the British for sure, just who was he dealing with.
- Oh sure we planned to rob some British aerodromes back in the day so I got some basic training on hand. Then in 1921 during the treaty negotiations if things turned sour we needed a means for a quick getaway for the Big fella and the Griff so bought a plane and parked it, fully fuelled and ready to go near London. I learned to fly as I was in and out of London on other business, thankfully it and me wasn't needed. Later on, in the 20s and 30s, I got plenty of opportunities to practice though, heavenly days – Dagan smiled at the memories.
- Opportunities! - berated Václav - this heist is asking a lot from someone who dilly-dallied.
- Maria - Dagan implored - did I get many opportunities, tell our friend.
- Now you are going to get me in big trouble with my father, I never told him about us flying around Europe, he thought we were in the dacha.
- No, I did not, I'm self-absorbed, not blind – Kessler put years of doubts to rest.
- You knew! – Maria gasped
- You don't need sterling and francs and lira and what not to go to the country house – Kessler said matter of factly.
- Well you know the Palm Beach set, half that lot were confirmed Earhart fans and spent their money on birds not cars, you should see the places they have. They've built entire neighbourhoods around airstrips, it will catch on here for sure - Dagan was on a roll - And don't get me started on Howard Hughes, a bit of an odd fish really but he loves planes and loves people who love planes so don't'

worry about the piloting I've got it covered. This is what I plan to do - Dagan proceeded to lay out what he hoped would happen to the three fellow travellers.

- Is that possible how you expect to find it, what if we are approached during the day? – Václav asked the pertinent questions.
- Planes are quite hard to steal I believe and German ones even more so - Maria chimed in.
- Does the British secret service know anything about this? – Václav continued in concert with Maria.
- The less they know the better and not because somebody might let it slip or some Czech person might be turned or just plain bad luck. This was always my main plan and not a midget submarine down the Adriatic for Christ's sake. Talk about a slow boat to China.
- And how did you think you were going to get a plane without this letter – Václav quizzed the Irishman.
- Devils luck this letter to be sure but there are private planes and pilots and small airfields all over Europe just waiting for the end of hostilities to start their true passion again. It took a lot of visits and donations to London's Catholic parishes, tapping into the oldest network in Europe I was and money was plentiful, the British are very open-handed these days.
- There's one way to find out if this plan works and that doing it – Václav started down the road while taking off his German coat and helmet - some petrol down in the village first, we can't arrive pushing the bike but I'm not going to get it as a German – he said to explain - I'll be a Czech one last time before I put my head in the mouth of the lion.
- I'll come with you - Maria suddenly piped in and took off with him - I feel like a walk – she said over her shoulder as she took his arm.
- I'd appreciate the company - Václav genuinely surprised said while winking at Dagan.

He's not as funny as I am thought Dagan, what does she see in him? Maybe not being me is what she sees in him, anyway with a twinge of sorrow and regret it's for the best, I was never what Maria needed me to be. Did I even try to be? Maybe for a brief instance but it delayed the slow decadent untangling, full of reproachable behaviour on his part and quiet suffering on hers.   He still remembered the acute embarrassment when she'd found out that he had gone out with drinking buddies the day before her birthday and had got falling down drunk. It was three days before she saw him again, musing on his amorous reverses left Dagan feeling very uncomfortable and knew exactly what he needed.

- Well, that's that sorted, why don't we brew up, a nice cuppa tea is an Irishman's manna from heaven – he said turning to Kessler.
- Ireland and the Irish, tea drinkers' par excellence, if I ever needed to leave a note for an Irish colleague in the lab I would leave it beside the kettle – Kessler, as usual, nailed it.

As the forest canopy would shield the rising smoke so Dagan went to work lighting a fire from the leaves and branches nearby while Kessler got water for the camp stove from a stream nearby. They boiled it up with some tea leaves Dagan had kept through thick and thin and once brewed passed it from one to the other. As they sipped the scalding dark brown liquid they spoke about the futility of war, the march of science and the long drawn-out suffering of the Jewish nation. Dagan was in an agreement with the first, a witness may times of the second and aghast at the last. The constant humiliations heaped on that collective, petty and not so petty and institutionalised by state-regulated guidelines was on a level rarely seen since the age of civilization had arrived (back) in Europe.

But some civilization. What was happening was well known so why weren't they telling the world by shouting it out from every newspaper Kessler wanted to know but Dagan didn't have the answer. Dirty politics or some strategy to their advantage is holding them back Dagan hazarded but he wholeheartedly agreed people know the Nazis are doing this and don't care. Heck, it was how they'd swung him on board the cynical fucks, the Olympics for Christ's sake was held in Berlin in 1936 well after Dachau had opened its doors, both men were so absorbed in this discussion, the possible reasons, the ins and outs of the personal and political lives of the world's leaders that they barely heard the spotter plane return till it was right overhead. Dagan shocked roughly dragged down Kessler who had failed to react to Dagan exhortations to get under cover and during which the scientist's glasses had fallen landing upwards on a low bush. Toast jam carpet Dagan had time to think. As fate would have it the sun choose to make one of its flitting appearances low in the sky behind the plane lighting up the inner edge of the forest as it did, a stage performance about to start, the rays of light glittered off the eyeglasses just as the spotter's vision looking away from the sun was drawn from the left and turned right to where Kessler and Dagan were.

The spotter and Dagan exchanged surprises before the German patted his pilots arm emphatically and started radioing the back the coordinates. Dagan saw this from the overhanging branches, the plane was at a crawling pace barely 200 meters distance, just enough for the

317

MP 75. Dagan could clearly see the spotter speaking rapidly as he consulted the map, he had one chance before the coordinates went over the wire, he stood up, rested the MP 75 on a low branch, lined up the plane, moved as it moved and let off a burst. Birds flew up from the meadow as the bullets went low and wide, he adjusted and let off another sustained burst, this time the hail of fire missed at first but then the arc crashed into the fuselage behind the spotter who looked over his shoulder wide-eyed as the noise of the shattered perplex glass broke to his left. The pilot reacted immediately by banking away and skipping low over the meadow the huge wings scant meters off the ground heading away from Dagan and presenting the smallest profile to the direction of the ground fire. Smart pilot Dagan thought as the plane rapidly went out of range with no more damage apart from several holes in the fuselage and canopy, the pilot pulled back the stick and disappeared over the treetops. Dagan hadn't managed his original proposition of bringing down the spotter, a long shot but had succeeded in scaring them off so they couldn't see the direction they were taking. He quickly got Kessler moving down to the village to rendezvous with Maria and Václav, Dagan pushing the bike with his help until Kessler couldn't anymore and hopped on. Dagan's face was a riot of reds and whites, chest heaving, damp sweat licked strands of black hair on his neck, luckily for his cardiac palpitations the ground gave way to a fairly flat path that started to slope down to the collection of houses that formed the village. As they made their way down Dagan sat on top recovering his breath freewheeling the bike down a side street that led to the big central square, a fair-sized market taking place every Tuesday he read as they cruised by. In the centre was a large two-piece fountain with a Neptune holding a spiral shell on its shoulder as a centrepiece, the water on special occasions would shoot out from the shell it seemed. Today however they just cascaded from four fish mouths at each corner of Neptune's upper fountain level down to larger lower one. The quiet gush and splash of water was the only sound to be heard, cars had stopped in 1939, no horses and carts were insight and as they entered windows and shutters closed, locks on doors drawn over and bolted. Must be the swastikas. Over the other side, Maria and Václav were crossing with a can of petrol.

- Why didn't you stay where you were? You are out in the open and don't speak German or Czech - Václav asked.
- You're out here as well, a German officer alone on foot with a pretty local girl.

- I haven't been called pretty since the takeover - Maria giggled but you could she was pleased, the last week had done wonders for her complexion and spirits.
- Whereas you have a bike and an old man on it and now some petrol - he got busy taking the cap off and set about pouring it from the jerry can to the tank as Maria helped. They worked in time quietly and effectively, Maria anticipating her compatriots every move and helping him do it. Dagan felt another twinge of regret as she looked over at him and their eyes met briefly. Nothing too obvious to the neutral observer but Dagan was a practised hand as much semi-hidden signals. In no time the empty square reverberated to the roar of the 730 cylinder BMX engine, no children playing hopscotch, no adults walking to shops, church, work. The solitary cafe deserted since their arrival as the proprietor had chosen this moment to poke around in the cellar.
- We've been sent to Coventry lads - Dagan said as they mounted up.
- I hope they don't – Kessler said mishearing - that poor city was bombed to bits.
- Sent to Coventry is what we say in Ireland when people ignore you, not sure why it's that particular city means persona non grata. Where did you get the petrol dressed like that anyway?
- I made use of my charm and powers of persuasion - Václav said ambiguously.
- He identified the village big man in the café, followed him home as everybody left and stuck a big gun in his face – Maria said less ambiguously.
- I did say please and I pointed out that he'll be helping out his country if he did. End of discussion – Václav finished off; both he and Maria laughed conspiratorially. Cue another twinge!

Gestapo HQ, Prague, Radio Incident room

10:03 am: Sir, a report has come in over the radio, a spotter plane has been fired on, light damage, pilot and spotter reported to be unharmed, radio damaged.

10:05 am: A patrol near Sumperk; came across a band of armed men, shots exchanged, the patrol has called for reinforcements, giving pursuit.

319

10:09 am: Raid on buildings in Lidicka Street, Ceske Budejovice; has returned, negative nothing suspicious found, no propaganda or illicit material.

10:12 am: Klokocov mountain pass; well-known smuggling route, a group of men encountered, shots fired.

10:15 am: Zlin checkpoint; fights broke out between gipsies' and peddlers waiting in line to pass, two soldiers injured trying to separate them.

- Tempers flare so easily, people are getting sick of restricting searches and checkpoints – one of the junior officers opened up.
  Do you suggest we let lawlessness run riot and resistance go unpunished - Hoffman freshly shaven, black coffee in hand after three hours sleep replied acidly.
- Well, I didn't mean quite that Sir – the officer in question blanched.
- Do you believe our soldiers are tried and need some barracks time? Soft beds, soft tack and soft women is that it? Do you believe they want to shirk their duty? - Hoffman kept up.
- Absolutely not Herr Sturmbannführer the men are ready to die for the fatherland, Sir.
- All of us are all of us - Heiser added who knew Hoffman's mood was caused by frustration.
- 10:16 am: Sir, Prubezna police station, elderly lady reports that neighbours very friendly with Jews, might be worth searching. She wants the reward before she gives the number.
- Show her the cells and tell her she'll be in one if she doesn't start behaving, rewards are for those who have given something in return – Hoffman retorted.

In the hours that had passed, they'd returned to the radio room again and again. A huge map of Bohemia and the surrounds was spread on the table. Due to the intense state of control that was being imposed over such a large area the resulting incidents, disturbances, shootings and arrests were coming in over the wires nonstop. The build-up was so large that only the most serious and related incidents were being reported directly to the control centre but even still the volume was crippling.

- Hang on, the plane that reported shots being fired, anything more on that – Heiser said after thinking over what he had just heard.

- Why? Don't you think it's the preening boys in the Luftwaffe playing to the audience, I mean we are 500 miles from the nearest enemy aeroplane - Hoffman's ears pricked up.
- Give or take the odd bomb raid – Heiser pointed out.
- Well yes, but they must feel a bit out of danger, getting an easy ride while the rest of the services do all the hard work and take all the risks – Hoffman pointed out.
- Who can ever say with the flyboys, all silk scarves and soft beds at the end of a day but they said multiple shots, sounds a bit odd. Two separate marksmen are not going to find the mark at the same time, the plane must have been flying really low and somebody with a machine gun fired at them. AND we know who's got a couple of MPs – Heiser surmised.
- What should we do? The firing was reported and then the radio gave out. Where could they have landed?
- Around here – Heiser pointed to the map. Hoffman looked over deep in thought.
- From the camp to the farm to this location - he traced the route with his finger and a measuring tape, he didn't need a string to see if was just where Heiser would have placed them.
- Pure coincidence you think? - Hoffman ventured to Heiser.
- No way, you're the betting man not me, put my artillery support on it though.
- How soon can we get to the zone?
- Looking at the map and state of the roads I'd image four to five hours at best, they went by track over the mountains on a bike but obviously that's not an option for us.
- Four to five hours that's that - Hoffman ran out of steam, he took a sip of coffee chicory made – Is there an aerodrome nearby the zone? - Hoffman asked the adjutant.
- Sir, I'm sure the plane would have landed here if it was damaged.
- Call the Prague aerodrome tell them in 15 minutes they'll have two passengers to fly to....what's the place called? Jedovnice. Okay, Jedovnice.
- Are you sure you want to fly with the Luftwaffe, you're not exactly in favour with them after the other day.
- It seems to have worked either way which is what counts.
- The cars! – Heiser shouted.

Same time 60 miles away near Jedovice

Lt Gruber and his flight operator Zink had the shock of their lives. You expect to get ground fire over the front but here in Bohemia! The Czech army hadn't even fired on them when we took over the country. Gruber had flown over the Rhine, Austria and Prague and it wasn't till Poland had anyone shot at him and it was only the British over Belgium who'd come close. Zink was eighteen and thought all Gruber's stories were very boring, he had a local girlfriend and was enjoying his war especially on leave nights.

- Wait till I tell Pavlina she'll be outraged – he said teeth chattering in semi shock at his first taste of action.
- Play it up, girls love a hero and having their man in dangers way makes them very open to all sorts of suggestions.
- The radio's gone, just as I was reporting. Was that really somebody in German uniform? – Zink instinctively looked around.
- It was definitely a German gun – Gruber could only look at the trees he was skimming over and not the trace of bullet holes arching from the left side of the cockpit over Zink's head and coming down in the radio. It was a miracle neither had been wounded though Gruber had a nick in his flying jacket and the wind came whistling in the holes.
- You were too low – Zink accused.
- You said to go in for a closer look - Gruber sometimes felt like an old married couple, they spent half their flights arguing like two fishwives. How did this happen? He was older, an officer and well outranked his spotter.
- The nearest field is Jedovnice, small and just used for training, 16 aircraft in total, 9 Aveno trainers, 3 Storchs like us, an Italian biplane, 1 Czech relic from 1938 and 2 transports. Base commandant Lekerby – Zink stated - direction due west by south-west, you'll have to turn around and circle the area we've just flown over.

Zink hadn't been to university but he was ship smart, it was as if he'd swallowed the whole Luftwaffe depositions register. The plane had drifted far left and wide, Gruber climbed over a small wooded hill and headed in the direction Zink had indicated and after a time spotted the airfield. They approached at 300 meters and flew over the watchtower with their flaps down, the signal of distress. There was no need to clear a runway as all the aeroplanes were hangered for the night. The tower signalled by semaphore that they could approach on the east runway. Gruber lined them up and put it down gently on the grassy strip, a textbook landing, Gruber was a natural pilot, the plane a pleasure to fly and there was nothing wrong really except for a few holes and a broken radio.

He taxied to a halt beside the rapidly converging paramedics and firemen as they opened the door he was able to shout to the paramedics 'Stop! At ease. We've got a broken radio that's all and some bullet holes' he added. The now relaxed paramedics and redundant firemen milling around started smoking and offered them a warm welcome, Gruber was invited to the officer's mess while Zink was to get the run of the men's canteen, hot showers and a warm meal. The plane was to be towed to a hanger and taken care of by a group of mechanics who arrived grunting at each other as they looked over the plane and its damaged parts. In a couple of hours were the verdict and no major repercussions it'll be fit for a field marshal they said. Gruber and Zink were separated by their distinctive counterparts and escorted off. The officers and NCOs alongside them were unusually talkative. Gruber managed to ask about the radio room as they had to report in on their 'incident'. 'They'd been fired on?' came the indignant replies, 'happens more often these days, the honeymoon is over in these parts, you're radioman will take care of it'. Gruber thought if fitting and right, it was Zink's job to radio and report in the air and so it should be on the ground. Zink for his part thought it fitting and right as he settled into the NCO's mess that the bloody commanding officer, bastards one and all as his hosts vehemently asserted, should be filing the fight report, ground fire incident and all. Such were the small vagaries of military command lines that define the fate of nations. Finally, the message wasn't sent.

While Gruber was having his first refreshing pilsner 4.2% lager in the cosy officer's mess Zink was having his second, a 5.2% volume dark premium quality Frome beer. 'Damn fine stuff this and that's saying something, I come from the home of the *Weihenstephaner Hefeweissbier* and I know everybody says that about their homebrew but damn this stuff is good'. Messes and canteens were stocked by NCO quartermasters so the quality of the food and drink is always better in the NCO's mess something no officer suspected as they never set foot in them, officers did, however, have better cutlery and table linen to compensate. As those beers were being drunk Hoffman and Heiser were mounting a plane to fly the short distance to the airfield, all the while Heiser was wondering why Gruber's flight report hadn't been filed

323

and just at the moment they ducked in under the overhead canopy of the plane parked in Prague aerodrome Václav, Dagan and the Kesslers arrived at the gates of the airfield. As they wore German uniforms and drove a German bike the sentry didn't unhoist his rifle but asked them politely to state their business. Václav gave a perfect Heil Hitler and asked the soldier to do the same saying it would be a discourtesy to the Fuhrer otherwise. The soldiers pulled up straight.

- Of course Sir, Heil Hitler - apologizing to the "Lieutenant".
- None needed - Václav spoke in a reasonable tone as if it was a between two companions - Germans should always greet each other in that way to start off correctly and do honour to our glorious leader.
- Of course, Sir, if you be so kind as to state your business, please.
- We need to see the base commander - Václav answered rapidly and importantly in a decided tone - acting under the highest orders.
- The base commandant is on the airfield I will ring through.

The sentry went to the guardhouse to ring the base commander's office but the Sergeant in charge, a veteran of the last conflict who'd lost a boy in France, was more suspicious less willing to take on face value all that was said to him unlike his adolescent sentry indoctrinated in the Hitler youth. His grey close thatched hair was covered by the helmet he put on as he stepped out of the guard post. Dagan noticed two-day stubble and deep brown stained lips and gums from chewing tobacco or what went for tobacco, slowly he approached making a vigorous Seig Heil quickly answered by Václav and silently with Dagan raising his arm.

- Excuse the interruption Sir but what do you want to see the base commander about? - Politely but firmly said.
- We are acting under orders Sergeant and are not permitted to say who's to anyone but the base commander.
- With all due respect Sir, I must ask under whose orders as you have not been on this base before, have not phoned ahead and are accompanied by civilians. No offence – The gate commander stood his ground.

An SS uniform commanded instant respect even in the most dubious cases but the Sergeant had glanced at Maria and Martin Kessler and was obviously puzzled, they didn't fit in this situation but he didn't venture to ask least he might accidentally put his foot into the brown stuff, he hadn't been in the Hitler young but had lived eight years in a

National Socialist paradise. Václav then played a full house, slapping it right down on the table.

- Of course. None taken. The answer as you ask is Reich's Marshal Goering and Reich's Fuhrer Himmler – the twin pillars at the top of the hierarchy around Hitler.

The two sacred figures mentioned, names to be feared and treated with the utmost care and attention and said together in this way, the effect was devastating however strange it was to have Goering and Himmler working in unison, sworn rivals at best, enemies at worst, Goering never forgot what happened to Thurm in 1934. Václav took out from his inner breast pocket the envelope Dagan had been given by Goering's brother. The insignia of the castle Christina more than evident on the heavy rich creamy paper... the Sergeant had seen enough.

- I'll ring the office and tell them to expect you. Raise the gate - he shouted at the sentry on the other side – I'll escort you myself to the commander's office, be so good as to follow please – It was as if they were talking to another person.
- There's no need, we'll find it ourselves, just tell me where it is and we won't disturb your work any further.
- Sorry sir, There is every need; we can't let people wander around the base, it is too dangerous for them. Your accent? I can't quite place it, Lower Saxony - the Sergeant asked.
- Placing ascents isn't asked of you either but not lower Saxony – Václav didn't bat an eyelid and didn't tense. There was enough conviction behind it to deflect the question - And you won't be able to place my batsman's accent either I'm afraid.
- Why not? I pride myself on knowledge of German speakers – The sergeant's curiosity was piqued.
- Your knowledge would do you no good, Rolf here is mute. A blessing for me as I don't have to put up with the prattle I put up with in my last batman. NO OFFENSE - he said loudly and slowly to Dagan. The non-deaf always thought they could overcome deafness by shouting. Dagan/Roff shrugged petulantly, the two sentries watching beside smiled ever so slightly.
- I wouldn't have guessed just by looking at him - the stubby headed Sergeant added, he and the guards laughed themselves silly. Dagan had to hand it to Václav, he'd managed to turn up with a mute, two straggling civilians, a stolen bike wearing stolen SS uniforms and was about to see the commandant - The commandant's strict instructions is to accompany all non-base

personnel at all times. Airfields are dangerous places and it's for your own protection as well.

- We would not have it any other way; we're winning this war because we are well marshalled, it is our order and superior organization. We'll follow you – Václav gestured to continue.

They mounted a car parked just beside the gate.

- The lady and gentleman and Lieutenant with me, please. You will all be much more comfortable than on the bike.

The Sergeant took Maria by the hand and sat her in the back, then helped Kessler as both expressed their gratitude in High German. The might be dressed less than sartorially but they had breeding. Dagan was left grunting at the others while he started the bike and followed the car, the gatehouse gave over to a series of single-story prefabricated buildings that served various functions as the signs outside indicated, storerooms, machine workshop, mess hall, officer's billets etc. in between each building the gravel path was beautified with borders of small round stones painted white and enclosing the verges of the grass lawns in front of each building. It looked as trim and tidy as naval ships of old. The base's large hangers were past these areas and opened out onto the grassy runways stretching out over hundreds of yards. Through the open doors of the hangers planes could be seen in various stages of maintenance with fuselages on the ground and engines laid bare. Most of the activity revolved around a smaller plane that had six or seven mechanics and ground crew swarming around it.

A chill went down Dagan's back, that had to be the plane he'd shot at and the pilot and crew couldn't be far off. I just hope they didn't pay a courtesy call to the commander. Serves me right for shooting first and not asking questions later. If he hadn't, the plane would have landed at its own base; too much of a coincidence if it were from here. Dagan turned away from the hanger and continued following the rest.

Maria beside Václav in the back of the car and out of earshot whispered into his ear.

- That tower is new - she was indicating with a slight nod of the head towards the camouflaged tower, three stories high with a wooden veranda running around - and some of the buildings and the green and black paintwork of course but the rest is the same.
- You've been here before? - Václav was astonished.
- I think so yes – Maria replied – with Dagan and some of his flying buddies. He always knew so many people from so many

backgrounds. It was such a blur with him, one minute in a Bishops palace the next in a roadside drinking hovel.

Václav thought over all that. That damn Irishman planned this the whole time, there was no submarine then though it was the silliest idea he'd heard in a long while. They should have gone out via Switzerland even if the Germans thought the same and put up a veritable minefield of obstacles and patrols, roadblocks they'd have got through. Double-dealing two faced Malone had led him right to this place and even worse had made it seem like his idea! Insult to injury. Did he even arrange to run out of petrol as well right beside the aerodrome? Devils alive, this man must have sold his soul to have such luck. How did he know his contact would be a Sudet German Czech? London did ask he now remembered but still, you couldn't plan this if you tried. Václav felt like rabbits coming out of a magician's hat. His revelatory revere was brought to a close by their arrival at the bungalow signposted – *FlugMesiterBurof*, as he got down he glanced over at the damn Celt and his expressionless face, Václav knew he was playing dump but what composure realizing what they were going to do; ask a German Luftwaffe base commander to give them a plane no questions asked. If they somehow managed to get out of this Václav would never play poker with 'Rolf'.

They stepped over the portal of a half wooden half glass door. The glass part with white tape fixed diagonally for bomb blasts, inside was a bright spacious room with light from both sides. The door on the left led into the offices while another door in front to the flight area hangers and runways, more vehicles were parked on that side in keeping with the functions undertaken on the base, strange multi-wheeled chaises designed to transport explosives and ammunitions from underground dumps to the planes, fuel trucks, small carts for flights crews, ambulances and so on all attended by animated crews gathered round. Leaving that scene they entered the spacious office, bright and airy and manned by three clerks each with a phone and typewriter on their desks. In the corner were filing cabinets and on all the walls could be found, maps of the local area, a swastika with an eagle in the middle, symbols of the Luftwaffe, the customary photo of Hitler and a larger photo of Goering. The adjutant, a fresh-faced thin tall bespectacled figure turned his round face to them.

-   The base commander will see you now. Your 'guests' can wait outside if you like with your batman.
-   No such need - Václav replied crisply- they are part of the reason we've here and hence most relevant to the proceeding, my batman

can stay or come if he likes but I'm sure he will come, like mothers they have to know everything so better he knows it now than nagging me for days.

- I have met many SS officers and you don't seem like any of them - the chubby officer who's desk nameplate had the aristocratic von Zichert printed on it replied, a chilling challenge it was too and said in high German.

They remained rooted to the spot facing each other, Václav had the mission in his hands and while Dagan could cajole and prompt in private now his fate was in entirely in the hands of Václav and he couldn't even say anything. Václav though didn't give signs of being intimidated but Dagan slipped off his trigger guard all the same.

- Himmler himself said to me that the SS is a broad church when he asked me to join, he'd read a book of mine on mysticism. I was an archaeologist and didn't understand that at the beginning but it is true and my promotions as a coal miner's son going to prove the SS is elite but not elitist.

Bravo though Dagan, Václav had pitched the tone just a shade below indignant. Everyone knew Himmler had a fascination with Teutonic myth and archaeology to lay the foundations of the superior race, no expense had been spared in investigating freemasonry and encouraging expeditions that had even arrived to far off Tibet. It was not usual to find historians, linguists, and writers, experts in the occult and what not drafted into the ranks of the SS. Any veneer of academic respectability to bolster the national socialist racial and humanist theories was avidly sought out and once co-opted used.

- Interesting background detail - A voice came over the intercom - Zichert don't detain our guests any longer, have them shown into my office.

Thus they were ushered into the adjoining room, again well lit with walls covered with photos of current Luftwaffe aircraft and their specs, famous German aviators were another favourite subject. Goering was prominent among those, the Red Baron another, along with more recent ace's from the Polish, French and Russian campaigns. Dagan's heart gladdened to see Koehl and von Huenefeld, the Germans who were first to fly West to East over the Atlantic because right beside him was their comrade in the endeavour, an old family friend, the Irish man James Fitzmaurice. A good omen thought Dagan a friendly face so far from home and so near to danger. Conspicuously absent were photos of the other leaders of the party. Another good omen. Along one side of the office was a bog-standard desk and chair but dolled up with a smart Bakelite phone, white no less, a fancy dark red leather mat held the plotter paper which was covered in calculations. In front of this was a photo of the family, wife and two small boys all in traditional Bavarian outfits and beside them was arranged a line of top quality silver Swiss pens harnessed in a row of silver beak holders. Each of the three wooden chairs, one behind and two in front had four wheels and was finished with leather buttoned upholstering. The rest of the furnishings were by a table in the corner with a bookstand each side, the table held copies of the pre-war flight magazines, a water carafe and three glasses on a tray. In the bookcases were pictures, books, model aeroplanes, a gyrocopter and another tray with a half-full decanter of whiskey and a dozen Bohemian cut crystal glasses. A comfortable office not overtly ostentatious, the office of a senior officer in command of themselves and quite un-Nazi like in appearance.

The commandant Lekerby by name rose from his desk and greeted each person in turn; even Dagan the lowly mute got a correct turn. Not a standoff type when Václav explained why Dagan couldn't reply the medium stature powerfully built officer had stood even more erect and replied directly to Dagan saying it was very sad but truth be told what most people who can talk do end up saying isn't of much interest.

- A small consolation I'm afraid but there it is – Lekerby even sounded sincere too, his thick neck and fleshy upper body were kept trim by an active life, the tendency otherwise was running to fat; the eyes were blue and clear and sparkled lively with intelligence. The left ear was mashed and cauliflowered - I'm half deaf after a crash but I have two ears so I got away with it - The goatee was an unusual sight on a senior German officer as was the Christian cross on one wall - We are not used to so many visitors in one day and such a variety, tell me what exactly can I do for you, petrol for the motorbike perhaps – this was said jocularly – a decent meal, a bath, a change of uniform, a car to take you to Prague. We are always at the disposal of the hard-working servants of the state - He spread his hands out, palms up saying he'd help but not because he wanted to help the SS but had no choice like everyone in Germany.
- That is most generous of you, we truly appreciate your most welcoming reception - Václav replied with diplomatic unctuousness, was this the same curt abrupt man Dagan had met last week. This was a different side of the Czech he hadn't seen, what did he do before the war? Engineer he'd said, farming background, he certainly spoke well, military bearing, well

dragged up as Dickens used to jest about Pip in his Great Expectations.

- In that case, what could I possibly do for you? I've been told you are here on orders from the highest authorities - Immediately and without batting an eyelid or changing his tone he directing himself to Maria and Kessler - You seem to be from the protectorate. How did you come to be involved with my new friend? I'm lost, the SS isn't usually on such good terms with runaway Jews especially those they had in their custody until recently and that they've been actively looking for these last few days.

The atmosphere in the room tensed, the commander knew who the Kesslers were yet he didn't call his guards. If he bought the fact that Václav and Dagan were Germans they still had a chance. Maria looked aghast and paled, Kessler seemed unperturbed and was 'observing' without interfering like the good physicist he was. Václav, on the other hand, flashed a set of conflicting emotions, he was obviously surprised and involuntarily inhaled a breath before smiling suddenly and nodding at his adversary. Jesus wept Dagan thought on seeing it all, this guy is something else. Where did London get him from?

- I hadn't finished answering your first question about what you could do to help us – Was what he cooly said in reply.
- What were you going to ask for before the situation changed so much that asking for anything apart from a quick death would be the best you could hope to obtain – the Luftwaffe commander came back with but still didn't call the guards.
- We need a plane, enough for the four of us and with a range of at least 450km. We'll leave it at the nearest airfield to Castle Karina – Václav said which caused the commandant to burst out laughing.
- That is all!! This is such fun. I haven't laughed so much since my cousin Alfie, the pompous ass, fell in the water when out rowing my aunt on a Berlin lake. – This was said in such a loud voice that the four guests and even the adjutant was taken aback.
- I'm perfectly serious and fully expect you to give me one, once I've have explained to you one thing and once I've shown you another.
- Oh, I'm immensely enjoying this farce and hate to bring it to a close so suddenly, the guards outside will be here in a second but let us continue, I'm intrigued - he said turning to Maria – the gentleman in me and some do still exist in this new Germany would be loath to condemn such an obvious lady to the same fate she just managed to spring from – Then Václav again - Pray work

your conjurer's tricks, do magic, pull a rabbit and then a plane out of a hat – Václav cleared his throat, he'd get one chance no more.

- Certain people pictured on the wall, without mentioning names don't share certain polices with other people on the SAME wall. This is normal but the situation has changed, some people are rising further and higher whilst others have fallen behind after being blamed for the first reverse of our glorious advances being checked over England's skies.

- I'm just a plain pilot so your riddles are obtuse and confusing, smokes and mirrors I think I'm getting the picture, I've stopped laughing you'll have noticed, I knew lots of brilliant flyers that are now resting at the bottom of the English Channel so be very careful how you proceed. We'll not permit the slightest disrespect towards them – the Commandant warned Václav to watch his words, Dagan didn't know why he didn't just show him the letter, what was he talking about? He was going to talk them into a cell, a nasty interrogation and a quick limed lined pit behind the prison.

- They were the bravest of the brave, honoured now and forever. Part of the reason that things went wrong was the advantage the British had with radar. Technology can make the difference between defeat and victory, for the British it meant surviving, for Germany our first defeat. A valid observation you will grant, if not I need not continue.

Václav feed him some lines and left him wanting more. This was excellent sales work and he really needed to make this sale. I hope Václav knows that he's doing, Dagan had a strange air of dislocation, his fate was in the hands of others and it was like it didn't matter all that much, maybe the cyanide capsule was a worry remover, he instinctively moved his tongue around to where it was for reassurance. He did that a lot lately.

- Go ahead – the commander said slowly after what seemed an eternity.
- In fact, Germany is embarking on the creation of new weapons, superweapons, technologies like radar that will render any numerical advantage the enemy might have null and void. This is even more important now that the Americans have joined in the fray. I am sure you are aware that the piston-driven engine plane is reaching its limit and will be superseded by new ways of power – Václav stumbled a bit on the jargon, his discourse passionate but not rehearsed – one that projects the plane through the air in

a new way that is close to development but requires some of the finniest minds we can muster to develop these and other weapons. My friend here and his daughter – Václav gave a short bow - are two of the best physicists in Bohemia and just happened to be vital for a program a certain person is developing. By a quirk of faith these talents are completely disregarded by other elements of the state, solely bent on their removal from society, hence the current apparently contradictory friendship and collaboration you are witnessing. The SS is not my first claim on the loyalty of my heart. This explains why I said I am acting on orders of someone on the wall, the man behind and above you and explains why I'm asking for the plane, fully expecting it to be granted to me. Which explains why I have a letter to show you which I was given only to be used when the state is in danger – Václav's eyes blazed, Dagan was stunned he'd thought he'd heard all the kooky science he was ever going to hear on this mission but Václav of all people has beaten him to the drop. Dagan called himself back to the realities of the moment.

- What you say is not without a grain of truth but I'm still not giving you a plane at the moment and it's open to debate whether I call the guards or let you walk out of the door and off my base.
- With your permission – The ace was being put on the table with a dramatic pause, Václav made to take out something from his inside pocket, his hand hung about the gap made by holding the label outwards slightly. The commandant nodded, the hand went in slowly and even more slowly withdrew the now rumpled envelope and handed it to the commandant who took it and held it up in the air.
- What can a letter possibly say that would make me change my mind - he opened it, unfolded the page with a flourish and started to read, at first the look on his face was one of playing along with the game, he'd started – Ahem oh let's see now – his eyes moved back and forth over each line, rapidly at first then as if paying more attention, he finished with a finger over the last line - *Got im himmel* – he said in a low voice and started to read again. In the end, he looked up at Václav and reached suddenly for his intercom - Dressler come here - Václav and Dagan were both startled – Dressler - he said as the door opened - Please have refreshments brought here, coffee and sandwiches and stay with our guest at all times. I'm going to the radio room as I need to make an urgent call to Berlin HQ - he got up while carefully

folding the paper sheet in his hands - You don't mind if I kept this for a moment.

- By all means, would expect no less - Václav said as the commandant left the room.

Just then over at the mess, Gruber was drunkenly saying to his new friends - I must see the commandant – *Ja Ja* - they said – But not in your state and anyway the commandant has just ordered sandwiches and coffee from the mess, coffee phah better beer yes! Anyway, he has guests so best leave it for later.

Chapter XII

Flight Control Tower

Flight 751T to tower: Unscheduled in-coming Prague flight requesting permission to land.

Tower to 751: Why is your flight unscheduled; please state reasons for landing request. Base shut down for operations today.

751 to tower: Carrying two senior officers, Hoffman, Sturmbannführer in the SS and Heiser, Colonel of the Ninth Army Group. They need to be the area in the shortest time hence unscheduled flight from Prague. Repeating request for landing permission.

Tower to 751: Of course, request granted, request a mere formality, approach on the east runway.

751 to tower: Adjusting nose to new coordinates, ten minutes to touch down. Will advise.

Tower to 751: Check. This is unusual, anything needed on arrival?

751 to tower: There is a war on we must be flexible and not stuck in the rule book or shut down at night. Please provide any reports of aircraft fired on in your operations area. You are the nearest field to a recently reported incident.

Tower to 751: The flight that was fired upon landed here a short time ago over.

751 to tower: Hoffman here, were there any fatalities.

333

Tower to 751: Both crew members unharmed over.

751 to tower: We were waiting for further updates in Prague, why didn't the unharmed crew members make use of the base radio facilities to report in?

Tower to 751: Unable to verify over.

751 to tower: Contact the crew and put them on over.

Tower to 751: Will take commensurate action over.

751 to tower: What does that mean over?

Tower to 751: We can continue to answer your questions or do what you asked us to do over.

751 to tower: Proceed.

Hoffman handed back the headphones to the pilot who shrugged.

- Control tower people are like that, the civilian ones even worse – the flyer said.
- Where do you think the flight crew are? - Hoffman asked him.
- Officers mess, enjoying the hospitality of their fellows, another characteristic of airfields – the pilot answered.
- You just have to look at Goering to see who much good living is appreciated in the service – Heiser added.
- I am hoping to get invited when we land – the pilot put in.
- And why didn't they report in? –Hoffman repeated.
- Maybe the pilot thought the radio operator would do it – the pilot suggested.
- And why wouldn't the spotter do it on the ground? – Hoffman came in with the obvious next question.
- Because he'd assume the senior rank would, the Luftwaffe works that way – the pilot right on song again.
- How are we winning this war! – Hoffman shook his head.
- The army doesn't do it that way - Heiser pointed out - or we wouldn't be winning and the Luftwaffe is one of the reasons we haven't won yet. No one could believe it when they told us to stop right in front of Dunkirk. We had the whole British army at our mercy, a step away from total liquidation, they were beaten and that would have been England out of the war there and then. Blast and bother! The Luftwaffe is no substitute for a column of tanks.

The pilot banked hard to the left so both Hoffman and Heiser were thrown hard against the side, emitting grunts and curses before the pilot righted the plane.

- Your pardon gentlemen - the pilot said - I had to readjust for our approach vector, I wandered off course distracted as I was by all you're gabbing.

Hoffman and Heiser both glared at the pilot who just flew on imperviously.

Commandants Office

Maria and her father fell on the sandwiches with undeniable relish, ten minutes passed without a sound. Dagan conscious of his inferior rank stayed on his feet and ate his sandwich from a plate. Never had a 'hambo' tasted so good. It came with a curious savoury vegetable shredded in such small bits that the Germans added to everything. He reckoned it was cabbage and damn it went very well with the ham, picnic food normally but in a war it was haute-cuisine. The tea he drank in a mess mug. As a last meal, it wasn't very elaborate but it was damn welcome though. After the food and drink had been finished another mess servant came and removed the plates and crockery.

Now with nothing to do time seemed like an eternity. Conversation wasn't an option under the scrutiny of Dressler who didn't attempt to make any small talk. Maria and Kessler sat back and held hands; they spoke quietly in German about mundane things, only later would it occur to Dagan that he was giving parental advice to a child as if that child wouldn't be seeing the parent again.

'Careful with sugary foods Maria, you know they are bad for your blood pressure and remember to keep in touch with the foundation' along those lines, what foundation was Kessler talking about? Before Dagan couldn't pay close attention footsteps rang out from the other side of the wall and a clash of boots as the office staff jumped to attention to salute their commander. But the door did not open immediately, voices were heard, something was happening, if the previous minutes had passed at a snail's pace such was the tension underlying the whole enterprise that the seconds transpired in hyper-chaotic moments. The recently eaten food now felt like lead as the stomach muscles tightened. Dagan felt inside his pocket for the Mauser, he'd have time to take out Maria and a few Germans before he'd be overpowered and pill crunch. The double doors burst open, the commandant followed by three junior officers swept in. Everyone in the room startled even Dresler the baby sitter.

- Splendid I hoped you enjoyed your refreshments and we would love to entertain you further and at a level way above mere bread and ham but we can't detain you a minute longer. You are expected by far higher authorities and we have your aeroplane prepared. The recent landing has provided us with an extra aircraft, it has been repaired, refuelled and the bullet holes covered up and we put four parachutes on broad should the unexpected happen and now please come with me – Kekerby announced.

Maria and Kessler looked at each other still holding hands, could it really be happening they thought or was it a pretext to get them moving docilely to the cells something which happened a lot in the camps.

- Come come there is no mistake although I have never seen anything like it in twenty years service but there is no error, your plane waits. As it is nearly nightfall would you like to wait till the morning? – Lekerby asked.
- We'll be on our way in the shortest time possible – Václav was understandably keen to move on.
- Just what I thought you'd say, this way - the commandant turned to Maria and Kessler and indicated the open door with his hand.
- Everything was in order with the call? - Václav asked him.
- Surprisingly as much as it could be, I'll keep the letter if you don't mind - Václav who still couldn't quite believe the turn of events. A Czech residence fighter who'd turned up on a stolen SS motorbike with two of the most highly sought Jews in middle Europe plus a renowned infamous Irish American spy who had only tried to kill the leader of the 3rd Reich, was about to borrow a plane from the Luftwaffe. The commandant hadn't taken it on word alone but had done some checking and the letter had held up. Incredible, it was the last thing Václav had expected if they were actually being given a plane, the same thought crossed his mind as Maria's. Was it a rouse to jolly them along at the outside office but then Dagan and he were handed back their MP 75s, that's when they started to believe. Dagan could tell by the weight that the cartridge was full, the weapon was loaded, they all marched out preceded by the escorts and accompanied by the Lekerby.

- Your flight plan has been filed and you are expected at the aerodrome in the early hours of the morning. Are you sure you don't want to wait till the morning? It would be much safer.
- Again thank you for your concern, we'll be fine – Václav told him.
- If you were my pilots I wouldn't hesitate to ground you by force if necessary but you aren't so I wash my hands of the affair, flying across Europe at night isn't easy at the best of times - Václav just nodded his head at that - We left a thermos flask with coffee, real coffee, my very own. You'll need it to keep awake and alert; I hope one of you is a good navigator.
- North is north on anyone's compass – Václav said cryptically – and thank you for the coffee.

As they passed through the doors from the outer office Dagan could see in the near distance a plane being pushed out of a hanger by mechanics and ground staff in overalls, sweaty and with greasy hands, signs of honour befitting their profession, white vests visible in the crisp chilly evening with overall tops pulled down and overhanging the waist. Even in the twilight, it was visibly the reconnaissance plane, the Stork like Storch, maximum velocity of 300kph and a range of 700 kilometres normal load. With four adults you'd have to half those figures but still, Dagan was relieved, this plane could land on a dime and take off on a nickel. Just what he needed. It'd be tight inside but Kessler and Maria could squeeze in the back seat and Václav and Dagan upfront but he knew they'd have filled the tank to bursting. The Commandant looked over at the landing tower curiously.

- The flag on the left means a plane was approaching, more visitors, we've never been so popular! – Lekerby joked – You'd best be on your way – this said seriously, a warning in his voice perhaps.

By this stage they had reached the plane and Dagan could plainly see the arc of bullet holes freshly painted and covered over, this WAS the aircraft he'd shot at! 'Damn me' Dagan thought 'if this is the plane where are the crew? Five minutes more and it won't matter, I just hope they stay out of sight five more minutes.' Over on the left, faint sounds of singing and music could be heard from a building more elaborately decorated than the rest. All its lights were ablaze, the shutters were a pleasant green, white curtains gave a glimpse of animated figures moving in the rooms behinds, the walls glimmered a fresh cover of whitewash and the main door had a tavern sign over it, Dagan couldn't make it out but a plane was evident on it, obviously the officer's mess and right as they reached the plane a group of bawdy deep throated singers came out into the twilight looking for some fresh air, Lekerby was embarrassed and uncomfortable at such a scene being witnessed on his base though it happened in messes on both sides of the conflict all across Europe. 'Two more minutes' Dagan thought as Václav did a quick inspection of the exterior of the aircraft as he had been coached to do by Dagan.

-   Everything's in order – the commandant assured him.
-   Force of habit – Václav countered.

The Kessler's mounted up and sat in the back, Maria from her previous aerial jaunts with Dagan was able to buckle herself up and then her father.   The knapsack with the thermos, bread, cheese and smoked ham as well as pickled cucumbers and onions was in front of them. Dagan put himself in the pilot's seat beside Václav who climbed up beside. The Commandant leant into the cabin.

-   Tight squeeze – as he surveyed Václav taking the control and Dagan sitting sideways so he could – I wish you luck, please convey my best wishes to the....well to whoever you meet - he shut the cabin door and shouted – CONTACT - A mechanic pulled on the end of the propeller blade and Dagan indicated the contact button to Václav.

The motor roared into life as the propeller started, oil and smoke sputtered out of the engine exhausts. The mechanics gave the thumbs up and removed the chocks. Dagan put his feet on the rudder pedal and took out the choke a bit increasing the tone of engine and the plane started to move slowly as Dagan used the flaps pedal to turn towards the runway. Over on his left amid the cluster of half-drunken officers, a pair of hands started gesticulating wildly and somebody in-flight uniform started to separate from the group and make his way unevenly towards the gunning plane, this flying officer rapidly started to sober up and began running while manically waving his arms trying to attract the attention of the people around the Storch. Dagan swung the plane around in an arch and righted the plane on the lit-up take-off runway. Dagan quickly told Václav how to contact the tower. As they swept through and past, the onrushing Luftwaffe Officer reached the within twenty meters before the plane took off in the opposite direction. The German stopped dumbstruck as his plane was being flown away and being flown by the same man who shot at him an hour or two ago. He recognized him straight away; Dagan looked over smiling and waved discreetly as the stupefied German started swearing profusely. As Václav was getting take off approval the plane arriving touched down just then and was taxiing along towards them parked at the end of the runway. The new arrival also passed some twenty meters in front and Hoffman did a double-take recognizing one of the occupants while his plane swung left and away, his face registered complete shock. Dagan waved and smiled at him too.

- Bumping into lots of old friends today – Václav said to the consternation of his fellow passengers and the Germans who'd just recognized Malone.

Behind the officer was still running after and was close to reaching them. The tower gave permission and Dagan gunned the engine, they rapidly began to move off as the red-faced officer stopped, vomited, then took out his sidearm and started firing while at the same time wiping the spittle from his mouth with his forearm. Pop pop pop the sidearm was ineffectual over forty meters and the Storch was now piling down the runway leaving heaving Gruber with some tricky target practice which he rapidly gave up and ran towards the commandant. Gruber spoke frantically to Lekerby who sensing the charade was up reverted to role, after glancing at the plane on he waved at the tower to abort the flight.

- Tower to Storch: Permission to take off cancelled please taxi to take-off point.
- Tell them we're past the point of safely stopping, we'll take off and land again – Dagan advised.
- Unable to abort tower, will fly around and touch down again – Václav repeated the sham.
- Tower to flight. The runway is long enough, please abort.

Václav turned off the radio as they hurtled along, Hoffman in the other plane was frantically indicating to his pilot to turn around and take off again while Heiser stuck his pistol out the window and started firing a few rounds.

- Just as well it's only pistols at the moment – Václav said as he turned on the radio.
- ABORT OVER ABORT - the tower was shouting, Václav turned it off again.
- What's taking so long, why are we still on the ground? – Václav was frantic, the end of the runway and the trees just after were approaching all too quickly.
- We've to get to 80 knots with the double the normal weight, shit we're going to make it overloaded and full of fuel but it won't be pretty – Dagan surmised.

- 73 knots – Václav looked behind – The Germans are shooting away at their own planes, that can't be good – he could see that the commandant's escorts loosening their rifles and joining in the firing - That other plane has turned around and is now barrelling along the runway after us – he added uneasily. At that, a bullet whizzed through one of the recently repainted holes.
- 78 knots! Fuck it – Dagan pulled back on the control shaft and at first nothing happened.
- Those pretty trees are getting awful close - Václav shouted
- 7.2 seconds to be precise - Kessler leaning forward and shouting in a jocular voice - not bothering with wind resistance and snow cooled air, denser of course and harder to..... woooo we're...somewhat... - The plane had left the ground as Kessler had perceived.
- Just over tree height – Dagan said as the audible pine tops brushing against the wheels.

Maria had been physically imploring the plane to rise and now relaxed, the 'OOHH's changed into 'AAAH's and an exuberant 'we did it!'. Maria arched to one side as Dagan banked the plane south as they slowly gained height.

- The plane right behind us! - Maria warned before it disappeared from view.
- It's an old friend of mine who's keen to see me.
- I don't like your German friends - Václav shouted - we're heavier and slower but not by much they'll take a while to catch us and night time is coming.
- He's throwing what seems to be seats and bags from the aircraft – Kessler informed - losing weight to fly faster.

Václav reacted immediately and started to throw everything overboard not tied down through the finicky side window, the Kesslers looked around and handed him manuals, tools and the empty knapsack. The second plane came up and started firing at them while Václav opened the window again and let off a burst as the wind rushed in, the other pilot swerved to the left and fired again. Hoffman's pilot brought them right level and tried to tip a wing an audacious move, all the while busy with their with pistols, Dagan slammed down his flaps, braking the plane and Hoffman's shot forward.

- Keep down - Václav said to the Kesslers – What about if you climb as high and as fast as you can.

- Why the frigging hell would I do something that crazy. Pardon my French
- Just do it. Look don't make me put more holes in you – Václav whispered in his ear as he stuck his Lugar pistol in Dagan's ribs.
- Don't want your beauty queen thinking what a prick you are – Dagan hissed back.
- She knows what a prick you are, I still have the benefit of the doubt – Václav hissed back jabbing the barrel in Dagan's gut. Maria looked on confused sensing differences.
- What's going on? – She hollered.
- Debating a strategic switch of direction – Václav said diplomatically.
  Fuck it you might even be right – Dagan said, his language getting cruder - It's the stupidest thing to do so they can't be expecting it – Václav looked on as Dagan pulled the stick back the aircraft soared into the sky leaving Hoffman's plane trailing as it had been swopping in and down. The gap grew wider.
- I stand vindicated – Václav smiled.
- Over at 1000m...1100m...1400m...shit this is burning up a lot of fuel, won't matter though if they catch us – said Dagan as he strained to keep the craft climbing - Give him a burst – Václav did as Dagan continued climbing on full throttle to 1500 meters which was when Václav started putting on the parachute. And then "he saw the light" Dagan thought to himself and knew why Václav hadn't dumped the food and thermos. Maria saw what he was doing and after a look at her father started to copy Václav.
- You're off your head – Dagan said looking at Maria - both of you.
- You need to lose weight or they're going to ram us, a few sandwiches and a heavy cheese aren't going to make a blind bit of difference but we will – Václav rightly pointed out.
- Where the hell are you going to go – Dagan didn't bother arguing, Václav was part of his mission but wasn't its objective, if he jumped all the better for him.
- I know this land like the back of my hand – Václav shouted - and my country needs me, to be very honest I am glad to return, I don't want to leave, we need people for the struggle. As we high enough?
- 1500 meters is enough, count to three to get clear and pull this cord - Kessler realized what Maria was about to do, he indicated the ripcord by holding a hand on it.
- I'm sorry Papa I can't go with you either, I have to try and save all the Jews I can by fighting for my country, I couldn't stand to be safe, to be the lucky 'one'.

- *Milacek* - said Kessler tenderly to his daughter and cupped her face with his hand he started to help her strap into the apparatus – jump away from the moving object, the plane in this case, count to 3 and pull this – he copied Dagan's instructions, and if that doesn't work then this. You are to be moving rapidly and approaching another much bigger moving object, the Earth. You will land with a force that will be responded equally so buckle your legs and land flat on your both feet to spread the reacting force then rollover. That should do it
- How do you know all this, you're never been in a plane before - Maria looked at her father in amazement one more time. Maybe the last.
- The laws of physics are everywhere, you were far too young but I sat on the committee which calculated the optimum height and size of the parachute, we were so sure that Broz offered to jump but they didn't take us up on that offer.

Before Kessler could continue the plane lurched to the right violently the plane of Hoffman scant meters away sailed by, the roar of its engine acted like the call of the wild.

- Jaysus we're got some rough ones in tonight, sorry about that, just saw the b**t**d in time. He fired some shots, anyone hurt - Dagan looked around and saw Hoffman's plane circling for another bite of the apple.
- Open the door – Václav shouted above the noise, Dagan could see a dark red patch on his arm.
- Are you okay? - Dagan asked.
- Doesn't matter, you and me even now – Václav pointed to Dagan's arm wounded in the forest ambush.
- We're expendable that's our problem brother – Dagan held out his hand and Václav took it.
- Brother – Václav smiled as he shouted this, the land below was now drained of colour and looked unreal, Václav turned and jumped out. Maria moved forwards to the open door. Dagan had banked and they both could see Václav hurtling downwards. Maria lent forward and kissed him on the lips.
- Thank you - was all she said but her eyes told a bigger story, she then turned and jumped out, rapidly falling after Vaclav, in seconds she was just a speck on Dagan's vision before he banked the other way to close the door, he caught sight of Václav as he approached the land and Dagan turned and descended rapidly away in the opposite direction, with a last look at Maria's parachute he gave a self-pitying sign, the things you have to do to

be forgiven. Now considerably lighter the gap between the planes edged a bit wider, Hoffman wasn't going to catch him nor would he have time to chase down the parachutists whose white mushrooms could be seen in the far distance seconds away from landing in the dwindling twilight. Dagan flew in the opposite direction to give Hoffman a clear choice of who to chase. Dagan banked as the specks were about to land in the pasture fields, the dozy cows were going to get a rude shock.

The Germans would be at the landing zone in half an hour, Václav was injured but Dagan didn't doubt he and Maria would manage to get away somehow. Now their plane could manoeuvre quite well Dagan started to put distance between them and Hoffman who followed suit and started to eject seats but too little too late. Kessler stopped looking at where his daughter had landed and reported little flashes of light from the pursuing plane, they were trying to hit the engine in a last desperate futile effort to bring them down. The popular myth of early WWI of biplanes shooting at each other with pistols like knights of old in the lists was engrained in the common physic but never once had one downed the other that way. It's virtually impossible given the movements of the plane air resistance, the speed of approach, and short-range of pistols. Dagan could rest assured on that but still pulled back on the stick and quickly rose to cloud cover. Suddenly they were enveloped by the fluffy wet marsh mellow dense whiteness. Dagan put the window screen wipers to work and continued on this course briefly before changing direction.

- Are we going to Russia? - Kessler asked as he clambered in beside the pilot – There's fresh blood here is it yours? - He asked Dagan as he looked at his red strained fingers.
- Not mine thankfully or Maria's either but Václav's, it's not fatal, no vital organs or anything he'll be okay.
- I do hope so he's stuck with my girl now so he has work to do and him being dead is not in her plans - Dagan looked at the elderly man, he was a lot sharper about people that the fuddie duddie scientist exterior lets on.

A break in the cloud showed in the last light of day a speck that was the blinking lights of Hoffman's plane's, Dagan had turned theirs off, back in the cloud cover Dagan banked 270 degrees.

- We're on our way to the Mediterranean. I hope you have your swimsuit and sandals! – He announced.

- It's hundreds of miles, we'll have to land, are the British sending us an aircraft carrier? Am I that important? The power of the atom, you were there in Dublin when Earnest came to tell us about splitting what he split. Are the British going to build the fission bomb? I can't believe it, even the Germans are baulking at that as it would take a thousand men a hundred years to manage that.

- I think the plan is one hundred thousand men and four years and you're right about the British not being able, they can barely stay in the war but the Americans can do what the hell they like if they see fit. I hope you like the desert climate now what would you like for dinner. I thought spaghetti or pizza would be nice. A change like – Dagan pondered the evenings culinary options.

- Pizza? Never heard of it, what are you telling me?

- Pizza, you'll love it, a very popular Italian dish. Personally, I think it has lots of potential if only people knew about it, so easy and simple, leftovers with tomato and cheese on rolled out bread dough done in the oven and hey presto.

- You were always one crazy boy.

- This crazy boy believes in your genius – Dagan dropped down to one thousand feet still under cloud cover, it was raining and water leaked in the bullet holes along with the wind, the cockpit was freezing but that was good, it's hard to sleep with chattering teeth - That's the Pula peninsula down there - he pointed to that distinctive outline of the coastal inlets, rivers and headlands.

- Now you say it, yes it's true but only because you just told me. Do you have the whole topography of Europe memorized? – Martin Kessler enquired.

- Even a London cabbie couldn't get that far - Kessler just looked at him. The "knowledge" wasn't something Kessler knew or cared about - I just memorized certain sections and hoped they are the ones I was going to need them. Now we have to turn South West, cross the Adriatic, follow the coast and when we come to Rimini, another distinctive coastal reference point, we have to head inland exactly twenty miles and try to land. So what I need is you to take note, airspeed two hundred and fifty knots, wind speed twelve knots, outside temperature six degrees, here's my watch, the best mamma Malone could buy for my 16th birthday and still going strong, the mammy and the watch, so note the time, base estimates on knowing we've gone 156 miles and we're 216 to go.

- Why don't we just look down – Kessler wanted to know.

- Because we have to be in the cloud cover just in case. Our fuzzy misty cloak.

Dagan took the plane up into the skies and changed direction towards Italy, anti-aircraft guns from the coast fired some shots at the direction of the engine sound. The flack explosions were well off but Dagan was relieved to gain cloud cover again and leave behind the eerie sensation of a war-torn continent below, silent, dark, hungry, people in their beds wondering what the new day will bring, one which could easily be their last.

The sound of a plane overhead was generally bad news but one alone at night, a solitary traveller was a mystery that didn't fit in the usual circumstances. Could it be a reconnaissance plane on its way to England and freedom or a transport bringing Germans troops home or any number of possibilities? But it could just be an Allied plane on a secretive mission, some small action against tyranny or putting it another way; a ray of hope. However, Dagan in the teeth-chattering cold didn't have much time to look down on the dark land while Kessler was muttering to himself as he looked at the watch now and again. He poured out coffee for Dagan whose hand shook as he brought it to his lips.

It tasted of glory and surged right through him, he felt a buzz in his head; Kessler kept working on the home comforts, blocking the holes with black straps, strips of seats, the lifebelt, whatever came to hand. It made a huge difference to the cabin but Dagan sorely missed having a pair of gloves. After thirty-one minutes seventeen seconds Kessler told Dagan that they were over the coast and Dagan descended and saw it was true.

- Just where we want to be – Dagan kept the plane far enough off the coast not to trigger a vacuous buzz to some listening ear on the ground - You are a perfect co-pilot, you don't talk much – he added.
- I'm counting – now another nine miles to go, three minutes, you're a tired boy I know – Kessler placed a fatherly hand on Dagan's shoulder - Don't think me unkind or ungrateful, you saved me from hell and more importantly Maria as well and you did it at some risk to yourself, words can hardly express the gratitude. Back there I was faced with a choice of a slow lingering painful death or a fast painless one. The worst was knowing that Maria was in the same position, I'm old I've lived but the children, the babies born every day in the mouth of Satan. I could discuss it but you are tired, you need to conserve your energies for our forced landing in the sea, then to drag me to the shore and carry me on your back to the end of Italy. After that I don't know,

you're such a clever fellow, you'd borrow Mussolini's yacht or row me straight across the Mediterranean! You're implacable but if I am talking it diverts precious energy to your ears that you need to fly.

Dagan smiled at the inexorable logic of the man, everything was measured and analysed from the point of view of Newton's three laws and the rest of those unbending truths that ruled the known universe. The truth was he was shattered, and flying at night was difficult, the false horizon confused even the best so he tried to fly by instruments as it was safer that way than flying visually but even thus he found himself drifting downwards and had to pull the nose up more and more frequently.

- Dagan – Kessler called out – now – Dagan took the plane down and inland over the coast straight at the mouth of the river Fiume below.
- Just where we should be, you nailed it – Dagan said admiringly - Now I have to turn seventeen degrees and fly on a straight line for nineteen miles. Can you tell me when?

Kessler nodded with a 'what a stupid question' shrug which Dagan didn't notice as he was banking and descending past the Rimini's coastal batteries and lookouts. A searchlight arched around in their direction but once he descended to two hundred meters the beams were overhead and soon left behind.

- The lookouts will ring inland, however - said Dagan - so we have to be quickly on our way.
- Quick? For what, aren't we just putting down and going to some safe house.
- We're putting down and refuelling, we've only 10 or 15 minutes of airtime left – Dagan had other plans than waterlogging a perfectly good plane.
- And you are just going to land at an airstrip, in and out of Axis airports like you own them – Silently they flew on - Times up.
- Perfect, look around for a lantern light, we'll circle till we see it.

Both Dagan and Kessler peered intently into the darkness below, the pale half-moon gave them the positions of the peaks and troughs as Dagan followed up over the river. They could make out small towns, dwellings, farm buildings, some roads. The river was a silvery snake and up and down they went as they looked intently at both banks and the higher ground Dagan didn't dare fly over it.

- I don't see anything, they should have heard us by now – Dagan said worriedly.
- You are varying the circle, the circumference is 3 miles, widen it to 5 and you cover more ground – Kessler put science to good use once again.

Dagan did as he suggested even though he was getting closer to deep dark ridges and up slopes, instant death if they made a mistake and he ploughed into something solid. Seconds passed, Dagan sweating despite the cold, he'd had to leave off looking to pilot them safely. He hoped Kessler's eyes were up to this. Another minute, now Dagan didn't know which way was upriver or down.

- I'll have to put us in the river soon, as close to the bank as possible and then as you say to drag you to the end and beyond – the Irishman spelt out the most likely outcome of their predicament.
- Won't be needed, look over there, do you see it, there look! Kessler called out – no it's gone.
- Keep looking, they might be flashing.
- No, nothing, it was somebody who heard the plane, opened a window and shut it again.
- We're barely enough fuel to get over the river... Dagan started before Kessler jumped up.
- THERE, that's it. It's a blazing torch, not a lantern.
- That's it – Dagan agreed – that's the arranged signal - He didn't waste a second but flew directly at where the light was coming from.
- You're going to land? Sorry it's obvious you are, I don't know but I had to say something, this is so unbelievable - Kessler was flabbergasted at the undertaking as he looked down on the murky dim land below - It's nearly pitch dark!
- That is a pointer. I have to line it up with another smaller one twenty meters beyond. There you can see it – Dagan said relieved as hell?
- I do now left go left to line them up - Kessler said.
- We've just enough gas to get us there, brace yourself it's going to be rough.

Dagan eased off the engine and kept the slowing aircraft straight, this is where the Storch came into its own like earlier over the meadow field, the plane was barely going forty knots as it came up and now Dagan and Kessler could clearly see a curved road at the point of the torch then straighten out into the murky darkness. On both sides, small fields and verges could be made out then dense dark tree-ness and behind them loomed larger hills under a starry night.

- The second torch is 20 meters past did you say? – Kessler asked to which Dagan assented with a nod - You're 120 meters out.
- Okay, my man that helps big time.
- Seventy...fifty...thirty meters – Kessler kept marking all-important distance as Dagan looked out the side window and pushed the stick down ever so slightly, the ground was coming up fast and crowding around them.
- Ten meters, here it comes – Kessler gave out a final warning and seemed surprised to see the ground so totally engaged in the exercise was he.

Dagan knew it was time and pushed it further, the wheels touched down on surprisingly smooth tarmacadam and cement road, Dagan struggled to keep it straight on the narrow as he slammed on the brakes and put his flaps fully down. They jarred and bounced along as Dagan fought the stick and used the rudders to correct the times they seemed to swerve. They zoomed past the second torch and Dagan had to keep dead centre in the dark with only the dim cabin lights to show the five meters directly in front. What seemed ages were over in seconds, they only needed about fifty meters to stop?

- Well done! Fifty-three meters - Kessler said as he had calculated the distance visually.
- Thanks to you too, couldn't have done it without your help - Dagan let out a puff of breath - Not done yet - Dagan gunned the engine and they moved forward – have to get to the end and then we can turn the plane for takeoff – Dagan moved along for another 50 or so meters - plenty of space but take off needs more legroom – he stopped just as the road sloped ominously downwards and to the left.
- Let's see where we are, I've haven't been to Italy in a long time – Kessler bounced down and disappeared.
- Don't you go slopping off we're not out for a country stroll – Dagan got down taking the machine gun with him, he saw that the wheel was just over the edge of the surfaced road and the huge nose of the Storch stretched into the void - Got to turn this around – he said looking over the precipice.
- Someone's coming – Kessler said.
- I should hope so, it wasn't the fairies that put the lights out for us and they're supposed to bring dinner with them too.
- Lucca – a whisper in the dark beyond the end of the road.

- Tosca – called out Dagan - *Andiamo Danilo.*

Out of the gloom came an elderly figure smiling broadly, in this late '60s, well preserved, white grey stack of hair still thick and strong, the face was covered by a similarly coloured beard. The face was brown from long hours in the sun with surprising pale blue eyes giving an outer-worldly look. To keep warm Danilo wore a heavy poncho over a rough white shirt, dark jacket and knee-length pantaloons; those were met by tough leather boots that Kessler thought fitting of a Dumas hero, all buttons, straps and flaps.

- Old friend I can't believe it, you came from the night like a Valkyrie settling back into its eyrie folding its huge wings - The new arrival said as he and Dagan embraced.
- Thanks to you we could Danilo, how are your goats?
- Bored waiting for weeks in the same spot, they like to move around you know and have eaten every damn blade for miles. Up the valley down the valley but always to the same stop at night here just in case. The blessed fathers were insistent; I had to be here for you – the man said in a slow determined diction.
- I could have left the pilot lights on just in case, we aren't visible here from down the valley – Dagan said looking around.
- Ah but if the high prefect had passed in his car which he tends to do after visiting the bakers wife, what then?
- He's not 'visiting' tonight I hope. But Danilo you are a good friend and we have some little things for you – Dagan handed over the coat hanger and cuff links and tie clip – Bring them to the Count, he will know what to do. This is my esteemed friend Professor Martin Kessler, Professor this is Danilo Costante, an old friend from days gone by.
- A pleasure to meet you - Kessler bowed and shook Danilo's hand – I feel the trees so close, how is it we didn't clip them with the wings.
- You wouldn't think it but at times we had five or six planes up here, people would fly from all around Europe for a weekend, the Count was famous for his hunting, there used to be a petrol pump but it's long dry now – Dagan reminisced.
- Here let me help you turn around the plane and put some nourishment in its entails – Danilo proposed.
- Just like old times.
- And after I have some good dinners for you, gnocchi *favoloso* my beautiful wife of thirty-eight years cooked it just like her mama and her mama's mama – He pulled up a mule behind him – Marta come on girl, she got such a fright with the noise – into the light

came a semi bald grey-brown donkey of reluctant port, laden down with fine dining and bulging canisters poking out from under the blankets on each of her flank's.

- Not just gnocchi – said Dagan to Kessler as the pulled back the rough blankets which dated from the Risorgimento – this is what we need to keep us up in the air till our next stop. Amigo this is something I can hardly believe or express my thanks with words - he said putting a hand on Danilo's shoulder.

- Not my doing and please stop you are embarrassing me, the good Count and the good holy fathers clubbed together the petrol from their stores and I added the good olive and nut oils to make it up, we didn't need asking, would gladly have done it, anything to poke a stick in the eyes of the black shirts. Come we will work and then eat - The three of them quickly unstrapped the jerry cans.

- Where did you manage to get so much petrol – Kessler, who' been out of earshot earlier asked – since the war started....?

- Petrol! - Dagan and Danilo said at the same time – Yes there is some too, that and lots of oils, olive, pumpkin seeds, sunflower, bacon fat, cooking fat, everything we could find, we have been saving this for months – The Italian answered - The Count collects the left over's from the estate's kitchens, from the olive groves, from the sunflowers. His cars never have to stop and the fascists have more reason to leave him alone as he keeps their cars running too.

Danilo produced a hand pump and put one end of the rubber tube in the first jerry can and the other end he handed to Dagan to put into the fuel tank which he had located on the back of the fuselage. Dagan went to open it, he cupped it with his hands and heaved and heaved and heaved some more, sweat broke out on his forehead. The biggest plans fall on the smallest details.

- Jaysus tonight, pardon me Danilo, but that's tight and I think we dumped the tools earlier – Kessler came over with a knowing look on his face - Kessler can you manage it, stuck solid though.

- I'll get it turning in a second – Kessler said emphatically.

Dagan had a face of whitewashed Connemara stone, the bags sunken under his eyes, his eczema flaring up leaving a red rash he kept picking at, making it worse but the momentary relief was nearly worth it. Danilo saw the red raw skin took some olive oil in his ancient hands rubbed it into Dagan's ruptures, 'Mani de Santi' he said, meanwhile

Kessler had taken the end of the tube and pumped some very carefully under the latch.

- Good idea to lubricate but I'll never get a hold on it after - Dagan said looking on.

But Kessler just ignored him while he dribbled a few more drops took a lighter from his pocket and set the liquid ablaze, the kerosene part flashed up first then the cooking oils gave a slower blue burn, in five seconds it was all over, the blackish-brown mush left was soaked up by Kessler's handkerchief as he gave a firm tug to remove the tank stopper.

- Open sesame as you say in the West End – Kessler exclaimed.
- Thank for that practical demonstration of thermal stimulated metal expansion and contraction – Dagan said relieved and laughed.
- *Erudito erudito* – said the Italian admiringly.

They all quickly set to filling the tank with every jerry can one after the other, intense work, Dagan could feel sweat all over his body even in the chilly winters night, he'd been lucky with a Mediterranean location as winters frosts were rare. Three more jerry cans were stored in the back of the plane, Danilo as well gave them a round loaf, salami, hard-boiled eggs, delicious olives, two jumpers and God love him a pair of gloves.

- Just leave the containers behind the tree there – he said.

The last thing done had been to tie a rope to the back wheel of the plane so Marta could put some mule power into helping them turn it around ready for take-off. Danilo and he hugged while Martin shook his hand before the old man took Marta down through the forest path. Danilo's parting shot had been to tell Dagan to be ready to fly at any minute and to watch out for the brigands and poachers. 'A lot of people are going hungry during this winter'. Dagan and Kessler ate the food in silence, the gnocchi peppered with chilli made it tough going for Kessler who was unused to spicy food.

- Leave it for later if you want to - Dagan suggested while he mournfully remembered the pepper left for the dogs.
- I've eaten a lot worse, this is delicious – Kessler replied - the cheese mixed in with the gnocchi and the sweet smooth olive oil makes it a succulent if hot dish - The bread they decided to keep for short rations later and the oranges that finished the simple meal was like finding a half-crown going through your pockets when expecting just coppers.

351

- Kessler you'll have to take lookout for an hour, I need a bit of sleep unless you want to pilot the plane for a while. Hmm maybe the most prudent option, we're safer up there than on the ground, we like fledgelings chirping and hopping around, very venerable, we've been very lucky so far but this is a road after all - Dagan handed him the machine pistol.
- I will not have blood on my hands – Kessler said rejecting it.
- After all, what's happened you're still an idealist! Just fire it in the air – Dagan said resigned.

The shattered pilot climbed aboard and hunkered down. Kessler didn't feel much better but the food had perked him up, it was 20 minutes later as his eyes lids were beginning to drupe when he heard bird calls, dawn was near but...he poked Dagan awake with the muzzle of the gun.

- Hey, it can't be an hour already and watch what you are doing, that's a loaded gun you are jamming into my ribs – Dagan said bad tempered.
- Sorry, it's only been 20 minutes but now shhhh and listen.

Dagan listened out, far down in the valley below the headlights of several vehicles were visible coming in their direction. Still fairly far off though.

- It was only a matter of time till they get here, good work quick climb up, we'll be away with the fairies long before they're here.
- Fifty minutes up those roads but it wasn't them I woke you up for! Listen again, those bird calls are too uniform and in the wrong key – Kessler hissed, Dagan listened and his expression changed.
- Shit, that's something else altogether, too low and too damn close. You know what key birds sing in? – Even as the call to action galvanised him he still had time to be marvel at the old man.

But still, it was more to himself than anyone as he sat bolt up, kicked the starter and gunned the engine into life, the roar was deafening in the predawn silence and set off a chain reaction, the bird sounds stopped, a light went on in the dimness, voices started shouting, shots were fired; the cars and trucks down the road accelerated and blasted their horns. By the time Kessler perceived all this Dagan had put the plane charging along the road and quickly reached the point of the second torch. That left forty meters of road before the drop, Kessler knew it and thought it better not to look, and he still couldn't imagine how they'd managed to land on the short stretch of road. He started doing so maths in his head as a waving figure started running out of the trees. Flat cap, jacket and web belting full of shotgun charges.

Before this new player on the scene had time to point his shotgun the plane had flashed by and they were up in the clean air again. Dagan banked directly right just as a blast rang out so avoiding buckshot all over their flying bird. The mountainside gave way and Dagan pulled right, swept down the valley to the river below and in passing flew over the approaching group of vehicles lit up by their headlights. As they flew directly over a dumbfounded gunner on an armoured car tried to swivel his mounted machine gun upwards while pulling back the catch and firing. Again the burst was aimed at where they had been seconds earlier as Dagan had banked left and upwards, rapidly getting out of range and out of danger.

- They must have heard the plane earlier and come looking for it, same as the gamekeeper types, we're very popular – they'd made their getaway but the relief was short-lived, now his next dangerous antagonist was hazard-prone night flying.

Dagan took the plane down the valley and up over central mountain ridge of Italy. Thanks to his foreshortened siesta they had time to get to the other coastline of Italy and head south under cover of darkness. He was racing the rising sun at 200mph and again took them up into the clouds to keep out of sight.

- A renegade's best friend – he said of his fluffy cloak.
- Where are we going now, what route are we on? I am most intrigued, how did you know where to land and that they'd be waiting for you, that wasn't British intelligence or anything planned by them. I know you are a person of resources, means, high abilities who knows a lot of people but this is like Bulldog Drummond – Kessler didn't read a lot outside of academic journals.
- I prefer the Riddle of the Sands, good old Erskine, God love him. Well, it's a long story as always but time we've plenty of and it'll keep me awake and avoiding mountains. Thousands and thousands of those. At the start of the century and well into it illegal car races were all the rage among the highest levels of society, London to Paris, Paris to Prague, Prague to Berlin and so on. The next big rush after cars at 100km per hours was aeroplanes at 350mph, the sheer exuberance of it and thanks to the Great War cheap second-hand biplanes were tuppence to a penny. Do you know how many surplus biplanes they're after the

war? You could crash one and have another sent in days – Dagan recalled.

- Sometimes you brought Maria along, I suspected something was going on from the odd coins she would have and flying was the only logical solution to the evidence. You see a person at breakfast and six hours later they come back smelling of Parisian scents, some French coins to hand and a bag from a store on the Avenue Foch. The only way to do that is by flying. I just didn't know you were doing the flying if I had it would have been another story.
- Breakfast in Prague, lunch in Berlin and dinner in Paris. The parties and the people were so splendid – Dagan fondly reminisced.
- A long way off your rebel days – Kessler pointed out
- Oh, those never went away either, I just like to mix it all up, enjoy life to the full, it's two *siestas* long as my Spanish chums tell me.
- So what was illegal about flying around Europe – Kessler asked – surely you had licences. permits.
- It was where you flew, the destinations got crazier, the authorities more annoyed, the incidents graver. People wanted to get on so waiting around for customs officials and paperwork was so ennui they didn't care, they had the money and influence to get around it creating a sort of semi-hidden network of 'landings', straight bits of road or flat fields in isolated areas with a friendly castle nearby to bunk over in and a petrol pump on hand. And if there wasn't one they'd rustle one up, we're talking about presidents of oil companies, friends or major stockholders. Petrol pumps popped up in the strangest places. We called it the Mittelholzer as he was one of the maximum exponents of landing anywhere and one of the best in designing routes, good old Walter, Swiss aviation's biggest gift to the world. Thanks to him and his mountain hopping expertise an alternative secretive pan European route map was born.
- But this was back in the 20's – Kessler pointed out.
- Roaring they were, the '30s killed off all this fun, the stock market crash got rid of the money and the plane crashes got rid of the few brave souls who remained.
- Yur friend Danilo hasn't been waiting around with torches since the early 30's – Kessler pointed out.
- Since early December just, I reactivated part of the network using British gold. Works wonders it does. Danilo is up around that area anyway with his flock, so no suspicions, he stuck around longer than normal.

- Re-activate you say? From London in the middle of a war! How did you manage that? – Kessler knew nifty footwork when he saw it.
- Another long story but one I can't spill, too many people involved, suffice to say that I had to go to confession a lot to move things along – Dagan hinted.
- There's older networks than your Mittelholzer – Kessler said sagely taking things on board.
- Damn right and if they've been around so long it's for a reason.
- By the way how far have we flown since we took off - Dagan looked out.
- 93 miles - Kessler intuitively replied.
- Good, its three hours to our next stop, Sardinia, you'll love it, an out of the way place that Mussolini hasn't been able to tame.

Flight 90 minutes in.

- One and a haaaaaaalf hours to our next stop, Saaaaaaaaardinia - Dagan was so far gone, so lacking in sleep and rest that odd malapropisms escaped without him even realizing – you'll love it, then Sicily all going well and there's no reason to suppose it will. Ha ha ha. Did I say will or won't. Lap of the Gods my good man. And then home. Ah home is such a wonderful concept, mine is long gone but I will go where you lead me.
- Are you okay? Let me feel your pulse, I think I will put a pin in your collar, your head droops and ouch – Kessler was worried, every once and awhile the plane juddered violently as Dagan fell in and out of microsleeps and tensed on the stick.
- *Ceart go leor* - Irish was now making regular appearances on Dagan's side of the conversation – All the pins you like, I'll be human colander by the end. Hell, you're right you know – Even though Kessler hadn't said anything on the subject - Home's where you hang your hat damn it. I hope I can get some shut-eye at the next stop, excellent Ravioli. Take over for five minutes; keep the nose on this heading.
- Me?
- No one else in the plane is there? They jumped out remember, was it something I said, the Irish are gas and full of it sometimes, bad diet, hard to look after yourself on the run, dodging bullets, woe is me, Okay! Here it is. How to fly in 20 seconds. Altitude, setting and orientation – Dagan pointed out the three instruments – make small slow adjustments to the stick to keep same. Any

big problems call me, fighters, storms, angels, Santa Claus. Give me ten minutes and our chances will improve 40% - With that Dagan pushed back, put a cap over his head and closed his eyes. If this dumb Mick can do it can't be that difficult. Theory is fine but sometimes it's good to go to the practice - Kessler spoke more to himself than anyone as Dagan was already deeply asleep.

Chapter XIII

January 4th, 1942, Maltese coastguard lookout point.

Juan Lapita spent most of his days and nights on the highest point of the island scanning the skies for Italian planes. Since the kingdom of Savoy had joined the war last June Malta being smack bang in-between it and its African colonies had been one of its first targets. It had taken two days before an Italian Savoia-Marchetti put in an appearance over the island's skies. That one was shot down but soon after daily visits to the rocky outcrop became the norm. Sicily was a hundred miles away, thirty minutes by bomb-laden plane, Joan scanned an arc of one hundred and eighty degrees almost always towards the North, towards Italy and its Southern isle, the Maltese were suffering terribly but suffer they must suffer they would, surrender was not an option as they were vital for the British presence in the Mediterranean. They had been for centuries the link between British Middle Orient, Gibraltar and the home seas. Their valour was to earn them the highest honour available for civilian bravery, the George cross but that was in the future and while it would make the Maltese feel extremely proud on its own it didn't stop the bombs failing or the daily struggle to survive.

Thankfully the Italians normally came in a eight thousand feet, just above flak and let loose their bomb loads from that height. The Roman legions do or die ways not evident nor the legionaries pointed sword stroke as due to the time it took for the bombs to fall they drifted off course. Only one in every ten fell anywhere near Valletta and its vitally important port. The sea and the fields around gobbled up the vast majority meaning the worst damage was being done to the sorely needed vegetable crops, potatoes were being blown sky high and their prices followed suit. The Maltese could also take solace and comfort from the large number of dud bombs added to the lack of precision and the height of the attack was keeping Valletta from complete destruction. Imagine then Joan's surprise when for no great reason or need he changed tack looked down and spotted a small plane skipping along the ocean barely meters off the sea. Joan blinked and did a double-take, the plane was now barely a mile from the coast and coming in fast. Joan fell quickly into the drill first trying to identify the plane from the silhouettes drawn on the wall, too small for a bomber, its shape was at odds from those of the regularly visiting Italian fighters or biplanes. It didn't seem to be Italian at all, the black cross on the wing could only mean a German plane but over Malta? He put down his cup of pasty

357

tea and picked up the phone connecting him to air defences HQ located on Valletta's much-bombed airstrip. There three Hurricane fighters armed and crewed up were standing in underground bunkers ready to go.

- Observation One: Small plane, possible recognizance aircraft, German markings, approaching on North-East direction. Correction, plane has crossed the coast, approaching Valletta over. Markings confirmed, visual on the plane, confirm two people on board, over.
- Central over: What the blue blazes Juan, where you asleep. Two crew on board, how can you tell? Over.
- Observation One: It came in skipping over the waves, impossible, a miracle they didn't ditch, the plane just flew around my position, both crew members waved and gave thumbs up, showing international distress signal over, now heading to the aerodrome. Over.
- Central over: Fighters scrambling. Taking no chances. Receiving distress calls in English claims to be a British agent bringing in a valuable scientist on orders of Churchill, Roosevelt, the knights of Columbanus and God knows who else. Eloquent babble.
- Observation One: Could be true although unlikely over, can confirm that plane is a recon plane and is unarmed. Over. Clear a runway? Over.
- Control over: Not a threat! The crazy pilot asked for a warm bath, a hot whisky and a hotter woman when he lands, he is singing baldy sailor songs as well. We take this risk very seriously, the plane will be shot down to avoid any chance of a crash landing on the tower or bunkers or fuel installations or the runway.
- Observation One: Surely that will cause the exact civilian or military damage you are trying to avoid. Over.

Joan didn't near what happened till later as he realized control weren't answering. Was that his imagination or did he get the smell of cooking in the air, a pleasant aromatic rich odour of oven-roasted meats and rich stewed casseroles.

On the east-west runway full of patched up bomb craters, the Malta 'fighter' group was lined up to take off. The three of them began hurtling across the open expanse almost side by side, this dangerous manoeuvre, a simultaneous take-off was due to the lateness of the warning and the urgent order to scramble.

- Dagan Air to landing tower, control, whoever happens to be happy and listening, I've had 95 minutes sleep in the last three days plus a cat nap I stole while I handed over the stick to my elderly co-pilot who's never flown before and who narrowly avoided ditching us in the sea... – Said in a slightly slurred way.
- I did not! Lies, calumnies, falsehoods, I was studying schooling patterns of dolphins beneath and went for a closer look, I am a better pilot than you! – Another very indignant voice come over the air. Song then broke out.

> *- I will cross the briny ocean, I will whistle and sing*
>
> *And since you've refused the offer love*
>
> *Some other girl shall wear the ring....-*

- Lads, so apart from whaling me songs laddies I want a whiskey filled lake the size of Loch Derg, Irish whiskey of course not that half made mush the kilt-wearing ninnies make and a soft bed with clean white sheets. I'll have to bath of course to get rid of the fleas, a shave too just the job, must be presentable for society, in which I mix with consummate ease. My last bath was in Prague in a fantastic middle European hotel, hot stuff, big brass legs, ended up having a huge soak so you Maltese have a lot to live up to.
- Control to approaching aircraft. Identify yourself please.
- Sure you said please, that's a great friendly start, I notice your fighters are scrambling, that's not so nice. Identify, identity, how do you define a person, did you like my singing by the way, my friends say I am the belle of the ball, light of their lives, a true pal, an outstanding citizen of the world, a clean shot, a coffee and whisky drinker, water is for cattle. My friend's legion, call me Dags and I'm happy to make your acquaintance. Excuse the unannounced house call, just turning up at the door so to speak, did you get my card, I rang earlier, how remiss, I am a bit dizzy, Sicilian food is very heavy and leaves one with a thirst, I am spitting feathers. Dagan Malone, bon vivant, lover of fine wines and fine long-limbed women. How are the ladies of the island anyway while we're on the subject – All said in a rush.
- Will you shut up for heaven's sake – The other voice broke in again.
- Excuse me Sir I have the word, as I was saying in Sicily they say the Maltese femmes are stout of leg but also stout of heart.
- Control, this is a militarized zone. We are scrambling to intercept and destroy.

- Tush, I can see that, you're a hard man and a terrible set of manners you have by the way. Damn your eyes and hang your heads in shame, I've told you till I'm blue in the face, Dagan Malone Esq. lately of the Holloway men's club New York, seconded to the Allied war effort against his will and better judgement but here I am, claiming to be a British agent, may God and Arthur Griffith forgive me it's the only time in my life I've claimed to be British anything. Don't you want to be civilized and let me land first and then we can have a gentleman's chat over a cup of tea before I smack you insolent head and have my bath, whiskey, barber and ladies company, did I leave anything out?

> - *Oh Father John*
> *Stuck his long*
> *In sister Mary's ha....*

- Would you please shut up, you are not even in key, more like two off – the other voice in the cockpit make its self heard again.
- Are you a musician or physicist or what, I'm beginning to have my doubts.
- Unidentified German aircraft! – The voice of the tower betrayed signs of end of tetchiness.
- Yes German of course, very clever of you to spot that, of course the plane is German, who else has planes you can borrow in Europe these days. If there'd been a Brit plane I would have asked for that. Ah I can see the planes you are scrambling you have no secrets from me up here. Three in fact, just for little old me! You have no secrets from me. Did I say that already? What a waste of fuel, one would bring this sucker down.
- Control desist from your present flight path.
- A cat among the pigeons I know but I'm coming in on the same runway those lads are bombing along on right now. They're young, I'll try to keep out of their way like I've no choice though I'm flying on olive oil vapours since a while back.
- Control desist desist, he's landing .....

Control then witnessed the chaos caused as the German plane came down on the runway among the fighters, in the tower they could barely look as the middle one of the formation took off right over the incoming Storch while those on the left and right aborted in time and pulled away. The Storch's left wheel gave way and it skidded to a halt. The returning planes turned and taxied back past the stricken enemy plane stopped dead bang right on the middle of the runway. Two figures were emerging and saluting them. The third plane came round and put itself down as fire trucks, ambulances and jeeps full of armed military police careered up put out the fires, tend to the wounded and stop the invasion.

- Malta at long last, Dagan Malone at your service send you best car, our wheel gave way at the last moment and we must importune some transport.

Control took up his binoculars and spied the shabby figures jubilantly dancing and throwing their hands in the air. He could hear the scene over the open microphone

- - *I'll take you home Irene* - was part of what could make out.

Epilogue 1: Berlin SS headquarters, Late January 1942

Hoffman sat at his battered wooden desk, working feverishly on an equally battered metal typewriter, he'd never been very adept at that skill, normally people did it for him but this was too important and too urgent, they were coming for him and he had to finish. Sitting where he'd sat since the night before, his plain white shirt's sleeves rolled up, jacketless despite the intense March cold, he'd turned off the heating to stay awake and sharp, finally, the last page was done and Hoffman stubbed out his umpteenth cigarette. He carefully extracted the page from the machine and added it to the pile beside him, punched a hole in the sides and weaved string through it and the rest of the sheets along with two harder brown cardboard covers. Finally, after rubbing his eyes he got up stiffly and walking around the silent office. Magda his secretary would not be here for hours yet. He walked over to the sideboard and the tins upon it which he opened and began wiping up the congealed meat fat of a stew with some bread. Even now stone-cold it was delicious, incredible he'd never heard of Maxims before. A final swig of beer from the jug and on the sofa for brief rest. His eyes were drooping but he couldn't sleep just yet or so he thought.

Suddenly he awoke as he heard footsteps and voices in the outer office. It was now late afternoon, how long had the slept? He jumped up and put on his jacket as his interoffice buzzer sounded. He picked it up thinking he had just been in time then with the report his timing right on as if divinely orchestrated.

361

- Sir, there are some people to see you, they don't have an appointment but they are insisting quite vigorously – Dear Magda sounded indignant and annoyed.
- That's okay, let them in but first put me through to Reich's Marshal Himmler's direct line – Magda knew the number, a secretaries club they belonged to.
- I will try sir but I'm not sure at this late hour, Oh they are pushing past, how dare you...Please! Excuse... - with that, the double doors opened and four SS entered, two officers accompanied by two rank troops armed with MP 75s. Overkill.
- Welcome gentlemen, I will be with you in just a minute please – The unfazed Hoffman addressed the group.
- Put the phone down Hoffman, we will not delay our duty one second for your convenience – The Colonel in charge bombasted.
- Would putting on my jacket delay your duty? - Hoffmann's evident serene state was disconcerting.

The face of the senior officer all repressed ire and disgust, the junior officer glaring silently with this month twisted in rage while the two soldiers more stoic just pointed their guns at him. This was the moment he knew would come since the plane with Malone and Kessler had disappeared into the darkness in the clouds over Slovenia, Hoffman that day had watched on in disbelief as his prey again escaped from his clutches by a matter of minutes and he knew that it would be his last opportunity. The British and especially Malone would have a plan and even if they were recaptured it would be by somebody else. Hoffman vividly remembered the cramped cabin of the plane filled with the smoke of the pistols.

- You did your best - Heiser had put a hand on his shoulder as they returned empty-handed to the base.
- My best isn't good enough by a long way, I'm a dead man now, persona non grata, they'll come from me and it will be the headlights of a truck, a wall in a courtyard and a platoon in front of me aiming at the piece of paper pinned on my coat above my heart. I hope you don't get pulled in by my failure – Hoffman said genuinely.
- Don't worry about me. What a waste though, a firing squad. I never shoot anyone even deserters, they go to a penal battalion, handy formations to have for the dirty work as they are dead men anyway, first into battle, over minefields if they have to, unarmed even they have to kill a Russian by hand, spade, knife whatever to get one. Clothes and food from Russians also mostly, dead men don't eat we say so why give them rations. And if they survive

ninety days they are exonerated and re-join the ranks! A boy are they tough bastards. They deserve it if they make it – Heiser finished on.
- Ninety days – Hoffman repeated slowly.

After returning to Berlin Hoffman had spent the weeks it had taken the justice machine to catch up with him by visiting eminent scientists in the city and elsewhere, those working on secret projects, investigating the possibilities of other miracle weapons such from the power of the atom. He had gone over again and again what the British had done via their surprising agent and why, this gun for hire Irishman rebel traitor, sure Malone knew Kessler and had been a gallant for the daughter but why go to all the trouble and how did the British convince Malone to throw in his lot with them, Malone had a long history of antagonism towards the British. Why help them out? And the more he thought about it, the more he'd found out, the clearer some self-evident conclusions became.

The British were trying or were going to try to build a special bomb, a city destroyer according to what he'd been told. The power was unimaginable, only those who've witnessed a Krakatoa or a Pompey could and they didn't leave descriptions because they had all been immolated. The result would be immense but so were the problems on the road to a workable weapon, insurmountable according to many of the top physicists but Hoffman had concluded that with more people like Kessler working alongside the best Germans, the Japanese and captured Russians it could be attempted. All this had gone into his report.

- You are through to the Reich's Fuhrer! - said a surprised sounding Magda – Hoffman wasn't, he knew Himmler's interest in his career, its meteoric rise and fall and would be following events out of morbid curiosity from his office.
- Hoffman, are you still at your desk at this hour? – Himmler said coldly.
- Yes, sir, my dedication to the state is total - Himmler knew exactly where he was, to direct the arresting party.
- Mine too but the state also expects devote Germans to perform and produce. If not we must move them aside and let others take the lead. Are there people with you? Have you had visitors? – said the Cat.

- Not expected ones but yes some gentleman, colleagues of the internal affairs bureau I believe want to talk to me. No idea what it could be about? – said the Mouse.
- I'm sure its routine, nothing to be worried about. Why are you ringing me? I am very busy – said the not busy enough Cat.
- I have doubts about how and why Malone got so close to the Fuhrer and anything touching on the safety our leader is not to be taken lightly by anyone - The mouse roars - You are busy but I've left instructions that certain information be passed should I be unable to do so myself.
- And why would that be? – Me-ow.
- Well it brings me to the second matter, I'd like to make a personal transfer request to join the *Disziplinschlagkraft* formation, Germany needs everyman it has to do the most they can to defeat its enemies, even those not currently in its favour.
- A transfer?
- Yes, I fear my ability to inflict damage on our enemies might be severely affected by my next assignment in the SS.
- I know little of this but perhaps you are right.
- The *Disziplinschlagkraft* division units are always first into attack, imagine the glory. Please consider this unorthodox and tardy request but I think it would be the best for Germany.
- And for you perhaps but don't be so sure. That ticket is nearly as one way as the one facing you now but I am a gambling man, transfer request granted, pass me to the senior officer with you. I am sure he is quite upset already at being so delayed in his work.
- Upset would be one word, he looks like he's having an apoplexy but thank you Sir, I will pass him the phone presently if you would indulge me on more matter – Hoffman made a gesture to the fuming man in front of him, holding the hand over the receiver – RF Himmler would like a word in a minute. You can wait at ease till then and so can both of you too – Hoffman said to the men pointing their weapons at him. The SS detachment stupefied by the turn of events just stood gaping.
- The situation there is tense I take it, what is this final matter, Hoffman, my time is limited – but Himmler's voice betrayed eagerness.
- It's the question of why go to all this trouble, the British I mean, I have drawn up a report about the events and the conclusions are quite surprising and maybe it will be my last service to the Fatherland and my greatest – Hoffman's voice soared.
- Your services have been many and varied so this report must be quite something.

- A way to win the war no less – Hoffman affirmed.
- Quite a claim, now pass me over to Erzht, he will be livid seeing his prey escape before his eyes. Hoffman good luck, you have saved Germany some bullets but notwithstanding, I don't expect to see you again – Himmler signed off.
- He wants to speak to you my dear Erzht - Hoffman passed the phone over. Erzht listened and said nothing except at the end.
- Of course, my Reich's Fuhrer – Erzht hung up and looked at Karl thoughtfully while seeming to come to a decision after a pause – Major Hoffman you are to accompany Lt Klotz to a holding station till you are transported eastwards to your new 'posting'. I wish you luck, you will need it but it seems you have it already, no one has sidestepped me like this before. Please this way.

Erzht indicated that Hoffman and Klotz should wait outside as he closed the door. Alone in Hoffman's office, Erzht waited a couple of seconds just looking around. You could tell a lot from a person's office but Erzht soon turned his attention to the desk. Himmler said Hoffman was having flights of fantasy and had written it all up in a report. Erzht was to look it over and see if it warranted being passed on to other departments. Himmler didn't want to be a laughing stock if it was a ridiculous proposal. Erzht sat down at the desk and took up the report left dead centre on the blotter.

The name was *Wundergrosesentotenbombe* and its use to end the war. Erzht grunted at that hyperbole and was amazed at the sheer neck of Hoffman to give a report a name like that. AMAZINGBIGGESTKILLINGBOMB. Who was he to take such liberties, Erzht stared leafing through the report but was against the proposal from the word go. He was soon lost in deep waters, a career bureaucrat and ardent Nazi he owed his lofty current position to his ability to read the wishes of his superiors and make them happen. He knew that Himmler thought this a load of tosh and nothing he read led Erzht to believe otherwise, at the heart of the argument was the central premise of a huge explosion that could somehow be worked up from radioactive rays, the details were vague but Erzht remained very sceptical. Radioactive elements were fantasy weapons unless you looked at Flash Gordon and that was it. He put the report in his bag, passing it to RF for reading would only damage himself vis-à-vis that august and all-powerful figure. He decided to quietly burn the report later in his office.

Epilogue 2: Sidi Haneish airfield, south of Alexandria, Egypt, Sept. 14th 1942

- That will be him – One of the waiting ground crew Charlie Everett said to his nearest colleague.
- Come to visit this section of his fiefdom so we can doff the cap – Billy Cantwell wasn't terribly taken with Bernard Montgomery the new commander of the 8th Army.   Charlie looked at him.
- Bit hard on him aren't ya – he just said.
- He's up against the desert fox and he looks like one whack of the skillet from my old Mam would knock him silly – Billy replied defiantly.
- Your Mam could knock Joe Louis out in three – Charlie said reverently – You're miffed cos you liked Auld Auck.
- Damn right, won the battle of El Alamein already he did and here's Bernie with tanks galore, the Germans on the ropes and all the glory for him – Billy fairly spat it out.
- Give him a chance, funny looking plane, huge bleeding wings on it. If it weren't for the RAF marking I'd swear it was a Jerry aircraft coming in.
- Well spotted, it is and it isn't or it was and now it isn't.
- Talking riddles Billy.
- That there is a German plane that was robbed of them and brought in
- No kidding, still and all why give it to our head honcho don't we have planes like that of our own.
- We do but not as reliable as this one, look how it nearly stops while landing, a thing of beauty – they both stood and admired the huge wingspan of the British plane of German origin as it gracefully glided into land – As light as a kiss on the hand touching down, smooth as silk and that's even after it got shot up when the mad bastard who swiped it from under Goring's nose took it past a storm of fighters and landed in front of the airfield tower like he was the Lord Mayor on procession. They say he left a litter of broken-hearted frauleins behind, pulled the wool over German intelligence's eye, brought out the smartest man in Europe for us and to cap it all jumped out on landing with a cigar in one hand, a brandy glass in the other and a card in his pocket from Herr Hitler wishing him well. Before they fell out of course.
- You talk awful shite Billy you really do – Charlie said sadly.

Epilogue 3: Wolfs lair, Eastern Ukraine, Nov. 12 1942

The conference room was replete with high command officials of the Wehrmacht, Kriegsmarine, Luftwaffe, Waffen SS, cohorts and hangers-on, highly connected party officials, the Japanese military attaché was also there along with representatives of the Eastern European Axis Allies. Today was a dramatic one not to be missed as news of the Russian envelopment near Stalingrad had reached HQ. Outside the temperatures were dropping and the snow-covered trees would soon be receiving another layer. Included among the throng were two pivotal figures of the regime, Himmler and Goring. Ardent diehard Nazis both, each vying to be the acknowledged indisputable number two and today both were anxious to learn about the development and how they could reinforcement themselves vis-à-vis each other and the Fuhrer. In court fighting at its highest, they assiduously avoided each other of course and kept to their respective clichés while awaiting the entrance of the supreme leader. Goring as a renowned military figure from the First war allied to his Prussian high-class background fitted right into the heavily militarized atmosphere despite his expanding waistline, covered by a grandiose uniform adorned with numerous decorations and medals, a tad too ostentatious for the day to day German army general. 'Some of those medals he even earned' – was one biting comment.

Himmler had his entourage and the SS military attaches for company, a former chicken farmer, the army never forgot his humble origins, finally, Himmler approached Goring and the figures around them started to melt away.

- My dear Herman, I've been meaning to talk to you about that letter I mentioned – Himmler opened with and Goering seeing he had no alternative said goodbye to his colleagues and feigned nonchalance.
- What letter would that be, I receive hundreds if not thousands each day.
- Not from me but a letter you wrote yourself. A *Sondersauftrag* no less – Himmler clarified.
- Show me the letter? What special mission, we have dozens of those every day, we are busy on the FRONT line – Goring exclaimed.
- I don't have it, your commander refused to pass it over but it was first seen in the hands of a known Czech resistance leader, the last of the three kings plus a renegade Irishman whom we considered a friend previously along with two Jews escaped from

Theresienstadt.   What can you say about that? – Himmler wanted to but didn't point his finger.

- Letter? I can't be expected to comment on every letter I am purported to write.   Hundreds, thousands – Goring habitually dealt and spoke in multitudes.
- The commander said he would send the letter to his superior and was quite off-hand with the requests for cooperation with our investigation.   He did, however, let us take a facsimile, terrible quality but that we expected from such a truculent source.
- I don't know where you are going with this my dear Hendrick?
- The commander gave them, enemies of the state no less, a plane after confirming the validity of the letter with you – 'dear Hendrick' got to the point.
- With me? I don't take calls from every base commander I have. Hundreds, thousands – Goering blustering started to swell up his enormous girth, the colour rising on his face.
- He rang castle Karina and was put through to you after mentioning a personal letter for you was in his procession - Himmler told a step back and in a less accusative voice added.
- Put through to my secretary I would imagine – the head of the air force said.

Goering's face was not a picture of placidity but just then the door connecting the conference room to the private quarters of the supreme leader opened, Hitler, entered with his private secretary Bormann and he approached the table covered with situation maps dedicated to the South Eastern Russian front.

The bombastic shouts of Heil Hitler and a veritable barrage of smashing heels that greeted him were met with an indifferent barely perceivable raising of his arm. It was past noon as the Fuhrer suffered chronic insomnia and went late into the night talking with his bleary-eyed secretaries and personal staff. They had to be at work at 8:30 and couldn't stay in bed as much as they would have liked to.

- What is the latest situation – the supreme leader asked in a tired voice?
- The encirclement is complete.   As of now the Sixth army is surrounded in the city seventy-five miles behind enemy lines - The senior commander Von Rundstat replied.
- Counterattack and join up with them, throw back the Russians – Hitler's voice was rising.
- But my Fuhrer our Allies on the flanks the Romanians and Italians - Von Rundstedt indicated to a group of high ranking

officers furthest away from the centre of the table – have taken huge casualties and are we are struggling to stabilize the front – At that Hitler diffidently acknowledged these guest officers.

- Noble defence - he muttered.
- My Fuhrer we need to regroup, the Sixth needs to breakout and we will counter-attack with everything we have, the link-up is more than possible before the Russian lines solidify - He pointed to a spot forty miles from Stalingrad where the forward supply base was overrun two days before. Cooks, mechanics, secretaries, chauffeurs and nurses running for their lives ahead of streams of incoming T34 tanks and Russian infantry.
- Sir - the staff officer of the 6th Army - General von Paulus has indicated that they are preparing for such an order but many of the vehicles are in a bad way after being immobilized for so long. Rodents have eaten through cables we are told - The cholera visibly rose on the Fuhrer face.
- What are you doing against the Russians? NOTHING!! And now the excuse is the rats. Germans soldiers are ready to give everything. I declare this city on the Volgograd be renamed Germania, it is to be a defensive strong point, you will remain in position. I will not hear the word retreat from those defeatists and traitors riddling the Fatherland, German sacrifice calls for drawn blood and no retreat.

Spittle blowing like a barrage while small white dry amounts of foam was visible in the corners of Hitler's mouth. No one dared contradict him until the lowly ranked officer assigned from the 6th again insanely saw fit to mention the banalities and read out the small print.

- My Fuhrer, eighty tons of supplies are needed every day, we only have ten days' supply left as it stands – The bravest man in the room said putting himself in the eye of the storm.
- Another brave soul looking for a way of saying retreat with saying it - mouthed one officer close to the 6th Army liaison.
- Sir, we could ask the 6th to regroup closer to the current front line ready to retake Stalingrad in the spring – the liaison continued his hopeless charge. Hitler was not slow to react.
- REGROUP, RETREAT, ABANDON – The heads of the German military knew what was being asked, Hitler paused to get his breath back to wind up his fury and here Goring seized his chance to have the Fuhrer see him again as his greatest bulwark and at the same time put Himmler back in his box.
- My Glorious Fuhrer there is a better solution, leave the 6th in place, your most devoted Luftwaffe will deliver everything that is

needed to the heroic 6th while we wait for the push from Von Manstein to relive them.

Hitler saw his unbending will being obeyed; backstabbing words like retreat banished and he was bowed up by the wholehearted support of the Luftwaffe's chief and old comrade, the supreme leader grasped the lifeline thrown thus avoiding having to admit defeat.

- Excellent, excellent, you see that example gentlemen, you see somebody who believes in Germany and her people, not like some of you, cowards the women would call you and would they be wrong? Villains, traitors, defeatists, comforters of the Bolshevik enemy, sullying the name of the glorious soldiers who have given the greatest sacrifice. Make it so, have von Manstein start planning the counter attacks to re-establish the front on the Volgograd and organize the supply bridge. We moved the Spanish army over the Gibraltar strait, this should be a lesser task. My own Fokker plane will be seconded to the operation. We will have NO MORE TALK OF RETREAT. Now excuse me.
- But Sir the North African situation?
- Deal with it Rundstat. Do I have to do with everything - Hitler muttered as he left the room.

A beaming Goring looked at Himmler's stony-faced exasperation before turning away as dozens of high ranking officers started to congratulate the head of the airforce who basked in the attention. Nearby the 6th staff officer who earlier couldn't ignore uncomfortable facts turned to his closest colleague.

- We're just thrown away the eastern front – he said in a whisper.
- And that means the war – the colleague whispered back while making sure no one overheard them.

Epilogue 4: Los Alamos, New Mexico 18th July 1945, 8:13pm

The day's events at Trinity were still reverberating throughout the scientific community of Los Alamos, people crowded around the witnesses and lapped up any scrap of information given or incident recalled. Only now hours later had the fervour died down a bit, Kessler finished his cigarette and went to the restroom, he waited till the last cubicle of the line of six was empty and went in locking the door. He loosened his tie and sat down on the latrine, more to rest than anything, he was now 65 after all; the three years since he'd arrived had involved long working days. They couldn't have done it without the near superhuman effort by all, he like most also spent his free time working away, slept at 11 pm, the same time every night and woke up at 4 am, it was all he needed. Ate a regular varied diet without overindulging, he needed to look after himself for Maria and his unseen grandchildren and for his great contribution to mankind to see the light. Not for the personal glorification of his scientific breakthroughs but for something much more important.

After a couple of minutes, the cubicle next to him was occupied as he heard the latch being locked. A dusty boot came slowly under the partition like the man was lounging, the boot softly tapped the ground four times as if following the beat of a song. The laces were red, he'd never seen anyone wear red laces on the Los Alamos site, he didn't want to know anything or anybody, no names, no faces just dry messages then wet faceless contacts, he studiously avoided anyone who professed socialist ideas or who admired Russia (As the Red Army smashed through the Germans in 1943 and 1944 it had to begrudgingly admitted by even the worst red baiters that the Russians were fighting a hell of a fight) or who knocked the USA. For such a secure location full of vetted personnel it was surprisingly common to find all three. He wondered if the other boot was red laced as well. Kessler tapped his own shoe five times and took the microfilm in a thin case from the hidden space inside the lining of his jacket; he placed it on the floor, extra security, he didn't physically give it to anyone. A rough workers hand, calloused and one dead black nail among the other chipped ones came over and quickly took the file. This was the moment he could be caught, jam on his lips, so he always held his breath, the toilet beside flushed, the door latch opened and the person left. Kessler breathed a sigh of relief, no bashing on the door by the FBI this time. He had been told to wait five minutes so Kessler put it about that he suffered chronic constipation to cover his long visits, the fault of the awful camp diet

371

he said. As he mentally counted down the time he sat and pondered his current situation.

He worked for the Americans who treated him very well, paid him very well and had gone to so much trouble to extract him and his daughter from the jaws of the extermination machine. The camps the Soviets had overrun in the East left little doubt as to what would have been his final destination. The films of liberated camps still shocked, he'd seen he'd never mentioned Theresienstadt to Oppenheimer because he wouldn't have comprehended such barbaric behaviour by anyone. That and the guilt because Kessler felt guilty, he woke up nights in sweats his heart beating wildly, he was alive, why him, everyone else was dead. And not only for that, he was also passing the Americans most prized and sensitive secrets to the Soviets, allies now but as soon as the hostilities stopped nobody was fooled about what would happen next.

The US and the USSR were polar opposites and would soon dispute the political hegemony of the new world order. So why betray the US and Kessler knew the Americans wouldn't see it any other way, those who'd saved him would just as quickly see him swing. But Kessler simply thought that this knowledge was the key to world domination and no nation should monopolize it, second and more prosaically, scientific advancement was for all mankind, it can't be kept hidden away in the dark recesses. Finally and something no security check would ever be able to find Kessler was a communist sympathizer. Today the Soviets had naturally been desperate for news of the test. It seemed Truman won't be giving quite the surprise he thought to Stalin. On the contrary, it was Stalin who could give his American counterpart a shock if he told him just how much he knew. But that old fox knew how to feign surprise to gratify his allies temporally. Kessler stood, flushed the cistern and left the bathroom. The information passed encoded had formulas, yields, procedures, Soviet scientists were very good in this area and they'd use this information to jump the steps that are not obvious or easy. The microfilm made the task quite simple. This time he had done it at night, scientists on-site often worked late into the night and Kessler always made sure he had some experiments to attend to, so when he was alone he just put the latch on the door and worked away on the microfilm.

Balance was what he was working towards. Night and day, sweet and sour, USA and USSR, one alone could not be allowed remain as the single world power, it was unbalanced and equations had to balance. All good scientists know that.

Epilogue 5: October 1926 Prague University

- Let's put on the radio for once why don't we? – Kessler suggested.

He was in a very good mood, he'd ascended to the Copernicus chair of Physics, his darling Maria passed her exams with excellent results, it was a lovely evening for early October, the lab was bathed in golden evening hues, to boot it was Friday and the weekend loomed.

- My pleasure sir – Boron his new lab assistant replied cheerfully.

Boran had been in the Czech legion in 1914-19 fighting for an independent Czechoslovakia and much to his delight Janacek's monumental Simonetta came on over the radio, dedicated to the Czech army and as such close to Boron's heart. It soon filled the lab with soft smooth festive rhythms that had made the country take it to it straight away and had made it wildly popular.

- We'll soon finish up, its Friday and you must be very keen to get home – Kessler looked at the clock, 7:45 pm, well past the hour he thought guiltily but he was right in the middle of an experiment and needed Boran to calibrate instruments and take measurements.
- Oh, I'm in no rush – said Boran amiably, he knew how much he was needed, even though his leg was very sore he kept quiet about it stoic soldier he was.
- Excellent, are you sure? – And without waiting for an answer Kessler continued - the radio will help pass the time.
- Of course, what we are doing is advancing mankind, something dear to my heart, I would do anything I could to improve us as a species and make the earth a paradise for everybody – the white-coated lab technician said breathlessly and with evident passion.

Kessler knew Boran was politically motivated but as Kessler was completely apolitical and never liked politics brought up in the lab he'd never exactly discovered where Boran's convictions lay. He feared they'd be extreme, science was Kessler's God but for some reason today he decided to delve into his assistant's political makeup intrigued by the correlation of advancement scientifically and socially and said so.

- I'm sorry for speaking out of turn and won't again - Boron was still hesitant however.
- Nonsense today we make an exception and what we talk about will go no further.

Boran like many was taken by Kessler's affability and avuncular nature started slowly but then passionately told his story.

- I really didn't care for politics or politicians but in 1918 I found myself in Moscow in the middle of glorious change, tyrants and aristocrats who'd lived off the sweat of the worker for centuries were thrown out, the land was given to the farmers of the land, literacy was spread to all. Prostitution eradicated, do you know how amazing just that is, why I could go and find five houses of sin within five minutes of here, women enslaved for the needs of weak men.
- Really! I had no idea – Kessler exclaimed.
- Yes but in Russia, women were the co-authors of change, votes for all. The first half of 1918 was the advent of the workers utopia before the suppression of the assembly and the murder of the Royal Family. The ex-Tsar was much to blame but his young daughters and son did nothing any other children of the aristocracy did. I meet a man who dazzled me with his ideals and beliefs and to this day I firmly believe in what he theoretically wanted but practice denied him, Vladimir Lenin. We of the Czech legion saved his revolution more than once, let me tell you.
- Please do! – Kessler had no idea of this either and it had been barely eight years ago.

Kessler and Boran sat down together, the physics experiment forgotten, two men unequal's on all levels according to the society in which they lived in but on that day they sat and talked and talked like brothers late into the night as the socialist preacher expounded on the excitement of those days, the idealism, the zealousness of the new comrades, Kessler was struck again and again by the ideals, so simple, so equitable, so balanced, he saw the righteousness of the whole massive undertaking. Their conversation planted a seed in his mind that he carried with him silently, undetected as it was never repeated and he barely saw Boran again. Shortly afterwards the laboratory technician took ill, his war wounds weren't just confined to his legs, and moved back to his naïve village.

One long discussion in his long life had gone unremarked, he hadn't told a soul not even Maria about that night through the years seeing what was happening in the world those ideas resonated further so when he had learnt of the width and breadth of the project he had been snatched from Europe to help with he knew the equitable, fair, just thing to do, it couldn't be one nation's personal belonging, it was the printing press, gunpowder, the cotton jenny all over again and he knew that the flawed Soviet experiment would have to have this knowledge. Kessler thought every time he placed the microfilm on the toilet room floor that Boran would have approved and every time he did it the sound of Janacek's Simonetta came to his mind as he stared at the cubicle door and waited out those five minutes.

Epilogue 6: Checkpoint Delta, Berlin, August 1947

The car on the other side of the closed barrier flashed its headlights three times.

- That's it then, showtime - Donovan turned to the attractive defiant blonde in the back of the car – You'll be back in your workers' paradise in a minute, all the cabbage soup you can handle. No more Washington delis I'm afraid.

Anke twisted a smile painfully on her beguiling face, she actually looked quite well considering how roughed up she'd been during interrogation, she had conserved her stunning visage. The smile, a laconic screw you funny guy one.

- Wanna escort her over? – Donovan asked the man in the passenger seat.
- Certainly will, sure it wasn't to take the night airs you asked me here? – Dagan Malone answered. He opened his side of the car, went around and helped Anke out – Permit me, my dear?

Anke put a hand on his arm and heaved herself up. She still couldn't walk that well, wasn't use to it after months in solitary confinement.

- You'll be right as rain in no time – he reassured her.
- And what would you know? – Anke answered with disdain, still plucky,
- Oh if we had more than twenty meters to share I'd tell you tales of goals and jails and daring-do you wouldn't believe and as it happens here we are.

The small side gate had been opened and on the other side were two men. One of them had an aspect very like Anke, shaky on his feet, pale as a sheet, sweat running down his forehead and looking about to fall over. That didn't surprise Dagan in the least. He hadn't expected the American to be in great shape but as only a couple of days had passed the mental and physical damage of his capture was going to be minimized.   What did surprise him though looking through the gloom was noticing the man who was holding up the faint American.

- Herr Malone, how good it is to see you again, fit and well – the tall man said smiling broadly.
- I would like to say the same but it would be a lie and there are enough of those in our business – This was a turn up for the books.
- Not too worry my old friend I understand I seem out of place but we're all friends now. We ended up on the same side, didn't we? After we conclude this business we are sure to meet again – The English was excellent though time had added a Russian lilt to the accent.
- To talk about the good old times no doubt – Dagan knew this was trouble with a capital T.
- Oh some of them were and then a twisty interesting tale you played an important part in. I nearly forgive you taking off in that plane, nearly mind I got into such trouble – Anke and the American looked at them both in amazement.
- Nearly forgive? – Now all three looked at the German as his voice took on a sombre threatening tone.
- Oh yes nearly, be unchristian not to try, but I'll still have to make you pay ever I get the chance, no hard feelings – Hoffman said in a sing-song half-serious voice.
- No hard feelings at all then if I plug you first – the Irishman replied - One friendly Christian to another mind.

Epilogue 7: Trinity College Dublin, summer, 1932

Both of the men sitting on the steps of the Physics department had a look of gentle satisfaction.

One of them turned to the other pointing with his pipe.

- Again well done Ernest. You and Cockcroft deserve the highest merits, you've managed to disintegrate the lithium nucleus – he said with evident delight, his English accented.
- They are calling it 'splitting', gives it a more common feel to it, something the man on the Clapham omnibus can get to grips with – Ernest Watson replied.

- And if it wasn't enough Einstein has come to say that it is the proof for his E=Mc² business. In Prague they will be ravenous for details – continue the second beaming from ear to ear.
- Come up so to the tea room and I'll tell you more. I'm only in town for a few days and then back to Cambridge again to continue with the next phase. Carbon's up next.
- Of to Trinity College in Cambridge, curious is it not? To TCC from TCD, Dublin's Trinity College.
- Trinity's pops up all over the place. By the by, I think I can spy out your daughter coming along with that Malone fellow – Ernest peered over the cricket ground to the pavilion.
- Goodness gracious me. Come on so let us go take that tea while I'm still in a good mood – Kessler sprung up and opened the door for his esteemed colleague and quickly they both went in.

Made in the USA
Columbia, SC
30 May 2020